M. K. Hume is a retired academic and is married with two sons.

KING ARTHUR: DRAGON'S CHILD

M. K. Hume

headline
review

First published in Great Britain in 2009
by HEADLINE REVIEW
An imprint of HEADLINE PUBLISHING GROUP

First published in paperback in Great Britain in 2009
by HEADLINE REVIEW

1

Cataloguing in Publication Data is available from the British Library

ISBN 978 0 7553 4867 1 (B format)
ISBN 978 0 7553 5643 0 (A format)

Typeset in Golden Cockerel by Avon DataSet Ltd,
Bidford on Avon, Warwickshire

Printed and bound in Great Britain by
Clays Ltd, St Ives plc

Headline's policy is to use papers that are natural, renewable and recyclable
products and made from wood grown in sustainable forests. The logging
and manufacturing processes are expected to conform to the
environmental regulations of the country of origin.

HEADLINE PUBLISHING GROUP
An Hachette UK Company
338 Euston Road
London NW1 3BH

www.headline.co.uk
www.hachette.co.uk

This work is dedicated to my friend, Julienne Marie Gleeson, who left this life on 5th February, 2004.

She was my beloved friend, my second self, and my unsung hero. Julie gave me backbone when life seemed darkest, and she taught me that there is great beauty in the struggle to fulfill a dream. She had resolutely survived death, fierce adversity, animosity and violence, until cancer finished her life struggle before her fiftieth birthday.

The fairest flowers are 'born to blush unseen and waste their sweetness on the desert air', but I recognized Julie's rareness and cherished every memory of our time together.

This book belongs to her because she fought to persuade me to write it. Without her, it may never have been born.

Ave, Julie, where you rest after life's suffering. I hope you approve of my offering.

ACKNOWLEDGEMENTS

I appreciate the simple fact that many readers avoid this section of any book. In this case, however, I hope you make an exception!

King Arthur: Dragon's Child, as the first volume in *The Chronicles of Arthur: King of the Britons*, would never have seen the light of day had my husband, Arthur Michael, not given it his inimitable editing and criticism, even when battling a serious illness. There are no words to thank him for his support, even though his oft-repeated words, 'What does this crap mean?' will always make me smile.

To Margot Maurice, and those members of the Independent Publishers of Australia Network who assisted me to achieve my goals – my thanks for your professionalism and excellent advice when it was most needed.

I am indebted to all the great writers of Arthurian Literature, from Gildas to Charles Williams and beyond, who made King Arthur, the High King of Britain and Dux Bellorum, such a fascinating hero in my imaginative other-life. Even when I cursed the dead languages I needed to learn to know him better, I became obsessed with the glories of his epic as I struggled with post-graduate research. Without those histories and literary masterpieces written during the past thousand years to fall back on, I could not have hoped to write my own version of Arthur's life and times.

Without the support of my friends, Penny Cranitch, Lyn

Baker, Robyn Jones and Pauline Reckentin, and many others, I would have crumbled long ago under the weight of this project. To my friends – I thank you for your love and support, despite my many faults. To those who would have done me harm – I thank you also, for you have taught me the valuable lesson that life is neither fair nor just, and that only by opposition to that which is immoral and wrong do we grow as people. I know you did not intend to spur me on to achievement, but the end result is ultimately the same.

My thanks must also go to the innumerable students at various High Schools over the years that enjoyed my stories and shuddered at the more gruesome of my plots and ideas. They always liked my more eccentric and grim visions, and they collectively set me on a path that avoided the pitfalls of writing stories that were simply 'nice' and 'acceptable'.

Finally, thanks to my high school English Teacher, Mrs Lapa, who tore my facile essays and short stories to shreds and taught me to write for me, and for me alone, and to give a whole-hearted effort in every task I attempted. She only taught me for one year, and she never graced students again with her unique viewpoints. She was a great loss to Education Queensland, especially in the public education system where the standards in teaching expertise are often narrow and inadequate – at best! But this excellent teacher of English taught me how to swim upstream, and to understand that populist visions usually involve a compromise. I hope that Mrs Lapa, wherever she is, is happy and at peace, although she will probably never know just how much I admired this lady for her professionalism!

Of course, how do I thank my agent, Dorie Simmonds, or my publisher, Jane Morpeth, and the whole crew at Headline? They have given substance to a dream.

King Arthur of the Britons was the second great love of my life, and he has driven me hard for over thirty years. My interpretations of how he lived and loved are just that – mine alone – viewed through the kaleidoscope of time. They are coloured by the demands of our current age, one that has little time for duty and less inclination towards nobility.

Myrddion's Chart of Pre-Arthurian Roman Britain

Trimontium

Bremenium

Onnum
Hadrian's Wall
Magnis

Bravoniacum
Lavatrae
Verterae

Eburacum
Bremetennacum

OCEANUS HIBERNICUS

Mamucium

Mona
Lindum
Deva
Aquae

Causennae
Ratae
Durobrivac
Viroconium
Venonae

Salinae
Camulodunum

Moridunum
Venta
Silurum
Isca
Glevum

Corinium
SABRINA AEST
Abone
Londinium
Aquae Sulis
Calleva Atrebatum

Lindinis
Venta Belgarum
Cadbury
Glastonbury
Sorviodunum
Noviomagus
Tintagel
Anderida
Isca
Vectis
Dumnoniorum
Durnovaria

Site Plan of the Villa Poppinidii

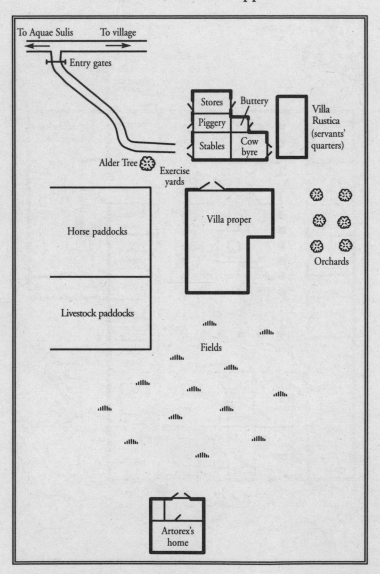

Floor Plan of the Villa Poppinidii

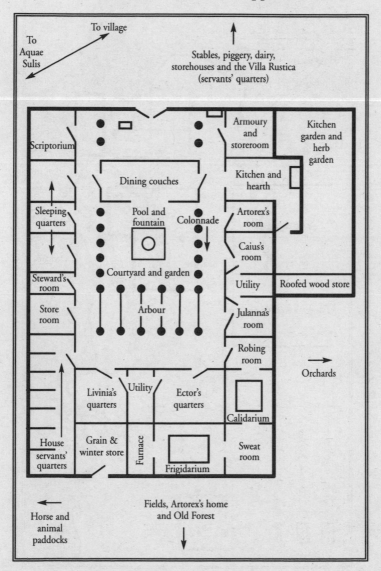

To village

To Aquae Sulis

Stables, piggery, dairy, storehouses and the Villa Rustica (servants' quarters)

Scriptorium

Armoury and storeroom

Kitchen garden and herb garden

Dining couches

Kitchen and hearth

Sleeping quarters

Pool and fountain

Colonnade

Artorex's room

Caius's room

Steward's room

Courtyard and garden

Utility

Roofed wood store

Store room

Arbour

Julanna's room

Robing room

Orchards

Livinia's quarters

Utility

Ector's quarters

Calidarium

House servants' quarters

Grain & winter store

Furnace

Frigidarium

Sweat room

Horse and animal paddocks

Fields, Artorex's home and Old Forest

The Route from Venta Belgarum to Anderida

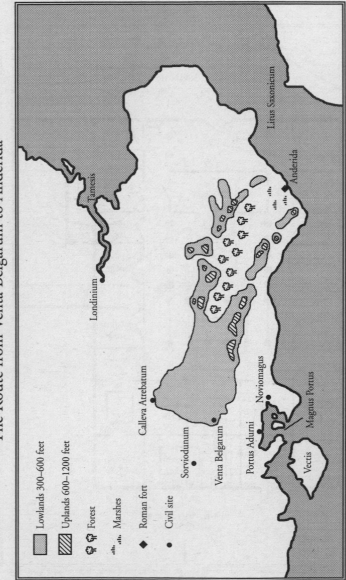

Lowlands 300–600 feet
Uplands 600–1200 feet
Forest
Marshes
Roman fort
Civil site

Tamesis
Londinium
Litus Saxonicum
Anderida
Calleva Atrebatum
Sorviodunum
Noviomagus
Venta Belgarum
Portus Adurni
Magnus Portus
Vectis

Glastonbury and Environs

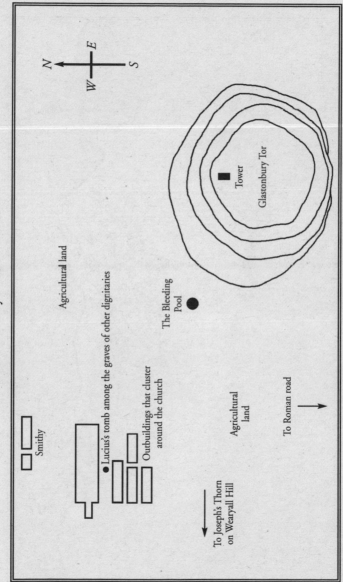

Smithy

Lucius's tomb among the graves of other dignitaries

Outbuildings that cluster around the church

The Bleeding Pool

Agricultural land

Tower

Glastonbury Tor

Agricultural land

To Joseph's Thorn on Wearyall Hill

To Roman road

N
W — E
S

CHAPTER I

THE EDGES OF MEMORY

> 'For a certain order embraces all things, and anything which departs from the order planned and assigned to it, only falls back into order, albeit a different order so as not to allow anything to chance in the realms of Providence.'
>
> Boethius

The forest embraced the boy like an ancient cloak, ragged at the hems, but still serviceable and strong in the weave. The roots of the oak trees twisted out of the deep, mouldering earth, and their branches were so thick and tangled that the boy felt as if he had plunged into cool, green water after the humid brilliance of the fallow fields. The threat that this adventure would lead to stern punishment meant little to him, for he would be punished anyway. If not for these hours of sensual pleasure, then some half-forgotten sin would stir his foster-father to wrath.

In a dense canopy of alder and oak, the trees starved all grass of the necessities of life. The boy walked through a perilous coverlet of leaf drifts, fallen branches embroidered with the verdigris of moss and strange, fleshy flowers that covered hidden badger setts. The eerie beauty of this half-lit world fascinated the boy and set his heart racing with the promise of danger. Anything could dwell in these sudden hollows of almost midnight blue. Within the shadows, anyone could be close enough to touch him in this half-imagined landscape where his foster-father's power was reduced to less than dust. He himself could be anyone, and he could dream whatever he chose without hindrance. Here, he was neither safe nor unsafe, but most truly himself.

The boy found a favoured natural glade, some ten spear shafts across, where tree trunks mimicked pillars and a slender blade of light reached to the forest floor. A great rock, covered in white lacy lichen, squatted off centre in the glade, and the boy ran his narrow hands over its surface until he felt the worn whorls and lines roughly hacked into its flank. For some half-instinctive reason, he chose to seat himself as far from those barely visible patterns as he could while he stared hard at a hollow, barely the length of his hand, which had been chipped out of the rock at its centre. It was tilted strangely, for the boy had once sacrificed a little liquid from his goatskin water carrier to fill that shallow, manmade cup. He had watched transfixed as some of the water drained away, following the spirals and whorls until the rivulet fell on to the forest floor.

Something dark always flexed its wings in the boy's mind when he touched that hollow. He could imagine a sticky, viscous thread of blood snaking away from his fingers into the pattern, and filling his nostrils with the unsettling scent of iron.

'Things have died here,' he whispered to break the sepulchral silence of the glade. 'But they are so old . . . perhaps as ancient as the trees themselves.'

He loved to frighten himself with his imaginings, even though he was a sturdy boy who was taller than his birth age of twelve years. Already the shape of manhood was coming upon him, and he drove the Saxon serving woman, old Frith, half crazy as he outgrew his leather trousers and strained the stitches of his tunics at the shoulders.

'A great lump of a boy,' his foster-father explained to the

occasional visitor. 'Half wild as well ... a little wanting, if you take my meaning.'

The master, Lord Ector, was himself tall and broad in shoulder and girth, but Lump, as the kitchen slaves called the boy derisively, threatened to tower well over six feet in height.

'A little barbarian,' his foster-brother would drawl to his friends, from his advanced age of seventeen and the impregnable reality of full manhood. 'He scarcely uses the baths – and his hair! Once his beard grows, he'll be a walking mop!'

The young men laughed, for Caius aped the airs of an aristocratic dilettante, although the Dracos Legion, the last to protect Britain, had been gone for many years. Roman by birth, as he described himself with pride, Caius had no time for Lump, who appeared to have none of the true blood in his veins. Caius conveniently ignored his own Celtic paternity.

'Why my pater accepted him defies imagination.'

Caius smoothed his shining black hair which he kept militarily short and carefully curled over his forehead.

'When he was an infant, he cried constantly until the women put him in a linen chest. Then, when he grew older ... well, look at that vacuous face. He's learned his letters, it's true, for Mater would not tolerate an ignorant son, foster or no, but he never reads the scrolls or conducts himself as a well-born youth should. Targo beats him regularly, for all the effect it has on him, for Lump just stands and takes the blows with that vague expression on his fat face.'

Caius and his Celt father, Ector, were wrong.

The boy read the scrolls in the meagre scriptorium, but only when the rest of the house was asleep and he could steal a little oil for his lamp. The flickering light made the Latin words dance with a life quite apart from the ancient memories they shared with him. But he had eaten the stale crusts of charity for every day of his twelve years, and they made an unpalatable and indigestible meal, scrolls or no scrolls.

So Lump simply *went away* whenever he chose – either to the woods or to the deepest caverns in his head.

The boy stretched his long, smooth legs on the rock's spine. What hair his body grew was certainly very pale, so his limbs were burned to a rich bronze by hours in the sunlight. His face was neither fat nor featureless, but was broad and already sharply angular at the cheekbones. His hair curled so wildly that no amount of combing could completely tame the spiralled ringlets that formed a red-gold nimbus around his head. His eyes were unusual in a world of largely brown, hazel, green and black-eyed people, slaves and masters both, for they were so pale and grey that they seemed almost blind in his smooth face.

Those eyes trapped the light, but nothing of the soul behind them escaped as a warning to those who would torment him.

With regret, the boy left the glade as the blades of light narrowed, then slid behind the dense foliage that towered above him. The air had a sultry heaviness, as if a storm was coming. He would have welcomed the steady driving rain from a downpour, but his empty stomach was warning him that he must return to the villa – or else go hungry for yet another night.

'Farewell, rock,' he whispered to the body-warmed stone. 'Farewell, trees.'

Arriving in the forest was always more pleasant than returning to the villa. As the boy pushed his way through the waist-high grasses of the western field, avoiding the stinging nettles that grew in dense patches, he put on his 'family face' as he called it, and assumed his accustomed untidy shamble.

When he reached the outbuildings of the Villa Poppinidii, his back was bowed and his feet scuffed the crazy stone pathways between the stables and the piggery.

'You're wanted, Lump,' a pert housemaid giggled at him as she emptied slops into the swine trough. 'You've been wanted for hours. The master has visitors.'

'Ugh!' was the boy's only reply.

Now he would have to bathe. He'd need to find a clean tunic as well, if Frith had found the time to mend his second-best clothing.

He eyed his filthy toes in their ragged sandals with ill humour. He'd be late – and Ector would not tolerate a tardy foster-son.

I'd best be moving then, the boy admonished himself with little enthusiasm. He sought out Frith in the kitchens where she was most usually seated, warming her old bones.

'It's a good thing I am fond of you, young rapscallion,' the old woman mumbled through her broken teeth. 'I've mended your tunic and found you a leather belt to fit that waist of yours. And don't forget the perfumed oil,' she called out after him. 'Perhaps it will train that hair of yours – it's full of twigs.'

'I thank you, good Frith,' he called back over his shoulder. 'Sleep well by your fire.'

'That Lump will never amount to much,' the sour-faced cook snapped as he fiddled with a brimming pot filled with boiled eels and root vegetables.

'Ah, but it's amazing how balanced his temper is when he is treated with kindness,' Frith replied tartly. 'It's also remarkable how agile the boy becomes when he thinks no one is looking.' She had been nurse to the last Roman child born to the House of Poppinidii, the sweet and tiny Livinia, and she knew all the secrets of the villa.

'Go back to sleep, Grandmother. You've been out in the sun too long,' was the cook's acerbic reply.

Pausing only in his narrow, airless cubicle to gather up his clothing, his old strigil and a small bottle of rather rancid oil, the boy ran to the very end of the east wing of Villa Poppinidii, taking care to skirt the atrium, the eating couches and the scriptorium in his haste. In truth, the boy loved to hear stories of the world beyond the villa, which only visitors brought. For him, a little scrubbing was a small price to pay for a night in the corner, listening to the men talk of strange and alien places.

Hastily, in the mosaic pool of the calidarium, the boy stripped and heated his skin in the hot water. He had scant regard for the proper civilities and order of the bathing rites, but concentrated on opening the pores of his skin, rubbing in the sickly oil while he tried not to breathe the stench in through his nose. The boy then dragged the old strigil over several days of accumulated dirt. He even paid cursory attention to his nails so that, eventually, the worst of the day's excesses were removed.

Then, after a quick splash in the frigidarium to cleanse and close his pores, he gave himself a rough towelling and attempted to tie back his wet, wild hair with a leather thong. Finally, he donned a tunic, belt, loincloth and sandals, and ran through the silent colonnades to the room where all visitors were entertained.

'There you are, boy,' Ector snapped. 'At least we must be grateful that you are clean.' He smiled at his guests to soften the effect of his harsh words. 'And now you can assist with the serving,' he ordered. 'As is your duty.'

Ector was a big man, thick in the body and broad of shoulder, but his legs were unnaturally short and bandy. His face was florid and almost smooth of wrinkles, for the master of the house rarely fell prey to extremes of emotion. His mouth was good-humoured and his pale, blue eyes were slightly protuberant, giving his face an expression of perpetual surprise.

But only a fool underestimated Master Ector, a man raised in the warrior tradition, to which the hard muscle of his body bore witness. Having served his time in the fortresses of the north, Ector now enjoyed his broad acres, his fat cattle and kine and the peace of a quiet middle age. However, should external peril threaten his house, like an old battle hound Ector would rise to fight with merciless glee.

Ector and his wife, Livinia, their son, Caius, and three unknown gentlemen were all reclining in the Roman fashion on carved couches around a low table that was piled high with delicacies. Eel in aspic, a boar's head splendidly presented with boiled barley, a sliced haunch of venison, salted vegetables and periwinkles that swam in exotic sauces were displayed on the low, central table.

The dining room was quite large, as befitted the honour of Livinia's ancient family, and gave directly on to the atrium where, under a pale moon, water danced and splashed from an imaginative bronze statue of a monstrous fish. Sweet-smelling oils burned brightly in rare glass vessels, and the best torches hung on heavy iron wall brackets, yet no unsightly stains of oil smoke marred a fine fresco of an olive grove. Ector might be a bastard Celt, but he had married the last child of an ancient family, and had taken the Poppinidii name as his own. In the nearest town of Aquae Sulis, he was deemed to be a man of significant wit – and extraordinary luck.

'Yes, Foster-Father,' the boy replied neutrally, then bowed formally to each guest, even the hateful Caius.

He sought out the villa's steward, a Greek slave called Cletus, and collected large jars of honeyed wine from Gaul and the crisp, clean vintages of Spain. Ector was noted as a connoisseur of good wines, and it was the boy's task at these functions to ensure that the gilded cups of the visitors were kept full to the brim.

The boy was also adept at becoming invisible. As the meal progressed, his presence was soon forgotten.

'What news from the east, Myrddion?' Ector asked with no little interest.

'The wolves from over the narrow sea come to pillage almost every spring,' a thin-faced man answered. 'Fortunately, the barbarians rarely venture far inland, but I fear one day they will arrive with their women and their broods and build their own settlements.'

'Then they will die here,' Caius drawled in a way that he believed showed his sophistication.

'Perhaps,' the man called Myrddion replied vaguely.

'Oh, come, Myrddion. What are a few savages to us? Londinium, Eburacum, and Camulodunum are heavily fortified, and the native legions are well trained. We'll smash any naked barbarians like roaches.' Ector plucked up a sliver of venison with a dainty knife.

Another stranger, notable for the long brown plaits that hung from his forehead, suppressed a grim laugh.

'I don't think anything amusing was said, Luka,' Ector retorted, his face flushing under what was left of his chestnut hair.

'My pardon, friend Ector,' Luka replied. 'I meant no offence – but these little toys,' he paused, and made the eating dagger spin in his neat hands, 'are no match for the war axes of the barbarians. Their swords are almost of your height – and they have iron, too, my brother.'

Caius began to speak, but Livinia quelled him with an imperial lifting of her narrow brows.

'There is no offence taken, Luka. I served with your father on the Wall, and we shared the same wet nurse for some seasons in Lavatrae. We both grew tall hearing the horror tales of Boedicca of the Iceni and the nearness of her victory when she rebelled against Rome. But that bloodstained bitch was one of us. She was civilized in her fashion, and not some ignorant Saxon pig-stealer, or a dog from Jutland who comes hunting enough grain to feed his filthy brood.'

'Luka is merely asking that we heed the warnings, Ector,' Myrddion soothed, although his expression, to the boy's mind, lacked compromise. 'Warned, we are strong; complacent, we are soft in the belly.'

'Rome owns the entire world, including Britannia,' Caius cut in excitedly.

Ector shot a swift glance of disapproval at his only birth son.

'But would the might of Rome come to our aid if we were under attack? I believe they'd leave us to our fate,' Luka replied, with a casual intensity that gave weight to his words.

'Uther Pendragon still holds the south and the west of our land under his foot,' Myrddion answered. 'But he grows old and frightened. God help the west should Uther fail.'

Caius and Ector both snorted. Neither possessed a flattering opinion of the High King who held the tribes to treaties won by bloodshed during his vigorous youth.

'I don't think we should ever discount Uther Pendragon,' Luka added.

'And your villa lies safe because of the protection of his rule,' Myrddion reminded Ector.

'Villa Poppinidii lies strong because it is in my hands,' Ector retorted, his face reddening.

'And very well-provisioned it is too,' Luka soothed. 'I admit I have longed for a civilized bed for many weeks during my travels.'

Somewhat mollified, Ector allowed the conversation to veer on to safer ground, with talk of fashion and trade in the south. Lady Livinia, especially, was starved for tales of civilized Gaul, and she managed to dominate the conversation for some little time, mainly by right of the purity of her breeding.

The three travellers acknowledged Livinia's superior qualities by the deference they showed her. She was small, even for a Roman matron, but her posture was so straight and uncompromising that few visitors noticed her diminutive form. Like all gentle domestic tyrants, she was possessed of great charm and wit, making her a hostess of distinction. Gracefully, she ensured that Myrddion Merlinus and his friends would find nothing amiss in the hospitality of the house.

The boy filled the gilded wine cups from his jugs and listened to the words of the guests with his senses all aquiver.

The third visitor, a dark-complexioned man, remained silent throughout the conversation that swirled around him.

Llanwith poured water into his cup, brushing aside Artorex's proffered wine jug with a flick of his huge beringed hands. His black eyes were watchful and intent, even when the other guests spoke of women's matters, as if the Villa Poppinidii held the answers to secrets he had yet to discover through stealth.

The boy felt his stomach muscles contract with nervousness when the dark-faced man stared covertly at him across the succulent meats and rich sauces. Black eyes forced grey eyes to meet and be examined.

When the honeyed sweetmeats were served, and the men lounged in comfort with the edges of their differences blunted by good food and wine, the silent stranger chose to speak.

'Who is the boy?' he asked in a voice that rumbled from his wide chest. It was a voice of command that demanded an answer.

'He is my foster-son,' Ector replied sleepily. The villa normally held to farm hours, and the water dial showed that the hour was now late.

The boy almost dropped the Spanish wine in surprise as all eyes flickered towards him.

'What is his name, good Ector?'

'Artorex. His name is Artorex.'

'But we call him *Lump*,' Caius giggled drunkenly.

'He bears a noble name. Stand under the wall sconce, young Artorex, where I can see you properly.'

'He's a good enough lad,' Ector mumbled. 'But he's not a sharp dagger, Llanwith pen Bryn, if you take my meaning.'

Llanwith son of Bryn, the boy thought to himself, as he moved to carry out the stranger's bidding. I'll not forget you quickly.

'He is a tall young man. What is his age?'

'Twelve – I believe,' replied Ector carelessly. 'Yes, he makes fair to be strong and large. But why are you so interested in the boy?'

Myrddion Merlinus smiled enigmatically and waved a negligent hand in Artorex's direction. 'Bishop Lucius is curious to know how the child grows. He expected that you'd see to his learning so we may assume he knows some letters. We're simply finishing what was started when we brought the babe to you – how many years ago?'

'It's been too many years, old friend, too many years!' Ector was disposed to be sentimental, but Llanwith was still staring at Artorex as if they were alone in the triclinium.

'Speak for yourself, young Artorex,' Llanwith demanded. 'Are you strong?'

'Aye, master, I'm strong enough,' the boy replied bluntly.

The stranger ignored the boy's effrontery, although Ector frowned in his direction.

'Are you fast, Artorex?' the stranger continued. 'Strong lads are rarely fast.'

Caius giggled.

The boy felt his face flush. He straightened his shoulders and raised his chin.

'Fast enough, master.'

The narrow eating dagger flashed from Llanwith's large hand across the light in a neat parabola that was aimed directly at Artorex's heart.

Unblinkingly, the boy watched the blade arc towards him. Acting on instinct, he moved to one side, and dashed the blade aside with his forearm. The knife clattered to the floor, where it lay like a silver reptile with the dragon aglitter on its hilt.

'Aye, you are fast enough, young man,' Llanwith replied with a laugh as the boy retrieved the dagger and handed it to him, hilt first. 'You bleed, boy.'

'It is only a scratch, master. A nothing.' The boy's face was as inscrutable as the bland features of Llanwith pen Bryn.

The other guests were momentarily robbed of words.

'These are strange dinner manners for an honoured guest, my lord,' Livinia chided. 'If the conversation is to be so surprising, I will leave you for my bed. We keep country hours here, good sirs, and I must supervise the wool bleaching in the morning. Come, Caius, you also would be better served by sleep.'

'I apologize for the want of manners in my friend,' Myrddion replied diplomatically.

Llanwith pen Bryn did not concern himself with words of apology but simply inclined his head towards mother and son with a brief, regal dignity.

As Livinia and a sullen Caius left the chamber with a hiss of sandals on tessellated floors, the mistress paused briefly at the door.

'Don't keep the boy up too late, Ector. I want him fit for work in the morning.'

Ector merely grunted in acknowledgement.

Silence fell after mistress and son departed.

Artorex shuffled awkwardly. He was uncertain how to respond to the visitors, so he stayed in position beneath the sconce.

'We now know that the boy is strong and fast,' Luka said conversationally to Ector. 'But does he read? Does he receive an education?'

'Why this interest in Artorex, my friends? I took the lad into my household as a favour to Lucius of Glastonbury when the child was newly born. The priest has never asked for word of him, nor has he shown any interest in the lad since that distant time.'

'I know his history, friend Ector,' Myrddion said. 'But I need to know if the boy can read.'

'Well, yes, he reads as well as can be expected,' Ector growled peevishly. He was unused to being questioned so autocratically in his own house.

'May we judge his ability, my friend?' Luka asked with a conciliatory smile.

The boy was totally bemused by the conversation that was taking place around him. He was conscious that he was being tested, but why? He was just Lump, of little more value than a good hound. In time to come he might be considered worthy of becoming a steward in the place of Cletus, but why should these great ones care a whit for his strength, his speed – or his intelligence?

'Fetch a scroll from my baggage, Artorex,' Llanwith ordered with barely a glance in the boy's direction.

The boy stood, unsure of how to respond, or where to find such an item.

Ector, grumpily, waved a hand at Artorex to indicate that he was to carry out Llanwith's bidding.

The boy ran from the room to seek out Cletus who took charge of all domestic matters. He escaped from the suddenly dangerous room with surprising agility.

Cletus had obviously been eavesdropping for his master's orders, and a kitchen slave had already been sent to the guests' quarters in the west wing to collect the scroll.

The steward said nothing to the boy, but glared at him suspiciously.

Enclosed in a fine hide case, the scroll was quickly found and thrust into Artorex's hands.

'Obey your masters, boy,' Cletus hissed, and Ector's foster-son slipped back into the dining chamber where the visitors were again speaking of matters in the east.

'Master.' Artorex offered the scroll to Llanwith pen Bryn.

'Read for us, young Artorex. For our entertainment.' The stranger did not even deign to look at him.

Artorex fumbled with the lacings, even clumsier than usual in his nervousness. The scroll was eventually unbound, and the boy stared down at the bold Latin script that marched across the fine hide. He was immediately seized by panic, for the text was totally unfamiliar.

'Read,' Llanwith repeated, his eyes on a stuffed egg speared on the end of his knife.

Haltingly, Artorex began to read the unfamiliar Latin script, becoming faster as he began to recognize more and more words. He had heard of the commentaries of the great Caesar in the Gaul Campaign, but he had never thought to have a copy in his hands.

'I want you to read this scroll and translate it into the common tongue,' Llanwith ordered.

His heart in his mouth, the boy obeyed.

Despite his confusion and fear, Artorex became caught up in the blunt, forthright description of the great Julian's battle campaign.

'Enough!' Llanwith ordered. 'What do you think, Myrddion? You are the scholar amongst us. Does the boy read well?'

Ector was staring at the boy with blank astonishment; there was more depth to his foster-son than he had ever imagined.

'Surprisingly well,' Myrddion replied. 'You are to be congratulated, friend Ector,' he added, turning to face the master of the villa.

'I don't see how, for I never heard him read so well in the past.' Ector may have been a hard man, but he was also bluntly honest.

'Have you read the memoirs of the great Caesar?' Luka asked the boy.

'No, my lord. But I am certain that I would like to do so,' Artorex managed to reply.

'Then keep this small gift, in payment for your diligence,' Llanwith stated casually, as if this strange conversation had been insignificant. 'Now leave the wine jars and get yourself off to bed. That is, if your master will give you leave.'

Ector waved Artorex away, his eyes troubled and gleaming in the light.

Clutching the precious scroll and its case to his chest, Artorex scurried to the door and was gone. Yet some wickedness in his curious nature caused him to pause outside the room and continue to listen. Even though he was aware of the presence of the faithful Cletus at his back, he could not bear to miss the last of the peculiar conversation.

'We have intruded upon your hospitality, friend Ector, but you must believe me when I vow that we would not have imposed on you if our reasons were not of the gravest importance.' Myrddion spoke with a statesman's glibness overlaying a current of urgency.

'Nor can we explain further tonight, Ector,' Luka continued seamlessly. 'Great affairs of state are marching on, old friend, and you and your family are a part of them, whether you will it to be so or not.'

'I don't understand any of this,' Ector grumbled through his beard.

'You must trust us until such time as we can reveal more of what is to come. Twelve years ago, the good Lucius of Glastonbury sent you a gift, and asked you to take care of it. You have done well with that charge,' Llanwith responded gravely.

'Besides,' Myrddion continued, 'perhaps nothing will come of our fears, and you will have an admirable steward to serve your family when you are gone from this world.'

'But it would be profitable for us all if childhood ceases for Artorex at this time,' Luka stated. His companions nodded in agreement. 'We ask that you commence to teach him those skills of the warrior that we ourselves learned as boys, old friend. Blade and shield! Horse and fire! Pain and bravery! Would you undertake such a task for us?'

'Aye, but—'

'And the boy must no longer be referred to as *Lump* by any member of your household,' Llanwith interrupted. 'He will be of no use to us without self-respect.'

Ector recognized the sound of command in the voice of his guest.

As Artorex turned to leave his listening point, he saw Cletus bow his head low. The boy turned. Llanwith pen Bryn was leaning against the doorpost, regarding him with fathomless black eyes.

'Learn your new duties well, boy. And remember that those who listen to private matters can sometimes hear more than they would wish.' Then he grinned at Artorex, and returned to his friends.

'He speaks wise words, young master,' Cletus hissed with frightened respect. 'You could yet get us all hanged if that black-eyed devil has any say in it.'

Artorex ran.

Back in his sleeping cubicle, he tried to chase the faces of the three strangers from his mind. Nothing had changed. He was still a fatherless son, not much higher than a house slave and only permitted to sleep in the main body of the villa complex on sufferance. He dwelt in the no-man's land of Roman life, a foster-son without status.

Then he reached down and felt the scroll beside his sleeping pallet, and knew that his life was changed forever.

CHAPTER II

THE BLADE AND FIRE

Although Artorex's sudden change of status was the talk of the villa for several weeks, masters and servants soon forgot him, and the narrow world the boy inhabited soon returned to its mundane unswerving routine. Wood had to be chopped into kindling for the kitchen ovens, the kitchen gardens required persistent, tedious weeding and birds stole the new fruit from the orchards and must be deterred with well-aimed stones. Mistress Livinia ensured that Artorex was never idle.

Except in one significant detail.

Each morning, after drawing water for the kitchen, currying the horses and feeding the hounds, the boy was ordered to attend on Targo.

Targo was a scarred veteran of indeterminate race who had served a lifetime in the noble art of soldiering. Small, bow-legged and deceptively white-haired, Targo had been washed up at the river port of Glevum, at the end of the Sabrina Aest, and had sold his skills to Ector as arms trainer to his son and captain of the small troop of men-at-arms who served the dual roles of field workers and protectors of the villa. The veteran had married a local widow from the nearby village, and was a man feared for his quick temper when drunk, and his even faster blade when sober. Who he was, and where he was originally born, was unknown to all save Ector.

The boy didn't enjoy his morning hours spent training with Targo. After being given a short, wooden sword and a wicker shield, Artorex was forced to learn the fighting positions practised by the old legions.

In spite of his ageing body and a limited reach, Targo managed to beat Artorex black and blue with the flat of his sword every day until, out of sheer desperation, Artorex began to take his training seriously and to learn the rudiments of thrust, parry and guard.

At first, these simple exercises in the farmyard were a source of loud amusement for the servants from the Villa Poppinidii. As they wandered out to the fields, or brought the cows to the barn for milking, the farm workers were entertained by the sight of young Artorex, awkward and frustrated, swatting at empty air with his wooden sword, while Targo danced negligently away. Even Caius dallied on his way to the stables to watch the red-faced and sweating boy as he tried to dodge Targo's flashing weapon. But the predictability of the entertainment soon palled, so teacher and student were left to practise the manipulation of blade, spear, shield and dagger in relative peace.

Gradually, albeit painfully, Artorex realized that the exercises were similar in nature to a village dance and, soon, he found himself captured by the grace of weapons drill. Then, just as his superior reach began to give him a little confidence, Targo changed the rules and, once again, the boy found himself pinned to the ground or stripped of his weapon, with Targo's sword held firmly against his throat.

'Remember, boy, any fool can pick up a sword and learn the motions. He'll live just as long as it takes for him to meet an enemy who thinks faster than he does.'

'Is that how you were cut across the nose?' Artorex panted as

Targo attacked from a new, and totally unexpected, direction.

'Of course, boy. You either learn or you're dead.'

'Then I had better start to learn.' Artorex stifled a cry as Targo used the flat of his sword across the back of his right knee.

'You are now crippled for life. What are you going to do to live?' Targo asked, and swept the boy's feet from under him.

Artorex hit the ground with the base of his spine and even old Targo had the sensitivity to wince.

'You're cheating,' Artorex complained as he drove his wicker shield towards Targo's nose, a move that would have smashed that scarred feature if the blow had ever landed.

Targo merely took one step backward.

'That's better. Remember, cheating is just good common sense. Only a short-lived idiot pretends to bring honour on to the battlefield.'

Targo set Artorex strengthening exercises with small ingots of lead to force muscle on to his growing frame. The weights were tied to his wrists so that collecting eggs or picking the last of the apples became a painful chore.

Nor was Artorex permitted to fight only right-handed, for Targo would switch sword hands regularly and, on occasion, would instruct his pupil to wield his sword with both hands.

Artorex soon learned the deadly disadvantage of fighting a left-handed enemy.

'If one arm is wounded, you must make do with the other. Now raise your sword.'

Artorex underwent many further weeks of bruising until he learned to fight with his left hand. To build up its strength, Targo tied his right arm to his side. Artorex suffered innumerable cuts and bruises as he endeavoured to separate the whey from the cheese during threshing and as he struggled to keep his balance while feeding jostling pigs. He learned how to use the distribution of his weight to his advantage, just as Targo had planned.

Artorex's days were now measured by the severity of his cuts and bruises, his weary muscles and the field work that Targo invented to strengthen his spine. Reaping was a particular Targo favourite and, in the afternoons, Artorex used his razor-sharp hook until his back was one long scream of pain. For the whole of autumn, all household tasks were done at a run and, although Artorex dreamed constantly of grinding Targo into splinters of bone and flesh, he was aware that muscles that had once been whipcord thin were now beginning to harden and thicken into ropes.

Meanwhile, his thirteenth birthday passed unnoticed.

'Will I ever be strong enough to be an able opponent for you, Targo?'

'Aye! Else we're wasting our time. But are you fast enough, boy?'

'Oh, shite!' Artorex swore, as Targo disarmed him once again.

Then, just as he was becoming comfortable with sword and shield, Targo changed the rules once again.

'A good fighter hacks away with either hand, judging his enemy accurately, and predicting his next move.'

Artorex nodded, as Targo grinned evilly, exposing long, brown canines.

'But a great fighter is agile, fast and unpredictable. He chooses the ground on which he might die, and he turns the worst footholds into an advantage.'

'I suppose that makes sense,' Artorex replied, trying to interpret Targo's words and discover what this lesson had to do with a farm boy on the outskirts of a city.

'Do you want to be a great fighter, Artorex? Or simply good?' Targo asked, without his usual sardonic grin.

The boy realized his tutor was in deadly earnest.

'I . . . er . . . great . . . I suppose. I cannot see the point of all this effort otherwise. I . . . er . . . I sort of promised . . .'

How could Artorex explain to Targo how the three travellers had questioned him, their responses and the odd look of measurement in their eyes?

Targo had to look up into Artorex's odd grey eyes, for the boy already stood several inches taller than his tutor.

'As you age, you'll become a big man, taller than most warriors who go to battle. And you'll be strong – and you're faster than most. Mithras gave you the bone and the reflexes for brute force. But those skills are as nothing.'

'So why have I sweated to learn them?' the boy asked plaintively and received a cuff across his ear from Targo's calloused hand.

'To begin, boy, to begin.'

Artorex fell naturally into the familiar pose of a servant who was being chided, and stared at his dusty feet. He received a cuff across his other ear for his meekness.

'The greatest fighter I ever knew was a Scythian woman who was no taller than my shoulder.'

Against his better judgement, Artorex smiled momentarily – and found his ear really throbbing from a particularly vicious blow.

'You might laugh, but she nearly cut my throat.' Targo pointed at a long scar that began at the side of his throat and trailed down into his rough tunic. 'If she hadn't slipped in a puddle of my blood, I'd have been worm food before I was twenty. I was very good, you see, and I underestimated her agility. It was many months before my wounds had healed.'

'So what happened to the Scythian woman?' the boy asked warily. He was making a vain attempt to imagine a female with warrior skills superior to those of Targo.

'I slit her belly open as she was falling down. Damn, but she was one fine woman,' Targo reminisced.

Artorex saw the old man smile fondly for just the briefest of moments.

'What was her edge?' Artorex asked.

'A good question, boy.'

'Ow!' Artorex yelped, as Targo cuffed him once again. 'What was that for?'

'A little pain now might make you think of my mistake at some future time when you believe you have an enemy at your mercy. I underestimated her. You mightn't get the second chance that I received.' As he spoke, Targo scanned the farmyard until his eyes stopped at a rough fence, some five feet high, around the field where the horses exercised.

'A test for you. Your life depends on it! I want you over that fence, as fast as you can. Now!'

The boy saw the fence was just a little too high for him to leap, and climbing was certain to make him look foolish.

'It's too late! You're dead! The enemy has taken you!'

Targo tripped the boy neatly and Artorex felt his bones rattle as he hit the packed sod.

'But to climb that fence I'd have to use my sword hand. I'd be dead anyway!'

'Your prime task is to get over the fence in one piece.' Targo whistled between the gaps in his old teeth as he walked away. 'And don't you ever drop your sword again. If you do, I'll give you three lashes.'

'Oh, shite!' the boy swore under his breath.

Of a sudden, a simple post and rail fence seemed more impregnable than the walls of the villa.

Artorex thought feverishly.

He approached the fence from several angles and noticed that the rails were sturdy enough as a barrier for horses but could easily collapse under the weight of his growing body. The horses saw the fence as a solid structure, so the rails were allowed to weather and split.

'Hurry up, boy. The sun is moving – and I'm tired. I don't want to find new shade.' Targo was sprawled comfortably under the cool cover of a young alder tree.

The posts are the key, Artorex though desperately. But how do I use them?

The answer came to him suddenly, so he decided to charge at the fence post before he lost his nerve.

Artorex's left hand hit the top of the post with a satisfying thud, and he was thrust upwards. Unfortunately, his feet did not rise quite as high as he imagined, and he clipped the rail with his foot, causing him to tumble in a wild cartwheel to the other side of the fence. He landed squarely on his backside with enough force to jar the teeth in his head.

His developing instincts ensured that he kept his sword firmly gripped in his right hand.

Targo laughed and leapt to his feet with far more speed than his youthful pupil was displaying.

'Boy, once again you're dead, but you now have an idea that you can work on. I want you to practise its execution until you perfect it. Forget haymaking for this afternoon – and get this task right. Consider today a holiday.'

Artorex grew to loathe that fence before the evening meal. He realized that, unless he could raise his whole body parallel to the rail, he would continue to land on his backside or, as the day continued, on any other part of his body that he treasured.

Targo wandered off in an unusually good humour, leaving him to charge at the fence until his left arm felt as if it would never bend again.

Darkness had almost fallen when Artorex finally arrived at the solution.

He realized that he would have to change sword hands to

successfully complete the jump. If he moved the sword to his left hand during his run, he could use his stronger right arm in the leap, then lift his legs high, land cleanly and change sword hands once again during the descent.

Eventually, Artorex managed to elevate his weary body over the obstinate fence in three successive attempts.

'Excellent work, lad! Well, perhaps we should say passable.' Targo laughed from the lengthening shadows. 'Tomorrow, you will work on your technique and you'll learn to use both hands.'

Over the long months of his training, Artorex discovered the true, manly pleasures of the Roman bath. The mineral waters eased the constant ache of bruises and the odd broken toe or finger, while the oils released the tightly bunched muscles of shoulder, thigh and calf. Even the steam emanating from the calidarium unknotted the abused nerves and tendons that stretched less willingly as his body grew. Where once cleanliness was cursory, it soon became a compulsory element in his daily routine.

Master and servants noticed the changes in the routine of the young man, and they delighted at his discomfort on those many occasions when they gently teased him.

'If the boy holds out,' Ector joked, as Artorex limped over to fill his master's proffered wine cup, 'Targo will have managed to wash him clean.'

Artorex's hands were trembling with weariness and he barely managed to hold the wine jug steady. Ector took the heavy vessel from the boy's unresisting fingers and replaced it with a pottery bowl of rabbit, root vegetables and barley stew. Artorex smiled briefly with gratitude and served the plain, workday food to the mistress of the house.

'If the Lump lives so long,' Caius said quite clearly to no one in particular from his seat alongside his father.

Both Ector and Livinia turned their eyes reproachfully towards their son.

'I swore an oath that the name you have just used would not be spoken in this house, young man,' Ector hissed. 'You will respect my wishes!'

'I agree with your father,' Livinia chided Caius. 'You will not be uncouth, my son, for Artorex has earned a measure of respect for the hard work he does. I might add that he doesn't complain or whine, but attempts to conduct himself like a true Roman warrior.' She tapped Artorex's hand gently with her index finger as he served her a small ladle of the stew. Her touch was respectful and affectionate, and Artorex felt his eyes fill with gratitude.

'Eat, Artorex. This good, plain food will bring the colour back to your face,' Livinia ordered kindly as she spooned out a bowl of stew with her own hands.

In truth, Caius was more embarrassed by his mother's reprimand than by any debt he felt he owed to his father's oath. He scowled and would have protested, but Livinia fixed him with her wide, dark stare and he lapsed into sullen silence.

Ector's attention returned to Artorex.

'I swear you grow longer in the leg than a barbarian,' he murmured. 'You'll be an asset to me, boy, if you hold to your training. Yes, a considerable asset.'

Artorex blushed hotly. He was unused to words of praise from his foster-family.

And so the boy learned.

As fast as he defeated one obstacle, Targo invented another to tease his strengthening mind. He was set tumbling exercises from which he must rise in attack mode, using whatever hand or weapon that Targo dictated on that day. On another morning, Artorex was left standing on his hands for an hour, a dagger clenched between his teeth, for no reason that the boy could fathom.

Later still, Targo told him to ford a deceptively shallow

stream that flowed through the western fields. Artorex almost drowned in a deep hole before Targo relented and taught the boy the rudiments of swimming. Then he must learn to swim one-handed, with his blade held high above the water. And, in his spare time, Artorex was taught how to care for his weapons, to oil them against rust and to sharpen the old, pitted blades with a whetstone.

Artorex almost wished he had been left with his original wooden sword.

At midday on the day after Artorex had reached his fourteenth birthday, two of the travellers returned to Villa Poppinidii. Shortly after their arrival, Artorex was summoned to the practise field.

Luka was speaking casually to Targo, who was uncharacteristically humble around the younger man. Artorex saw the gruff old warrior bow his head as he listened with deep respect.

Both men turned to examine Artorex as he approached.

Luka was forced to raise his eyes slightly to meet the gaze of the sheepish Artorex while his inscrutable, flat stare calculated every change that had occurred in the young man's body.

'He's grown since last I saw him.'

'Like a weed,' Targo agreed.

'Are you stronger now, boy?' Luka asked.

'I'm strong enough, master,' Artorex replied in the same fashion as on that strange night when his fortunes had changed.

'And are you faster now, boy?'

'I'm fast enough, master.'

'Then let's see, shall we?' Luka stripped off his tunic and stood bare-chested in his leather riding trousers and soft boots. He drew his short sword from its scabbard with a little menacing hiss, exactly like the warning from a marsh snake.

Artorex had brought his weapon, but neither combatant had a shield.

He must be very confident, the boy thought to himself as he concentrated on maintaining eye contact with the stranger. But I dare not cut him – even though he can't imagine that I could do such a thing to him.

Luka fell into the fighting crouch.

Without any further thought, Artorex moved warily sideways, circling until the waning sun would strike Luka's eyes, and not his.

'That's very good,' Luka muttered reflectively, and immediately resumed the attack. The boy realized that this opponent was in deadly earnest. One slip, and he could easily be filleted like a fish.

The boy parried and moved as he searched for a weakness in Luka's fighting skill. Targo had instilled in him the truth that every warrior had a flaw and that, once found, that weakness could give his opponent an edge.

Artorex changed hands and reversed direction, thrusting carefully as he moved into a different attack mode.

'Very good.' Luka also changed hands.

This is unfair, Artorex thought to himself. He's older than me – and he's stronger. And he knows I cannot fight back.

Then Targo's steady voice echoed in the boy's mind: 'Fair doesn't enter into the battlefield! Life is unfair! Find an edge or you're dead!'

His mind suddenly clarified, and the consequences of failure outpaced all the jumbled images that were scrambling for prominence in his brain.

This field of combat is all there is. This man and his weapon are all there is. He's my enemy and he must be defeated – by any means!

So easily comes the end to childhood.

Even as this coldness overpowered all other thought, Artorex continued to move, his feet falling naturally into the patterns dictated by the shape of the field. One particularly wicked slash from Luka could have removed his arm if he hadn't evaded the blade by throwing himself into a tumbling arc and rising to his feet almost at Luka's back.

Almost – but not quite.

Luka's torso glistened with a light sheen of sweat, and Artorex knew his skin must also be slick and wet.

The minutes continued to drag on as each man probed, until both were breathing heavily.

Artorex never took his eyes from Luka's face.

Suddenly, he found his edge.

Luka showed the smallest fraction of his forward planning in his eyes and in his free hand which twitched away from the intended direction of his next movement.

There! It happened again. Luka's mind revealed the nature of his next attack.

Now is the time to wear him down, Artorex ordered himself as he attempted to control the thud of his wildly beating heart, although in truth he was near to exhaustion himself. I have a height, strength and speed advantage over him, Artorex reasoned. I must wear him down until he makes an error.

And then, suddenly, Luka lowered his sword.

'You speak truthfully, Artorex,' he panted. 'You have strength and speed enough.'

Luka turned his back on Artorex and ambled over to Targo. Artorex, still in the fighter's crouch, was left feeling confused and foolish.

Luka clapped the veteran on the shoulder.

'Damn me, but he'll be good. You are to be congratulated.'

'I'll grant you he's a good enough student,' Targo replied complacently.

Artorex shook his head to clear his concentration, then sheathed his sword with an angry thud.

'His eyes say nothing, Targo, not a blessed thing,' Luka muttered. 'I think he had my measure – and I'm not really ashamed to admit it.'

Targo nodded ruminatively. 'You're right, master. I believe he'd have held off your attack for some time.'

'Good. Good. And now I think we old soldiers deserve some wine.'

After the men ambled off companionably, Artorex was left alone on the field of combat.

'That's it?' he asked the descending sun. 'Nearly three years of work – and that's it?'

But the trial by combat was not quite *it*.

The feast passed much as all such occasions did at the Villa Poppinidii. A supply of fresh fish had been delivered to the villa and the mistress had ordered that the finest sea bass should be stuffed with spicy fungi and a concoction of herbs, bread and chestnuts for the banquet. Against all his finer thoughts, Artorex's mouth watered at the smell of succulent roast piglets and honey-glazed venison covered in sauces so exotic that the villa cook had screamed curses at anyone brave enough to interrupt his ministrations.

Serving women struggled under full platters and Artorex followed in their wake, checking the oil burners and wall sconces automatically. As usual, he prepared and served the wine, and exercised considerably more deftness than on the first occasion when he had met Myrddion Merlinus and Luka. The lad tried to remain invisible, as was his custom, but he was forced to hear himself being discussed openly as if he was mere smoke and shadows.

'You have our congratulations, and our thanks, friend Ector, for your foster-son has grown in stature as a fighting man.' Luka smiled across at his host.

'We are quite aware that the training the boy has received has been expensive, Ector.' Luka crossed himself sardonically for, like many sensible Celts, he paid lip service to many gods. 'The good Lucius has sent a purse to recompense you for the effort you have expended on his behalf.'

Myrddion turned to face Livinia. 'Our friend, Llanwith pen Bryn, is acutely aware of his rudeness and failures in gallantry towards you, my lady,' he said. 'He sends a gift as a peace offering between you.'

Both Livinia and Ector received their gifts with some perplexity.

When the mistress of the villa opened the oiled wrappings, a pair of pearl earrings caught the light with their extraordinary exotic lustre. Screws of gold were designed to fit through holes in Livinia's ears and Artorex winced when he saw the thickness of these plugs of precious metal.

Women are very strange creatures to endure such pain for physical adornment, he thought as he watched Mistress Livinia's face blossom delightedly at the gift. Then she rewrapped the oilskins and hid the irregular, refulgent pearls from sight with a sigh of regret.

'I cannot accept such a gift, Myrddion Merlinus. I've done my duty by my husband and my family; courtesy towards my guests does not warrant such a reward.'

Myrddion waved an elegant hand in her direction as if to dismiss her qualms.

'Pen Bryn thought you might refuse his gift on such grounds. So he asked me to thank you, in advance, for your part in polishing the social skills of this young man. Our plans for him are such that he'll become much more than a fighting machine and should learn the skills of courtesy, nobility and patience. My friend asks that you accept these trifles as a small reward for the efforts that you will spend instilling these qualities into our young protégé.'

Lady Livinia bowed her head in acquiescence, and Artorex groaned inwardly.

His mistress spent much of her day presiding over the smooth running of her household and weaving fine cloth on her looms, and Artorex did not relish being confined to the villa at her beck and call through the winter months. Any thoughts of leisure when snow shrouded the villa were fast disappearing in the pleasure reflected in Lady Livinia's eyes.

Ector expressed his gratitude at the honour bestowed on his family.

'I ask that you thank Lucius and Lord pen Bryn for the courtesy they have shown our house, not only for your fine gifts, but also because you have given us what we might never have anticipated – a strong arm to protect the Villa Poppinidii and keep it safe if ever violent hands are raised against us.' With age, Ector had discovered that he, too, could speak with a suave polish, especially when he felt totally beyond his depth.

'Of course, the boy still needs some ... rounding out,' Luka added.

'Of course,' Ector agreed cautiously.

'We feel that horsemanship is a vital tool in the arsenal of the warrior, especially as barbarians always travel by foot.'

Artorex gasped.

'Er ... yes, I can see your argument,' Ector agreed, his confusion now clear in his bluff, red face.

'But Artorex isn't a gentleman!' Caius protested.

All eyes, apart from those of Artorex, swivelled towards Ector's son.

'Young man, would the good Lucius, priest of the Christian god at Holy Glastonbury, have sent the son of a slave to be reared by a man as worthy as your father?'

Myrddion's words cut far more deeply than Luka's sword could have done. They sliced open the youthful pride of Caius.

He flushed unbecomingly and opened his mouth to speak but, as one, the men turned away from him as if he was of no account.

Only Livinia stared fixedly at Caius, and she raised a finger to her small mouth to silence the young man.

She had no inkling of the importance Artorex held for these great ones, but she instinctively realized that his person was vital to them. Villa Poppinidii, of all the great houses, had been chosen to nurture a cuckoo in its nest, and her husband and son could only profit from that choice – especially if Caius could be forced to relinquish the prejudices of his childhood and birth. Lady Livinia lived and prospered through her duty to her house so, from this point on, she would give Artorex the benefit of her full attention.

'How old are you now, Artorex?' Myrddion asked, as the boy filled his wine cup.

'I am in my fifteenth year, my lord.'

'So young,' Myrddion mused. 'And so tall.'

'He's a little too tall,' Luka stated. 'He will draw the greatest warriors towards him when he is on the battlefield.'

'Unless he's truly exceptional, or mounted on a large horse.'

'It would have to be a very large horse – once the boy is fully grown.' Luka laughed. 'Else it will soon grow swaybacked under his weight.'

As he listened to the discussion flowing over and around him, Artorex wanted to scream and shout questions at the honoured guests. It was only with the greatest self-control that he managed to hold his curiosity in check.

Although Artorex's eyes said nothing, they had lightened with his mounting anger. He was still very young.

Luka saw the start of red spots high on the boy's cheekbones.

'These changes must be difficult for you to understand, Artorex. We come out of nowhere, make decisions that change the order of your life and then disappear without providing any explanation for our actions. However, you can be assured we do have our reasons for monitoring your education.'

Artorex lifted his chin. His face now reddened further in embarrassment and confusion.

'That may be true, my lord. But any man would wish to understand his place in the world in which he lives.'

'Then ask your questions. If it is in my power to answer, be very sure that I will do so. It is far better than listening behind closed doors.'

Now, Artorex flushed hotly in acute embarrassment.

'You wrong me, my lord. I was only a curious child when last we saw you here – one of no account. You treated me like an untrained hawk, not yet fit for the glove. But I must know what is intended if I am to serve whatever purpose has been ordained for me.'

'The boy speaks truthfully and Luka did resort to a low blow.' Myrddion laughed easily.

Artorex clenched his jaw, for even the scholarly Myrddion was still treating him like a performing animal.

'Who is my father?' Artorex snapped.

'It is not in my power to give you that information. However, you may be assured that he was a man of extraordinary gifts, else you would not be here.' Luka spoke with conviction, and Artorex understood that, at last, the northerner was taking him seriously.

'Where was I born?'

'In a fortress to the south.'

'Why was I taken from my mother? Is she still alive?'

'Your mother lives. You were brought here to save your life.'

'Oh!'

Luka recognized that Artorex's size belied his maturity, and the warrior felt a pang of sorrow as he realized that this amenable and talented young man had no place in the world to call his own. A wealth of hurt feelings and sad experiences, both past and present, were compressed within Artorex's regretful sigh.

But the boy also knew how to speak with a voice of unconscious command. For one short moment, Luka had almost slipped under the force of the boy's personality, and had nearly revealed information that, for now, must be kept secret.

'So you must continue to listen and learn, young Artorex. Perhaps we shall meet again soon, at which time you will almost certainly be able to defeat me in equal combat,' Luka added, with surprising gentleness.

Myrddion Merlinus leaned forward and engaged the master and mistress, the heir and the foster-son with eyes that were hooded and brooding.

'The Villa Poppinidii is far from the centre of the world,' he declared. 'It's also far from the deeds of the great ones of Briton – and Briton is far from the Rome that was once the centre of the world until the barbarian hordes stripped the legions of their invincibility. You, Caius, speak of Rome with pride as if it will last forever. But the glory of Rome is gone, just like the empires of the Carthaginians and the Spartans before them, so that Constantinople is now the only city in the world where dreams of past glory still have some shadow of life. Odoacer and his Germanic sons now rule the Forum, and the great fortresses of Gaul are deserted.' He gazed round at his audience with eyes that were infinitely sad. 'The legions of Rome will never return. The end of times has come.'

Ector shivered and Livinia raised her hands to her eyes, but Caius shook his artful curls in denial.

'No, Caius, what is done is done! The barbarians have been nibbling away at your world for two hundred years and now the end is near. Do we go down to the Saxons? Does our civilization fade and rot away under muddy, barbarian feet? Do not doubt me! Artorex has been trained for battle, for all men of the Celtic peoples must fight to ensure that the world we know is not obliterated, as Rome was!'

Blank, shocked eyes met Myrddion's direct gaze and then looked down at the fine food and the good wine on the tables before them. Their world had changed, even as they dined, because they suddenly understood that men were fighting and dying so they could eat in peace.

'We've often talked of Uther Pendragon and his failure to stem the Saxon tide that moves inexorably towards our peoples. The High King is old, and he is exhausted by a lifetime of attempting the impossible, for chaos has come upon us as the wild hordes of the north continue their march. Without Caius and his friends, and without Artorex and his kind, how shall we hold back the darkness when you and the High King go to the shadows?'

Ector blinked, and then shook his leonine head in understanding of what loomed before the Celtic peoples. Livinia gripped his hand across the eating couch.

'Artorex, continue to learn.' Myrddion added, and then smiled. 'You will be needed. But we must not forget to praise you for your studies, young man. Our friend, Llanwith pen Bryn, had no doubt that you'd pass any test that Luka could devise, so he sent you a trophy of victory. He hopes it will be a small compensation for your many unanswered questions – and our unspoken motives.'

'Did Lord pen Bryn truly use those words?' Artorex asked. 'Or do you embroider them in his name?'

Ector gasped at the effrontery of his foster-son, but Myrddion simply rose, lightly tapped the boy's cheek and offered him a scroll case.

'Much to my surprise, he said those very words. You have my

word on it, Artorex. Llanwith pen Bryn is in no doubt of your value to our plans.'

'You should thank the masters, boy, and you should remember your manners,' Ector ordered. He had understood very little of the conversation except for the imminence of the Saxon threat, but the purse sent by Lucius had held seven imperial gold coins, a vast amount, and Artorex was obviously favoured by fortune.

Artorex did his foster-father's bidding and courteously thanked Myrddion.

Soon, the feast was over and the villa became still. The night had a cool privacy that enfolded the boy in his own thoughts, lending him the illusion of autonomy. In the quiet of his cubicle, Artorex opened the scroll case and discovered another part of the Commentaries of the great Caesar. He hugged the scroll with a pure and child-like joy.

On silent, bare feet, Artorex moved out into the colonnades, and thence to the atrium where he could observe the stars of the autumn night.

The midnight air was chill, and Artorex wore only his loincloth, but the gelid cold steadied the hot blood that thundered in his veins and denied him sleep. The moon was waning and now it appeared like a sickle or some strange silver blade that curved low towards the roof. Artorex's breath steamed in the night. He was too weary for fear, and too confused for questions. He must consider the information Luka had given him during the coming days at times when his brain could dissect and measure the message behind his words.

And tomorrow, he would begin to learn the art of riding a horse.

CHAPTER III

CHILDHOOD'S END

In the early morning, winter announced its arrival with chill, white fingers that left serpentine trails of frost in the drying grass. The days shortened noticeably as the corpses of leaves fell in great, scarlet carpets. A single gate barred the path to the villa, although it was never locked and any child could raise the long, iron tongue that held it closed. The path was deeply rutted by farm wagons and, in winter, it was a frozen agony of hardened mud and dried grass. Settled firmly on deep foundations, the villa and its outbuildings, its rich storehouses, its capacious servants' quarters and its herds of horses, cattle, pigs and fowl hunched on the low hill overlooking the Roman road, brooding in the fading light.

Provident masters of the Villa Poppinidii had scorned to hide the villa and its wealth behind a strong exterior wall but, ever mindful of the dangers in an outpost colony, they had built their home to last. Over a foot thick, and largely free of any openings, its frame offered a blind, uncompromising face to the casual visitor. Its neat, fruitful orchards, the fields that were a patchwork quilt of prudent agriculture and the verdant kitchen gardens might promise a warm welcome, but the villa's heavy, studded door was prudently locked at night. The Villa Poppinidii looked inward at its fountain and its atrium garden, rather than outward at the long road that led to Aquae Sulis. In the eyes of its inhabitants, the enclave was their whole world and was complete as it stood.

But, beyond the fertile orchards and fallow fields, the Old Forest brooded. Artorex's refuge was a constant reminder that the land was not completely safe and, now that Myrddion Merlinus had opened their eyes, Ector and Livinia surveyed their small kingdom with hearts that were weighted with foreboding.

Caius ventured into this winter landscape of grey skies and misty, skeletal trees with his customary elan. Unlike his parents, Caius refused to accept that Rome was dead, so he enjoyed his days with the same careless pursuit of pleasure that had always motivated him. With his hunting hounds and his trained hawks, he rode into the wilderness to harry his prey. He rarely returned with the boars, the foxes or the stags that he killed, preferring to leave their corpses to rot on the bloodstained, frozen earth. The local villagers learned to follow his blood spoor which unerringly provided them with enough fresh meat to last them through the winter months.

At other times, when he was bored with hunting, Caius spent his days and nights with a coterie of young men who were noted for their epicene habits and their conscious, offensive arrogance. Wealthy, idle and bored, they drank, whored and terrorized the villagers with stupid pranks that amused the young men hugely but embarrassed their elders when complaints inevitably came to their doors.

But even a much-loved and cosseted son couldn't avoid all responsibility, and Caius was expected to put aside play to learn the duties of the villa, although he protested at first. Maintaining inventories, supervising crop rotation and planning new villa facilities crowded the days of the young heir as he learned the myriad responsibilities of a master. If he chafed under the yoke of his birth, Caius chose to hide any impatience under a glacial, patronizing composure suitable to his station.

At the other end of the social scale, Artorex stared out at the delicate winter landscape and envied the few scavenger birds that hung in the fog-wreathed air like black rags. Their freedom mocked his busy schedule of toil, study and the endless, irritating challenges that kept him from the fields and the forest. Even the heady promise of horsemanship was small recompense for a life of tedious, inexplicable tasks that left Artorex confused and frustrated, even when he successfully completed the many tests set by Targo.

Gradually, Artorex learned to ride the working farm horses that were the pride of the Villa Poppinidii but he soon discovered that a steady trot was the best they could manage, no matter how hard he beat the sides of their flanks with the flat of his sword. Easy-natured as these horses were proving to be, Targo attended to the young man's training with his usual order and precision.

When the old legionnaire led Artorex up to Plod, the farm stallion, with his fringed hooves and massive bay shoulders, the boy felt his knees turn to jelly with fear. The horse stood ruminatively chewing grass with huge, yellow teeth, or piddling amazing streams of hot urine wherever he pleased. By the size of the huge droppings scattered through the stables and fields, Artorex decided he did not want to be near Plod's backside when he lifted his large, coarse tail.

'He's big, isn't he?' Targo stated reflectively.

'He's too big for me,' Artorex said flatly.

'People always think that big means savage,' Targo murmured. 'How many times have you been called a barbarian, boy? But it's not true, is it? Well, Plod here is like his name, for all that he's a stallion. He's as sweet as a nut, ain't you, you old faker.' Targo proceeded to beat on the horse's belly and flanks with his open hand, so hard that dust rose from Plod's winter coat in little puffs and drifts.

Artorex waited for Plod to pound Targo into shreds of raw, bloody meat, but the beast simply snickered his enjoyment at the attention he was getting.

'See? He's a pleasure to be around, is this old boy. But he's useless, mind, except for siring more big bastards like himself, or pulling logs from the forest. Now, lad, I want you to mount him.'

'How? He's as big as a small room,' Artorex retorted. 'I'll need a ladder.'

'You won't be finding a ladder on the battlefield.' Targo laughed and wandered off in his usual, aimless fashion.

Unwilling to even touch Plod at first, Artorex approached the huge horse from one side. Placing his hands on the horse's back, the young man tried to jump on to its broad haunches as he had done with the smaller farm horses. He ended up sitting on the ground with the horse's tail switching in his face. Plod turned his head and eyed Artorex with a wide, long-lashed stare of amazement.

Even the horse is laughing at me, Artorex decided.

Then he gripped the base of Plod's mane in his left hand and tried to hoist himself on to Plod's back by brute strength.

Inevitably, he fell on his backside again.

Plod continued to gaze at Artorex with a total lack of comprehension.

Think, idiot! Artorex admonished himself, not even bothering to rise to his feet. It's like the post and the rail. There must be a trick to this business of riding a horse as big as Plod.

And so the boy considered his position logically, for he was by now becoming comfortable with devising solutions to Targo's problems. He determined that he needed to approach the large horse from the front, grip the mane and leap on to Plod's back, turning as he did so.

The solution worked and he was successful at the first attempt.

Plod ignored Artorex once he was seated painfully on the horse's very sharp spine. The young man was soon slapping the stallion's shoulders and trying to discover how to entice or, better still, order the beast to move.

Plod continued to munch on some green shoots near the fence. If he bothered to obey the command to move at all, it was to search out sweeter grass.

'Aaaah!' Artorex screamed with frustration after five minutes of fruitless pummelling and shouting; Plod, being well used to the strange ways of humans, took no notice.

Then, in pure frustration, Artorex kicked the beast in the flanks with his heels. Abruptly, Plod obeyed, and Artorex, who had not thought to grip the stallion's mane, fell backwards over the horse's flanks.

The horse stopped and turned its head to look back at the boy as if Artorex was mentally retarded, a gaze that was mirrored in the laughter and expressions of two passing field hands.

'That's the way, Artor – show him who's the boss,' one guffawed as they carried their reaping hooks and hoes out to the fallow fields.

For the first time, Artorex heard the shortened form of his name used by common field hands instead of the regal-sounding name that Lucius had chosen for him at birth.

Artorex persevered and soon began to unlock the secrets that allowed him to control his horse. He practised hard and began to experience the pleasure of feeling such a huge creature move on his command. While Plod's great muscles surged and bunched under Artorex's knees, he soon became familiar with the exquisite pain that men experience as their bodies become fused to the unbending spine of a horse.

Not surprisingly, Artorex managed to fall off the workhorse

on many occasions, and was almost crushed against the fence until he learned to manipulate the horse's halter and pull its head back when he wanted the beast to stop.

And so the young man and his giant horse began to learn the rudiments of riding.

Targo allowed him no time for self-congratulation, because the veteran now arranged for Artorex to meet Aphrodite.

This slightly smaller mare had a nasty disposition and hated all men, especially tall, vigorous specimens like Artorex. She gazed balefully at him with a jaundiced, narrowed eye at their very first meeting, and then managed to regularly throw him off her back with casual disdain.

Aphrodite was definitely not the Greek goddess of love.

'Who's the smarter? You or the horse?' Targo asked, with a wicked leer plastered over his seamed and wrinkled face.

'I am,' Artorex snarled through clenched teeth.

Then the horse stood on the boy's foot. Artorex was sure she had broken his toe.

'Who's stronger? You? Or the horse?'

'She is – unfortunately.'

Targo laughed, coughed and then spat on the ground.

'So how do you control something that is far stronger than you?' Targo asked.

'Cheat a little?' Artorex said hopefully.

'You must convince her that you are stronger and nastier than she is,' Targo lectured. 'Horses are like little children. And how do you stop little children from misbehaving?' Targo mimicked the slapping of a naked bottom. 'For truly difficult horses, trainers use a quirt, or a small whippy branch. They don't use it overly much, mind, for if you brutalize a horse you'll only make it dangerous. Just a taste is all you will need, not enough to hurt but sufficient to demonstrate to Aphrodite that you're in charge.' He smiled. 'Here's a suitable branch. I'll return when you've mastered her.'

Targo walked away with his usual lack of concern, but he had just handed the boy his greatest test – and the most dangerous temptation to date.

Targo was a hard man, in fists, in swordplay and in the business of living. He had few illusions about the goodness of heart of the people with whom he mixed, nor was there much love left in him. But to those he did love, he was faithful forever.

During his long life, he had seen men who appeared to be honourable on the surface but who took unnatural pleasure in the infliction of pain and brute force. Targo had never understood such flawed creatures, for he hardly considered them to be human. They brutalized anything and anyone within the ambit of their power, so they would beat a horse until it was a quivering and broken-spirited creature, simply because they had complete mastery over the animal.

Targo didn't know if the boy was such a person. Often, these human beasts had felt inadequacy as children, or had been bullied and brutalized themselves. Targo knew that Artorex had never been forced to exercise power over anything that breathed, so he hoped that the boy wouldn't fail this crucial trial. The snake-eyed Luka would be certain to ask the question on his next visit.

Artorex could never have guessed the fearful tenor of Targo's thoughts, so straight was the old man's back as he strode briskly away.

As was becoming his custom, Artorex approached this latest problem with logic and reason. He cut his own quirt in full view of the wild-eyed mare, slicing his hand with the thin wand of alder in the process. It hurt!

Yes, he thought to himself. No horse would enjoy a blow from this weapon.

Then, for the very first time, he looked at Aphrodite with real attention. She was an ugly mare at best, and it was obvious that she had felt the quirt before, judging by the narrow scars on her shoulders and her flanks.

The horse looked back at him defiantly and Artorex recognized that the mare's hatred was directed at the narrow wand in his hand. In clear view of Aphrodite's rolling eyes, he turned his hand and dropped the branch to the ground before showing Aphrodite his bare palms. Then he swiftly leapt on to her back, grabbed her mane tightly with both hands and wrapped his legs about her barrel belly.

As usual, she tried to throw him, but this time her heart didn't seem so set on drawing his blood and maiming him. Artorex pulled hard on her mane, thereby yanking her head upward. The horse corkscrewed and twisted, but the boy continued to pit his will against hers. Even when she eventually threw him off, he went through the same procedure as before, again and again, until, just when Artorex believed his aching bones couldn't bear another fall, Aphrodite surrendered her will to his. He felt the sundering of her defiance flow through her body and into his hands which were still tightly knit into her mane. He kicked her flanks, and the horse broke into an obedient trot and then a comfortable canter. Artorex began to exult in the pure joy that a man can only experience when a powerful creature gives itself to him, to do with as he pleases.

When Aphrodite had demonstrated that she was a more mobile and speedy animal than Plod, Artorex threw himself from her back and approached her frontally to stroke her great cheek and forehead.

At first, Aphrodite pulled her head away, and the boy could see all the whites around her untrusting eyes, but he persisted until the horse reluctantly permitted him to caress her.

An hour later, when Targo returned from the villa to rejoin his pupil, he discovered a guilty Artorex feeding the horse a stolen carrot top from the kitchens.

'So she took to the quirt, then, boy?'

'You're an evil old man, Master Targo,' Artorex replied evenly. 'You knew this horse wouldn't respond to that sort of treatment.' His voice was a gentle murmur to spare the horse from nervousness.

'You did very well with this task, lad, and I'm pleased.' Targo smiled. 'The best horsemen I have encountered had no use for whips and quirts, but controlled their beasts with the bridle, the reins and the sure touch of their heels. I've seen Scythians who can guide horses with the reins in their teeth – and empty-handed – so that they can use their murderous bows while on the gallop.' He grinned at Artorex. 'Some men say those devils were centaurs once but I believe they're just excellent horsemen who regularly practise their skills.'

'Someone has scarred this horse very badly, Targo. Who ruined her?' Artorex asked.

'It's not for me to say, boy. But I think you could make a good guess.'

It's what I'd expect of one such as Caius, Artorex thought to himself but, like Targo, he wisely kept his opinions to himself.

Aphrodite and Artorex gradually became friends – of a kind.

The boy brought her a carrot every day, so the kitchen staff began to keep the misshapen or slightly elderly vegetables for Artorex's use. Artorex always rewarded her if she kept her temper with him, and he knew that this was all the consideration that he could ask of her. He understood that she would never fully trust him, for a damaged horse, like a betrayed child, cannot ever be quite whole.

The next spring, after Artorex turned fifteen and had become quite a competent rider, with or without a bridle and rein, Aphrodite broke one of the weaker fence rails and escaped. For a weary and interminable week, Artorex searched for her, expecting to discover that she had been killed by boars or was hobbling on a broken leg in the Old Forest. But when he finally came upon her, he found that she had inexplicably found her way to his secret glade in the forest, where the old stone still drew his eyes with its strange carving, and the grass grew fresh and green wherever the sun's rays penetrated the treetops.

Amicably, Aphrodite submitted to the bridle and placidly followed him home. Behind them, in the deepest groves, Artorex heard the challenging whinny of a stallion, as if some strange centaur really did inhabit the ancient places. Superstitiously, he didn't look back, and Aphrodite quietly ambled behind him without any fuss.

In time, the mare bore a colt out of season, a long-legged, tiny thing, with slick black hair and an unnaturally large head. Once Aphrodite had cleaned the curly coat and nuzzled the colt to her dugs, Artorex stroked the short, wiry curls on the little creature's flanks.

Aphrodite snorted her displeasure just once, and then permitted Artorex to fondle her foal.

The colt grew and grew, as different from Plod and Aphrodite as Artorex was from Caius. The small creature would never be quite as tall as its dam, but it had inherited the same length of leg. It was also cleaner of limb, with legs that were unmarred by thick hair above the hooves, although its body coat was still rough and curly. Its head was smaller and more delicate than its mother, yet, for all its apparent fragility, the young horse appeared strong and heavy-boned.

'She must have found herself a wild pony when she was in season,' Targo decided. 'Perhaps it was a descendant of the horses brought from Gaul, or it might have been one of the hillside beasts that are still found in the high places. I don't know if he'll be any good, but he's a handsome colt.'

'He's beautiful, Targo,' Artorex breathed, as the foal nuzzled his arm with soft, questing lips.

'I hope he's not too beautiful or else the young master might be tempted to take him off you,' Targo murmured regretfully.

'Master Ector has already ordered me to become a horseman, so could you ask him if I could be responsible for the foal's training?' Artorex asked.

Artorex expected Targo to reject his request outright, but the veteran pursed his lips, then bit on one calloused knuckle until, finally, he came to a decision.

'I'll ask him before the young master decides to take the foal for his own use.'

Privately, Targo had already determined that he would keep Aphrodite's foal safe from the grasping hands of Caius. His gorge still rose whenever he remembered Aphrodite's coat, slick with blood and sweat, after Caius had beaten the mare almost to death. Targo had believed the mare would die with her spirit crushed, but she had found a well of hatred within her being that kept her alive. This foal wouldn't be spoiled like its dam if he had any say in the matter.

When Targo approached Lord Ector with his request, the master was inclined to be generous. For several months, Ector had been concerned that Artorex's riding lessons were inconvenient for the smooth running of the villa and this small, bastard horse was of very little value, except to solve the problem. If his foster-son could make something of the unpromising creature, then Ector would be advantaged once again.

And so Coal, as the young man named him, became Artorex's horse.

'Why did you give him that particular name?' Targo asked curiously. He had expected a far more grandiose title, even for such an awkward little colt.

'Coal burns hot and it fires the forges that make iron. It's stronger than wood and yet it is glossy and easily shaped. Yes,

Coal is his name, for he is my fire,' Artorex answered with perfect seriousness.

'Well, he's your horse, boy, so you can select whatever name you like for him,' was Targo's non-committal reply.

Horsemanship was the least of Artorex's newly acquired skills. Golden limbed, cleanly muscled and fair of face, Ector's foster-son drew the eyes of the villa women with little effort or conscious use of charm. Perhaps his innocence contributed to his attractiveness, for the lad had no notion of his sexual power. But Lady Livinia recognized Artorex's burgeoning manhood and, belatedly, remembered her promise to Myrddion Merlinus.

Towards the end of one long, tiring day, as Artorex trudged back from ploughing, slick with sweat, soil and the cold water he had sluiced over his head and shoulders, Lady Livinia left orders for her foster-son to attend to her in the atrium once he had bathed. Artorex was surprised, but he complied as quickly as he could, joining Lady Livinia and her maid on a limestone bench under a single linden tree. Lady Livinia was working her large floor loom while her maid was spinning degreased wool on a simple, wooden spindle.

'You asked to see me, my lady?' Artorex asked carefully, his grey eyes watching the flicker of coloured thread as her shuttle passed across the loom.

'Yes, Artorex.' She smiled in welcome. 'I've been remiss in your education. As Lord Myrddion explained, a true gentleman should understand how to speak to both servants and masters, how to practise courtesy and economy, and to display the good manners that oil the wheels of society. From tomorrow, you will attend me in the atrium each afternoon after the noontime meal.'

She smiled inwardly as she glimpsed the frown of chagrin that the lad attempted to hide by dropping his head. From

Artorex's point of view, hard work was preferable to such pointless activities.

'Don't fear that I'll keep you from your duties to the villa. An hour a day should be more than sufficient to correct any deficiencies in your deportment or manners. My woman, Delia, will oversee the more ... physical ... aspects of your education.'

Artorex was truly horrified. The words 'physical aspects' had an embarrassing, terrifying ring and the lad turned to face Livinia's maidservant with trepidation.

Delia was well past thirty years of age and seemed very old to Artorex, although her skin was still fresh and her hair was rich with an auburn sheen. She had served as Lady Livinia's servant from childhood and was devoted to the interests of her mistress, so Artorex had known her for years, at least from a distance. As Delia stepped forward into the light of the setting sun, Artorex had an opportunity to gauge the kindness in her mild, brown eyes.

Delia had borne five living children and her body was plump and strong. Her hands were her great beauty, although they were calloused from sewing, washing and the women's work of the villa. Her fingers were long, with sensitive pads and almond-shaped, pale nails, while her palms were unusually large and well fleshed. Those hands were clasped together firmly as she smiled at the thunderstruck young man.

So, in the noontime, Artorex learned how to dance, to turn a courtly sentence and to take a lady's arm. He mastered courtesy and deportment, and found nothing shameful in conversation with an interesting and intelligent woman. Lady Livinia's lessons would last the boy for the rest of his life and serve him well as he grew to manhood.

More importantly, Lady Livinia taught Artorex the woman's point of view, filtered through the Roman matron's idea of female duty. Without conscious effort, Artorex absorbed

Livinia's values, her style, her respect for family and her uncompromising ability to face painful truths. A single caress upon his hair, as light as thistledown, was cherished as he luxuriated in her regard.

After an afternoon's toil, Artorex would report to Delia at the servants' quarters. There, over a period of two weeks, the cheerful and motherly woman taught Artorex the pleasures of the bed. Her warmth, her good humour and her earthy common sense revealed many of the mysteries of women to the round-eyed boy, and for the first time he grew to appreciate the strength and pragmatism of the other sex. Wisely, Lady Livinia contrived to end these special lessons before Artorex teetered on the brink of lovesickness, for this clever matron understood that teacher and pupil might begin to care for each other if their arrangement continued overlong.

Artorex continued with Lady Livinia's lessons and discovered that he enjoyed his new friendship with Delia. Although any sexual liaison was over, he discussed the relationship with Frith who explained that Delia loved Lady Livinia, not him, and had taken him to her bed for her mistress's sake. Artorex should be grateful to these two women of such different stations, and free himself from any residual sentimentality.

Artorex examined Frith's amused blue eyes closely and saw no sign of mockery or falsehood in their clear depths. As he kissed Frith's withered cheek, Artorex realized that women like Frith, Delia and Livinia, who seemed so delicate and easily shocked, were actually stronger than iron and far more ruthless than a man could ever be.

'The mistress is a marvel,' Targo informed the young man after Delia had completed his education. 'She knows a boy needs guidance or else he'll likely develop some silly ideas.'

Artorex blushed hotly and wondered what Delia had let slip to her friends.

'Don't colour up, boy.' The warrior smiled at his protégé. 'I'm reliably told you've no cause to be ashamed of your performance.'

Artorex wished fervently that the earth would swallow him whole.

'It's a pity that Mistress Livinia didn't see to the education of young Caius so sensibly. He spends too much time with whores and catamites.'

'Gossip, Targo?' Artorex goaded, grateful that Targo had veered off the subject of his sexual education. 'I thought you disapproved of idle sniping at your betters and their habits.'

Targo responded with a quick clip to Artorex's ear.

'Don't be impertinent, *Master* Artorex. I see what I see, and a wise man stores away useful information in case he needs it later. Mistress Livinia should have entrusted her son to someone worthy, like Delia – or me for that matter. I'd have been a better guide to the beds of willing maidens than that Severinii brood.'

Wisely, and before Targo became really cross, Artorex changed the subject.

When Artorex turned sixteen and the colt was a yearling, they made a unique pair. Artorex stood at well over six feet and was still growing, and his wild hair was now plaited to tame its curls. He was shapely and strong, yet not so fair as Caius in face and form. But, alongside Artorex, Caius seemed insubstantial and a man of straw, although he was five years older – and had recently brought a wife to the villa.

Coal was still outsized in head and length of leg, but his coat shone from constant brushing and he trotted after Artorex like a dog. Even as a yearling, nimble and unafraid of the most treacherous terrain, he was faster than any other horse at the villa, save for the Gallic gelding owned by Caius. In the Old Forest, his coat made him almost invisible among the shadows of the trees, while he was sure-footed even where the forest was almost impenetrable.

When Artorex reached his seventeenth birthday, and the full duties of manhood, Ector set his foster-son to work. Cletus, the villa's steward, had succumbed to a lung disease that often kept him to his bed, so the master realized that the time had come to train Artorex as his replacement. On his good days, Cletus taught Artorex the role of steward while the young man served as the steward's ears and eyes outside the walls of the villa. Artorex rode around the estate checking provisions, supervising the rotation of crops and serving his master with diligence and speed.

Artorex began to understand the responsibility of leadership and the command of men.

Ector blessed the day when Lucius of Glastonbury had sent the boy to him.

Mindful of the promises he had made to Myrddion Merlinus, Luka and Llanwith pen Bryn, Artorex still practised the art of weaponry and horsemanship with Targo on a daily basis, and conducted all farm business from the back of a horse.

The young man's days were full and he was now permitted, on rare occasions, to eat with the family. These marks of favour occurred at those times of the year when he was required to report on the success of the harvest and the well-being of all those souls who lived at the Villa Poppinidii. Unlike Cletus, who was a slave, Artorex still existed in an odd no-man's land, neither fish nor fowl, neither slave nor master. As Cletus weakened, Artorex learned how to manipulate the many cogs that made up the machine that was the estate. He also learned to lead men with firmness, fairness and efficiency. He worked with them, when need be, and they appreciated the care he took to protect their interests.

At first, the field hands had resented a young man who

issued instructions on irrigation, planting, crop rotation and provisioning. But Artorex brooked no insolence and was only forced to break the jaw of one malcontent before the men accepted his superior leadership qualities and strength. After that, he set out to win them over to him.

Nor did Artorex prove to be insensitive to the constant dangers faced by the ordinary workers who served their masters so faithfully at the Villa Poppinidii. When the servant, Brabix, fell from the colonnade when securing a loose tile on the roof, he lingered for a week before dying. His belly swelled and he howled in agony until Frith mixed a draught made of sap from the bulbous heads of poppy plants to ease his suffering. Artorex kept watch over Brabix with the rest of the servants and promised the delirious man that his wife and child would be welcomed into a lifetime of service at the Villa Poppinidii.

Livinia was heard to say to her woman that the house had not run half so well in the hands of Cletus, but Artorex was always careful to defer to the old, failing man whose skin had turned to parchment, and who seemed to be burning to ash from within.

Only one cloud blotted the blue skies of Artorex's life. The new wife of Caius, Julanna, whose father claimed to be an unrecognized scion of the Julian line, came to the Villa Poppinidii boasting of the purity of her blood. At first, she seemed the perfect mate for Caius.

The marriage was arranged between the heads of both families, and little Julanna was a mere thirteen when she was wed to Caius in the old Roman fashion. She was a pale little creature with clouds of soft, nut-brown hair, but behind her initial arrogance she was really a frightened child, completely over-awed by her husband's family and the life into which she had been thrust.

Her eyes were very dark but without the hard shine of her husband's pupils. Every line of her face and her plump, soft body was curved and gentle so that she seemed a negligible creature, unable to hold her own in the world of the Villa Poppinidii, where conversation was witty and politically aware, and personalities were strong.

Poor Julanna was outmatched. The servants ignored her, and the mistress smiled kindly and treated her like a child. Her husband was bored within a fortnight, relegating his new wife to the role of an inconvenient visitor.

Nor was Caius a kindly husband. He saw no pressing reason to change his lifestyle now that he was married, and continued to carouse with his friends from Aquae Sulis on every available occasion. Caius considered the running of the estate to be an unfit task for a gentleman and spent his days, and sometimes whole weeks, away from both the villa and his wife.

One morning, Julanna didn't rise to eat with the family and, when she found a quiet corner of the atrium to work with her distaff, only Livinia and a sharp-eyed Artorex noticed that she had covered most of her face with a gauzy matron's shawl. Both mother and foster-son saw bruises on her cheeks and jaw through the sheer folds of cloth but, when Livinia asked how she'd been injured, Julanna twisted the wool in her lap and blamed her own clumsiness for an accidental fall.

I'll wager that Caius is being far too ready with his fists, Artorex thought to himself but, as always, he did not dare to question the word of a respectable matron.

Livinia glanced upward at Artorex as he made his bow to the ladies, and he recognized the resignation in her large, still-brilliant eyes. The mistress identified the weaknesses in her only son, the last of a long line of honourable Roman gentlemen, and she was ashamed of what she'd seen in his nature.

As for Artorex, he had been kept far too busy for years to even contemplate marriage to any woman. Sexual adventures were limited to hasty couplings with kitchen maids in the cow byre. These were satisfying, but hardly lasting. Love for any female hadn't yet entered his heart, and Artorex was content that this state of affairs should continue. He was happy, his horse grew swiftly under his tutelage and the villa blossomed under his guidance. What more could a young man of seventeen years desire?

Time meant less than nothing to Artorex, except for the change of seasons, the foaling, and the tasks of supervising a large and profitable farm. He would have been content with what he held, were it not for rumblings from the east.

One autumn day, a ragged woman came walking slowly up the road from Aquae Sulis. Her shoulders were bowed with weariness and her hands and feet were wrapped in makeshift mittens of rags. Her age was indeterminate inside the shadow of her hooded cloak

Seated high above her on his horse, Artorex greeted the beggar on the rutted track that led up to the Villa Poppinidii.

'Master,' the woman lowered her head. 'The nights grow cold for a friendless wanderer. May I sleep in your barn before I continue my journey to the north? I will work for my keep.'

What one so ragged and weary could do in recompense for shelter defied Artorex's logical mind, but the nights were unseasonably cold and he didn't wish her death on his conscience.

'Welcome then, mother. Villa Poppinidii can always find a little extra food and somewhere for a stranger to rest.'

Artorex missed the flash of a pair of midnight-blue eyes, as she bowed her head once more in submissive gratitude, for he hadn't yet learned the full measure of women.

'When you reach the villa, you'll find Cletus, the steward, at the kitchens. You may tell him I've given you leave to stay one night, and he'll see to your needs.'

'And who do I say sent me, young master?'

'Artorex, foster-son to Lord Ector.'

The woman slowly bowed, as if her spine pained her.

As soon as she trudged away, Artorex forgot her entirely.

That evening, as the family sat down to dinner and Artorex began to supervise the serving of a simple repast, the woman came to him once more. She was now swathed in black, obviously her best clothing which she had carried in a sack during her journey.

'Master, I tell fortunes and carry news of the world. Would Lord Ector and his noble family desire a little entertainment?'

'I'll ask them,' Artorex replied doubtfully. The ragged beggar appeared to be younger than he'd first thought, although most of her face was still concealed by the shadow of her hood.

While Ector and Caius were uninterested in fortune telling or women's stories, Livinia chose to be charmed by the offer of amusement and, with a quick glance at Julanna's pallid face, she decided that the child might be entertained as well.

'Yes, Artorex,' she replied imperiously from her couch, for Livinia was the master of the Villa Poppinidii in all but name. 'You may send the wise woman in to us.'

For reasons that Artorex did not understand, the black-clad woman caused frissons of fear in him and raised the hair on his arms. He ushered her into the family's presence and then stood against the pillar of the doorway.

'What is your name, wise woman?' Livinia asked, with her usual bland courtesy.

The woman raised her head and lowered the cowl that had concealed her face. 'I'm called Morgan, my lady,' she replied evenly.

Even Caius, bored and slightly hung-over after a day with his friends, was disposed to stare at the wise woman. He felt his loins harden as her knowing eyes slid over his body.

Morgan was not old, nor even middle-aged; she was beautiful and timeless in the light of the wall sconces. But it was a beauty that both attracted and repelled. Artorex was immediately reminded of Targo's tale of the Scythian woman and he decided, prudently, to watch her movements very carefully.

Her hair was midnight-black with a long streak of snow that started at her right temple and ran the full length of her head. Her eyes were blue-black and strange, for they sucked in the light and allowed nothing to escape. Her mouth was full-lipped and promised delicious, forbidden pleasures.

Carefully, she removed a silver mirror, a long band of pale, baby-soft leather and a handful of knucklebones from within her robe.

Even Ector leaned forward, curious at last.

'Ask,' she said simply. 'And I will try to answer.'

Livinia deferred to her husband.

'Will the Villa Poppinidii remain fruitful?' Ector demanded autocratically, for he was a little afraid of this small woman.

Morgan tied the narrow band of leather over her eyes and stared sightlessly at the mirror's face. She crooned under her breath.

Artorex stared fixedly at that narrow, pale band.

What is it? he thought to himself. It looks like . . .

His mind was too revolted by the image of soft, human skin to continue with his thoughts.

'The Villa Poppinidii will last for a long, long time. Its fields will bear for generations to come and, when it is dead at all but the heart, still it will live on in legend, until men in a far off time will find it and make it bloom once more.'

'Well, that's a fair prospect,' Ector replied, seeing none of the menace and all of the good – as usual.

'Will I bear a son?' Julanna asked timidly.

Once again, Morgan seemed to listen to silent voices and see strange shapes in her mirror with her covered eyes, although Artorex swore to himself that it was not possible.

'You will bear children, lady, in pain and travail, and you will hold them in your arms and suckle them. Yet no son will live to spare you from later pain.'

'But will Villa Poppinidii have children to hold it strong, children that are of my blood?' Livinia asked, for this question meant more to her than any other.

'Aye, my lady. You will know that they are yours before your ending – and believe yourself blessed. You have earned the forbearance of the gods.'

Artorex shuddered, despite himself. Why did the family smile, refusing to recognize the poison in Morgan's prophecies?

We hear what we want to hear, Artorex heard Morgan whisper in his head.

Not I! he thought, savagely.

Not you! was the soundless, laughing reply.

Caius was restive for his own turn.

'Will I be a great landowner and warrior?' he demanded. 'And will my name live on after I am dead?'

Morgan stared hard through her leather band. Her hands made strange patterns in the air, and Artorex saw that they were long, clean and comely.

'Under one form or another, your name will endure down the ages. You will be steward to a great king and the whole world will know the truth of you.'

The truth of you? Artorex thought furiously. Spare even Caius from such a fate!

But the young master was delighted.

'Steward to a great king. Renown for ever. Could a man ask for more?'

'And what of you, Master Artorex?' Morgan asked softly. 'Do you have a question for me?'

'None!' Artorex snapped. His response was far rougher than he intended.

'Come, Artorex, it's only a game,' Ector admonished.

'Are you afraid to learn that you will make me a wealthy man, Steward?' Caius filled the title with enough venom and contempt to poison all the persons present.

'I fear nothing,' Artorex retorted.

'Then cast the bones,' Morgan demanded evenly and without challenge.

'Why should I do so? Can you not see my future, as you did for the family?'

'My gift is not easily mastered. Cast the bones, Master Artorex, and I will tell your fate.'

Unwillingly, Artorex picked up the knucklebones.

They were smooth and slick under his fingers and seemed to quiver as if they were still alive. Instinctively, Artorex knew they had once been part of a human hand.

As the great Caesar had cast dice many, many years before, Artorex threw the bones on to the mosaic floor.

Morgan took off her ghastly eye-band before rocking and moaning over the pattern the bones had made on the tiles. Her voice seemed to come from far away.

'You bear poisoned blood, Great One. Beware of a woman with yellow hair, for she will lead you to ruin.'

'Surely you can give me something better than that,' Artorex challenged her.

Morgan stared at him through the lamplight. Her voice changed, and became deeper.

'Greater even than thy father, and greater than thy son, you will save your world for a time but it will be at the cost of all that you hold dear. Time will not change you, nor shatter your promise. You shall live, though your body be dead, long after the might of Rome has fallen into the dust.'

The family was struck dumb by the enormity of Morgan's prophecy. Caius's mouth was twisted into a sneer of jealousy and Artorex knew the master's son would make him suffer for the promise in the words of this wise woman.

'You can spare me your promises, for today is enough for me,' Artorex snapped, annoyed by the riddles in her words. 'And what of you, Morgan? Do you dare to turn your gift upon yourself?'

'I will cast also,' Morgan replied, still staring enigmatically into the eyes of the young man.

She swept up the bones in one eloquent hand, and cast them down.

'Blood calls to blood, whether I wish it or not. You should call on me, should you ever have need of me. My life skein is tangled with yours, and my name will endure as long as yours lives. I am bound inextricably to you by old wrongs.'

Caius rose to his feet. His temper and resentment was clearly exposed in his dark eyes and Julanna flinched away from his peremptory hand.

'Well, I'm sure this little game has all been very interesting, but Julanna and I are for our bed,' Caius ordered, and led his reluctant young wife from the eating chamber.

Livinia and Ector also rose to their feet.

'We thank you for your gifts,' Livinia said for both Ector and herself.

As the mistress led her husband away, Morgan bowed low until she was a dark puddle of shadow on the bright floor.

Artorex snapped his fingers and servants scurried to clear away all signs of the family meal. He noticed that the women gave Morgan a wide berth and one old grandmother surreptitiously made the age-old sign to ward off the evil eye.

'Come, Morgan.' Artorex offered his hand. 'This evening's charade is over. When are you going to tell me what you really want?'

'I wanted to see your face,' Morgan answered, with her head tilted upwards so she could see his unusual eyes.

'And?'

She took his hand and rose to her feet, the accoutrements of her trade having disappeared inside the voluminous black robe. Her fingers were soft and dry, like the skin of a snake, but he sensed the strength that lay under the surface.

'I have nothing else to tell you, my lord. Nothing you do not know for yourself.'

'I have no idea what you are talking about,' Artorex said irritably. 'But I do not believe you came to Villa Poppinidii by accident. We are some little way east of the road that leads to the north.'

Morgan smiled. 'I believe now that you have not been told of your birthright. How surprising! Sometimes the ways of men are very strange. Now that I look at you, I can see a little of your mother in you,' she added. 'It is in your eyes, Artorex.'

'You are speaking in riddles yet again. Perhaps it is the language of all charlatans.' Artorex paused as Morgan's pupils flared for a moment with an intense white fire. 'Or perhaps you believe what you say. Who was my mother?'

'It is not my place to tell you, my lord, if greater ones than I have kept silent.' Morgan smiled and, for a brief moment, her face lit up from within and she was very beautiful indeed.

'You should not invest me with titles that are not mine to claim,' Artorex replied evenly, although his hand tingled from contact with her slim fingers. He frowned at her. 'Where is your home?'

'I am from the Fortress Tintagel, lord. I tell you nothing by saying this, for you have probably never heard of such a place.' Morgan slid to the doorway.

'You're correct, Morgan, but I will not forget you,' Artorex promised grimly.

At his words, she paused for a moment, and stared back at him with eyes that drew the light to her face. 'Of that, I have no doubt. There is no forgetting with those of your blood – as you will come to learn.'

And then she was gone.

Artorex arose early next morning, before the sun had banished full darkness, but Morgan had left even earlier while the night was still wholly black. He would be a man full grown before he heard of her again. When he looked at the empty road, he crossed himself in the Christian manner. It did no harm to take precautions against the evil ones.

Life at the villa continued in its seamless patterns of nature. It seemed, to Artorex's young heart, that nothing could ever change. Occasionally, a message would arrive by a courier for Ector, and the master would look grave for days. The same courier sometimes brought another scroll for Artorex from the mysterious Llanwith pen Bryn but, mostly, Artorex was content with his world, and all that existed within it.

Julanna was to effect the changes that would shatter Artorex's calm. Little Julanna, already pregnant, and frightened as the child swelled within her belly, begged leave to invite a friend from Aquae Sulis to visit for the duration of her confinement.

As Lady Livinia could not bear to deny anything to the mother of her grandchild, she agreed that word should be sent to the trading house of Gallus, so that the daughter of that wealthy family should be invited for a long stay at the Villa Poppinidii.

And so fate decided that Artorex would meet Gallia, daughter of a Roman trading family, and his life would change direction once again.

CHAPTER IV

GALLIA

Spring had come and the whole world of the villa bloomed anew. Buttercups appeared under trees in the lower meadows and the cows grazed belly deep in waving grasses and wild flowers. Trees exploded with tender pink and pale green shoots, while the fields ached to produce the crops that would ripen in late summer.

Frith led the women in the collection of herbs and simples that were hung, upside down, to sweeten the villa as they dried. Meanwhile, Julanna checked the long track from the Roman road every day, pining for the companionship of her friend, and Mistress Livinia watched her daughter-in-law with concerned, apprehensive eyes. The villa held its breath ... and waited for change.

Artorex was far off in the south pasture when a heavy wagon struggled up the road to the Villa Poppinidii. It was loaded high with chests and boxes, so even Livinia wondered if the child meant to stay forever, so deeply were the wooden wheels of the cart driven into the muddy track.

Under a small, tent-like structure, Gallia reclined on cushions amidst the piled excesses of her luggage. Only when the wagon drew to a halt, and her maid and manservant helped her to descend, did Livinia clearly view the changeling that Villa

Poppinidii had welcomed into its family. From her vantage point at the thick wooden doors of the villa, Lady Livinia watched their guest approach in a flurry of shawls, wrapped packages and restless fingers.

The new arrival proved to be an extraordinary young girl, for all that she was a bare fourteen years of age. Her face was small and unbalanced by a long nose, but there was great sweetness in her rosebud mouth and kindness in her amber eyes that were so out of tune with her curly black hair. That hair, unbound except for jewelled pins as befitted a maid, seemed to crackle with wildfire, as did her compact little body.

Gallia was tiny, even by Lady Livinia's standards, but her body was almost vulgarly lush at the breasts and the hips. She took great pride in a tiny waist, pinching in her pleated peplum with a belt of freshwater pearls from the north, embroidered on leather-backed linen.

Now here's a little miss, was Livinia's first thought as the child approached her at a rush. But then Gallia smiled, and even the cloudy day seemed brighter for her unalloyed joy in all those marvels she had yet to experience.

After bowing low to the master and mistress of the house, against all the rules of good manners Gallia had clapped her hands, giggled delightedly and then kissed Lady Livinia's cheek.

The mistress was momentarily taken aback by Gallia's forwardness and presumption, but the girl smiled so sweetly with her head cocked sideways like a colourful bird that Livinia felt her reservation melt.

'I beg your pardon, my lady. My father would be ashamed of my rackety ways, but I've waited so long to see my sweet Julanna that I could burst with excitement.'

Lady Livinia frowned and Gallia looked chastened.

'I'm gabbling again, aren't I? I shall be apologizing every day,

I'm sure, because I can't bear silence and I always fill it with chatter – or so my brothers tell me.'

'Never mind, child,' Ector chuckled in avuncular good humour. 'We don't stand on ceremony here.'

'No, indeed, Gallia,' Lady Livinia began kindly. 'Good heart counts for more than empty manners.'

'Oh, I do hope so,' Gallia said with an impish grin. 'I'll try to avoid talking too much.'

Scarcely pausing for breath, Gallia proceeded to regale Lady Livinia with tales of her journey, the appalling condition of the roads and the beauty of Villa Poppinidii. How Gallia talked. Silence was not her métier and she filled the villa with her tinkling laughter. She was enchanted by the atrium and was charmed by the sheep and cows as only a city girl could be, and very full of reminiscences of her friendship with Julanna.

Despite her natural reserve, Livinia found herself smiling as the child prattled on – and on.

Her servants soon stowed her many belongings into the best guest chamber and, once again, Gallia was delighted by the comfort of her quarters.

'For I can actually hear birds, Lady Livinia,' she smiled. 'Real birds, not those poor things that languish in cages. I do think they sing more prettily when they are free, don't you?'

Scarcely pausing for breath, Gallia fell upon a simple pottery beaker filled with wild flowers.

'Oh, how kind you are. The flowers have no smell in Aquae Sulis, but these are heavenly.' She smiled again. 'Thank you, Lady Livinia, I know I will be very comfortable in your wonderful house.'

'Hush, child!' Livinia replied when Gallia seemed to run out of superlatives. 'Julanna picked these trifles from the fields at dawn. She has desired your company so desperately, but I fear you will find little to divert yourself in our quiet country life.'

'Oh, I don't care a jot for entertainment. Games make me queasy and Father keeps parading young men before me as if I were a prize heifer. I will so enjoy a holiday from marriage proposals and the smell of fish.'

Unwillingly, Lady Livinia laughed. The maid was so outspoken and so frank in her observations that even the mistress's Roman reserve fell away under her charm. Gallia might well prove to be the perfect companion for Julanna, for who could be sullen or sad around this laughing girl?

'And is Julanna well?' Gallia asked more seriously. 'I, for one, wouldn't care if I never saw Aquae Sulis again. She is fortunate to live in Villa Poppinidii, for the air here smells so sweet.'

'Julanna is a little afraid of her coming labour, although it is five months before her child is due to be born. She needs a companion to make her laugh and help the days pass more easily.'

Gallia so forgot herself as to wink at Lady Livinia, but the mistress lacked the heart to chide this engaging child.

'I'll cheer her up, never fear, mistress. I have brought gifts from my father and any number of amusements with me. We shall be as happy as the birds in the trees.'

When Julanna saw her friend in the doorway of her room, she leapt to her feet, wrapped Gallia in a desperate hug and promptly burst into scalding, wrenching tears.

Unobtrusively, Livinia left the friends to re-acquaint themselves after more than a year of separation.

Livinia was stricken with guilt and was apprehensive of the warnings of trouble to come. Julanna was a dutiful girl and she was carrying the first Poppinidii child since Caius had been born over twenty years before. Try as she might to justify her son's actions, Livinia knew that Julanna didn't deserve the cruel treatment inflicted by Caius. Uncharacteristically, now that she had faced the facts, she hesitated about what course of action to take.

Caius was male and therefore had more status than his mother in a Roman household. His wife had even less standing. Livinia had spoken to her son, and he had sulked for several days, refusing to speak to her because she had chosen to taken his wife's part. However, after an epic fit of debauchery with his friends, he had returned to his mother's side, unshaven, contrite and smelling of stale wine to beg her pardon.

'My little wife is too meek, Mother, and so little like you.' Caius had laughed softly. 'I beg your forgiveness – and I promise to be more patient with her in future. There. Now, will you smile for me again?'

Livinia had allowed herself to be wheedled and placated, but she worried constantly when Caius was at home and at loose ends. She knew her son's mercurial, restless nature and she wondered if she should have discussed this intensely family problem with Ector.

She loved her husband, although few acquaintances would ever realize how passionately she adored him. Even Ector's cronies in Aquae Sulis would have laughed to imagine that the bluff, rather credulous Celt was the only man that Livinia had ever wanted. In her youth, her wealth ensured that she could have her pick of many eligible young men, and her handsome looks ensured that she would also be desired for herself. But Livinia had chosen Ector, a man with scarcely any coin in his purse and no useful land to call his own. He had a mane of plentiful red hair, a smile that was slow and brilliant, and a pair of wide blue eyes that had spoken volumes about his honesty and sincerity. Livinia was lost as soon as he smiled at her.

Now her dear Ector was arthritic in winter and his hair was thin and grey, but she loved him even more, now that the fires of youth had banked and cooled. Ector still clung to a frail hope that his son would be a credit to him, and Livinia was determined that her sweet old man shouldn't suffer further disappointment. No, she would handle her beloved, wayward son herself and shield her husband from his excesses for as long as she was able.

Her decision made, for right or wrong, Livinia squared her narrow shoulders and lifted her indomitable chin. As was her custom, she would do what was needful to protect her family and her home.

Later that afternoon, as the soft breezes of spring sweetened every room of the villa, she led Artorex into a quiet corner of the atrium. Around her, drying herbs scented the air and dappled shade softened the inflexibility of her jaw.

'I've spoken to my son, Artorex, concerning that troublesome matter with his wife. I believe the situation is now rectified.'

Artorex bowed his head. In truth, a load of guilt lifted from his broad shoulders.

'As always, mistress, your actions are noble and good. Mistress Julanna is a sweet and gentle girl.'

Livinia stroked Artorex's face with the tenderness of a mother and he felt his eyes moisten at her touch. Her fingers were cool and dry, and Artorex was surprised at the affection that enlivened her quiet face. The expression was fleeting, leaving the young steward unsure that it had ever existed.

'We shall let my son's failings be our secret, Artorex,' she murmured. 'My husband would be very concerned if he realized that Caius can be so intemperate. I trust you in this matter, Artorex, because I know you have the well-being of the villa at heart.'

'Of course, mistress. I'll carry out your wishes.'

At dinner, on her first evening, Gallia was uncharacteristically subdued, thus earning the approval of both Ector and

Caius. Had the men known that she had been told Julanna's most shameful secrets, Caius may not have been so complacent.

'He ... he beats me, Gallia, when I displease him. No doubt I'm very stupid and I cause him much irritation. Pray, tell no one, for he has the right to do as he pleases.'

'Nonsense!' Gallia retorted, with a martial glint in her eyes. 'You were always too sweet-natured for your own good, my petal. What decent man could hurt such a lovely girl as you?'

'I try his patience, Gallia, I really do. He spends most of his days with Severinus and his friends, and what little time he does spend with me puts him out of temper. I wish I knew how to be a good wife to him.'

'You quicken with his child, don't you? Caius should be pleased that he will soon become a father.' The sharpness of Gallia's voice emphasized the bluntness of her reply.

Two tears trickled down Julanna's cheeks.

'I suppose he is proud of me and our marriage, but he never says so,' Julanna sniffed wetly. 'I know I'm not very clever, not like you, but ... but ... he strikes me when I annoy him. Nothing I do ever seems to be right.'

Privately, Gallia believed that any man who hurt the mother of his child was no man at all, but she kept her opinions to herself.

'I wish he'd spend more time with me instead of spending it with his fine friends. I don't believe he loves me at all,' Julanna wailed.

'Does he seek out other women?' Gallia asked practically. Julanna blushed hotly and would not meet her friend's eyes.

'There are no women that I know of, but ...'. Julanna's voice trailed off miserably.

'Perhaps he prefers boys,' Gallia suggested matter-of-factly, a statement that shocked prim little Julanna. 'No one who knew you could treat you so badly if he was a true man.'

'Gallia, please, don't even suggest such a terrible and wicked possibility. I couldn't bear it if Caius had a male lover, truly I couldn't.'

'I'm sorry, my sweet. You know my tongue – always running away with itself. Of course Caius doesn't have a sexual interest in boys.'

But, privately, Gallia determined to watch Caius closely.

Julanna glowed with happiness at dinner. Gallia had brought her a little clockwork bird in a gilded cage. A golden key wound up the delicate automaton and it whistled in a high treble, while flapping its tiny wings. She could scarcely stop speaking of it.

Caius barely disguised his impatience, while Livinia thanked Gallia with simple dignity. The young master retreated into a prolonged, sullen silence.

When a very tall young man joined the family, Ector introduced him to Gallia as his foster-son.

Artorex saw a tiny, child-like girl with clouds of curly dark hair and eyes that were very sharp and critical. Within a few moments of meeting Gallia, her chatter irritated the steward and he dismissed her as a foolish, trivial prattler. Nothing she said, or did, during that first meal improved his opinion of her.

The next morning, Gallia rose early, flustered the kitchen staff by descending into the cook's domain to beg a simple meal, and then volunteered to carry a morning tray to her friend. Julanna ate sparingly for she was still wracked with morning sickness, but Gallia had no intention of allowing her friend to submit to a little nausea.

Gallia gazed curiously around the spacious kitchens with the keen interest of a townswoman. A huge brick oven, stoked by a cavernous firebox, dominated the simple, flagged room. Another large brick hearth served to cook any meal, from a whole, roast pig to small delicacies in gravy which simmered in small iron pots hung from brackets over the open fire. A scarred wooden bench dominated much of the room and Gallia realized that this table was the domain of the cook, a small, animated man with a pot belly and wildly gesticulating arms. Servant girls ran to obey his slightest gesture.

Gallia tripped into the organized chaos of the kitchen with scarcely a thought for the commotion she was causing. One plump girl dropped a fish that she was bearing in a basket filled with cut grass, causing the cook to sternly box her ears.

'Tell me, Master Cook, what will cure Mistress Julanna's vomiting illness yet nourish her well?' Gallia asked the worthy servant, who was shocked to be involved in women's matters.

Frith cackled in her warm corner.

'Don't be asking that long-faced bag of rubbish, my lady,' Frith began. 'I cared for Mistress Livinia when everyone in the house thought she would die of starvation as she bore the young master. We shall give her cold water, a little dry bread to settle the stomach, some milk with just a taste of honey for strength and then a platter of fruit that is cut small to tempt her. That'll set the young mistress right.'

'I thank you,' Gallia replied with a sunny smile that warmed the old woman. She turned back to the cook. 'I can't believe that you would be prepared to let our sweet Julanna suffer. I know you'll find just the right fruit to tempt her.'

The cook unbent so far as to summon servants to fetch crisp apples from the cold store, some nuts and the blackberries that had been put down in the autumn.

'You are all so very kind to me,' Gallia bubbled, and swept away to Julanna's rooms, bearing her repast.

Julanna was still abed and very miserable.

Undaunted, Gallia coaxed her to drink a little cold water and try a few mouthfuls of fresh, warm bread. She then engaged

Julanna with tales of her prospective suitors, and their many faults, until the expectant mother was giggling despite her nauseated stomach.

'I told my father that if he wanted me to marry a man with a face like a cod, I would drown myself.' Gallia giggled as she pressed Julanna to drink her milk. 'As for the old goat, Preopius, who owns the fleet that trades from Sabrina Aest, I reminded Pater that if he wanted more grandchildren, he'd best find a man capable of siring them.'

'You are truly wicked, Gallia,' Julanna laughed. 'How you dare.' She found herself nibbling crisp slices of apple. 'I think I'm hungry after all,' she said in wonderment.

'So you must eat every mouthful, and dress warmly, and then we'll go for a little walk. It will do you good, I'm certain, and it's far better than remaining within these four walls and dwelling on your fears. Hurry, my dear, else I will be forced to dress you myself.'

'How have I survived here without you, my crazy Gallia?'

'Not very well, it seems, when you're living in such a paradise as this villa.' Gallia replied, and tripped out of the door, much pleased with her efforts to cheer her charge.

Julanna was some little time being dressed by her maid, but before the hour was up, well wrapped against any stray winds, she was taken forcibly on a leisurely walk around the villa buildings, surreptitiously followed, at a safe distance, by Gallia's manservant.

Julanna had never bothered to take much notice of her surroundings at the villa, but now, through Gallia's joyful interest, she saw the sheep, the placid cows, and the squabbling fowls through freshly opened eyes. The two young women foraged for eggs in the hen house and filled an old basket. Gallia cooed over the lambs – now almost as large as their mothers – and both were fascinated by butter churns, cheese wheels and the huge horses already hard at work ploughing the fields in preparation for planting.

Gnawing on a late carrot, Gallia seemed to find magic in every corner of the villa, for she was city born and bred. Every colour enchanted her, the bronze and scarlet leaves, the high white clouds and the rich brown loam of the fields.

When Julanna began to appear a little tired, Gallia also claimed weariness, so they retraced their steps towards the villa.

In the horse field, Targo and Artorex were practising their swordplay.

Both girls stopped to watch.

'My!' Gallia said with a laugh. 'Your steward is a large young man. And quite handsome, now that I look at him more closely.'

'Gallia!' Julanna gasped, quite shocked at the flirtatious eye of her friend.

'Well, he is, my dear. He has a fine, strong body. And he fights very well, does he not?'

'Our Artorex?' Julanna asked vaguely. 'Yes, I suppose he is quite skilled with weapons, although I can't see why he wastes his time with so much practice.'

'Surely as a steward he should be about Lord Ector's business?' Gallia asked. Her curiosity was piqued by Artorex's odd, ambiguous position at the Villa Poppinidii.

'Well, he's not exactly a steward, although he very well might become one in time. He is Ector's foster-son and, if you believe the gossip of the servants, his patron is Lucius of Glastonbury.'

'The Christian priest? Does Artorex follow the teachings of the Nazarene?'

'I don't know, for he's never expressed an opinion one way or another. But he is treated with much favour by the great ones who come at intervals to check on his progress.'

'How strange,' Gallia muttered under her breath and sucked

the knuckle of her thumb, a habit from childhood that signified she was thinking hard.

'Now that I come to think of them, the prophecies of that wise woman, Morgan, were truly quite odd. She seemed to imply that Artorex was destined by the fates for some future greatness,' Julanna continued, her fine brow furrowed in unusual concentration.

'You must tell me everything, Julanna. I find I'm agog with curiosity,' Gallia chirped eagerly, and whisked her charge away to her quarters.

As Julanna began to spin fine wool, Gallia set up her loom to weave the delicate yarn into a soft web to be made into clothing for the baby. As they worked, Julanna told Gallia all that she could remember of Morgan's prophecy.

Gallia was unusually quiet as she digested Julanna's tale.

When Lady Livinia found the two young ladies before the noon meal, both dark heads were close together and they were working diligently, as good girls should. Livinia was pleased to notice that Julanna's face was quite rosy with health and her timid smile was wider and more unforced than usual.

'The girl might talk incessantly, but she is good for Julanna. I am glad she will be here until the babe is born,' she told Ector as he checked the farm inventory with Cletus.

The steward seemed to be breathing more easily in the cooler air.

'She's an engaging little thing but I wager she could be quite a handful,' Ector replied distractedly. 'I'm told she has her father wrapped around her little finger.'

'Gallicus has five strong sons, so he can afford to indulge her. Still, I cannot help but like her,' Livinia decided.

Caius, on the other hand, did not like Gallia at all.

He had risen in the afternoon and strode into his wife's quarters in a surly mood to find the two young women together.

'What do you make, wife?' he demanded impatiently.

Julanna was immediately reduced to incoherence, but she was saved further embarrassment by Gallia's neat intervention.

'She's making the woollen wrappings for your new child, Master Caius. See? Your wife spins the finest yarn imaginable. The wool is as light as thistledown when it is woven on the loom.'

Caius grunted in disdain.

'Will you be with us this evening, husband?' Julanna asked timidly.

'No. Severinus expects me to attend his feast,' Caius retorted rudely.

'Oh! I had hoped that we would see more of you, now that Gallia is here.'

'The gossip of women is of little interest to me,' Caius snapped. 'I've better ways to spend my evening.'

'Of course, husband,' Julanna replied soothingly.

'Of course! Of course! Of course!' Caius mimicked her cruelly. 'Can't you speak of anything but babies and weaving?'

'You asked the question, sir,' Gallia replied, tossing her head high, her amber eyes cold with disdain as they met Caius's stare unflinchingly.

Julanna tried to hide the tears that filled her eyes.

'Your wife is not well, Master Caius. Surely she means more to you than a mere feast?'

Gallia knew she had gone too far, but the young master was insufferable in his arrogance, and some devil in her nature encouraged her to tweak his unbearable superiority.

Caius flushed unbecomingly and his mouth drew down in a scowl of contempt.

'It is obvious to me that your father has not schooled you to know when to speak, young woman, and when to be silent.'

By now, Caius was having difficulty controlling his anger, as his twitching fingers attested.

Gallia lifted her determined chin to show that she was not intimidated.

'If I have caused any offence, then I beg your forgiveness, Master Caius. But Julanna is not well and she pines for your attention.'

'Well, she will have to pine alone,' Caius snarled, and swept out of the room to take his bad temper out on any hapless servant who crossed his path.

'Oh, Gallia, how do you dare to upset him?' Julanna breathed, quite amazed by her friend's composure.

'Him? I will not say anything against your husband, dearest, but I would dearly love to box his ears. He behaves like a spoiled child.'

'But he's the master's only son and he'll be the paterfamilias when Ector is dead.' Julanna appeared quite terrified at the prospect.

'He's a bully, and I won't permit him to frighten you – and that's the end of it!'

'I'm so glad you have come to stay, Gallia.'

'Hummph!' was Gallia's only response.

That afternoon, when Julanna had retired to her bed to rest, Gallia decided to explore the Villa Poppinidii in earnest. Followed by her manservant, and completely oblivious to the stares of the field workers, she trudged through the acres of grain to the open paddocks where flowers grew in profusion near the edge of the forest. As she plucked a posy for her friend, her quest drew her closer to the deeper shadows surrounding the great oaks.

'You would do well to stay clear of the woods, Lady Gallia,' a curt voice intruded into her thoughts.

Gallia barely suppressed a flinch of surprise.

Turning, with the skirts of her peplum full of wild blooms, she was forced to look up at the smiling face of the steward mounted on a large black stallion.

'You startled me, Master Steward. My mind was elsewhere, I'm afraid. Are these woods so dangerous?'

'Very,' Artorex replied. 'You will find yourself lost before you have taken twenty paces into the trees. And there are many dangers for unwary fools.'

Gallia smiled as engagingly as she knew how, for she was an accomplished flirt and the steward brought out the very worst in her nature.

'You own a fine horse, Artorex. He's quite large.'

'Yes. He's big. But he's still smaller than his dam,' Artorex responded uneasily.

He was discovering that this frank young woman possessed the ability to make him feel awkward and uncomfortable simply by gazing intently at him with her neat head tilted sideways, as if in surprise.

'Surely not,' she replied limpidly.

'Oh, yes. Aphrodite is his dam, but his sire was a wild horse who mated with her in the forest.'

'Aphrodite?' Gallia invested the name with a coo of surprise that showed her small, red lips to advantage.

Artorex mutely pointed towards a very large workhorse contentedly dragging a wagon loaded with harvested hay through a nearby field.

'Well, he's much prettier than his mother, I'll grant you that.' She laughed, and affectation fell away with her mirth.

Then her expression changed entirely, leaving Artorex even more confused.

She turned to her manservant and gestured to him to move out of earshot. Well used to the moods of his mistress, the burly man obeyed.

'Would you walk a little way with me, please, Artorex? I have wanted to speak with you all day but I would not willingly trouble you.'

Artorex decided that he'd never known a woman speak so much and say so little, apart from polished compliments. She was unstoppable, and similar to Plod when the mares were in heat. He felt no envy for the man who would become her husband at some time in the future. But, despite his reservations, he dismounted and led Coal by the reins, shortening his stride to match Gallia's smaller steps.

'I'm sure the farm will do without me for a time, if you desire my attention.'

The last traces of Gallia's flirtatious manner fell away like a discarded shawl. Her eyes pinned him so directly that Artorex was forced to halt.

'I'm glad you have the time to speak to me.' She smiled disarmingly before continuing. 'You're aware by now that I'll be living at the villa as companion to Julanna. She's my friend of many years' standing, but even in the short time I've been here, I've become curious about the nature of her life in the villa – and especially her reliance on her husband.'

She smiled guilelessly up at Artorex once again, so her next words left him gaping.

'Does he beat her often?' Gallia asked bluntly.

'That's not a question for me to answer, my lady,' Artorex replied. 'I act as the Steward of the Household and it's not my place to comment on the actions of my masters.' Artorex closed his eyes for a short moment. This girl-child had no tact at all.

'Come, Artorex. Who at the villa will answer me if you do not? I have always preferred plain speaking – it saves so much time.'

Artorex examined her determined face with narrowed, opaque eyes. What would this child say next?

'Caius is the son of Lord Ector,' he said. 'And one day he will be my master.'

'But you are free-born. Have you no brain under all that hair?' Gallia retorted tartly.

For no reason in particular, Artorex laughed. As an angry young woman, she reminded him of a speckled hen, dashing here and there, with her beak on the ready to peck at the nearest enemy toe.

Gallia saw his laughter for what it was – patronizing indulgence – and she stamped her feet in frustration.

'Even a woman can reason, Steward,' she hissed.

'In answer to your question,' Artorex shrugged, 'Caius is ... just ... Caius. He is an only son of a wealthy Roman family, and he believes himself to be important in the world.'

'Is he too important to spend some time with his wife who is gravid with his child?'

'He feels he is far too important for all this good earth as well.' Artorex's outspread arms encompassed the Villa Poppinidii and the lands that surrounded it. Bitterness lay under his sarcasm and Gallia could clearly hear the gall in his response.

'Then he's a fool,' Gallia replied, somewhat mollified by Artorex's frankness. 'He trusts his wealth to the honesty of others.' She turned on her heel and began to stride in the direction of the villa. Artorex was forced to follow.

'You are also being foolish, Mistress Gallia, if you speak harshly of your host inside his own house.'

She stopped abruptly, and stared directly into Artorex's eyes.

'Do you deny the truth of what I've been saying?' she demanded.

'No. But it's not your place to say it. Mistress Julanna is the wife of Caius, and she's his property to do with as he wills. We live by the old ways, and the Villa Poppinidii follows the ancient traditions.'

'Even you, Artorex?'

'Caius and I are not friends, nor ever will be. I'll serve him as a servant, but only out of gratitude to my foster-parents. I don't need to love Caius to be his steward.'

Somehow, Artorex realized, this slip of a girl, so tiny and so inflexible, had wrung an admission from him that he would not have made to any living man.

'The blood that flows through my veins is purer than that which nurtures Caius,' Gallia retorted haughtily, with her head held high. 'I am all Roman, not a bastardized Celt. His actions are appalling for a man of breeding.' She looked like an angry pigeon.

Artorex was concerned about the direction their conversation was taking, and gazed around to ensure that no one could overhear the words this girl was uttering. Did she have no reserve in her nature?

'My brothers share my lineage, and they don't assert the full rights of a husband on the bodies of their wives.'

Artorex shrugged. Lineage was of little interest to a fatherless man.

'And so Caius is allowed to beat Julanna, and everyone in the Villa Poppinidii knows about it,' Gallia stated with conviction. 'How cowardly!'

Artorex shrugged once more. The truth was self-evident.

'Is there anyone here who can protect her from Caius?'

'No one at all, if the Mistress Livinia decides to turn a blind eye – as I believe you should, if you are wise.'

'I am not so mean-spirited.'

'I believe you, but what do you expect me to do? Lady Livinia has spoken to her son, so I expect no more violence from him. I can hardly insist that the son of the house should be punished, nor is it my place to be critical of those decisions made by the master and the mistress of the villa.' Artorex was frustrated with the discussion, mainly because he knew in his heart that Gallia was correct. Caius was a bully, and the poorest servant at the villa knew it. Artorex himself had seen the proof and he felt soiled by his complicity.

'As the steward of this noble house, I suppose there is nothing you can do if his parents will not prevent the cruelty of their son. It is all very sad, because I considered this beautiful villa as a little slice of Olympia, and it is disheartening to discover that wickedness is everywhere.' Gallia sighed deeply, and Artorex found his irritation had flown away on that gentle exhalation of breath.

But the girl immediately shocked him with her next question.

'Does he follow the Greek fashion?'

'What?' Artorex drew to a halt so quickly that Coal butted him in the back.

'Does he seek out love with small boys and effeminate men?' Gallia elaborated as if to a young and innocent child.

'I know nothing of the amorous preferences of Master Caius. His friend, Severinus, may be another matter – but I am never invited to consort with my betters.'

'How very convenient,' Gallia said softly, as if to herself. Turning, she smiled up at Artorex's scowling face. 'Thank you, Artorex.' She smiled once more in dismissal. 'You may leave me now. I wish to return to the villa.'

His abrupt dismissal irritated Artorex more than he could have expected.

As he mounted Coal and rode away, his mind decided on a number of stinging answers to her impertinent questions. But it was all too late.

'Damn the girl,' Artorex told Coal, who whickered his encouragement. 'She makes me feel like a fool.'

However, once an idea takes root, it begins to grow.

Despite himself, Artorex discovered his thoughts returning to Caius and his friends, no matter how vigorously he tried to rein them in. Thoughts of Gallia, too, intruded into his reading of Caesar's exploits against Versingatorex, something that had never happened before. In the days that followed, when he was in her presence he struggled to meet her wide amber stare – and realized that thoughts of her lush breasts were beginning to disturb his sleep.

Women are very, very strange, he thought to himself on several occasions. The other servants frequently noticed that he would stare distractedly at nothing in particular when he should have been concentrating on the running of the villa.

It was only natural that the servants began to gossip.

'The young steward is in love,' Frith cackled at him one morning after a frost had driven him into the kitchens to warm his chapped hands.

'Nonsense, Frith!' Artorex retorted, although the old servant noticed that her words had brought two spots of colour to the thin skin over his cheekbones.

'Methinks it is Lady Gallia that distracts you,' Frith replied complacently.

Her great age and the service she had provided to Mistress Livinia allowed the old woman some impunity against censure, so Frith exercised her tongue as much as she pleased. The servant was a natural aristocrat.

'I am a steward, Frith, and the Mistress Gallia is of an ancient lineage.'

'What nonsense!' Frith responded rudely. 'Her father, Gallicus, may be a lord but he has no class at all. He's a seller of fish,' she exclaimed, as if that explanation bridged the wide gulf that existed between Gallia and Frith's favourite.

Artorex kissed her wrinkled, rose-petal cheek.

'Please don't encourage gossip, Frith,' he said softly. 'If you wish me to remain free from harm.'

'And who would dare to touch you, young master, when you could cut them in two in a moment?' Frith answered practically. 'Now away with you, or the servants will start to talk about us.'

'You are fairer to me than all the beautiful maidens in Rome.' Artorex smiled down at her wizened old face.

'Away with you, you teller of tales.' But Frith glowed softly with love for him.

Artorex's mind was now fully occupied by the currents that seethed below the placid surface of the Villa Poppinidii, and he determined to discuss the matter with Targo at the earliest opportunity. If anyone at the villa would speak frankly with him of his concerns, then the wise veteran would be the one.

He joined the old warrior under his favourite alder tree, squatting easily on his heels beside the veteran, and searched ponderously for the appropriate words. Artorex had lived with Caius all his short life, and he had chosen to blot out the spiteful words and personal insults hurled at him by the young master before he was even half-grown. Targo was a servant of the house and would be made to suffer if he became involved in any attempt to openly chastise the young master. But Artorex understood the rat cunning and vindictiveness perpetuated through the ages by servants. A cruel master was often punished in various, surreptitious ways – a meal made a little too salty, or a nettle placed under the blanket of a fractious horse so that accidents bedevilled him.

But, in his fashion, Targo was an honourable man. He scorned to resort to a servant's revenge, and instead chose to store away the insults of Caius towards the inevitable day when the young master could be humbled.

'Ask your question, lad. Spit it out! I'll be on my deathbed before you find the pretty words you seek. What do you want?'

Targo was as blunt as Gallia. Momentarily, Artorex smiled at the thought of these two unpredictable people in conversation.

'I wish to speak to you of Caius. What rumours of the young master run through the village? What does he do with his hours? Where does he go?'

Targo raised a quizzical white eyebrow. 'So that's the way the wind blows, is it? I'll be arrow-straight with you, boy. The village has no love of Caius, but that sad fact is common knowledge. He's fast with his whip, slow to pay and his friends are men who are even worse than he is. I'll say no more.'

'If he becomes master, then I must know what breed of man I serve. Please, Targo. You are more aware than most men concerning what occurs at our villa.'

'I don't speak the half of what I hear,' the veteran replied, with a sardonic grin. 'That's why I've grown to be so old.'

Artorex waited, his relaxed hands resting on his knees.

After a short length of stubborn silence, Targo capitulated. 'You will tell no one what I say, for I have no desire to be found on my doorstep with an extra mouth under my jaw.'

'I can't believe that Caius could murder,' Artorex exclaimed. 'I know he's a bully, and his friends are drunkards and wastrels, but he's too weak to commit a mortal act.'

'Is he? Well, then, you hardly need me to tell you anything, young sir.'

Targo began to rise, but Artorex abjectly apologized, so the old man reluctantly leaned back against the trunk of the tree.

'The young master has been vicious since he was a boy. His mother is a great lady, and my Lord Ector is as easy in nature as old Plod there, for all that he'll huff and puff if he's in a temper. But Caius was born with a black hole inside his body and nothing in this whole land can fill it. He is not to be trusted.'

'You know this for certain?'

'For certain. Beyond doubt. Sadly, I'm aware of many matters involving the young master – matters that I don't wish to recount to any person. Because you're already aware of one particular sin of his making, I'll confirm with you that he ruined Aphrodite because she wouldn't answer easily to the bridle when she was a yearling. He beat her until her coat was blood-red.'

Targo shook his head at the memory.

'When Caius was younger, he tried to kill me on the first occasion I gave him a sword with an edge,' the old man continued. 'He approached me from behind, but I sensed his presence and avoided the blade. He couldn't find an opening – and then claimed that he was simply testing me. Caius is mastered by spite, and you, of all men, should never trust him.'

'But surely Lord Ector is aware of his son's nature?' Artorex had no good reason to admire Caius, but he was suddenly amazed at how little he had absorbed of life within the walls of the villa.

'Both Lord Ector and his lady are aware of the flaws in their son. They pretend otherwise, but I've seen the master watch the young man, and I know that look. He's ashamed of Caius. They both are but, like all parents, they love their son.'

Targo stared up at the branches of the alder tree. When he spoke again, it was as if he was releasing frightening thoughts that had been too long contained.

'Caius isn't particular who he hurts, if you take my meaning. It's the pain that's important to him, for it bolsters his manhood. Wine, blood and mating! Those three demons can make the world a terrible place.'

Targo was speaking in riddles, but Artorex didn't dare to break the flow of the old man's thoughts. The veteran's dark eyes were sad, as if he had seen too much of the brutal side of human nature.

'Some years ago, two little children went missing from a village to the east of here. Do you remember it?'

'I've some memory of it, but it didn't mean much to me at the time,' Artorex answered slowly. 'It was before you became my tutor. I recall that Frith warned me to stay out of the Old Forest or the evil spirits would steal me away.'

'You can thank Mithras that Ector ordered you to be trained for battle, or perhaps you would not be standing here, so strong and so unafraid.'

Artorex could only look confused, while Targo pretended to examine his calloused hands.

'The children, a boy and a girl, were brother and sister, the only little ones of a woodcutter. The boy was thirteen and the girl was eleven when they were lost.' Targo paused as the memories of that dark time came back to him. 'The villagers searched for them for weeks, but the children had vanished off the face of the earth, and the superstitious believed that a demon had eaten them. As it turned out, a monster had taken those poor little things who were never apart in life. We found the girl a week later. She'd been tortured and stripped of her hair and her hands. She was alive when that monster cut her veins, for the ground in the woods where they found her was soaked with her blood. Her face . . . it's one thing to kill in battle, and I've seen sights that would sicken the strongest man, but this crime was grotesque – and I recall it to this day.'

'Was she used?' Artorex asked, for children were often the prey of human beasts.

'No, she wasn't touched. But I'm sure that the man – or the men – who killed her must have hated women. They even cut off her childish nipples when they mutilated her. She bled freely from the wounds – and the dead don't bleed.'

'Agh!' Artorex could not help his exclamation of disgust.

'The boy's body was found some weeks later. He'd been

buried in a shallow grave on the edge of the woods over by Falcon Fold, but the coldness of winter had kept his flesh fresh, so his father was able to recognize him easily. None of us knew how to tell his fate to his mother, but the woodcutter was fair mad with grief.'

Instinctively, Artorex knew that this grim story was a long way from its ending.

'The boy had been raped repeatedly. There was still blood smeared along his pitiful little flanks. He'd been tied up, and had then been abandoned to starve to death.'

'But what have these horrors to do with Caius?' Artorex asked.

'I wonder you don't remember more of the Murder of the Innocents. No one, servant or master, seemed to speak of much else for many weeks. And then, one day, when Mistress Livinia warned Caius to take care – for there was a bloody murderer at work – I saw the young master smile. It was just a fleeting smile but I sensed that he was guilty of something. The villagers distrust Severinus and his catamite, but where the Severinii go, so does Caius.'

'I was feeling sorry for myself in those times,' Artorex explained softly. 'I was spending much of my time in the Old Forest, or avoiding work, so I cannot remember much of the lost children,' he whispered slowly, his mind consumed by the graphic cruelty of Targo's tale.

'Every year or so, another child seems to go missing. But there are so many children and wild rumours surface about their fates, each tale more unlikely than the last. We sometimes find their remains but, more often than not, the bodies are too well hidden by the beasts who commit these crimes.'

'Do you believe that Caius is part of these abominations?'

Targo glanced over his shoulder towards the villa with a harried, haunted expression. Artorex couldn't remember a time when the veteran had appeared to be frightened, but now his seamed face bore a number of changing emotions – and one of them was fear.

'Yes.' Targo spoke the single word reluctantly, and in a whisper. 'Either alone or, more likely, with Severinus, his friend. He was very young when the first children were lost, but he was already friendly with Severinus.'

Targo looked at his young pupil.

'I wouldn't be surprised to find that Caius doesn't have the balls to act in these atrocities. I think he's satisfied just to watch, like the suppliants at the more ugly festivals that were held on the Lupercal in Rome, before the barbarians burned it to blackened marble. What I'm saying, boy, is that either Caius is a murderer or his friend is a murderer. And, yes, I believe that Caius is an accomplice in the slaughter of these children. May the gods help me, but I pity Master Ector if ever he learns what the villagers suspect.'

Artorex was revolted, as much by the web of silence that had been thrown over the villa as by the vileness committed in the execution of the crimes.

'It's clear to me that you despise Caius, and yet you obey his orders with a calm face,' Artorex protested. 'How do you remain silent? Do you think Ector knows anything of the fate of these children, and would he remain mute to protect his son?'

'I hate Caius with an old soldier's loathing, but I've hated many men and I've still allowed them to keep breathing. The reason I obey the commands of Caius is because he is the son of Lord Ector, a true and noble man who took me in when I was near to falling on my own sword. My master doesn't know what his son does, for he doesn't have the face or the eyes that can easily tell lies. I swear that he doesn't suspect Caius.'

He gazed down at his hands which were twisting and kneading each other restlessly.

'I couldn't bear to be the one to tell Lord Ector the full measure of my concerns. I've no proof, as the villagers have no proof, so I wouldn't expect Lord Ector to believe anything that stains the character of his house. As for the mistress? No. Never. She'd kill the boy herself if his guilt brought shame on her family name.'

Targo's eyes were filmed with self-disgust as well as tears, and Artorex winced to see what his doubts had aroused.

'Now that you're aware of my fears, boy, you must promise me that you won't do anything until we can act with certainty. Too much pain would be inflicted on too many innocent people if we acted on mere suspicion.'

Artorex nodded. 'I agree. We must watch and we must try to keep the family safe from harm – even Caius. Like you, I owe my life to Lord Ector and Mistress Livinia.'

The morning breeze blew cold and raised the hair on Artorex's arms. He rose to his feet. His eyes were quite flat as he considered the problem of his foster-brother.

'Damn her!' Artorex sighed. 'I was quite content until she stirred me into thinking.'

'You speak of Mistress Gallia, I suppose.' Targo grinned through his yellowed teeth. 'A tasty little morsel of trouble.'

'Yes. She's an infernal nuisance, but she's sharp – and she's beautiful!'

'So sharp that she'll cause you to be cut if you aren't careful, boy. Young teasers like the Mistress Gallia are a curse to most men, for they'll drive you fair crazy.'

With much still left unsaid, the two men began to prepare for their daily sword practice.

Quite ignorant of the upheaval she was causing in the still pool of the Villa Poppinidii, Gallia helped to while away Julanna's long hours of enforced inactivity by showing her all sorts of trifles she'd brought from Aquae Sulis. Jewelled combs, a game of pegs, a tiny amulet of the Mother in whalebone and delicate threads from the East all found their way into Julanna's room.

Cletus died suddenly when spring was at its most beautiful. He had been ill for so long that the master and the mistress counted his death a blessing for the faithful servant. As he had no children and no kin, he was sent to his gods discreetly with only the family and the house servants as witnesses. Afterwards, his ashes were scattered over the fields he laboured to enrich. As quietly as he had lived, so Cletus passed out of the world of Villa Poppinidii. His death caused scarcely a ripple in his wake, for he had providently trained his replacement.

Over the next month, regardless of the disdain shown by Caius, Gallia kept close to Julanna, so the young father-to-be contrived to be absent from the household often, sometimes for days on end. Spring flew by on heady, scented wings and even Gallia was lulled into a protective aura of peace and contentment.

She sewed with a fine hand and the friends spent countless hours preparing baby clothes and embroidering fanciful designs that would beautify the fine wools and linens. The girls were rarely bored, for Gallia knew a wealth of stories that never failed to enthral her friend. Had she known how carefully Artorex watched over both of them, Gallia would have felt less comfortable within the walls of the villa.

When Julanna was less than a month from birthing and the start of summer was only days away, the three travellers returned once again to the villa.

Some days glister as if diamond dust is carried on the warm air. The fitful breezes had been hot all day and the family had spent most of the hottest middle hours in the atrium where the fountain offered some illusion of coolness. The ladies fanned themselves desultorily and gazed longingly at the visible square of sky that held no trace of cooling cloud. Even the birds were silent, as if the heat had robbed them of the power to sing.

The three noble visitors were a welcome distraction from the unseasonable weather. An excuse to laze in the baths and dress for the evening meal was a blessing after the hammer of heat that had bludgeoned the family throughout the day.

Ector greeted Myrddion, Luka and Llanwith pen Bryn with pleasure, for he realized that, thanks to these noble and powerful men, he now possessed a strong young steward who could safely manage his lands for many years to come. When Cletus died, the youthful Artorex immediately took complete control of the villa's day-to-day life and was performing his duties with distinction even before Ector confirmed his promotion to the position. Much that Artorex now was, Ector knew, was due to the intercession of the three lords, and he was grateful.

The presence of Gallia caused some consternation on the part of the three noble visitors. Obviously, they had not anticipated other guests during their visit.

Gallia was agog with curiosity at the presence of the three visitors, and her golden eyes gleamed as she noticed every tiny detail that marked the strangers as powerful men of influence. Llanwith's dragon dagger told her much, for if she was not mistaken the hilt was wrought from iron and pure gold. Luka wore a torc of antique shape and, although the metal was strange to her, the worldly little Gallia guessed that it was made of electrum.

As for Myrddion, who was now distinguished by a white streak in his black hair, Gallia recognized the manners of one who is used to daily contact with the mighty and the powerful. She knew a dignitarium, a high-ranking courtier, when she met one. He wore a pigeon-egg-sized ruby on his thumb as if it was a mere nothing, and one ear was pierced and filled with a strange spearhead of gold.

Yes, very peculiar indeed were these men from far away – men who came infrequently to observe Artorex's progress, and then departed as quickly as they arrived. Gallia knew there was some deep purpose behind their visits, for men of wealth and power never act impulsively. Gallia grinned delightedly. Mysterious strangers, rumours of the wider world of Britain and an opportunity to wear her best robes danced tantalizingly through her thoughts.

'Anything that occupies Caius and deflects his words,' she muttered aloud, sobering immediately. 'The heat is making us all irritable.'

But Gallia could never be gloomy for long, so she danced away to her sleeping chamber to consider the deficiencies in her wardrobe.

CHAPTER V

BIRTH AND DEATH

As had become customary at the Villa Poppinidii, a feast was held to honour the arrival of the three dignitaries. Artorex kept the kitchen humming and nimble maids prepared bed-chambers for the three visitors.

Gallia was obliged to sleep on a pallet in Julanna's room. She did not protest, for she knew that Caius had recently grown increasingly morose and she welcomed the opportunity to guard her friend from his temper. Artorex was also uneasy, for it was clear to him that Caius was distracted and his moods were growing even more unpredictable. The noble visitors only served to put Caius on edge; Artorex overheard him swearing viciously at a manservant who was laying out a fresh tunic for the feast.

As Artorex strode through the colonnades, ensuring that all the small details of the meal met Lord Ector's expectations, he saw Targo hovering in a patch of shadow near the stables.

The old man had swathed himself in a dark cloak so that only the keenest of eyes could spy him as he observed the comings and goings at the villa. Artorex noted that Targo carried his short sword and dagger in sheaths at his waist.

'What tidings, Targo? Shouldn't you be in your widow's arms, or seated by her fireside?' Artorex asked from the courtyard.

Targo looked alarmed at the loud greeting from his pupil. He raised a finger to his lips, and then pulled Artorex into the relative darkness of the stables.

'Keep your voice down, boy. You could cause us both to be killed.'

'Why are we whispering?'

Targo's eyes gleamed in the half-light. Had Artorex not known better, he would have believed that the older man was seriously frightened.

'I've just been told that another boy has vanished from the village, and his kin are terrified for his safety. The boy isn't one to wander far from his home so they're certain that he's been taken. His father, the Smith, won't wait quietly for his boy to be found. He'll be here before too long, prepared to choke the life out of Caius if that serves to find his son. The other villagers are also angry, and rumours are rife. If they believe that Caius is involved, and they do, they'll come here with the Smith to drag the master's son away, whether he's guilty or not.'

'When did the latest boy go missing?' Artorex asked abruptly.

'Yesterday, at dawn,' Targo replied tersely.

Artorex heaved a deep sigh of relief. 'Thanks to all the gods – Caius hasn't left the villa for two days,' Artorex murmured with simple truth. 'He's been a damned nuisance, in fact, and is driving his family demented with his moods.'

Targo laughed ruefully. 'Then I must be right when I say that Caius is a watcher of evil and doesn't have the balls to carry out these crimes for his own gratification. I'd wager my left hand that he is involved, especially if he's been anxious to visit his friend, Severinus. At any rate, the threat to the villa still holds. That's why I'm here. It's possible the villagers might turn against Ector and the situation could get completely out of hand if something isn't done to stop it. These murders have gone on for too long.'

'Then I'll try to keep Caius at Villa Poppinidii where Lord Ector can provide some protection for him,' Artorex decided. 'If you can convince the villagers that Ector's son was here at the villa at the time the young lad went missing, then perhaps we can avoid too much bad blood – for all our sakes. In this instance, you can tell them that I, Artorex, swear that the young master is innocent of this particular disappearance.' He paused. 'You're aware that the three travellers have returned to the villa and are with Lord Ector even as we speak?'

'Why does everything go wrong at the same time?' the old man muttered. 'It's best then that I go to the village to placate the boy's kin at once.'

'Yes. And I thank you for your warning. I'll watch Caius and ensure that he remains here at the villa.'

Turning, the old warrior took his leave, patting the trunk of his favourite alder tree as he passed.

Artorex stared after Targo until his form was lost in the deepening darkness.

The young steward returned to his duties, his sandalled heels striking down hard on the cobbles as he strode to the kitchens. He had work to do, and little time to ensure that no shame should be attached to the hospitality of the Villa Poppinidii.

That night, the feast had a tense atmosphere, despite the exquisite food.

Mistress Livinia had dressed with particular care in a peplum of pale blue that suited the remnants of her dark beauty. As was her custom, she wore few jewels, but the great pearls that hung from her ears and the two heavy bangles that encircled her narrow wrist were exclamation marks that emphasized her delicacy. Llanwith pen Bryn bowed his head to her when he recognized that his gift adorned her ears.

Master Ector was as hearty and as insensitive as ever,

completely oblivious to the undercurrents of bad temper, nervousness and watchfulness that pervaded the triclinium. He lounged on his carved and painted divan and waved to his guests to join him.

Julanna had pleaded a sick headache and had taken to her bed, but Gallia could not resist the impulse to observe the three visitors at close quarters. Caius seemed more distracted than was usual for him in the company of the great ones, while Livinia was occupied in surreptitiously observing her son, in spite of the gracious smiles and welcoming words she directed towards her guests.

Artorex summoned the first course of songbirds, glazed with honey and sweetened aspic of eggs and lambs' tongue, and the meal began. He joined the family once the first course had been served, but made no effort to engage in the conversation. His presence was ignored by the assembled group, so he fetched the wines, just as he had done so long ago as a young boy. He served guests and hosts alike.

'What news of the east do you bring, my friends?' Ector asked, as was his custom.

'It's bad, friend Ector, very bad,' Luka replied, as he daintily plucked a chicken wing from the meat platter and crunched its bones between his strong teeth.

'Tell us, friends,' Livinia asked in her gracious manner. 'For we hear little of the outside world at our villa. I fear we are so caught up in our safe little world that we know nothing of the troubles of others.'

After a moment of wordless communion between the three friends, Myrddion spoke for all, and his words offered little comfort for the future well-being of Lord Ector and his family.

'The Saxon hordes have invaded the eastern coast in large numbers and have taken Camulodunum and a number of smaller towns and villages. At the same time, the Jutlanders have landed in great numbers from the Metaris Aest. They've not moved far from their longboats and have held back from plunder – unlike their practice in the past. And they have brought their women and children with them this spring. We fear that they've come to stay.'

'This is nonsense. How could a fortress such as Camulodunum fall?' Ector protested. 'It's walled and garrisoned by the forces of the High King. How could the barbarians breach the rock walls of Camulodunum?'

'We have warned you before, friend Ector, that the Saxons have excellent fighting men – and women,' pen Bryn rumbled, as he waved away Artorex's offer of more wine. 'Many of their warriors are as large as Artorex here and they have spent their entire lives fighting for every crust and every slave since the day of their birth. They are ferocious, and their leaders control their soldiers mercilessly. When they hold the high ground, they're virtually invincible.'

'We've felt their ruthlessness before, during those days when Vortigern married his Saxon woman and opened the floodgates to her kin. The wars of Vortimer haven't been forgotten – and the Saxons still live in the wilder parts south of Mona Island.' Myrddion spoke gravely and with the conviction of absolute truth. 'I myself felt the sting of Vortigern's venom, and I experienced the Saxon lust for the land of the Britons when I was but a small boy. Did you truly believe that such a people would leave us in peace?'

Gallia shivered. This news was not the comfortable and interesting tales of the world that she had hoped to hear.

Luka observed her frightened face. 'Well may you be concerned, Mistress, for the Saxons and their allies will not be stopped until they have spread from sea to sea. More raiders will come next summer now that they have a foothold on both our eastern and western coasts. And the year after that, more still will arrive. They will turn our towns to bloody, smoking ruins, like Camulodunum, and then they'll build their wooden halls on our stone foundations. Our safe world is coming to an end, my friends.'

'And what are our great lords doing?' Caius snapped. 'Where is Uther Pendragon, the High King, who is supposed to be protecting us?'

His mother flashed a quick, eloquent glance of warning in his direction, but Caius was too angry to heed her silent caution.

'As usual, the Celtic kings are useless, just as they were when the legions defeated them easily in years gone by. What is needed now is a leader, one with the belly to put these curs to flight,' Caius concluded, his face twisted into a sneer.

Pen Bryn would have answered, but Myrddion placed a hand over his friend's forearm, and took up the argument smoothly.

'It's true that many kings of the Britons are frightened, Caius. But it is also true that it has only been the strength of Uther Pendragon that has held them together during these past decades of peace. It would only need a small mistake now for the lesser kings to break the High King's treaty – so we live in perilous times.'

'And Uther Pendragon sickens,' Luka interrupted abruptly. 'He is not the man he was last year, or five years before that. At sixty, his fires are almost quenched.'

'Then we truly need a leader to put iron in the spines of our leaders and fear in the hearts of our enemies,' Caius repeated. 'It is only strength and fighting spirit that can give these cowardly weaklings the will to face the Saxons.'

'Take care, Caius, or you'll cause offence,' Ector hissed.

'I speak the truth, Father,' Caius retorted.

'You speak like a child, boy,' pen Bryn growled and drove his dragon knife deeply into the wooden table; the gems in the dragon's eyes winked balefully in the light of the torches.

'Britain was ours long before the Roman legions came. It was ours when the Roman tribes crawled in their mud huts between the Seven Hills. And it was ours when it was under Roman rule. And they were quick enough to run when the barbarian hordes began to cross the Danube. You are half Celt, boy, so remember that you are only the bastard son of a family that was crawling in the dirt when my ancestors were kings in their own land.'

'You must mind your manners, Llanwith,' Luka admonished. 'Still, I agree with this young man that we need a strong leader in these perilous times.'

Caius leapt to his feet.

'Sir! I don't care for your insults,' he screamed. His eyes appeared half crazy in the light of the sconces. 'How dare you insult my mother who is Roman to the core and who is also your hostess!'

'Your mother is a Briton,' Myrddion interjected. He turned to face Livinia. 'Is that not so, my lady? You've never walked upon the streets of Rome, I know. In fact, Rome no longer exists as it was known in the past.' Myrddion spoke carefully to remove the sting from his unpalatable words.

'Our guest is right, Caius,' Livinia answered. 'I am a Briton, as are you. In Rome, we would have been as nothing to the senators, and even less than nothing to the curs who inhabited the subura. My great-grandfather followed the legions, and he made his home and his fortune within these walls. We will all live and die as Britons, for I fear the Saxons will not care to make a distinction between Ector and myself.'

But Livinia's words didn't mollify her son, whose face burned with raw anger and hostility. Out of a visceral desire to destroy, he ripped apart a delicate cloth that had been laid aside for greasy hands and flung the fragments on to the floor. Livinia whitened in apprehension and resolutely turned away.

Myrddion turned to question Artorex.

'And what say you, Artorex? What would you do if you were Uther Pendragon?'

'I'd strike, my lord. And I'd strike hard with all my strength before the Saxons have a toehold in the west. A battle fought at a later time on our own fields could be disastrous for all the Britons.'

'Yes, my boy, you're probably right. But Uther is old – and has no heir to succeed him,' Myrddion replied regretfully.

'Then one must be found, preferably one of Roman lineage,' Caius hissed through his teeth. He was almost standing over Myrddion in his rage.

'Even as we speak, young man, the search for a successor to Uther Pendragon is being pursued by men of faith and principle. One fact is certain, the kings of the Britons would not be stirred to follow a Roman-born leader. Such thinking is over-proud and impractical.'

Caius dashed down his goblet on the table and the lees splashed over Myrddion's tunic. The scholar merely mopped the wine stains from his garment and ignored the younger man. Ector started to apologize, and Livinia's face was stricken.

Caius stormed from the room, his fury a palpable, living thing.

Artorex was torn. Caius was in the kind of rage that made the man dangerous, but Ector had not given him leave to follow the young master.

Fate intervened, for Myrddion continued to address Artorex. He must stay.

'Your foster-brother is a hot-headed young man, Artorex, but in these dangerous times such men are often needed,' he said carefully. 'I am curious. What qualities of leadership do you feel are necessary in our leaders during these troubled times?'

'We should be searching for a warrior who has been trained from birth to lead. He should be one whom all Britons will follow because of his birthright – and through his strength of arms. You need a cold, calculating man such as the great Caesar, a man who will dare much and gamble everything on his will, and not just his anger.'

'True!' the friends agreed.

At this point of tentative agreement, the screams began.

The sound of those thin, wailing trebles would have chilled the hottest blood. The whole company stood in haste, hands searching out weapons, but Artorex and Gallia were first through the doorway. Both recognized the direction from which those terrified screams came.

Livinia was only a few steps behind them, and the guests brought up the rear.

Artorex burst through the doors of Caius's apartments to discover Julanna curled up into a ball as small as her pregnant belly would allow, while a foaming Caius kicked out viciously at any part of her flesh that was exposed.

'Stop, master!' Artorex shouted and plucked Caius away from his wife's bleeding face and body. 'You must stop!'

Gallia immediately threw herself over her friend's prone form and tried to cover her with her own small person.

'You cannot think to harm her, sir,' Artorex tried to reason. 'She is the mother of your unborn child.'

'I will kick her to death if I choose to do so,' Caius snarled, maddened beyond rational thought. 'She is mine to do with as I choose.'

In his incoherent rage, he howled and attempted to throw himself at his sobbing wife once again.

According to Roman law, Artorex could not harm or even restrain Caius, son of the paterfamilias, yet custom and rule were only a perilously thin veneer over the instincts of a man like Artorex. He had no intention of standing aside.

'You'll only touch her again when you have passed through

my body', Artorex promised quietly, in a voice as smooth and as sharp as a wire.

'The prospect would delight me', Caius screamed and drew his knife. Artorex easily parried Caius's blows, until a woollen mat brought him to grief when his foot slipped on its treacherous purchase.

As Artorex began to fall, Caius struck out at him, slashing his arm from shoulder to elbow. Still, he wouldn't have passed had he not managed to throw a sleeping coverlet over his foster-brother that completely enveloped him in its folds.

Gallia sprang to her feet like a tigress and faced Caius as boldly as any soldier.

'You'll not touch her, Caius', she snapped. 'Not if I can stop you'.

'But you can't prevent me, can you?' Caius said, almost conversationally. He gripped her hair by the crown of her head and tossed her into the corner of the room like a bundle of wet rags.

'Now, madam', he said in a voice so drenched with fury that Artorex struggled even harder to extricate himself from the suffocating folds of the bedcover.

'*No! . . . No! . .* '.

Artorex heard the thin voice scream, as the sturdy body of Caius connected with another that was smaller and infinitely frailer. Lady Livinia had stepped between her son's knife and her daughter-in-law. Both mother and son stared at the knife buried up to the hilt in Livinia's breastbone.

'Mother!' Caius screamed.

Livinia crumpled at the knees, and Artorex had time to lower her gently on to the sleeping pallet that Gallia had used. He was oblivious to the orders of the three visitors, to the wailing of servants, to the sobbing of Julanna, to the sight of Gallia being carried bodily from the room, while Caius was physically restrained and dragged from the sleeping chamber by pen Bryn and Luka.

Only Lady Livinia existed. Her dark eyes were intensely alive and pleading – and they were fixed on Artorex alone.

Ector prostrated himself beside his wife and was sobbing uncontrollably as he cradled his dying wife in his arms. Artorex tried to extricate his arm from the death grip that Livinia had placed on his wrist, but all her considerable vitality was concentrated in that one small hand.

'You must promise me,' she whispered.

'Anything! Anything, my only love,' Ector replied brokenly.

'No, not you. Artorex. He must promise me that when he is a great man . . . that he will care for Caius.'

'But he has sorely wounded you, my lady,' Artorex protested, brushing one hand across eyes that were wet. The wound was mortal although the blade was more decorative than deadly. Sheer chance had driven the short, slender shaft between Livinia's ribs and breastbone, and into the region of her heart. She should be carried to her room, but any movement might drive the dagger through her heart and still Livinia's voice forever.

'Caius is just a silly boy . . . a foolish boy . . . a child who needs saving from himself. I forgive him. Do you hear me? My death is an accident. You must hear me – and swear to all that I ask. I have raised you to manhood, Artorex, and I beg you to protect my son.'

Artorex could feel the tears in his eyes begin to run silently down his face. In every way but blood, Livinia was the closest thing to a mother he had ever known. Even now, with her face as pale as bleached linen, and the thin blade alone saving her from immediate death, her Roman duty held true. She gave no indication of pain or fear, and her only expression was one of regret.

'I can't meet my ancestors in peace until you promise me, Artorex. I can't go into the long sleep until my Caius is protected from himself.'

Her voice wheezed through damaged lungs and a thin rivulet of blood ran from her lips, even as Ector fruitlessly tried to wipe it away.

Under the spell of those vital, pleading eyes, Artorex swore his oath.

'I vow that I will keep Caius safe, and that I will endeavour to protect him from himself. I'll carry him with me down whatever path my life follows. Rest, my lady, rest, for I promise that I'll follow your wishes.'

'Stand back now, Artorex. You must allow me to care for my wife,' Ector ordered in a cracked and broken voice.

'Thank you, Artorex.' Livinia smiled painfully. 'Now, my dear Ector,' she breathed. 'You must remove the knife for me, my husband.'

'But you will die if I do, Livinia. What will I do without you?'

'You will always be my strong, kind husband,' she said softly. Livinia's breath was now coming in fast and painful gasps. 'Please, my dear. I'm bleeding inwardly, you must spare me my pain. I'd have liked to see my grandchild, but I know it will live. Care for it, my dear one, as you have cared for all my people in the past.'

She took one painful breath and generations of the hardy progeny of Rome seemed to stare out at the world through her calm, black eyes.

'You must take out the knife. Now!'

Artorex watched from the doorway, for he couldn't force his body to entirely leave the room. A weeping Ector put one giant hand over the delicate hilt of the knife, and Livinia wrapped her small palms around his.

Ector eased the narrow blade out of her chest. Immediately,

a great gush of blood bubbled from her mouth and the narrow wound allowed more blood to spurt free. Livinia briefly smiled, like a tired little girl, and then closed her eyes.

Lord Ector began to wail as Livinia took her last breath.

Outside, all was chaos. Llanwith pen Bryn had taken Caius into his bedchamber and watched his charge through narrowed, hostile eyes. Caius had thrown himself on to his pallet, his legs drawn up to his chin in his guilt and distress. He wept hysterically, because, although Caius cared for very few living things, he depended on his mother.

'What will I do?' he howled, and Artorex hurried away from the whining, self-absorbed voice.

Julanna had been moved into the dining room where the terrified servants had cleared away the food and covered a dining couch with fresh linen. The girl was now in labour, her eyes half-crazed and her swollen belly moving spasmodically with each powerful contraction. Frith had come from the kitchens and she and Myrddion had the childbirth firmly in hand.

Artorex ordered Livinia's maidservant to assist Lord Ector to move the body of his wife into their bedchamber and, although her face was twisted with grief and loss, Delia rallied to fulfil the needs of her mistress. Artorex longed to weep and to lay his head on Delia's capacious, cushioned breasts and cry for the loss of his mistress. But he was the steward, so he must put her house in order.

As the news of Livinia's death spread, the servants of the villa set up a great wailing, but Artorex ordered them to be silent.

'Your mistress was a great lady. She would expect you to honour her by washing her body and preparing her in her best peplum and robe for her funeral. Don't shame her.'

Their tears stopped on Artorex's command. Celts knew the

honour owed to the dead – especially to the heroic dead – and they ran to do his bidding.

'Take care of the master,' Artorex ordered the cook. 'Coax him to drink a little Spanish wine. He is broken-hearted, but I must entrust him to your care. I am needed elsewhere.'

'Of course,' the surly cook replied, his features freed of their habitual, disagreeable irritation. 'I will do all you ask.'

'You have my thanks, good man. Take him to the scriptorium where quiet reigns, while I attend to the guests.'

He found Luka in the guest room, across from the atrium and the colonnade.

'I have been seeing to the maiden,' Luka told him. 'She is aware, but her scalp needs mending. By the gods, what a madhouse we have seen this night.'

With a few long strides, Artorex crossed the central atrium to see to Gallia's wound for himself. He found her lying on a disturbed coverlet in her old room with one hand pressing a torn fragment of cloth that Luka had folded into a compress for her wound. Her hair was streaked with blood, but her eyes were bright, albeit frightened.

'Let me see your head, Gallia,' Artorex ordered curtly and, obediently, she pulled the compress away from her scalp. A long split in the skin was slowly oozing blood.

'The brain might be damaged within the skull, so she shouldn't be moved,' Luka cautioned. 'I've seen strong warriors who've died of head wounds.'

Artorex felt along the gaping edges of the wound, and Gallia bit her lip hard to keep from crying out in pain.

'Good girl,' he murmured, as his fingers carefully probed the skull around the long split. 'Your hard head seems intact. But Luka is correct. You should lie back, hold the compress to the wound and, when Myrddion is free, he'll stitch your wound together. He'll need to shave part of your hair away, unfortunately.'

'I don't care overmuch,' she mumbled. 'How is Julanna? Is she safe?'

'Aye, but she is in labour.'

Gallia tried to rise from the bed, but Artorex pressed her back.

'She has Myrddion and Frith with her, so she has no better aid in all of Aquae Sulis. Obey me, Mistress Gallia. Luka will stay with you.'

At the entrance to the room, Artorex pulled Luka aside and informed him of Livinia's fate. The older man shook his head in consternation. He had seen enough of the carnage in Caius's room to have guessed at the outcome but he frowned in distaste as Artorex confirmed her death.

'I need to set the villa to rights,' Artorex added desperately, for he knew that activity would keep his mind sharp and hold his grief at bay. 'It would assist me greatly if you could stay with Gallia and prevent her from any childish action. She's quite capable of ignoring the best advice if it pleases her.'

Luka merely squeezed Artorex's shoulder. 'Be about your tasks, boy. We'll talk later.'

'Aye. Later.'

Once Artorex had seen to the needs of all his charges, he set about putting to rights what could be salvaged from this terrible night.

In the barn, several stable boys had been woken by the din and the commotion, and were trying to calm the restive horses. Artorex sent these men to Julanna's bedchamber with the express task of cleaning away the blood-splattered evidence of the death of their mistress.

'Burn anything that can't be cleansed. Scrub the floors, to ensure that there's no sign of carnage that could further trouble the master,' Artorex ordered crisply, and the men lifted wooden water pails and rags and ran to do his bidding.

Delia met him at the doorway of Livinia's rooms and barred his entrance. The last dignities offered to the dead have always been the duties of women, and Artorex wondered sadly how this sex could bear the pitiful task of cleansing and straightening the lifeless flesh, especially when they were as beloved as the mistress had been.

'You may leave Lady Livinia with me, Steward,' Delia whispered. Her face was slick with tears, but she was controlled and fixed in purpose. 'My lady will go to the flames as she would have wished. Be about your duties, for her sake.'

'Oh, Delia. Her death is such a waste, such a mess,' Artorex began, his head bent and his hand tightly clasping that of the servant.

Artorex suddenly realized the impropriety of his actions and the inadequacy of his grief. He pulled his hand away and squared his shoulders.

'Spare no expense, Delia,' he whispered. 'The master would want you to use all the precious oils you need, for the last of the Poppinidii family goes to the shades to join her ancestors.'

'The women shall do all that she would have wished, just as if she were here herself,' Delia whispered.

The servant woman began to weep as she turned away from the granite-hard eyes of the steward.

As Artorex left the corridor, Julanna's childbirth cries began to echo through the villa, but the steward knew that he couldn't assist with the agonies of a new life entering their world. However, he could provide some service to the master. He found Ector weeping quietly in the scriptorium under the watchful eyes of Grunn, the cook.

The master's large, liver-spotted hands were folded around a wine cup, and his head was bowed low.

'Lord?' Artorex said softly.

Ector raised his leonine, balding head unwillingly. His blue eyes were filled with misery and wet with tears, as if he was drowning in sorrow.

'How can my Livinia be dead?' he asked feebly, and then burst into a fresh storm of weeping.

Artorex knelt beside Ector's chair and gripped one limp hand.

'Mistress Livinia is with her ancestors. I fear we'll never see her like again in these isles. But she died for what she loved and, even now, she holds me to my oath. She'd wish you to go on and to protect the villa in her name.' He squeezed Ector's hand. 'You must rest, master, for you'll need all your strength for the grandchild that comes.'

Ector bowed his head once more over his entwined hands. 'But what of Caius? What of our son? How can I bear to look into the eyes of the man who has killed his own mother?'

'You must trust me to put everything to rights, master. I have asked Grunn to take you to your bedchamber. I'll do everything exactly as you would wish it to be done, and I'll do it in your name.'

Reluctantly, Ector permitted Grunn to assist him to rise to his feet. Like an old, old man, Ector was led from the scriptorium.

Artorex automatically took up the pitcher of wine and the goblet, wiped over the desk and set all to rights within the room.

Then he returned to the kitchen.

A single maidservant was boiling rags in a blackened pot, her face flushed from weeping. Artorex paid her no mind, until a sudden shriek split the preternatural silence of the villa once again. It reminded him that a new life was struggling to come into his world.

The woman used a wooden stake to put the cleansed, steaming rags into a wicker basket, bobbed her head to the steward and then ran to tend to the needs of her mistress.

Artorex knew better than to intrude into the female business of childbirth, so he waited in the corridor, pacing in time to the beating of his heart.

The night was still and Julanna's final scream tore the darkness apart with her primal need. The frail cry of an infant was anti-climactic, but Artorex sighed deeply, muttered a quick prayer to Mithras, the soldier's god, and waited for Myrddion.

Instead, Frith came to the doorway. Her back was straight and her arms held a dark-haired babe wrapped in fresh linen.

'A child is born, my lord.' Frith held the baby out to him. 'You must bless her. Please, my lord, for she's a weak thing, and she mustn't die, for the shade of the mistress would never forgive me.'

'Don't name me by titles that aren't mine, Frith. You know that I'm only the steward. But if it will set your mind at rest, I'll bless the child for you.'

His large hands obscured the red, monkey-like face of the infant as he murmured the old blessing of birth over its head of dark hair.

'Now the child will live,' Frith exclaimed happily, her old eyes alight with something fey and strange. 'I'll take her to the master – for she has the eyes of my sweet Livinia.'

Myrddion watched the tableau in the doorway. His mouth was smiling, but his eyes were grave as he wiped his bloody hands on a scrap of cloth.

Artorex smiled gratefully at him. 'I thank the gods that you were here when Caius ran amok, otherwise more than one soul would have fled to the shades during this night. Once Julanna is safely abed, I beg you to tend to the head of Mistress Gallia, my lord.'

'You give me too much credit, Artorex. What of your own wound?'

Artorex looked down at the long shallow gash that ran from

just below the shoulder to his elbow. It had stopped bleeding some time ago, but was now beginning to redden with heat from the wound.

'I'll see to Gallia shortly,' Myrddion decided. 'But first, I'll clean and dress that trifling wound.'

As Myrddion cleaned the gash in hot water, Artorex continued to issue orders to the servants.

'Before you see the master, Frith, I wish you to oversee the moving of Mistress Julanna. Her room should be prepared by now. If not, inform the servants that I require them to work faster. You must also send one of the girls to the village for the wet nurse. And I want Targo here – I need him immediately, Frith.'

'All shall be done as you desire, master.'

'Stop calling me that, Frith. I am still that same grimy boy you forced to bathe.'

'Yes, master,' she replied, with perfect sincerity.

'Will this take much longer, my lord?' an anxious Artorex asked Myrddion while his wounded left arm was bandaged. 'I left Lord pen Bryn with Caius and the gods alone know how I shall deal with him.'

Around them, servants bustled as the stable boys carried a pale Julanna to her quarters, and the women struggled to put the dining chamber to rights. Frith issued orders with the clear commands of a general and, before Myrddion had completed his task, the entire room was once again bare and silent.

'I am still at your service, Artorex. Where do I find the Mistress Gallia?'

'She is in Luka's room. He is concerned that she should not be moved.'

'I shall see her immediately.'

After Myrddion left him to tend to Gallia's injury, Artorex sucked in the luxury of blessed silence – and tried to think. The dining room, where the whole tragedy had begun, had been restored to its usual state. Cleared of the bloody detritus of birth, it was simply a room of some opulence, with its couches awaiting the arrival of valued guests. Yet, Artorex was certain, it would never be the same cheerful place again. The benign graciousness of Livinia was lost forever.

Leaving the cursed room, Artorex waited in the lee of the alder for the wet nurse and Targo to arrive. The night was not yet finished, nor was its bloody aftermath even begun, and he desperately needed the advice of the rugged old campaigner. Artorex had never seen a living soul die so violently, least of all someone he loved, and his head swam in a vortex of emotions.

Some little time later, a small, pixyish woman from the village hurried out of the shadows with Targo as her escort. She was carrying an infant in a sling around her neck.

Artorex noted grimly that the warrior was still fully armed.

Directing the wet nurse to Julanna's quarters, Artorex instructed her to send Frith to him when the old woman could be spared. Then, flexing his suddenly aching arm, he turned to his old tutor.

'I imagine the messenger told you what occurred tonight?'

'Aye, Artorex, he did. What caused the young master to turn into a madman?'

Artorex grimaced wolfishly, his eyes suddenly flat and unforgiving. 'I've no idea but I intend to find out. Bring Luka and Myrddion to me from Mistress Gallia's rooms as soon as they've finished with their ministrations. I'll be with pen Bryn and the young master in his sleeping apartments.'

'Aye, lad. All shall be done as you require.' Targo gripped Artorex's shoulder with one hand. The lad's expression softened for a moment, and something wounded looked out of those glacial eyes. Then Artorex's mental shield dropped back into place.

When the steward entered the room where Caius was secured, nothing had changed in the sad tableau, although his foster-brother was no longer weeping. Llanwith pen Bryn leaned casually against the wall as he cleaned his nails with a dagger. His eyes never left the miserable form of Caius.

'Foster-brother!' Artorex used his most authoritative voice. 'The time for plain speaking between you and me has arrived.'

'Leave me alone,' Caius whined.

'Not this time, I'm afraid, foster-brother. Sit up and dry your eyes like a man, and then explain yourself.'

Caius reluctantly obeyed. The glint in Artorex's eyes promised dire consequences if he refused.

'It wasn't my fault! I never meant to hurt her! Mother stepped in front of my blade. Does she live?'

'No, Caius, don't treat me like a fool. You're fully aware that your mother is dead and that it was your hand that guided the blade. If you hadn't struck her, then you'd have murdered a harmless, pregnant woman in her stead.'

'What will become of me now?' Caius sobbed.

'Still thinking of yourself,' Llanwith rumbled, without taking his eyes from the dishevelled form of Caius. The Cymru prince was stiff with revulsion and contempt.

'You're the father of a daughter, Caius, and your wife is well, in spite of being badly bruised at your hands. Your father is prostrate with grief and the Mistress Gallia is even now in the hands of the physician, Myrddion. Tonight, you have torn apart all that was good in this villa, yet still your thoughts are only for yourself.' Artorex fairly spat the last words. Caius thrust his face into his pallet and continued to weep.

Targo and Luka silently entered the room.

Artorex had been patient enough for ten men throughout the long evening. He crossed the room to the pallet in two quick strides and dragged Caius up by the hair.

'Stand up and face your guilt, foster-brother. I'm sick of your puling and whining.' Artorex slapped the face of Caius with such force that the imprint of his hand stood out on the cheek of the young man.

'Your mother has forbidden me to kill you, Caius, but I can hurt you! And I will hurt you very badly, and then I'll lie to Master Ector without a shred of guilt. Now, I want to know what is maddening you.'

Caius collapsed as if his legs were made of jelly. 'They'll kill me if I so much as hint at their guilt.'

Artorex laughed drily and pointed to the travellers. Three pairs of cold, contemptuous eyes stared fixedly at Caius. Llanwith spat on Caius's pallet with contempt.

'I swore an oath to your mother. She forgave you as she lay dying, and she forced me to make a promise to protect you. These gentlemen, however, are not bound by my oath, and they are men of far greater powers than you would believe. They have the authority to punish a matricide in the name of the High King. Do you wish to discover what Uther Pendragon's law prescribes for any man who kills his mother? The Celts deem matricide as one of the worst murders – unlike the Romans. I'm sure that Luka would be pleased to explain the difference to you. Ector cannot protect you from these men, so you must answer before we lose our self-control.'

'I was angry . . .'

'That's no excuse!' the voice of pen Bryn rumbled from his position against the wall. 'We're not interested in your feelings. Try again!'

'I'm tired of being second best . . .'

Llanwith knocked Caius down with a swift blow to the side of the head.

'Second best? You're the only son of Ector, the lord who owns the Villa Poppinidii,' Luka said grimly. 'You'll rule the villa when your father goes to join his ancestors. You will act like a master – and not like a cur!'

'Artorex is fatherless, and lives on the charity of my father. But everyone at the villa obeys him and not me!'

Llanwith knocked Caius down again, and he began to bleed from the mouth.

'Have done with excuses! I had a great fondness for your mother.'

'But ... she listened to Artorex rather than to me', Caius wailed and pointed at the steward.

Artorex made an exclamation of disgust and gave Caius a back-handed slap across his face himself. It effectively ended the sickening whine.

'Jealousy isn't an excuse for the damage you've done, Master Caius', the unforgiving voice of Myrddion came from the darkness of the doorway. 'We're all aware that you spend little time at Villa Poppinidii and avoid taking part in its affairs. Who deserves the respect of the servants, a young man who spends all his hours carousing with his friends or the steward who controls the destiny of the villa and who works in the fields with the men?'

'The servants don't care for me ...'

'They believe that you and your friends are involved with the murder of children', Targo declared bluntly as he stepped into the room.

Caius recoiled and covered his face with his hands. What could be seen of his countenance was bone-white except for the red marks where angry hands had struck him.

Then, tousled and dishevelled as he was, he lifted his head and faced the accusing eyes of Targo. The expression on his face had all the cunning and slyness of a stoat.

'You can't prove anything! I've been here for days!'

At that moment, Artorex knew that Caius was guilty of more

than matricide, and he felt his gorge rise. What could he do? How could he save Ector? How could any honourable man save Caius from the consequences of his vices and yet retain a semblance of decency for himself?

'You know nothing of Severinus and my friends,' Caius blustered, his eyes downcast and shifty. 'I didn't kill those children. No! I had nothing to do with them! I'm not a monster!'

Artorex was revolted by his cringeing foster-brother.

'But we do know that you attacked your pregnant wife,' he said evenly. 'And we also know that you're responsible for the death of your mother. Enough! I'm tired of this whole charade, so I'll hand you over to Llanwith who'll decide what punishment you will receive for your crimes.'

Whatever self-justification Caius was about to offer died on his lips as five pairs of eyes bored into him. Llanwith straightened and reached out one huge hand and gripped Caius by the throat. Then, straight-armed, he raised the young master into the air so that his feet kicked feebly and his face began to purple.

Artorex glared at his foster-brother. 'I've sworn an oath to protect you, but that promise was for those sins committed this night, and this night only.' He paused. 'Will you speak now? Raise your hand if you wish to speak.'

Caius kicked, struggled and slowly strangled. His head bobbed up and down like a child's toy while his eyes almost popped out of his skull.

Llanwith tossed him on to his pallet like a piece of dirty rag, and Caius attempted to regain his breath with harsh, ragged gasps.

'The foul acts ascribed to Severinus – and to your own self – are matters we want to discuss immediately,' Artorex told him. 'Not only do you have to worry about those of us who are in this room, but you may have to face the wrath of the villagers who, this very night, are mourning the loss of another of their children. Should we be dissatisfied, we intend to hand you over to them for questioning.'

Even the impassive face of Llanwith pen Bryn looked a little sick at this pronouncement.

Haltingly, fearfully, Caius told his story. His eyes were shrouded so that Artorex was unsure what motivated his foster-brother.

'Severinus will kill me if he thinks I've betrayed him. You must save me!'

'Why must I save you?' Artorex snapped. His eyes were like grey slate.

'Because he's a murderer and a pederast – he's truly an abomination. I fear for my life each time I see him.' Caius huddled into the very corner of the room, oblivious to the drying blood of his mother that still stained his hands and tunic. He was a study in ugly self-pity, and his judges weren't convinced that this sudden capitulation was honest or sincere.

'When did you first know that Severinus was a murderer?' Artorex was implacable.

'Not until it was far too late to remove myself from his influence. You must believe me!' Caius's eyes turned from one man to the next, pleading for sympathy and mercy.

'Then you must tell us everything,' Artorex insisted. 'And I must warn you that Targo will know if you leave anything out. He's familiar with some aspects of your activities.'

'I've known Severinus and his friends for many years. He seduced me years ago with talk of epicurean manners and the Roman right to rule. By the time I realized that Severinus was a perverted aberration of nature, I was too deeply enmeshed to extricate myself.'

'Is that so?' Luka asked silkily. 'Many young boys are seduced but few ally themselves with a murderer.'

'I couldn't go to my father and tell him what Severinus had done to me'. Caius blushed with shame and self-disgust and, for a brief moment, Artorex felt a stab of pity. Caius could easily have been a well-born victim and to admit his rape would be to shame himself further.

Caius's eyes displayed no emotion. He was no catamite, his tastes ran to young women, as meek and child-like as possible. His rape had convinced Caius that he hated pain   unless he was the person inflicting it. And this twisted and frightened young creature feared Severinus, who recognized the flaw in the boy's nature and probed that weakness remorselessly until Caius was trapped in a nightmare of his own vices. No matter how fiercely Caius had thrown himself into debauchery, a part of his nature had remained frightened and ashamed.

Now, sensing that Severinus was under threat, Caius saw a way of saving himself from his friend's demands and diverting Artorex's rage at the death of his mother. Caius took pains to cower and beg, although the true core of his nature screamed furiously at his assumed compliance.

'At first, we sacrificed a few sheep at the time of the Lupercal. The sport seemed harmless enough. I felt truly Roman for having taken part in the ancient ritual, for Severinus was always casting doubt on the purity of my Roman blood'.

The silence in the room was absolute, and Caius schooled his face to appear pathetic.

'Years ago, Severinus and his catamite stole two children from the village. I became aware of it, and I was sickened by what they did. But I had no part in their deaths'.

'It's just as I told you, Artorex', Targo interrupted, spitting on the floor in contempt. 'He only had the balls to watch'.

'I couldn't believe what Antiochus did to that girl. It was horrible!'

'Was she attractive?' Luka asked slyly.

Caius looked revolted. 'No, of course not! She was only a child. Severinus gave me the task of burying her body, but I couldn't even bear to cover her with earth when I unwrapped her corpse.'

'Who removed her hands?' Luka asked. 'She was alive when they were hacked off.'

'Antiochus did it,' Caius whimpered. 'She wasn't dead when we unwrapped her. And Antiochus said the bitch would tell her kin in the village if she was allowed to live so he cut off both hands with his short sword. There was nothing I could do to stop him.'

'Yet you left her to bleed to death?'

'No! I stayed with her until she stopped breathing – and then I closed her eyes.'

'What did Antiochus want to do with her hands?' Artorex asked with sick curiosity.

'He told me that Mistress Severina wanted them for some woman's charm. I asked no more questions – I didn't want to know.' Caius looked at the sickened faces that encircled him and cowered back into the corner of the room. 'On my mother's head, Artorex, I was only seventeen. I didn't know what to do! Who would have believed me if I had spoken out? Please, I don't rape children!'

The last howled comment was true, Caius had no need to dissemble. Even Llanwith believed him, and the cold inner part of Caius rejoiced to trace the sickened acceptance in their eyes.

The need to purge his body filled Artorex's mouth with a taste of bile. He couldn't imagine any magical spell that would require the mother of Severinus to use the hands of a girl child. Like Caius, Artorex simply didn't want to know, and he believed his foster-brother's excuses – although he knew he was seeking the easy way out of his promise to Livinia.

'What Roman matron could act in such a vile fashion?'

'The mother of Severinus is worse than he is,' Caius whined.

'And what of the boy?' Targo asked. 'Did you take turns to pleasure yourselves with him?'

Caius was genuinely revolted. 'I never knew what happened to the boy until later. I threatened to tell my father, but Severinus reminded me that I had assisted in the disposal of the dead girl's body and I'd be judged guilty of the same crimes as he was.' Caius hesitated briefly. 'Every time Severinus takes his entertainment, I become ill with apprehension. He insists that I watch until I am sick, and then he allows me to take my leave. I'm kept fully in his power.' Caius was almost telling the truth.

'But your fears don't explain what happened tonight,' Artorex reminded Caius.

'I know that Severinus has taken another boy,' Caius whispered softly. 'He sent word that I was required tonight to attend his "feast", as he calls it, and that no excuses would be accepted. I tried to send a message that we had visitors at the villa, but Severinus didn't care. During our meal tonight, I had to endure the thought of what he would do to me because of my absence from his entertainment, and I was frantic with terror.'

Caius genuinely hungered to be free of Severinus and his friends. The Roman was drunk with his diseased pleasures and was taking greater and more unacceptable risks. Sooner or later, Severinus would be caught, and the justice meted out would be cruel and swift. Caius was, in truth, sick with apprehension that he would be caught up in the destruction of the Severinii family.

Now he saw a way out of the trap he had devised for himself so he kept talking.

'I just snapped when Julanna tried to stop me, and whined on and on that I loved my friends more than I loved her. I hate Severinus! I hate him! I wish he were dead so that I can once again become free. As Julanna nagged on and on, all I could think of was how I had to get away. But she set up such a crying and keening that I lost control of my senses – and I tried to shut her up.'

'Your feeble explanation is very convenient,' Luka commented, his face twisted with disgust.

'Severinus took an intaglio ring from me some time ago in payment of a debt. It is a jewel that could easily be recognized as my property, and he swore to leave it with one of the corpses if I didn't do exactly as he ordered. He terrifies me – even more than you do!' Caius's eyes darted from one unforgiving face to another. His cold, inner self hunted desperately for the words that might exonerate him from his manifold sins.

'Your friend is a brave man when it comes to killing children,' Artorex murmured sardonically. 'I wonder if his courage will stand by him when he is faced by men?'

'You can't confront him,' Caius panted. 'It would be the death of me.'

'I think we can, you know,' the baritone voice of pen Bryn stated coldly. 'Where is this Severinus? I have a sudden desire to meet him.'

'You must tell us, Caius,' Luka added. 'For, if necessary, we'll use means that you won't enjoy to force the answers out of you.'

As his eyes darted around the chamber, Caius realized that he had no choice but to comply, and information began to spill from his lips.

'He has a crypt, an underground room that he has devoted to Dionysus and other older and darker gods. He keeps the children there for the rituals, because he believes their suffering will make him stronger.'

'How do we find this crypt?' Artorex asked, his face carefully masked to hide his loathing.

'There's a trap door in the mosaic floor in his scriptorium at the Villa Severinii. The entrance is hidden under a floor rug with a large eye woven into it. He says it is the orb of the black god.'

'Your association with Severinus is about to come to an abrupt end, one way or another', Artorex said. 'Your father will never have cause to be ashamed of your actions and I predict you will soon become interested in Ector's affairs, as a good son should. No, don't argue, Caius, for you have no bargaining power left to you. You will stay here in your rooms with your wife and new daughter, and you'll consider earnestly how you intend to live so that your mother's shade will find peace. You can leave the rest to me.' Artorex smiled thinly. 'From this day on, Frith will be watchful in case you should ever decide to take your bad temper out on your wife and child. She will ensure that several stout servants will be on call if you are stupid enough to ever use your fists again.'

'And Severinus?'

'Severinus will soon be entertaining some important visitors,' Targo interjected. His mouth was a seamed wound of half-suppressed contempt and Caius flinched away from the old soldier's basilisk glare.

'And, in case he should wish to argue his rights, all five of us will be present to answer any questions he might have,' Luka added sardonically.

Caius cowered as the men saw to their weapons, but Targo watched the young man's hands, which clenched and unclenched as if they searched for something to grip and tear.

'You're not to leave the villa, Caius,' Artorex warned. 'I'll know if you even attempt to disobey me. And no warnings are to be sent to Severinus, for I'll soon become aware of your duplicity if you attempt to do so.'

'No! No! I wouldn't do that. I swear I'll obey you in all things.'

'See that you do obey me, Caius,' Artorex continued. 'For your mother's sake, I'll try to extricate you from the sins of your fine Roman friends. But should I discover that you, personally, have shed innocent blood, or lied to us, I'll expose your knowledge of these hideous crimes to your father, loath though I'd be to do so in his time of grief.'

'I haven't lied to you!'

'Then I'd suggest that your wife and daughter are awaiting your congratulations and your best efforts at reconciliation. You may be sure, Caius, that I'll kill you if you raise your hand against your wife or your child. As long as we are alive, you will be bound to your oath and you will act like a Roman gentleman. You owe your mother a change of heart and, by Mithras, you will honour her shade by making her death have some purpose. You'd be wise to understand that you are under threat from all who are here this night. Do you understand me, Caius?'

'Aye!' Caius muttered, his eyes hidden.

'Look at me, foster-brother! You'd be unwise to think that you can placate me and then go back to your old life. Your punishment is to live to prove every day that you can be trusted. I don't know whether I will ever believe you.'

Myrddion shot a quick, searching glance at the steward. Caius was being forced to become a penitent curled at Artorex's feet, but Myrddion couldn't see any trace of sympathy in the face of his protégé. To live on, to harbour one's guilt and to endure life under constant suspicion was a cruel punishment, even for an unforgivable crime.

Shortly afterwards, five grim men left Caius's rooms, pausing only to collect their arms and don dark cloaks.

Artorex spoke briefly to Frith. He instructed her to watch Caius with the stable boys on hand during his absence, in case his foster-brother should try to take his own life, or undertake some other foolish action. Satisfied that the villa was in order, he followed the others to the stables.

The night was thick with shadows, for the hour was well

after midnight, that time when the vitality of the body wanes, and even the moon seems like a pallid skeleton of itself in a starless sky.

The horses and men disappeared like silent wraiths into the fog that blurred the outlines of the Villa Poppinidii.

CHAPTER VI

Cleansing the Altar

After an hour's hard riding under a gelid moon, the party arrived at a sumptuous villa on a bare hill overlooking Aquae Sulis proper. Although no lights shone, the brick and stone of the buildings seemed to be awake and eerily sentient. In those dark hours preceding the dawn, the villa appeared to crouch like a jewelled toad on the spine of the hill, causing Artorex to suppress a superstitious shudder.

The floor plans of Roman villas, despite their thick walls, usually followed the natural variations of the terrain, so that they blended with their surroundings. With their orchards, gardens and running water, Roman homes were graceful and comfortable places.

But the Villa Severinii was unlike any Roman palace that Artorex had ever seen. The hill was bare of all vegetation and no sculptures were visible along the walls to soften the harshness of the bare stone. The structure hadn't been whitewashed, as was the normal custom; Severinus had ordered that a dark red ochre should be mixed with a skim of mortar, which might have been fashionable in old Pompeii but transplanted into Aquae Sulis gave the impression that the villa had been dipped in drying blood.

Boldly, but on silent feet, five grim men led their horses up to the stables. The silence was tomb-like, and the air seemed unnaturally prescient. Not a soul was stirring in the villa, not even an ostler. The horses rolled their eyes, sensing something unwholesome in the air, and Artorex was suddenly grateful that he had not come alone.

The humid weather conditions conspired to suffocate the intruders. It was the kind of warmth that rarely came to the north but, when it did, it left the weak or the very old short of breath and close to death. Within their light armour, the friends sweated profusely, even in these early hours of the morning when the cooler breezes should have brought some relief.

Perhaps the earth itself is sickening here, Artorex thought as he wiped away the sweat that streamed down his face.

The gate at the entrance to the villa had been left unlatched, perhaps in anticipation of the arrival of Caius. A drowsy steward intercepted the armed men as they entered the atrium, his eyes flaring in sudden panic. He would have run to raise the alarm had pen Bryn not picked him up bodily from behind, clamped one hand over his mouth and expertly snapped his neck.

'The servant could have been innocent,' Artorex protested.

'Not if he lived in this pestilence,' Llanwith whispered. 'Smell the air, my young friend. The corruption of death hangs over this villa.'

'The air is thick with a cloud of perfume,' Targo grunted as he dragged the body of the steward into the shadows. 'Damnation! The place smells like a whore's armpit.'

The same cloying heat accentuated the stink of attar, precious oils and something sweet, sickening and dead that pervaded the painted walls of the villa.

Llanwith pen Bryn slowly led the party through the imposing central garden.

No other servants seemed to be awake, for no one accosted the group as they slid into the villa's gilded, red-painted rooms.

Paintings of debauchery covered the walls, and bronze sculptures depicting obscene couplings were placed in niches along the walls of the colonnade. Priapic figures with grossly swollen organs stood leering in the shadows and even Myrddion, who had seen much human depravity during his life, was forced to turn away.

Artorex shuddered with disgust, while Luka silently disappeared into the right wing of the building.

Unlike the usual plan of a villa, the scriptorium of the Villa Severinii was sited at the very end of the left wing of the structure where the earth fell away, making a hidden crypt possible inside the slope of the hill. The scriptorium was almost bare, except for a wall of niches where the scrolls were presumably stored, a single desk, and a chair just off the mid-point of the room.

The only decoration in the room was a woven mat in the very centre of the mosaic floor, from which glared a large black eye. The air in the room was thick with a miasma of exotic oils and something else that roiled under the heavy, cloying scent.

With a soft exclamation of disgust, Llanwith pen Bryn removed the mat, exposing a trap door cut into the mosaic.

Luka slid into the room, his dagger in his hand.

'The sleeping chambers are empty,' he whispered. 'I found no one but a few terrified old women in the servants' quarters, so I locked them inside one of the storerooms. From the looks on their faces, they seem to know what their master is about – and they are relieved to be safely imprisoned.'

'Then it's time we joined the festivities,' Llanwith mouthed grimly through his beard.

Luka and Myrddion raised the trap door as silently as the mechanism allowed. A black maw yawned below them. Llanwith disappeared first into the darkness, down a ladder of some kind, while Artorex followed closely behind.

The ladder terminated on a sod floor at the end of a simple, timber-lined corridor. The smell was so thick that Artorex had to stifle a telltale, reflex gag.

As the others joined them at the bottom of the ladder, Artorex became aware of a low chanting. The sound was tuneful and not unpleasant, but the melodic voice only served to intensify the horrors of this secret, sinister place.

From the shadows of the corridor, Llanwith and Artorex peered cautiously into a large stone-lined room that had been largely carved from the rock of the hillside. The floor was constructed of packed earth and was bare of any ornament-ation, as were the walls. Two large braziers provided light, and one of them burned the nard that so thickened the still air.

For the first time, Artorex felt cold – chilled to the soul. The air in this underground cell was cool, but something else caused his flesh to shrink away from the walls, something primal turned the sweat on his body into a rankness that left him shivering.

A woman sat comfortably on a throne to their left. She held a wine cup in one beringed hand and would have seemed a normal Roman matron, except for a towering Egyptian facial mask and headdress that rose from her narrow shoulders some two feet above her head. Her silhouette made strange shadows across the floor to the edge of a small alabaster altar, which was at the very centre of the room.

Two men, naked except for ornate cloaks and grotesque head masks, capered before the altar of veined marble. One willowy form wore a headpiece shaped like the grinning head of a large black dog and the other, stockier man wore a grotesque mask that was black, shining and hideous, for all it was shaped like a massive human head. He had just drawn away from the body of a boy child who lay spreadeagled, face down, on the altar, his limbs held by chains secured to the four corners at the base of the altar by iron rings that had been set into the highly polished stone.

Except for the intermittent chanting of the woman and the panting of the black-headed suppliant, all that could be heard in the hideous room was the quiet sobbing of the child, his face pressed to the altar stone and his long pale hair hanging almost to the floor.

Llanwith drew his sword and the tableau froze as the steel hissed from its scabbard. Artorex and the others moved into the room in Llanwith's wake, their swords at the ready in their hands.

'What abominations do you enact here?' Llanwith roared, and the dog-headed man cowered behind his companion. Both men now looked ridiculous in their flaccid nakedness.

Only the sobbing of the child robbed the scene of its elements of farce.

Myrddion moved forward and knocked the black headdress sideways with an expert blow of his sword.

'This gentleman, I believe, must be Severinus, who is imitating Set, the Egyptian god of the underworld.' Myrddion raised his sword to the handsome, dark face that was revealed to the assembled group.

Severinus was in his mid-thirties, and he was gifted with a natural beauty of face and form, which was now running to fat after many years of self-indulgence. A thick pelt of dark body hair that partly disguised a grotesque little paunch marred the man's well-formed torso. His handsome face was completely plucked free of beard. Only his eyes belied the delicacy of his features, for they were flat and quite devoid of any emotion other than rage.

Myrddion turned slightly to face the other figure and used his sword point to dislodge the mask.

'And his companion must be his catamite, Antiochus, in the

guise of Anubis, another of the death deities. I think the dog motif is rather in keeping with this filth, don't you, Llanwith?'

As he finished speaking, the woman launched herself out of her throne with a screech. Her outstretched talons would have done Myrddion serious damage had Luka not tripped her and stripped the heavy mask from her face.

'And this . . . this . . . this lady is meant to be Isis, I suppose. All we need is Osiris to round out this very unpleasant little ritual.'

The woman, Severina, screamed insults through her thickly rouged lips and, under the lavish cosmetics that gave her face an illusion of youth, Artorex could see that she was old and raddled. The words she spouted out with such crude venom were so vile that Luka restrained her hands and gagged her with strips of her own gilded shawl.

'Release the boy, Targo, and take him upstairs into the clean air. Then find a blanket to cover him and give him something to eat and drink from the kitchens,' Artorex ordered.

'And you may release one of the servants to bring the city watch to us,' Myrddion added, without taking his eyes from the murderous face of Severinus. 'Choose one who is likely to do your bidding – but I'm sure we can safely leave that matter in your hands.'

With a grim expression, Targo pulled the black cloak from the shoulders of Severinus, while Artorex unlocked the chains that bound the boy across the altar with a key hanging from Severina's girdle. Targo wrapped the boy in the folds of the black cloak and, with the child pressed against his heart, hastened to obey Artorex's orders.

'What do you think you're doing?' Severinus snarled, raising his autocratic cleft chin. 'How dare you enter my villa and threaten me and my kin with your weapons?'

'We are citizens of good standing with an interest in the abominations that have been committed in this place,'

Myrddion replied without expression. 'And we have more than enough power to enforce the laws of the land and terminate your vile rituals. For the moment, that explanation is more than sufficient for lice such as you to absorb.'

Severinus narrowed his pebble-black eyes and peered at Artorex through the hazy torch smoke. His sweet, well-shaped mouth smiled to reveal white, slightly uneven teeth.

'I know you. You're that bastard foster-brother of Caius. He'll rue the day he sent curs down on me.'

Artorex stepped around the altar, nearly losing his balance on a surface that was slick with a scum he did not wish to identify. One fist swung out, seemingly of its own accord, and smashed the straight nose and cupid-bow mouth of Severinus.

'I suggest you keep your filthy tongue between your teeth. There will be time enough to speak your fill when the soldiers of the watch arrive. What will they make of your little playroom, I wonder.'

Severinus stared malevolently at his captors with eyes that were both crafty and amused. He licked the blood from his mouth with a long pink tongue, and seemed to relish the taste of its freshness. Artorex was forced to look away, or his stomach would have betrayed his will.

'The Council of Aquae Sulis will not raise a hand against me. I am not the only one who worships the Dark God, and my hospitality has extended to several prominent citizens in the past, including Caius, the so respectable son of the Poppinidii family.'

Artorex hit Severinus once again, with sufficient force to send the man reeling backwards into a long swathe of gilded cloth hanging against one of the walls. As Severinus clutched at its folds to regain his balance, the curtain tore and revealed a black opening in the wall.

Artorex spat with loathing.

'You mention that name at your peril, Severinus, for this night the Lady Livinia of the Poppinidii has gone to the shades of Hades. And her son has testified to your involvement in the rape and murder of children.'

But Severinus was not easily cowed. If anything, he seemed exhilarated by a twisted sense of power.

'None of you should dare to lay a hand on me, for you are nothing but Celtic dogs who amount to less than nothing. You are servants, fit only to wipe my boots, and I will have you crucified before I am finished.'

'I, Llanwith pen Bryn, son of the King of the Ordovice, dare to accuse you of child murder,' Llanwith intoned, his voice strong and cold in the fetid room.

'And I, Luka, son of the King of the Brigante, also dare to accuse you of child murder,' Luka repeated.

'And I, Myrddion Merlinus, Steward of the High King, Uther Pendragon of the Atrebates, also dare to accuse you of child murder.'

Overawed by the lineage of his companions, Artorex stepped forward to face the snarling face of Severinus.

'I, Artorex, foster-son of Ector and Steward of the Villa Poppinidii, do accuse you of the foul crime of child murder.'

But Severinus only laughed, a high-pitched whinny of confident glee that sickened the warriors and caused the fawning Antiochus to cover his ears in terror.

Llanwith bound the madman's arms behind his back lest he harm himself, while Myrddion did the same to the cowering Antiochus. But still the laughter peeled on until Severinus's voice began to grow harsh and croaking.

'It is best that you go upstairs, boy, and wait for the guard,' Llanwith ordered Artorex hoarsely. 'You can do nothing more in this pest hole.'

'But the ring that Caius lost is here. It must be found.'

'Leave that trifle to us, Artorex. Go outside and breathe some clean air,' Luka repeated.

Gratefully, Artorex retreated down the narrow corridor, up the ladder and out into the scriptorium. Pausing only to wash his face, hands and feet in the water of the atrium fountain, he made his way to the gates of the villa to await the arrival of the City Watch.

Dawn was brushing the sky with its fiery breath when a small detachment of armed men came marching up to the villa. Artorex raised his head from his hands, and ushered them through the entrance to the villa.

At first, the Captain of the Watch was disposed to treat Artorex like a thief, especially as the corpse of the Severinii steward was still lying where Llanwith had abandoned it at the threshold to the villa. But when Targo brought out a tired young boy, with deeply bruised eyes set back into his skull, and took the child haltingly through the tale of his capture, incarceration, starvation and rape, the captain was disposed to treat Artorex with more civility.

When the young man escorted the soldiers to the gaping hole in the floor of the scriptorium, several of the watch clutched amulets around their necks in superstitious fear.

'It's fetid down there. A number of other children have been held captive on the altar, as you will soon see for yourselves. Severinus is not a careful housekeeper. When I last saw him, he was threatening to name prominent citizens and soldiers as his partners in these heinous crimes. We were forced to restrain him.'

The captain paled. 'Good work, young man.'

Artorex smiled thinly, because he knew that the captain had no intention of hearing the names of powerful citizens involved in criminal activity, even if he had to personally cut out the tongue of Severinus to ensure his silence.

Thus, Caius, too, would be safe from wild accusations.

Artorex sighed inwardly. So this is the way that justice really works. Those persons who have the money, the influence and the real power always avoid the consequences of their actions. The steward felt nauseated. May the gods help me, but I'm a coward, he thought to himself. I must save Caius because I owe a life to his mother. Caius will be exonerated, when he's near as guilty as Severinus. He'll never be punished and he'll never suffer a single day for his brutality. How the gods must be laughing at us!

One by one, the soldiers entered the crypt, save for one lucky man who stayed with Targo and the boy in the kitchens. When they returned, the men were dragging their prisoners behind them, with scant care for scraped shins or skinned heads.

Even the old woman, the mother of Severinus, was bustled into the early daylight like a common whore.

Then Luka, Myrddion and Llanwith emerged from the darkened entrance into the daylight. Pale with nausea, Llanwith slammed the trap door back into place with an exclamation of disgust.

'Enough! I will be months getting the stink of that hole out of my nostrils,' he complained. 'And we will be forced to stay here at this villa until the magistrate of Aquae Sulis acquaints himself with its horrors.'

Luka called out to the captain who was swilling his mouth out with some wine that Targo had found in the kitchens.

'I searched the crypt while we were awaiting your arrival,' Luka told him. 'There is a low annexe, not more than four feet high, behind the curtain on the rear wall. You should send some men to dig there while we are awaiting the arrival of the magistrate.'

'But why should we dig, Lord Luka? What would be the purpose?' the captain asked, angry and insolent but still half deferring to Luka's rank.

'Because some of the ground has been disturbed in the annexe. As that boy was not the first child to vanish in this district, we suspect that some of those children who disappeared are buried in the crypt where they perished.'

The captain gave a grimace of distaste, but he barked out instructions to two of his more bovine men to re-enter the crypt, armed with digging axes and spades, to search the floor of the annexe.

So lavishly was the villa painted in grotesque and lascivious scenes that the group could find no place where they could rest that was free from the depraved decor. Artorex determined to wait in the atrium, his back against the pool, so that he wasn't forced to gaze upon the lewd fountain. He stared fixedly at a charming display of summer flowers in the garden as he considered the events of the night. One by one, his friends joined him there.

'No wonder Caius was terrified,' Artorex muttered. 'If I had to spend a few hours in that hellhole watching those monsters carry out their evil work, I'd be ready for the madhouse myself.'

'Here!' Myrddion tossed Artorex a golden seal ring with a red intaglio stone.

'Severinus was persuaded to remember where he had hidden it,' Myrddion said drily. 'Caius may be a spiteful and dangerous young man, but I'm beginning to believe that he was unwillingly under the influence of Severinus. That creature is vile, and I can easily believe that he might seduce a foolish young boy until, eventually, the victim was completely under his control.'

'Should we then acquit Caius of perversion?' Artorex asked.

'I suppose so,' Llanwith pen Bryn said guardedly. 'It seems as though Severinus kept the children for himself. Even Antiochus, by his own admission, was not permitted to touch their "pretty and holy flesh", as Severinus described them. In truth, I feel dirty over this whole business. And I'll never trust

Caius at my back for, whatever his fears, he surely killed his mother.'

'You prefer to kill cleanly, my friend,' Luka joked, until he saw Llanwith's jaw working.

'Did you notice that the catamite plucks the hairs from his entire body and face? He's far more womanish than my mother.' Llanwith ground his sandalled foot into the rich loam of a flowerbed.

'Ouch!' Artorex responded automatically at the cynical remark.

'You haven't met Llanwith's mother,' Luka jested.

Llanwith's mind was still in the crypt. 'If you're right, Luka, and if that annexe is the reason that the missing children from the village have vanished so successfully, then I'd like, very much, to be the one who executes Severinus, his vile catamite and his unspeakable mother – preferably all at the same time.'

'As would we all.' Myrddion sighed. 'But any execution must be public, so the villagers can be assured that justice has been done. For our part, we must divert attention away from the Villa Poppinidii, for there are too many reputations resting on a quiet, lawful conclusion to this ugly turn of events. May the gods help us all with this problem.'

Artorex was too weary to query the decisions of his three friends and his eyelids seemed very heavy in the early morning sunshine.

Within moments, he was asleep.

'Oh, to be a young man again and to sleep off horrors so easily.' Luka smiled kindly as he watched the young man doze in the sunlight.

'He won't rest so easily soon – perhaps never again – if he is to fulfil the destiny we've mapped out for him,' Myrddion whispered. 'He showed his mettle during the night, and I'm convinced that he has the courage and the wisdom to become the commander we seek. Caius hangs around his neck like a curse, but who knows what our lad will make of that young pretender.'

'What a raptor we placed in Ector's peaceful nest, with no one to recognize his qualities but an old barbarian woman and a battle-scarred veteran from who knows where.'

'I hope the oath Lady Livinia bound him to doesn't cause trouble in the future,' Luka responded.

'We've done our part, whatever the outcome of our actions might be.' Llanwith patted his friend's shoulder kindly and eased himself on to a stone bench where he gazed at the fountain with a jaundiced eye. 'Your plan was always risky, Myrddion.'

'How do men twist their bodies into such unnatural positions?' he asked of no one in particular as he observed the Severinii sculptures. 'They look damned uncomfortable to me.'

'You lack a certain erotic sophistication,' Luka joked.

'I'm a plain man – and I make no apology for it.'

Luka observed movement on the road leading up to the villa.

'If I'm not mistaken, the magistrate and a number of the town councillors have finally arrived.'

Myrddion nudged Artorex gently with his booted foot until the young man scrambled to his feet, childishly rubbing his tired eyes.

The magistrate was dressed in the Roman fashion, in a snowy tunic and a purple-edged toga that denoted his exalted position. Myrddion wondered idly how this provincial Roman had availed himself of the rich colouring that was so costly in coin and human life. Only the greatest men in the land wore Roman purple, for the dye was found in a certain shellfish that, unfortunately, killed the slaves who extracted it. Sardonically, Myrddion doubted that the magistrate had the breeding or the lineage that would entitle him to wear even a hint of imperial purple but, wisely, he held his tongue.

Aquae Sulis is a dying remnant of a shrinking empire, he thought. But even an anachronism has its uses, and Artorex may come to need every ally he can find.

When the magistrate was settled inside the villa, the captain made his report of what he had seen in the crypt. After he had concluded his observations and opinions, the three warriors informed the magistrate and the town councillors of their titles and their parts in the affair.

When pressed to explain why the five had descended on the villa, Artorex extemporized.

'The Villa Poppinidii, as you know, good sirs, is a seemly house and farm some little way outside the walls of Aquae Sulis. Tonight, a tragedy struck the villa with the death of Lady Livinia of the Poppinidii, a family of some repute.'

The councillors nodded, confused at the tenor and length of Artorex's explanation.

'After the death of his mother, and in great shame that he hadn't expressed his suspicions earlier, the son of Lord Ector confided that his erstwhile friends were practising unwholesome rites whereby the bodies and souls of stolen children were sacrificed. Caius had been pressed to join this vile cabal, but his natural distaste, and the pregnancy of his young wife, gave him an opportunity to refuse. He was terrified of the repercussions to his family and he couldn't bear the thought that yet another child had been taken, as so many innocents had vanished before.'

Once again, the magistrate and the councillors nodded at the common sense expressed in these careful words.

'Caius is only a few years into manhood, and he'd worshipped Severinus during his childhood. I believe that Severinus corrupted my foster-brother as a child but his breeding alone saved his life. Severinus terrified Caius into silence, and he failed to voice his suspicions lest he should shame his mother and sully the name of his family, and I'm assured that he never took part in any of the vicious rituals that we interrupted. After the death of Lady Livinia, he opened his heart to our distinguished guests and voiced his suspicions to us.'

Artorex paused.

'We left the villa at once, for we were determined to save the life of the missing boy. We arranged for Targo, the Arms Master for the Villa Poppinidii, to accompany us as the representative of the villagers.'

One ferret-faced councillor stared at the bland face of Artorex with obvious distrust.

'Why should we believe that Caius is guiltless of any involvement in this matter?'

'Sir, we are here at the urging of Caius,' Myrddion answered neatly. 'Before we gagged him, Severinus assured us that the council would not hold our evidence as true, as he had welcomed prominent citizens of Aquae Sulis into his cult. Of course, you and I know that his assurances are baseless, and we do not believe his perverted lies.'

The councillor coughed hoarsely, his face now pale below his oiled curls.

The magistrate wisely ordered the soldiers to ensure that the prisoner's gag and bonds were kept firmly in place. The felons were then locked into the wine cellar.

Artorex knew exactly what the magistrate was thinking. What were a few dead village children compared with the reputations of the mighty of Aquae Sulis? How would the magistrate fare if he meted justice to the guilty in equal and unfettered measure?

But why should I be critical? Artorex thought sullenly. For I've performed the same service for Caius. But I'll damn my soul to the shadows before I permit Severinus to go free.

He smiled artlessly at the assembled group and determined to confront the councillors.

'You gentlemen must remember that this matter will soon become public knowledge,' he said. 'There'll be anger in your community, and the reputations of those few who are considered part of any conspiracy will be sullied forever. You will soon see the crypt that lies directly below this building, and you'll be made fully aware of all that has taken place at the Villa Severinii. I myself wouldn't have believed that such a place could exist outside of Hades had I not seen it.'

The magistrate's eyes flashed, leaving Artorex fully aware that the official knew exactly what he was threatening.

'Lead on then,' the magistrate ordered. 'We must be seen to be doing our duty.'

Artorex would willingly have faced ten fully armed warriors rather than return to the crypt, but he forced himself to lead the way into the open mouth of the tunnel towards the scriptorium; the ordeal seemed no more than just in the light of his lies and prevarications. The sound of shovels came up out of the earth, intensifying the impression that the councillors were entering a tomb.

'Can't anything be done about this stink?' one older, hard-bitten merchant complained as he followed Artorex down the ladder.

'Severinus burned perfume on the braziers to disguise the smell. Unfortunately, they provide the only light down here,' Artorex replied.

The curtains on the far wall had been stripped aside and two burly soldiers were working on their knees in the narrow annexe. Artorex swallowed the bile that began to rise in his throat; the sickly reek of death seemed to be stronger than on his earlier foray into the crypt.

The magistrate eyed the small room, the throne, the stained altar and the discarded masks. He could see the evidence of other children in the dried slime of old vomit, urine, faeces and blood around the stone. There was a perceptible tightening of his narrow lips. Most of the councillors covered their noses with their robes of office, and several of them looked as if they would soon vomit if the smell intensified.

And so it proved to be.

One of the soldiers suddenly backed out of the annexe and heaved away his last meal in a corner of the crypt.

'There's another child here – and he's been dead for some months,' he cried, wiping his lips. 'God help him.'

The other soldier was made of sterner stuff. His spade explored the edges of the swollen, corrupted little form, and then he, too, was forced to scramble back into the chamber.

'They're piled up like cordwood in there, one on top of the other,' he reported. 'I can't tell how many but I'll wager there be five or six, judging by the stink.'

Several of the councillors had seen enough and bolted for the relatively clean air of the scriptorium. The magistrate clenched his fists, set his lips in a tight line and issued orders that the soldiers were to fetch what linen sheets could be found so that the tiny shells could be brought out of this hellish place.

'No wonder Severinus burned perfume. This smell would sicken all but the strongest of stomachs,' Artorex groaned.

'You may go, my boy,' the magistrate said kindly. 'I will see to the removal of the remains.'

'No, sir. I started this ugly search, so I must finish it. We must show the parents of these dead children that our actions were carried out in accordance with what they would have wished for the recovery of their kin.'

'As you choose,' the magistrate replied drily.

And perhaps I can cleanse myself in the process, Artorex thought silently.

The soldiers returned, dragging sheets and woollen cloth behind them.

When the first blackening and bloated body was eased on to a sheet, all the remaining councillors fled, leaving only Artorex and the magistrate to witness the exhumation of the corpses.

The bodies, in varying stages of decomposition, were systematically brought out into the light. Artorex struggled to ensure that his self-control should not betray him, but when one small form almost broke in two when it was moved, he was forced to turn away, or else run screaming back up into the open air. Instead, he bound an abandoned scrap of cloth over his mouth and nostrils, for even the perfumed stink of the cloth was preferable to the ever-increasing miasma of rotten, corrupted flesh.

At last, seven small shapes, the last three being little more than clean bones, were moved away from the ugly light and placed on the sod floor in all their pitiful nakedness.

Only then did the magistrate and Artorex leave the crypt.

In the atrium, the magistrate issued instructions that the soldiers were to bring the bodies up from the crypt, after first numbering the pitiful bundles in the order in which they had been exhumed. He also ordered that hanks of hair should be taken from each small skull to facilitate identification. The bodies would then be burned and the remains placed in terracotta urns for their final journey back to their families.

Artorex had gone into the crypt as little more than an untested boy. He came back into the daylight as an adult, and with a man's shadows embedded in his colourless eyes.

The soldiers set to work in the courtyard outside the villa, collecting wood to cremate the small corpses of the sacrificed children. One less doughty youth was sent to collect grave urns while, inside the atrium, the magistrate eased himself on to a bench, stripped off his clothing down to his loincloth and left his stinking robes of office to lie where they fell in the colonnade. He dispatched one of the Severinii servants to collect a fresh robe.

Artorex washed in the fountain once again and almost immersed himself in the shallow pool, but the stench of the crypt would remain in the back of his throat for many days to come.

'And now for the Severinii,' the magistrate said under his breath, no less impressive for the lack of his judicial robes of office.

The councillors clustered like frightened hens as far from the magistrate as possible; only Luka, Llanwith, Myrddion and Targo kept themselves firmly at his back.

'I will question the boy first. What is his name?'

'Brego, sir,' Targo replied. 'He's the son of Bregan, the blacksmith. I'm afraid he is very frightened, my lord, for he has lost all trust in powerful men.'

'Bring him anyway, for I need his account of what has happened here.'

'Aye, sir,' Targo answered, and he moved purposefully towards the kitchens.

The boy returned, wrapped in a woman's shawl, and clinging tightly to Targo's hand as if the old veteran was the only safe constant in a terrifying universe.

'Brego?' the magistrate asked in the kindest of voices as he crouched in front of the boy.

The boy met his eyes unwillingly and forced himself to nod. Artorex knew that the child wanted desperately to suck his thumb.

'Who brought you here, Brego?'

'A man.' The boy's voice quavered, for he was on the brink of tears.

'What did he look like?'

'He was the thin one, Anti ... Anti ... something. And another man gave me some milk to drink – and I fell asleep.'

'Who was the other man?'

The boy furrowed his brow. 'He was a servant. The master wasn't very nice to him, and kicked him when he spilled some of the milk.'

'The steward,' Llanwith pen Bryn recalled grimly. 'I'm pleased now that I broke his neck – although, on reflection, perhaps he deserved a slower death if he was involved with these murderous creatures.'

'What happened when you woke up, Brego?' the magistrate asked gently. He smiled down at the young boy. 'Don't cry, my lad, for you will soon be safely back with your father once again.'

'It was dark when I came here, and I was tied with ropes. I was thirsty and hungry, but nobody came for the longest time. And when they did come . . .' The boy began to sob uncontrollably.

'Sir,' Targo protested. 'This boy is exhausted. We may inflict lasting damage on him if he is questioned further.'

'I agree. I've heard enough.'

The magistrate turned to a soldier, while Targo picked up the boy and carried him back to the kitchens.

'Bring the servants to me, all of them!' he ordered.

With much wailing and sobbing, five women were dragged to the outer door of the atrium. They were all old – none under forty – and their grey hair and haunted eyes were proof of the hard service they had performed at the Villa Severinii.

The magistrate addressed the servants sternly. 'You are commanded to tell me what you know of the crypt. And do not think to tell me you know nothing, for no one could live in such a house and be ignorant of what has been happening here.'

One of the women, who seemed less terrified than the others, stepped forward from the huddled group and spoke for them all.

'We are slaves, sir. The master loathed all women, except for his mother, and she wouldn't permit young maidservants to enter the house. She was the only woman permitted to be young and beautiful.' The old woman smiled and revealed two broken teeth. An ugly, puckered burn that covered her jaw also marred her features. But, for all her ugliness, her eyes were a clear, clean hazel. They'd seen too much, and no longer feared anything, not even death.

The magistrate waited impatiently, one foot tapping on the tessellated floor.

'I've lived too long and heard too much in this place to care what happens to Master Severinus or to his mother. While the old master was still alive, the villa was a clean and contented house. But when he died ten years ago, it became a bad and frightening place.'

'Get to the point, woman,' the magistrate ordered, but not entirely unkindly.

'We never knew precisely what the young master did when he was in the secret places. We didn't want to know. And Longus, the steward, locked us in the kitchens whenever the master had his entertainments.'

'What of the crypt, woman? Surely you knew of that place.'

'Yes, sir, we knew of it. Workers came and dug it out, and then the master paid them to leave Aquae Sulis and move to other towns. I was the only servant who was permitted to clean the scriptorium, only me, although I was threatened on pain of death never to open the trap door that led down to the crypt.'

'Did you ever open the trap door?'

The woman shook her head so fiercely that Artorex had a sudden hysterical thought that she would shake her old head clean off her scrawny neck.

'But if I pressed my ear to the joint between the trap door and the floor, I sometimes thought I heard weeping coming from below the floor. The master caught me once and beat me half to death. I felt his cruelty and I was careful never to listen again.'

She pointed at her burned face.

'When I was a younger woman, Severinus Major took me to his bed. Mistress Severina didn't care overly for the touch of any man, so I became her husband's amusement in her stead. But when he died, mother and son made sure that no one would ever want me again. All of the servants in this house have been brutalized. We know that we belong to Severinus and he can do whatever he wants with us. These poor old women can show you their tears. No, sirs, we heard nothing. And we saw nothing.'

'You can speak now, woman,' the magistrate said quietly. 'Did you ever see children here?'

'No, sir. I swear. You may do with us what you will, sir, but we didn't dare to look once Longus had locked the kitchen doors behind us.' She raised her grey head and looked squarely at the magistrate. 'We've washed and fed the little fellow who was brought up to us tonight, and we know now what's been done to him. We know he was raped. If we were to be blamed for what has happened to the children, then I'd rather die than live in this villa another day. We wear the collars of slaves, but we're women, and some of us were mothers once.'

The magistrate rubbed the stubble on his chin and thought hard.

Finally, he came to a decision.

'You shall go free, all of you. I don't believe that you are guilty of any crime. Further, your collars shall be struck off, and you shall cease to be slaves from this day on.'

'Then we shall die, for we're too old to find new masters to care for us,' the old woman replied with dignity. 'It would be better that you should kill us now rather than force us to starve to death.'

'You may take anything of value that you can carry from the villa, as long as you depart before sunset. The contents of the villa are forfeit and before this day is over I'll order it to be burned to the ground and its foundations obliterated.'

The women bowed low, then scrambled away from him. The susurration of their bare feet on the tiles was the only sound in the atrium.

'Bring the Severinii woman to me,' the magistrate ordered.

The matron was dragged in. Her wig had fallen off in her struggles, and her bare, shaved head seemed pathetic in the morning light. The cosmetics on her face were almost blasphemous in their provocative ugliness.

One soldier took off her gag. She spat at him.

'Control yourself, woman, or you will be gagged once again.' The magistrate's voice was like ice. He had shared a dining couch with this woman in other, better times, but he had never seen such depravity in any female eyes before, or such cruelty, as he now observed in this woman.

'I have done nothing wrong. I am the widow of Lucius Severinus, a noble name even in Rome. How dare you let servants touch my person.'

'How dare you sanction the rape and murder of children in your house!' the magistrate thundered.

'I did not touch them,' she snarled at the magistrate. 'It was all my son's doing, under the influence of Antiochus, his perverted little catamite.' She paused. 'There are other fine gentlemen who have enjoyed the pleasures of the Villa Severinii,' she stated, her eyes alive with cunning. 'They are powerful men who will protect us.'

'You will be gagged, woman, so that I need not listen to your lies,' the magistrate ordered, for he was reluctant to deal with the wider ramifications that her loose tongue might unloose. 'I've heard enough from you.'

Two soldiers quickly applied a gag round the woman's mouth.

'I will now see Antiochus,' the magistrate continued. 'Since he has been accused of being the ringleader and perpetrator of these crimes.'

Antiochus was a pitiful figure when he was dragged before the magistrate and the councillors. His ragged cloak was still wrapped about his narrow body to hide his nakedness, while the cosmetics that had been smeared round his eyes had begun to run from his constant weeping, and served to make him appear as a pathetic figure in the raw light of morning. The blackening bruises on his face were evidence of the rough handling inflicted by his captors.

The magistrate looked at him with disdain. 'I'm told by the mistress of the house that you are the principal instigator of this vile cult.'

'That's not true, my lord! I'm merely the lover of Severinus – and nothing more,' Antiochus pleaded. 'We met soon after the death of his father and he invited me to enjoy the pleasures of the villa. I've never touched any children – I can't stand the vile little creatures.'

'But you did prompt the worship of Osiris in the crypt, didn't you?' The magistrate's disgust was tangible. 'Come, Antiochus, you come from Asia Minor, whereas Severinus has never left these shores. How else would he know of the Mysteries of Death?'

'When it first started, it was only a game,' Antiochus howled. 'But I couldn't stop the master from slaking his desires. When he began to take his pleasure with the boys, he no longer wanted me in his bed. I had no choice.'

'But the mistress of the house swears that she had no part in the murders, and the blame should be placed firmly on your shoulders,' the magistrate told him.

'She's a lying cow!' Antiochus shouted hysterically, his voice rising to a womanish shriek. 'She believes that the dying breaths of children will preserve her youth and her beauty. No, she never touched them, but she watched them die of starvation so that she could kiss away their last breaths. The woman is demented.'

Every man in the room was appalled. The mistress Severinii felt their sickened eyes upon her and her arrogance finally deserted her like ice before fire. She began to sob through the gag.

'It was Severinus! It was all Severinus! He always wanted newer pleasures. I warned him that rumours of his entertainments would boil over, but he wouldn't listen to me. He's turned into a monster, and I can't believe that I once loved him.'

Antiochus would have continued bleating, his eyes darting from stony face to stony face, had the magistrate not cut across his gabble.

'But you stole the children for him. You brought them here. And you were the one who took them to the crypt and tied them down, ready for your master – unless I'm mistaken. You're also a monster, Antiochus, and as a monster you shall be treated. Gag him!'

Finally, Severinus was dragged into the atrium. He was stark naked and streaked with blood from grazes and cuts all over his body. Yet, in a flash of arrogance, he shook his black curls back from his face and stood as easily and as proudly as if he were welcoming important and valued guests to sample his hospitality.

'You shouldn't bother to implicate others, Severinus, for I will simply gag you once again if you do, no matter how convincing you seem to be,' the magistrate stated mercilessly. 'However, in deference to your father, who was a man of honour and decency, I'm giving you this one last opportunity to explain yourself. Can you justify your actions?'

Severinus appeared to be a magnificent specimen of

manhood, for all that his body was too short and hairy for true beauty. His pride was a tangible and living element that was an essential part of Severinus the man. Artorex could easily imagine that this was the way that Mark Antony had stood as he faced his Egyptian and Roman enemies in the last days of the old Republic – immediately before he fell on his sword.

But when Artorex looked into the eyes of Severinus, the spell of nobility was immediately broken, for something filthy oozed behind the black pupils of the man's expression.

'I don't recognize the right of any of you to judge me for I am Roman!'

The magistrate smiled slightly and reflectively.

So smiled the old senators who sent Caligula and Nero to their ignominious deaths when their vices finally affronted the last vestiges of Roman pride.

'Is this bravado to be your only defence? Truly, you've made my task easier through your refusal to speak,' he stated. 'When Rome first rose out of the mud, she came to greatness through her courage, her piety and her strength. By all such standards, you're not Roman – and you never could be. You shall be punished like a common felon.'

The magistrate paused, knowing that he had the full attention of all persons present.

'Hear my words. The Villa Severinii is forfeit and will be burned, except for those items of usefulness that the servants can carry away on their backs or in the villa's wagon. All else will be consigned to the flames.'

His voice had the magisterial ring of one of the old lawmakers of ancient Rome, for all that this doughty man was half-Celtic by birth.

'Let no stone stand on another stone when the flames have cooled. And let the ground be sown with salt to cleanse this poisoned earth.

'The Severinii woman will be strangled immediately, and her body thrown on the city midden. Her callous cruelty deserves a worse fate . . . but I don't have the stomach for it.

'As for Severinus and Antiochus, let them be crucified, like the criminals they are, at this very hour. And they shall hang outside the gates of Aquae Sulis, so that all good citizens shall see the fate of those fools who sell their souls to the Darkness.

'And, lest their mouths spew poison, they will die in silence, with their tongues removed from their heads.'

The magistrate was a prudent man, and Artorex couldn't suppress a grimace of respect and black humour.

'I have spoken! So let it be done!'

CHAPTER VII

THE AFTERMATH

Artorex would have gladly ridden away with Targo, who had been charged with returning Brego to his father. He longed to climb upon Coal and escape, like Llanwith pen Bryn and Luka who were returning to the Villa Poppinidii to ensure that peace had settled within its walls. But he must take charge of the pitiful terracotta urns, each numbered in the Roman fashion but not yet filled with ash. He must take hanks of hair to grieving mothers, and watch the final death of their long and useless hopes.

Such was his penance for achieving freedom for Caius. Such was his self-administered punishment for lending his name to a lie.

The forecourt filled with smoke from the roaring fires that had been lit to consume the small, abused bodies of the sacrificed children. One by one, and still wrapped in their pitiful linen sheets, their remains were cremated.

Myrddion had stayed with Artorex and, together, they searched out what food could be found in the kitchens, eventually settling on cheese and a heel of bread as the simplest repast they could stomach on such a day as this. Around them, the villa boiled with activity as the servants systematically ransacked it for items of value, showing surprising strength as they loaded a wagon and several handcarts with all that they could carry. Before the three prisoners were chained and led away, the old spokeswoman for the servants didn't hesitate to tear the golden earrings from Severinii ears and prise rings from their manacled hands. Then, with grave deliberation, she spat in the faces of each of her erstwhile owners.

Neither Artorex nor Myrddion could deny that she had earned the right to perform this last vengeful act.

By mid-afternoon, the old women could load and carry no more. What items were left were worthless or too heavy to move. Even the villa's finest horses would be departing with the women.

'Will they be safe with all of their scavenging?' Artorex asked Myrddion anxiously, for it seemed unjust that these ancient women should fall foul of thieves and villains after all their years of suffering.

Myrddion walked up to the spokeswoman.

'Where will you go, good woman?' he asked. 'My young friend fears for your safety.'

'I am of the Dobunni, and I was born near Corinium,' she replied, as she tied her hair up in a scrap of fine linen. 'Perhaps there are some of my kin who are still alive. If not, then we old ones will be safe if we can come under the protection of the King. We've survived far worse than a week's journey through strange places.'

'Go safely, then,' Artorex called after her, as she flicked the reins on to the backs of the horses drawing her wagon.

'And you, young master. Verily, your coming to the villa was a fortunate day for us.' She laughed shrilly, and turned her back on her erstwhile home for the last time.

The two men watched the dust cloud of the little cavalcade as it descended the hill and turned on to a back road leading to the north. It was little more than a rough track.

'She is clever, that one'. Myrddion smiled his admiration. 'They will stay far from the main thoroughfares and likely find the sanctuary they seek'.

'I've no taste for further bloodshed, Myrddion, and I'm glad the magistrate will execute the Severinii outside the walls of Aquae Sulis. Crucifixion is a vile and a lingering death. I've never seen it and I don't want to'. Artorex sat on his heels and rubbed his reddened eyes with the heel of his hand.

'The Severinii have earned their fate, Artorex, but I grant you that I, too, take little pleasure in such necessary affairs. Let the mob howl for their blood. I prefer the quick ending of a sword'.

'May the gods grant that such is our fate', Artorex sighed.

By dusk, the soldiers had finished the grisly task of burning the small bodies, pounding the longer bones to splinters and placing the remains in the numbered urns. As he stared at the pitiful strands of hair, also numbered in the same fashion, it seemed to Artorex that the terrible night, and the day that had followed it, had been without end.

Yet, before they left the silent villa, the magistrate and the full complement of councillors returned, in company with a troop of soldiers and field workers who carried hammers and torches. Artorex shuddered, for the cruel day was still holding sway over the darkness.

'I see you gentlemen are still here', the magistrate noted, as the two men continued to stow the urns in a pannier hung over the withers of Artorex's horse.

'We're about to leave, sir', Artorex replied, and bowed low.

'The execution of the Severinii has been carried out. The son and his catamite hang on the road leading into Aquae Sulis. Both are still alive, and will continue to suffer. The mother died before their eyes'. He smiled in the direction of the stables. 'I see that the servants have departed – and not on foot'.

'They took all that they could', Myrddion replied with an

ironic laugh. 'Perhaps their spoils will bring them good fortune.'

'That old grandmother will have chosen carefully,' the magistrate stated with a smile. 'She has a deep store of vengeance in her heart, and I shouldn't care to cross her path.'

He patted Myrddion across the back to show his appreciation for the satisfactory outcome of what could have developed into a disastrous political scandal.

'The time has come to burn this pest hole to the ground,' he ordered without further discussion.

The group of workmen carrying the torches leapt to do his bidding and soon the building was ablaze from end to end. As Myrddion and Artorex rode away, they could feel the heat of its destruction on their backs and, long after night had fallen, the black sky was lit by a hellish redness as the villa on the hill crumbled into hot ash.

Two very tired men returned to the Villa Poppinidii shortly after moonrise. Myrddion decided that the hour was too advanced and Artorex was too exhausted to complete the final, sad task of delivering the urns to the villages. The parents of those children who had vanished had waited for months, even years, to learn the fate of their children; another night wouldn't matter, especially when it would end in tears and grief.

Artorex was almost asleep on his horse as he rode into the stables at the villa. The strong arms of the servants assisted him as he climbed down from the horse cloth, while other hands respectfully unloaded the urns from the pannier on Coal's back.

How could word have spread so quickly? Artorex wondered in his dazed state, before remembering that Luka and Llanwith had returned before him. Bad news always travels fast.

Stumbling and ashen, Artorex hastened to the baths where he cast aside his cloak, tunic and loincloth. He stepped out of his sandals and fell bodily into the cleansing waters. When a servant peered cautiously round the doorway, Artorex ordered that every stitch of his clothing should be burned, and new robes brought to him.

He finally emerged, cleansed, shaved and in fresh clothing, but his grey eyes still spoke volumes of matters no man should have to contemplate.

Artorex ate in the kitchens with Myrddion, the household having already gone to its rest, and even though fresh apples, nuts, cheese and milk were wholesome food and pleasant to the palate, he was not hungry. He could still feel the poison of the Severinii family working through his veins.

Myrddion laid a narrow hand upon Artorex's forehead.

'It'll pass, my friend. It'll pass.'

'Will it? Can it? I feel as if I've lived in a safe bubble my whole life. I wasn't able to recognize evil when I saw it. Severinus was just an annoying, patronizing pig. And what of Caius? What can I do about my foster-brother?'

'We've done all that we can, Artorex,' Myrddion replied. 'Caius has been given one last chance, for the sake of his mother. What he does with the rest of his life is up to him. My advice is that you should ignore him, if you can.' The older man paused before continuing in a soft voice.

'Sometimes, when a wound must be cleansed, the pus and corruption fills the nostrils with a rank odour that seems to endure forever. But new flesh eventually grows to replace that which was rotting. The Severinii have now been amputated from this world and they will soon be forgotten, and all will be healed again.'

'Until the next monster appears,' Artorex replied with a weary sigh.

'Until the next,' Myrddion agreed. 'Perhaps men such as we are born for nothing else but to bear witness, and then crush those human horrors, so that simple men, women and children may sleep safely in their beds.'

'Then it would be better to be a simple man,' Artorex whispered, exhausted almost to the point of tears.

'Of a certainty,' Myrddion agreed. 'But we rarely choose our own fates. Something else – something more powerful than we frail creatures of flesh and bone – does the choosing for us, and a man is measured by how well he bears the weight of the travails with which fate burdens him.'

'Is the whole world so simple then, Myrddion? Do the evil ones balance against those who would only do good? The magistrate of Aquae Sulis is a good man, but he knows that Severinus and his mother were merely the leaves of a noxious weed that is only seen above the ground. Too many evil men lurk where they can't be seen, and their roots are too strong to be easily dug out. The magistrate didn't even try to find all the malefactors associated with the Severinii. Is the earth, and all things that live upon it, bound in shades of grey, neither good nor bad, but just muddling on as best it can?'

'If I knew all the answers, I would be Emperor of Constantinople and all wars would cease at my command. But chance, I know, is not the balance of which you speak. Men and women choose how to live with what fate has given them. Did Mistress Severina always hide a streak of cruelty in her nature? Or did fear of old age create her viciousness? Does her motive matter? All I know is she chose to act as no man or woman should, and she paid the price for that decision.'

'I'm too tired for riddles, Lord Myrddion,' Artorex replied, and he rose to his feet and staggered away to his simple bed. He slept in little more than an alcove near the kitchens and the triclinium, at the heart of the house, where he could feel the beat of its pulse. Now, exhausted, he wished he were the meanest field worker, billeted in the servants' quarters and far from Livinia's cold body, the grief of Master Ector and the problem of Caius. Not surprisingly, on his lumpy pallet,

Artorex's sleep was disturbed by unspeakable, half-remembered nightmares.

He woke shortly before first light but exhaustion quickly drew him back into dreamless sleep.

He slept long past his usual hour for waking and old Frith set herself on a stool before the door to his small bedchamber. She allowed no man or woman, not even Master Ector, to disturb his rest.

'The boy is tired to the bone, master, what with setting all to rights in your household. Let him sleep as long as he's able and then old Frith will help him to break his fast.'

Wisely, master and servants permitted the old woman to have her way.

The morning was well advanced before a stray beam of light angled through the shutters, causing Artorex to stir in his bed. In an instant, Frith was aware of his movement and a servant was dispatched to the kitchen to prepare his meal. Soon, Artorex was faced by a huge selection of food.

'I'm a man with a healthy appetite, Frith, but only an Atlas could eat this excellent repast.'

'The village has sent it, boy, so you must try to eat a little of everything. The women who prepared these dishes will expect a report from me on what you eat.'

'But why?' Artorex asked, his confusion clearly written on his open face.

'Last night, you brought the children home, young master. The villagers know that you, above all men, were responsible for their return.'

'But there were other men at the villa – Myrddion, Targo, Llanwith and Luka. We all did what was required of us.' Artorex was quite shocked at the idea that his small part in the events that had unfolded at the Villa Severinii should assume such huge proportions in the eyes of the villagers.

'Get on with you, my little lordling,' Frith admonished him with the familiarity of long custom. 'Was it not Lord Llanwith himself who described how you went back into that nasty pit to bring the little ones home? You may gull some people in this house but you can't fool your old Frith.'

Artorex knew that it was pointless to argue with the old servant, so he tried, heroically, to eat as much of the meal as he could. Then, when he'd dressed and washed, he took himself off to find Lord Ector.

Ector and Caius were seated together in the scriptorium, and both faces were etched in lines of grief. Father and son had been checking the household accounts when Artorex entered, although they sat some distance apart from each other, locked away in their separate, lonely silences. Neither man knew how to speak to the other, and Ector's face bore the puffiness of weeping. Caius was unable to meet his father's eyes, and he stared at the scrolls with painful intensity. Ector gave Artorex a small smile of welcome, but Caius couldn't look at his foster-brother and stared fixedly at the wall.

Ector was the first to break the small, awkward silence.

'Does pen Bryn speak the truth? The Villa Severinii has been burned to the ground?'

'Aye, Master Ector. It was well alight when we departed. If the magistrate holds to his words, the foundations are being torn asunder as we speak, and the raw earth will be sown with salt.'

'Gods!' the bluff old man swore, ignorant of how close the Villa Poppinidii had come to a similar fate.

His head sunk low on his chest, Caius managed to suppress a sob.

'If their Osiris is a kindly god, Severinus and Antiochus will soon be dead, if they aren't dead already,' Artorex said softly. 'And the world is cleaner for their having left it.'

'Llanwith told me that there were seven children buried in

the crypt below the house', Ector replied. 'And two others who had been buried elsewhere.'

'Aye, Master Ector. Since his father died, Severinus and his mother have indulged in all manner of perversities.'

Ector turned to his son, who tried desperately to avoid eye contact with his father.

'Did you know, Caius? You've been in that man's company since you were a boy. He even ate food in our house. He breathed the same air as your mother.'

Caius flinched as if his father had struck him.

Artorex was watching his foster-brother very closely in the hope of catching him out in deceit or to discover a trace of guilt, but he couldn't tell what Caius was thinking. The handsome, chiselled face was sombre and closed, the eyes were lowered and turned inward, and his lips quivered, but Artorex had no idea what prompted his foster-brother's distress.

'I knew he was wild and had strange tastes, Father. I was afraid of him, especially when some of his moods took him. He was terrifying and dangerous, a pederast, although he never dared to touch me.' Caius looked up at this point, and stared directly into the eyes of Artorex.

'You said something else when we questioned you a mere day ago', Artorex stated with the same blandness of face that Caius had adopted.

His foster-brother paled. 'Very well, Artorex. I lied! Are you satisfied? Severinus raped me before I was fifteen, but I hoped to spare my father that shame.'

'Caius!' Ector gasped, aghast.

'It's better to tell your father the whole truth and be done with it, Caius. Your father is owed an explanation of why Severinus had such a hold on you.'

'I didn't know what Severinus did to those children, Father,' Caius swore.

Even Artorex, who knew about his foster-brother's role in the first murders, could have wagered that he told the truth. But the words were false, although those few who could prove it were now either dead or dying. With newly educated eyes, Artorex recognized the open face of Caius's guile.

'He had a terrible power over me, Father, that I cannot deny. He ordered me to attend a feast last night, and I was overcome by my fear of him. And now, neither you nor the gods will ever forgive me.'

In truth, Artorex wasn't entirely sure if Caius was deliberately telling a falsehood to his father or if he had already convinced himself that his sins lay at the feet of Severinus. And perhaps it was true that many of his faults were caused by his friendship with Severinus, Artorex thought to himself, knowing, even as he made this excuse, that Caius was still the young man who had brutalized the mare, Aphrodite, and beaten his young wife.

Artorex watched a tear trickle out of Ector's eye, only to be dashed away as the master wrapped his right arm around the shoulders of his son.

'Your mother forgave you, Caius,' Ector said sincerely. 'So it's up to you to justify the belief she had in you.'

So, Lord Ector has chosen to forgive his son's sins, Artorex marvelled. He is choosing to blind himself to his son's character for love of Livinia. But Caius is too old to change – and the mistress knew it.

Compassionately, he kept his thoughts to himself, for his mind was heavy with dread and guilt. How could he blame a fond father for trying to protect every father's dream – the heroism and success of his son? He himself had been complicit in the whole cover-up; Ector only knew what his steward and his friends told him. If Ector was at fault, so was he.

His respect and love for his mistress, as well as the oath she had wrung from him on her deathbed, was a yoke around his neck.

'I must ride to the village, master,' Artorex interrupted his circuitous thoughts with action. 'I have been charged to return the remains of the children to their families, and I must set their souls to rest.'

Ector nodded in understanding. In truth, Artorex welcomed the horror of this task as his punishment for his sins of omission.

'Of course,' Ector agreed. 'Do you think we should accompany you?'

No, by God! Artorex thought. The very sight of Caius would only rekindle all the suspicions that still lay just beneath the surface.

'No, master. The villagers may be embarrassed to show their grief when they are in your presence. You can trust me to say all that is needed. I'd lief not go myself but I've vowed to do so.'

'That's understandable, my boy, entirely understandable.' Then Ector sighed heavily. 'Livinia goes to the fire tomorrow. You may inform the villagers that food and drink is to be gifted to them in her name. Perhaps they might pray to their gods that her shade finds rest.'

'I'll relate your sympathy and good wishes to the villagers, my lord,' Artorex replied.

Before taking his leave, Artorex turned to Caius, and nodded to him.

'Young master, could I have a private moment of your time?'

Caius followed Artorex to the doorway, where Artorex slipped a ring into the palm of the young man's hand.

'I'd advise you to avoid such roads as those you have travelled in recent years,' Artorex warned. 'Even my fond memories of your mother won't save you from my retribution should you fail to heed my words. I'll always treat you with the respect due to the son of Ector but you must beware, Caius, for if you act in any way that is unseemly, I can promise that I'll find some way to bring you to justice, oath or no oath. Don't test my resolve!'

Caius appeared vulnerable in his humiliation. His obvious relief made Artorex long to strike him down.

'I'll gladly promise you that, and I thank you for your kindness.'

And those few words have almost stuck in your teeth, Artorex thought sadly, as he strode away to the stables to prepare for his visit to the village. Difficult tasks may only be tackled directly, Targo had taught him. But they need good preparation.

How he could possibly offer comfort to the parents of the vanished children was a daunting problem for Artorex, for he could not anticipate how their kin would react to the unexpected return of the children's remains.

Artorex realized that the innocents had already become the stuff of legend. In the wider world of the region, the common folk now whispered that the boys had been stolen away by creatures from the otherworld, wraiths that the superstitious swore dwelt in the chaos between the real world and an imagined place where the rules of men didn't apply. Those villagers who had experienced the actual loss of their children were driven by more primal needs for revenge and, for them, the loss of the vanished children was no tall tale designed to frighten children around the firepit. It was real. These villagers knew that men had ridden forth, had taken their innocents and had burned the lives of their families into ashes.

'I must find a way to bring them peace,' Artorex murmured. 'And still protect Master Ector.'

'Lord?' said a bright-eyed stable boy with tousled blond hair and strong shoulders in response to Artorex's words.

Artorex emerged from his dark reverie. He'd made his way to the stables without conscious thought, and now he stood before

Coal's stall with the reins hanging loose in his hands. The stable boy took the leathers from Artorex's limp fingers and began to prepare Coal for the steward's departure.

'I'm sorry, it was nothing. I was thinking aloud of how fair and good it would be to know nothing of the evil that exists in the ways of the world.'

The stable boy snorted in derision, just as Artorex would have responded in those long-past days before he had been forced to become a man.

'Begging your lordship's pardon, sir, but I'd rather ride a horse than walk.'

Artorex gave the boy an affectionate cuff about the ears.

'A wise answer, young man. Do you desire to work with horses when you are grown?'

'I want to ride with you, sir, whether to ruin or to triumph. Walking is for those who have no choice.'

Artorex stared with interest at this sturdy boy.

Under the grime and smut, a pair of very sharp hazel eyes gazed back at Artorex respectfully, but without a hint of fear. The boy's hair was almost white in its blondness, and his light eyes were very clear and pale.

'What is your name, young wise one?'

'I am Gareth, my lord, great-grandson to Frith of the Villa Poppinidii. She said I am now old enough to work, so here I am.'

'I am no lord who has warriors to ride behind him, young man. If you believe such nonsense, then you are bound to be disappointed. I was a boy, just like you, not so very many years ago.'

'Everyone knows that, sir.'

'A good morrow to you then, wise one. I will watch for reports of you.'

As Artorex kneed Coal into movement, the boy ran after horse and rider into the sunshine.

'My name is Gareth, my lord,' the boy called out once more. 'Pray remember me!'

'The world is very strange,' Artorex muttered to himself, 'when ragged boys want to follow me . . .'

The first village he visited was a drab cluster of wattle and daub buildings built around a well-defined roadway leading south towards Sorviodunum, which was situated on the Great Plain where the fabled Giant's Carol danced. The village, which was nameless because it lay upon a minor Roman road, boasted a clean alehouse and a village elder, who sometimes called upon the protection of the men from Villa Poppinidii when the wolves were on the prowl in the dead of winter. Well-tended fields stretched out around the conical houses, and the multitude of healthy domestic animals was evidence of a prosperous community.

When the villa could spare him, Targo lived here with his comfortable, laughing widow and her two grown sons.

Targo and the village headman were standing at the point where the road bisected the small settlement. Behind them, dressed in their finest homespun and bearing armfuls of summer flowers, every man, woman and child from the village had gathered.

Puzzled, Artorex noticed that the mood of the village was festive, and not funereal. One short, heavy-set man pushed his way through the crowd and stood beside Coal, his jaw working under a play of powerful emotions. He abased himself and, to the acute embarrassment of Artorex, kissed the steward's sandalled foot.

Artorex nudged Coal forward in surprise.

'This man is Bregan, father of Brego,' Targo intoned with all the solemnity that the occasion warranted. 'He does not have the words to thank you for the life of his only son but he swears to make you the best dagger that his skill will permit.'

'Good Bregan, you honour one who is the least important of those men who saved your son. I merely performed my duty.'

Bregan simply bowed his head in homage.

Artorex dismounted, for he was feeling uncomfortable, towering above the simple village people. Still, his bright hair, his height and his grey eyes marked him as one whose station in life was far above the simple expectations of ordinary folk, and they knew it.

Artorex led Coal, with his precious burdens, into the crowded sod circle before the tavern. As he made his way through the throng, women made haste to throw flowers at his feet and men drew two bench seats out on to the roadway so that Artorex could rest himself.

He seated himself and motioned for the village headman to join him. Targo took up a position directly between the two men, while eager hands unloaded the pannier and laid the urns at Artorex's feet.

'Are there families here whose sons have been taken?' Artorex called loudly, although the crowd was silent.

'They have been found, Lord Steward,' the headman answered formally.

He raised his right hand and the crowd parted to permit a small group of men, women and children to come forward.

'Felix was lost three years ago,' the headman intoned solemnly. 'He is the son of the soldier, Kester, who is now dead, and Iemar, his wife.'

'A noble name,' Artorex murmured as a short, dark woman, supported by a taller young man with mud-brown hair, sobbed tearlessly.

'What colour was his hair, good Iemar?'

Artorex drew out the hanks with their numbered tags.

The woman felt the texture of the pitiful remains between

her work-scarred fingers until she came to the fifth hank, a lock of hair that was chestnut-brown with just a hint of curl.

She wept openly against the breast of her son.

'That is the hair of our Felix,' the young man confirmed.

'Good Iemar, these are the mortal remains of your son. May he rest in peace.' Artorex lifted the terracotta urn with the Roman numeral V marked on the side. He handed it to the sobbing widow.

'Thank you, sir! Oh, thank you! Felix is home at last!'

Artorex bowed his head respectfully.

His grim business went faster then, with all the urns destined for the village finally being placed into the hands of their kin.

Afterwards, Artorex was offered fresh mead, which he refused, asking for water in preference. Then he stood among the assembled villagers and told them what they could bear to know about the Severinii family, their bloody fate and what had become of their children.

'Severinus and other noble young men rode through this village on many occasions. Most were men of quality who were simply going about their business. But Severinus was different, for he followed the rites of the black gods and he became a monster who preyed on your innocents. Fortunately, there were only two others who followed him in his pursuits, and all three of these beasts have been found and punished. Severinus, as well as his mother, Severina, and his lover, Antiochus, have all been found guilty of their crimes and have been put to death. Your children have been avenged.'

He paused before the assembled throng.

'Young Master Caius from my home, the Villa Poppinidii, grew up under the influence of this monster, but I swear to you that young Master Caius was the one who truly saved Brego. He was the man who sensed the evil that was being perpetrated by these monsters. And his suspicions led us to the crypt where we found Brego and the remains of the other children.'

The crowd muttered dully. Artorex could smell their doubts, like bad meat on the still air. Rumour-mongering is difficult to control, and the villagers had already heard how Mistress Livinia had died.

Targo registered that the steward's words were carefully chosen, to protect Caius without telling a direct lie.

'I ask that you bear no ill-will towards Caius or towards Lord Ector, his good father. The lad has been driven half crazed through fear of the Severinii, but Brego lives because Caius did his duty. And has Lord Ector not answered every call for assistance from your headman for many, many years? Have your sons and daughters not found honest work within, and without, the Villa Poppinidii?'

'That is true,' the village headman intoned importantly.

'Lord Ector asked me to offer you his tears for the vanished children, and to beg you to share in his mourning for the Mistress Livinia, who was the last child of the Poppinidii family. She will be sent to the flames on the morrow. Ector and Caius will send funeral meat and drink to you in your time of sorrow, and ask that you pray for the shade of an honourable woman who did nothing but good throughout her whole life.'

The murmuring in the crowd rose, and many heads slowly nodded in agreement.

'Ector's granddaughter is born and has been named Livinia, in memory of the mistress. Let all good souls mourn the passing of the innocent children and this wise and goodly woman in the time of tears that has come to us. But it is also a time to rejoice, for the young Brego has been returned to the bosom of his family, and a new young babe has entered our world.'

The village headman inclined his head towards Artorex. 'You may tell the master that we will always hold allegiance to the

Villa Poppinidii, to its master, and to the son of the master. And we will also hold allegiance to its steward, Lord Artorex.'

The crowd cheered and Artorex felt himself blush.

Nor was he permitted to leave until he had sampled the best food that the village had to offer, giving, in turn, effusive thanks for his morning meal and the bounty that now followed.

Finally, in company with Targo, Artorex was permitted to depart from the village.

Neither man spoke overly much on the short journey to the next village, but Targo's eyes reflected his concern for his young companion and the task that Artorex had chosen to perform.

The second village was smaller and showed clear signs of poverty, for it was situated further from the benign influence of Villa Poppinidii. Yet, for all its squalor, Artorex was greeted as before, and the remains of two more children were returned to their families.

Only one urn now remained. Only one hank of auburn hair rested over Artorex's heart as he took to the road once more. His long and painful task was almost completed.

'Gerna, the wild woman, lives by the sacred well only a few miles from here,' Targo told him. 'She is believed to be fey, and she is feared by many. Most sensible people try to avoid her, for she sees things in the waters that no one wishes to know. But her son was taken, and the village headman told me that she knew when he drew his last breath. She asks that we come to her.'

'Targo, I am weary of portents, death and the common folk who stare at me as if I could somehow ease their lot in life. Who am I to earn such respect? I'd rather avoid Gerna and her mirrors.'

'I'm tired also, boy. Perhaps we could leave the urn with the village headman if you'd prefer not to see her. I'm satisfied that you've done everything that could be expected of you.'

'No, Targo,' Artorex sighed. 'I'll see this quest through to its ending, for I owe all the families some words of comfort, at least.'

Gerna lived in a very wild and savage place at the foot of an exposed knoll of granite that resembled a half-buried skull. At its base, a stream gushed out of a cleft in the rock and filled a natural, fern-lined depression leading into a deep, black pool. A sacred hazel tree drooped over the waters, and shed its nuts into the lightless depths.

A crooning that appeared to emanate from a fissure in the knoll interrupted the eerie stillness of the woods.

Suddenly, a middle-aged woman clad in skins and wreathed in oak leaves heaved her thick body out of the concealed cave, then rose to her full height before Artorex.

Gerna was huge, both in girth and height, and her hair was such a wild, red tangle that only her green eyes could clearly be seen. Wordlessly, she accepted the urn from the young man and stroked the hank of proffered hair. Then, silently, she motioned for Artorex to sit on a mossy stone before the pool itself.

'Is she mute?' Artorex whispered to his companion.

Targo shook his head.

'They say she only speaks when she has something important to say.'

'Then she is a wise woman,' Artorex grunted.

Gerna filled a wooden dipper with water from the pool and handed it to Artorex, who accepted it gingerly.

'You need have no fear, Artorex, for the water is live and pure.' Gerna spoke in a voice that was cracked from disuse.

Carefully, Artorex drank the proffered refreshment.

The water was slightly brackish but not unpleasant on the tongue.

Gerna nodded and bared her teeth in a smile as he finished the water.

She stood before the waters of the pool and stared into its

black, mirrored surface. Then she turned back to the men, closed her eyes and began to speak.

'The tide turns and it will sweep you away, Artorex. Your father awaits you. He has waited overlong and has missed his moment, so your path will be the harder for his lack of decision. He has clung to power, like a drug, and so I warn you to beware.'

She paused.

'I see blood – rivers of blood – and horses – and fire. I see a great fortress and an army of men who will die to defend the west. Do not fear, for you will fulfil your destiny, until even your great strength is not enough. But your struggles will ensure that your world is not lost into darkness and decay, and those who are coming will become enmeshed in your legends. They will use your name for uncounted generations after your death, to seal these isles in safety against attack from those who would cause us harm. This gift I give to you for the sake of my son, although I pay for the giving with years of my life.'

'Will I be happy?'

Gerna laughed, but it was little more than an ugly croak from her long-unused vocal cords.

'What is happiness? But I tease you, Artorex. Yes! You will be happy for a little time. And, yes, I will answer the unasked question. A child of yours will live and breed unheeded by the vast issues of your future world. Though love is fleeting, you shall have it, but look not for contentment, for it is not for men such as you. Enough now. My voice is weary – and my son's shade is speaking to me on the wind.'

Then Gerna was gone, back into her cavern, and the pool was just a shallow bowl of water, caught for a time before it became a streamlet that disappeared back into the ground whence it had come.

'No one promises me wealth or happiness, only pain and struggle.' Artorex complained, for he was still very young.

'Never mind, young master. If the soothsayer is correct, you'll not be rotting at Villa Poppinidii forever,' Targo said with honest good humour. 'And who of us with common sense would wish for a safe life, anyway?'

'I would,' Artorex replied ruefully and only his heart knew that he spoke the simple truth.

CHAPTER VIII

A Convenient Marriage

Lady Livinia was buried with all the ritual and ceremony deserving of a great Roman matron. The clay facemasks of her ancestors were removed from their special cabinets and both paid and unpaid mourners rent their clothing and filled the villa with the eerie sounds of their weeping.

Livinia's pyre was built high and she lay, wrapped and waxen in her finery, until Ector and Caius lifted their torches and lit the fire that would send her shade on its long journey. Ector had purchased scented wood, regardless of cost, so his lady could depart her villa, and her life, in a manner that befitted a Roman noblewoman. As a sop to the sensibilities of the scented gentry of Aquae Sulis, Ector should probably have buried his beloved in the cold earth, but his heart cried out that his lady was a warrior of sorts, and deserved the old Republican way of cremation

After the prescribed days of mourning, life at the villa returned to a semblance of normality.

Two days after Livinia's cremation, the three travellers left, but the servants at the villa were accustomed to their strange arrivals and departures and did little more than comment that the visitors had stayed overlong on this occasion. They knew the delay was due to the death of their mistress and the respect that even these great ones accorded to Lady Livinia.

Before they left, the three travellers did much honour to Ector's household by attending the *Dies Lustricus*, the Day of Purification, when the daughter of Caius and Julanna was formally named. After days of mourning and sorrow, such a joyous feast promised that a better future lay ahead.

The infant girl was belatedly laid at the feet of Caius in the ancient birth custom of the Republic. Julanna's gentle face was tense as she watched her husband decide if this child should be acknowledged as being of his blood. Of course, the issue was never in doubt, but Julanna scarcely trusted her husband to touch her child.

When Caius lifted the *bulla*, a small, gold, double-sided shell that held the charms that would protect her through childhood, and placed its golden chain round the baby's neck, Julanna felt as if her heart would burst. Caius had touched her throat often enough, but he'd been cruel and had bruised her tender flesh. She shuddered to see his large white hands hold her daughter's small body with an emotion that was akin to paternal love.

So, with due ceremony, Ector presided over the feast of *Dies Lustricus*, and the three travellers each presented *crepundia*, small gold and silver charms that tinkled and rang as they were draped over the baby's head. Finally, Ector pronounced the infant's *praenomen*, Livinia, as a name favoured by her ancestors and given in honour of her grandmother.

As the feast progressed, Julanna smiled and was gracious to her guests, but her eyes followed the graceful shape of her husband with the blank stare of a stranger.

In the weeks that followed, Julanna remained frail, and inclined to panic if her child so much as sneezed. Still, the young mistress had much to do, for now she must shoulder Livinia's role long before her time. She must fill shoes that were far too big for her over-cautious feet.

The servants at the villa were fond of Julanna, so they nodded amiably as she issued instructions and ignored any proposed changes to their established routines. Only the hawk-eyed Gallia really noticed that the servants obeyed the rhythms that had been set in place by Lady Livinia over a period of three decades. When Gallia discussed their intransigence with Frith, the old woman was happy to explain.

'No one really disobeys Mistress Julanna, they just don't quite obey her. They know that the new mistress will never notice if they follow the old ways, because she spends her time doting on her babe. Soon, the wishes of Mistress Julanna will become the old ways practised by Mistress Livinia, and she will accept that it has always been so.'

Frith brushed away an errant tear, for Lady Livinia had been her charge from birth. Gallia patted the old servant's shoulder and wondered anew just how free the great ones of the world really were, for most were at the mercy of their servants and their own indolence.

Gallia was much changed since the Night of the Innocents, as those bloody hours had come to be called. The wound in her scalp had required some shaving of her head to allow for treatment of the wound, and the bald patch could be seen right on the crown of her head. Eventually, Gallia decided to break with Celtic and Roman custom. Early one morning, when her maidservant arrived in the bedchamber to dress her hair and hide her unsightly stitches, Gallia informed the young girl of her decision.

'Cut it off!'

'What, my lady?' the maidservant gasped.

'My hair! Shear it off so it is no longer than my little finger.'

'But I can't do that, my lady.' The young girl looked horrified. 'Your father would thrash me black and blue.'

'I doubt that, for my father is the kindest man alive,' Gallia replied with inescapable logic. 'Anyway, he isn't here, so he can't punish us.'

The maidservant was still unwilling to perform her task, so Gallia simply picked up the shears and began to cut off great swathes of black hair herself. But her efforts were so uneven and so unsightly, that the maidservant was forced to avert complete disaster by cutting Gallia's mane and coaxing it backwards to disguise the unsightly locks that remained.

At first, every person in the villa stared incredulously at Gallia's shorn head. Her long, black hair, with its blue lustre like fine grapes, had been her greatest beauty but, oddly, her pert little cap of curls, for that was how her hair gradually regrew, accentuated her fine throat and white breasts. Masters and servants followed her little form with their eyes as she danced through the villa, always in search of new diversions.

Of course, she should have returned to the bosom of her own family after the birth of Julanna's child, but Gallia wasn't ready to depart, and nor was Julanna ready to relinquish her steadfast yet unpredictable friend. Letters were penned between the two families and Gallia was permitted to remain for another few months at the Villa Poppinidii. However, with the arrival of the first chills of winter, Gallicus warned that his daughter must return to her home and resume the duties owed to her family and to her name.

'Father is determined that I should be married as soon as is practicable,' Gallia translated laconically. 'Once again, he has found the perfect son-in-law, so I'll hate the poor man at first sight. So far, I've been very fortunate to remain free of his male acquaintances, but life will become difficult once a dowry is offered.'

'Surely, marriage wouldn't be so very bad?' Julanna replied soothingly.

Caius had made every indication of a change in character,

having become an amenable husband since the death of his mother and his flirtation with disaster. But Julanna's slight frown was at odds with her encouraging words, for even after the passage of five months, she couldn't bring herself to trust the young master.

'That seems to depend on the nature of the person one marries. Believe me, dearest Julanna, my father's choice will look like a cod.'

Both pairs of female eyes turned to follow the tall figure of Artorex as he strode down the colonnade towards the baths.

Both ladies sighed – and then burst into rueful laughter.

'Perhaps your father could be convinced that Artorex is a coming man,' Julanna exclaimed innocently. 'Everybody says so.'

'Believe me, my father wouldn't be swayed. He is far more interested in gold coin, settled wealth and good family connections than marrying me off to a steward.' She sighed. 'But marriage to Artorex could never happen anyway because he doesn't even realize that I'm alive,' Gallia pouted.

'I'm certain that Artorex is very much aware of you,' Julanna assured her friend with a knowing grin.

For once, Julanna was correct. At the advanced age of twenty, Artorex was experiencing all the pangs of calf love. From the day he returned to the villa after fulfilling his duties with the missing children, the sight of Gallia's short and curling hair had inflamed Artorex. He had admired the girl's forward tongue and quick grasp of affairs long before Livinia's death, but now the sight of that small head atop her narrow, delicately sloping shoulders filled Artorex with an unfamiliar hot tide of lust and, perhaps, developing love.

Thoughts of her breasts consumed him night and day, and he could visualize the rosy thighs beneath her gown. Even the briefest of conversations with her became a contest between his growing desire and an unanticipated shyness that overcame him when he was in her presence.

To ease his pain, he sought out compliant servant girls and rutted with them in the stables, but no amount of sex dismissed the hot and erotic thoughts of Gallia that ate into him by night as he lay in his spartan bed.

Of course, the whole household was aware of his plight. General opinion among the servants was that Gallia was a flighty young woman, but strong and brave, and these factors overcame the disadvantages of her birth as the daughter of a fish merchant. And so the strange prejudices of family seethed around Gallia and Artorex, while they resisted the hungers of physical attraction that were driving them together.

Artorex was not alone in his yearning. Gallia's eyes followed his tall form wherever he went, and she dreamed of his bronzed arms embracing her and his body enfolding and dominating hers. Without the physical outlets available to Artorex, perhaps Gallia's fires burned the hotter, for they must be hidden under the smile of a well-bred maiden. But she knew in her heart that her father would never permit her to marry a fatherless steward.

Initially, it was fortunate for the two lovesick young people that Gallicus caught a chill a bare week before his daughter was due to return to her home. The chill proved to be a fever that ran like fire through his body, burning the ample meat away from his bones and filling his lungs with fluid.

Gallia was packing, in floods of very unvirginal tears, when a courier arrived from Aquae Sulis to deliver a letter penned by her eldest brother announcing that a deadly fever had taken the city in its grip, and that Gallia should remain at the Villa Poppinidii until all danger of infection had passed. The letter stressed the seriousness of her father's condition. In fact, she would have been on the road to Aquae Sulis, prohibited or not, had her brother not added that the house of the Gallica, as well as all other houses of infection, were locked to all newcomers by orders of the Town Council.

'The pestilence!' Ector intoned solemnly at supper that evening, once Gallia's plight had been explained to him. 'This curse has come before, usually through the ports, and over half those poor souls infected will die of it. Yet, I remember that some people are immune to its symptoms and suffer no ill effects. They remain healthy throughout its worst contagions.'

As the master spoke, the winter wind soughed outside the walls of the villa with a mournful sigh. Ector scratched his chin where his beard was whitening, a habit that warned he was about to make an announcement of some seriousness.

'I've seen the fortunate survivors as they pass through the villages, continuing their trades or their business as if death had not consumed their homes. And I believe that these souls who seem so hale and healthy often bring their contagion with them, perhaps in their clothes, or even on their skins. But how can we be sure, for we can't tell the sick man from the healthy? And we don't know where they rest their heads or sell their wares, and so the illness spreads.'

He paused, scratched at his beard once more, and then continued as the wind rattled the heavy wooden door on its hinges.

'The gates to the Villa Poppinidii will be closed to all visitors,' Lord Ector decided, just a little pompously. 'As of now, no servant may give even a dry crust to a wanderer, no matter how sad his story. No tinkers may set foot upon my lands and all contact with the village is forbidden.'

'Artorex!' He turned to his steward. 'Tell Targo to warn the village headman of the dangers of the pest, and what I've decided. A little prevention, as your mistress used to say, is worth a mountain of cure. Targo may stay with his widow in the village or remain here, as he chooses, as may all our servants. But once they have decided where they'll lay their heads, there they will remain until after the contagion has passed.'

No one in the villa even considered arguing with the master.

In the opinion of Artorex, the greatest advantage of old age was the accompanying experiences that came from a long life. Once Frith confirmed Ector's explanation of the spread of deadly fevers in past years, the folk of Villa Poppinidii considered they were fortunate to have such a wise master.

Julanna survived the weeks that followed in an agony of fear. For her, the villa must be kept in a state of constant cleanliness, for the courier from Aquae Sulis might have brought the pestilence with him, and even now death might lurk in some dusty corner, waiting to kill her daughter. For once, the servants implicitly obeyed the young mistress, not because they gave any credence to Julanna's fears but because Frith confirmed that where dirt and filth clustered, there the pestilence flourished.

Other than an orgy of cleaning, little disturbance marred the peace of the villa. But Gallia fretted and blamed her selfishness for her absence from the home of her family. In vain did Julanna assure her friend that Gallicus must be relieved that Gallia was safe outside the walls of Aquae Sulis. As an only daughter, Gallia accepted that her place was with her family and that it was her responsibility to tend to her father's needs during his illness.

To pass time, she began to take long, solitary rambles around the fringes of the farmlands and, during her daily explorations, she found herself wandering ever closer to the edges of the Old Forest. At Julanna's urging, Gallia's maidservant was hard at work scrubbing every dusty corner of the villa while her manservant was assisting with the storage of autumn grain. Few at the villa observed Gallia during her walks, while even the early winter landscape, delicate with a faint rime frost, failed to assuage her oppressive feelings of guilt.

Inevitably, Gallia's inquisitive spirit led her to enter the wood. Its impenetrable silence and brooding shadows so perfectly matched her mood that many hours would pass while she sat on a fallen tree trunk, oblivious to the mossy slimes that stained her skirts. The stillness was an anodyne to the bustle of the villa so that, enclosed by the lichen-draped trunks, Gallia discovered that she could think clearly in this sanctuary, free of domestic distraction.

Each day, she ventured further afield during her forays, for the frenetic labour of the villa, as it prepared for the quiet, fallow months, meant that neither masters nor servants thought to wonder where she took herself in the shortening daylight hours.

Inevitably, she stumbled upon the glade that Artorex had frequented during his youth, and she, too, sat on the ancient stone and traced the worn pattern of spirals and whorls with fingers that profoundly understood the spirit of this place better than her conscious thoughts ever could. While death seemed to live in the glade in the dying of leaves and the small things that dwelt in tree and grass, it was a death that was kindly.

'All things must die,' the Goddess of Death seemed to be whispering to Gallia, 'but the sun rises, the grass grows tall again and life goes on. Season follows season, and men are like flowers who bud, bloom and fade before the earth even recognizes that they live. Stone, trees and water go on and on.'

Gallia allowed her hand to trail over the cup that had been carved into the stone. A memory of warmth from direct sunlight soothed her fingers, while her mind was lulled by the deep, restful silence of the glade.

The face of Gallicus smiled at her with kind, brown eyes, and gesticulated with a wholly Latin flamboyance as he begged her to marry someone – anyone – before she was past marriageable age.

'I'll marry whoever you want, Papa, if you'll only be better soon,' Gallia told the trees and his remembered face.

She imagined the faces of her five brothers, all of whom were older and sterner than she was, with their tribe of wives, children and grandchildren at their flanks.

'I'll even try to be polite to the wives of my brothers. Please, be well when I return.'

Gallia was still daydreaming in the glade when another courier arrived at the Villa Poppinidii with word from her family.

Artorex met the rider at the gates to the farm.

'Stop, sir! This villa is closed to all visitors until Aquae Sulis is freed of the pestilence,' he ordered grimly, but kindly, for bad times cause decisions to be made which are not within the natural patterns of courtesy. The villa had always welcomed the poorest and meanest of visitors in the past.

The courier remained on his horse and wiped his chilled face with a muffler of greasy wool.

'The pestilence is dead, as are over half the citizens of Aquae Sulis,' the courier reported grimly. 'The city still reeks of funeral pyres, but no one has taken ill during the last ten days.'

Artorex shook his head in disbelief, for his ordered mind could not imagine such carnage.

'You may well speak the truth, my friend, but I must obey my master's orders. I regret the discourtesy of these days, which must send you back to your city without food or shelter.'

'In truth, steward, I'd as lief be at home with my wife and children, but Gallinus, son of Gallicus, has charged me to bring a message to his sister, Lady Gallia.'

'I will ensure that the message is passed to Lady Gallia if you read it to me,' Artorex told the courier.

'I cannot read, steward, but my master expected your caution, so my message has been learned.'

'Then you may inform me of the message, good sir, and I will faithfully deliver it to the Lady Gallia.'

'This is the message that Master Gallinus entrusted to me,' the courier intoned formally, and closed his eyes to ensure that none of the precious words were forgotten.

'Greetings to Gallia, sister of Gallinus, who is now the Master of the House of the Gallus. Our father has departed this world to join his ancestors, as have my son, and one daughter, four of my brothers and many other members of my family. Their shades have been honoured in the ancient ways, although in great haste as inhumation was not possible. Your absence at the funeral feasts and the cremations is forgiven. I will come to escort you to the House of Gallus as soon as I may be spared, for our affairs have been sorely struck by the displeasure of the gods. Lay these words to your heart – and farewell.'

After several repetitions, Artorex had mastered the message, so the courier departed on his return journey. Artorex sighed, for he now had another unpleasant task to perform.

He was no fool. The master of the house and four of his heirs were dead, including grandchildren and wives. Gallia had lost almost all of her family and much of her wealth. Although Artorex could scarcely imagine being part of a family of such size, either living or dead, he accepted that Gallia would be distraught at the loss of her father and brothers.

He dreaded the prospect of breaking such bad news. He would have preferred to pass on this onerous task to almost anyone else, but Artorex was no coward and Gallia deserved an accurate accounting of the tragic deaths of her kin.

The steward searched for Gallia for many hours, but no one in the villa had seen her. Tense with the first stirrings of serious alarm, Artorex took Coal out into the fields but, yet again, there was no sign of the wayward young woman.

'Not even Gallia can disappear off the face of the earth,' he muttered to himself, as he stifled a flash of mounting irritation.

But after a fruitless search of the farm and all the outbuildings, Artorex was considering mounting a major search using
the field workers when, by a fortuitous stroke of luck, his sharp
eyes spotted a small red ribbon on an overgrown path close to
where the Old Forest merged with the farm cultivation. The
path itself was ill-defined, but the tiny sliver of fabric twined,
serpent-like, around a clump of dying thistles, and Artorex
knew that the impetuous Gallia had wandered into the woods.

'You're a devil of a child,' Artorex muttered to himself. 'You
should know the dangers of these places – especially for a
woman. Why can't you weave, or sew or even clean, like every
other female in the villa?'

Ducking and weaving on Coal's back as he avoided low-
hanging branches, he rode Coal deeper into the woods.

Perhaps it's because she's not like any other woman, an
internal voice warned him.

The trees had no interest in either Artorex or Gallia, so he
received no answer to his questions except for the rustling of
small, unseen things that had been disturbed by the passage of
his horse.

'Gallia!' he roared at the top of his lungs, once he was deep
within the woods, knowing that he could search these wild
places for weeks and still not find her.

'Where are you? Shout if you hear me.'

Coal picked his way daintily over the uneven ground while
Artorex strained to hear an answer to his calls. When a response
came, it was unexpectedly clear – and very close. Artorex leapt
off Coal's back and led the stallion through the treacherous
tangle of tree roots and fallen logs, and into the silence of his
long-unseen glade.

Gallia was seated on his stone, her head lifted and her eyes
already flaring with panic. Instinctively, she knew that only a

matter of great urgency would cause the steward to seek her out when, under normal circumstances, she wouldn't expect to see him till the evening meal.

'What is amiss, Artorex? Is it Julanna? Or little Livinia?'

Artorex gazed down at his sandalled foot and fiddled with the reins of his horse.

'I . . .' he began, but Gallia leapt to her feet impetuously.

'News has come from Aquae Sulis, hasn't it?' she asked. 'Is it Father?'

Artorex nodded. 'Yes, Gallia, I have news from Aquae Sulis . . . and it's bad tidings, I'm afraid.'

He paused but could find no platitudes to ease the pain he was about to inflict. Gallia's eyes were wide and frightened, and the half-light that filtered through the tall trees cast a greenish light over her features. Artorex was stricken, but he knew that only the blunt truth would serve him now.

'Your father has died from the pestilence. A courier has just arrived with news from your brother, Gallinus, who is now the new master of your father's house. Several of your brothers, the son of Gallinus and one of his daughters have also gone to meet their ancestors. Other members of your family have also perished. Gallinus sent few details, except to warn us that it might be some time before he can fetch you home. I regret that I must bear these sad tidings and I wish I could say something to console you in your grief.'

Gallia stared at Artorex blankly.

'But Gallinus is my third brother. What of Gallicus Minor and Gallius? They must be dead as well – and Gallinus has lacked the heart to send word to me directly. Help me, Mother, help me!'

Horrified, Artorex saw that Gallia's eyes had rolled back in her head and she was falling sideways in a dead faint towards the depression in the rock with its strange and disturbing design.

Even as he sprang forward and caught her, he could picture her blood filling that cup and escaping along the spirals in a thin ribbon of crimson.

'Gallia!' he whispered in her ear as he effortlessly lifted her slender body. Her face was only inches away from his lips.

'Wake up, Gallia! Wake up!' he said urgently into her ear.

Gallia's eyelids fluttered but she made no sound. Artorex swung her soft, pliant body up into his arms and, whistling for Coal to follow him, he began to pick his way back through the tangle of trees to where the forest met the fields of the farm.

Gallia lay limply in his arms. It was almost as if she, too, were dead, like so many of her kin, and Artorex wondered how it would feel to lose someone who was so close in blood and affection. Try as he might, he couldn't imagine such a loss. He would mourn for Targo, Frith or Ector if they should die, for he had known them all his short life. He had mourned the loss of Mistress Livinia, and whenever he heard the swing and beat of the shuttle and the loom, his throat constricted with an emotion that was surely grief. But, with no blood ties to a family, he could never fully understand Gallia's loss.

Once he was clear of the trees, Artorex remounted Coal with Gallia still in a dead faint in his arms. She began to return to consciousness as they approached the villa, but her eyes were dry and glazed. Something essential to her spirit had fled away with the news that Artorex had delivered.

'They're all dead,' she murmured against his chest.

'Not all of them, Gallia. Not all! Your brother struggles to put his father's affairs in order, and he'll come for you when his duties permit. The pestilence decided that many of your kin went to the funeral pyres long before they were fated to do so, but I have been assured that all the burial rituals were observed exactly as your father would have wished.' He looked down at her upturned face. 'I'd take your pain away myself, Gallia, if only I knew how.'

Absently, she squeezed his arm to express her thanks, but her mind was struggling to comprehend the depth of her loss.

'I know you'd help me if you could, Artorex, but there's nothing we can do, is there?'

'No, Gallia, there's not.'

At the very least, he could present her with the truth.

At the villa, Gallia's maidservant came running and assisted her mistress into her quarters. Julanna had been disturbed by the fuss and now she listened to the report from Artorex with growing concern and horror.

'Will this terrible year never be done?' she moaned, and hurried to the side of her friend.

The evening meal was bereft of womenfolk. Ector was saddened by Gallia's tragedy, but was fully aware that there was nothing he could offer to assist Gallia in her time of mourning.

'We're very fortunate to be so distant from Aquae Sulis. If the pestilence has truly passed, as the courier suggested, our isolation has been instrumental in keeping us safe.'

'Aye, master. You acted wisely when you determined to keep us isolated from all contact with outsiders.'

'I wish Lady Livinia was still here. She'd know how to ease the burdens that little Gallia must carry. It must be nigh impossible for her to linger here in comfort when her family is such a short distance away and yet not be able to help them in their suffering.'

'Aye. The mistress would have known how to help little Gallia,' Artorex agreed. But Caius remained non-committal and silent.

Frith reported that Gallia was now awake but remained dry-eyed, shivering and distracted.

'Will she be well?' Artorex asked.

'Never fear, master, she'll start to talk soon, and then she'll remember the happy years and the joyful times she spent with her family. She'll shed some good, healing tears. The little mistress is young, and her body is not yet ready for death, although she's half mad with her loss.'

And so, old Frith, faithful Julanna and a few trusted maidservants sat with the grieving Gallia and tended to her needs. At first she was mute, and then the memories poured out of her as if the simple task of repeating tales of her childhood could keep her father and her brothers alive for a little longer.

The tears followed, and the nightmares, and yet more tears, until Gallia emerged from her bedchamber, pale, thin and as insubstantial as thistledown.

During her ordeal, a strange friendship had been forged. Julanna had the running of the household and the care of her child pressing down upon her narrow, girlish shoulders. Although she longed to ease Gallia's sorrow, time kept her from the side of her loyal friend more often than she wished.

But, smoothly and naturally, as if she had always been there, Frith sat with Gallia beside her pallet or coaxed her to eat. When the girl wept in her restless sleep, it was old Frith who woke her, held her gently to her withered breasts and soothed away her nightmares with kisses and kind words. The first thing that Gallia saw when she awoke each grey, winter morning was Frith's wrinkled, smiling face, and the last sound she heard before sleeping was the sweet sound of the old woman's singing.

Gallia had barely risen from her bed of grief when her brother suddenly arrived at the Villa Poppinidii. New streaks of grey now bleached his black hair and he was without even a single manservant to attend to his needs and comfort during his journey.

After a tearful reunion, Gallia took to her bed once again, too worn and weary from tears and misery to face the tangible person of her last sibling. To pass the time, Gallinus sought the advice of Lord Ector, seeking an older head to guide him, while Artorex took pains to ensure that he was also present at the meeting.

'I couldn't speak what is in my heart with little Gallia present. Ten members of my family are dead, and over half our servants have perished with them. The family business is in tatters. Oh, it is sound at the roots, for everyone needs fish, but I must labour hard to repair what the pestilence has stolen from us. The markets of Aquae Sulis are silent, the fleet from Abone is halved and the warehouses are stripped of those labourers who are necessary to carry out the physical work. Little Gallia knows little of trade so it will be difficult to tell her she is unlikely to have a dowry when she is eventually married.'

Ector rumbled his distress at this news.

'Gallia has always been the little singing bird in our house,' Gallinus sighed, and then continued. 'She's the youngest, and she has a tender heart.'

He paused once again, while Artorex grinned inwardly at the thought that Gallia was either fragile or tender.

'I lack the words to explain to my sister the true circumstances of the disaster that has afflicted our house.'

Ector nodded his sympathy and understanding, but there was little he could say that would alleviate this young man's concerns. Instead, in the Roman tradition, he attempted to keep his spine straight and his gaze direct.

Artorex watched Gallia's brother impassively. Gallinus was disturbed and frightened, as any sensible man would be who was suddenly faced with the task of salvaging an extensive trading empire that had inexplicably been brought to its knees. His brothers were dead, and he was suddenly forced to assume control of his father's many business interests at a time when he was ill prepared for the task before him.

After a few moments of silence, the young man began to explain his quandary over the future of his young sister.

'My most pressing problem is Gallia. Our father intended that she should be wed months ago, but all past arrangements have failed to bear fruit. Unfortunately, Father's most recent choice of husband was also a victim of the plague.'

He pondered his situation in silence.

'To be frank, Gallia will have no possibility of dowry until she is much older, for I must use our remaining gold as wages for those fishermen, artisans and workers who have survived,' Gallinus said softly. 'I must diversify if I'm to survive, but I'm at a loss to know what to do with my sister, for who'd wish to marry a woman who is no longer young and fresh?'

'She's welcome to stay with us for as long as you wish,' Ector replied. 'She's a charming young girl, and she brings much happiness to our Julanna.'

'I thank you for your generosity, but the problem will continue to grow. She's now more than fifteen years and will soon be past her first bloom of youth. By the time the family fortunes are rebuilt, she will be at least twenty years old. Heaven knows where I will find her a husband, for Aquae Sulis has been stripped of its suitable young men.'

Artorex interrupted before he had really considered the importance of the words he was about to utter.

'I would make an offer to marry Gallia – and would do so gladly – although you may not want a lowly steward as the husband of your sister.'

Ector, Caius and Gallinus turned to face Artorex as one. They were dumbfounded by the proposal, and stared blankly at him.

'I know I'm not worthy of her by birth and by wealth but I have a most sincere affection for your sister,' Artorex added. 'Nor will I always be a landless man, for I intend to make my mark on the world. But I will understand if you find my proposal presumptuous and insulting.'

Ector gave Artorex a fleeting smile.

'My foster-son is overly modest, and he need not be landless, for I can always settle a small parcel of Villa Poppinidii land upon him if he so desires. Further, the holy Lucius, Bishop of Glastonbury, would also settle gold on him if Artorex decided to take a wife of good lineage. It is a fact that Lucius prevailed upon me to raise young Artorex, and a priest of his renown wouldn't take such pains if Artorex wasn't of respectable birth.'

Belatedly, Artorex realized that Gallinus was actually considering his offer. He could readily understand that Gallia was one problem too many for a man beset by the trials confronting a younger son who was attempting to make his mark on the world.

As his stomach churned with a sudden attack of nerves, Artorex had no idea if he was more afraid of rejection or of acceptance.

'I'll sleep upon your proposal, good steward, and I'll give you my answer in the morning.' He smiled at Artorex. 'And now, Artorex, if you aren't offended, I'd ask you to leave me with Master Ector so that he can acquaint me with your character. I may be in desperate straits, but my sister is precious to me.'

'I understand, sir, and I'll leave you to your deliberations.'

What have I done? Artorex asked himself as he strode back to his spartan bedchamber. How can I take a wife when all I own is a horse? I must be moon mad!

The measure of the financial troubles besetting Gallinus was amply proved by his agreement to the marriage when he met Ector and Artorex the following morning.

Bemused by the unexpected turn of events, Artorex and Gallinus sealed their bargain with a clasp of hands and an assurance from Gallinus that, in time, a bride price would be paid so that Artorex could build his own small villa. Documents would be drawn up in Aquae Sulis and Ector had already agreed to give the young couple the field that bordered the Old Forest.

In truth, Ector gave very little, for the land was full of brambles and weeds, and would take a great deal of effort to set to rights. On the other hand, he would gain much from the match. His steward was now bound to Villa Poppinidii by the bonds of his coming marriage, and the villa had gained another Roman chatelaine.

Once again, the wily and affable Celt could not lose.

'But what of Gallia? Perhaps she will not wish to marry me?' Artorex suggested.

'Gallia is of Roman lineage and she'll marry whomever her paterfamilias chooses,' Gallinus stated abruptly. 'I know that Father indulged her but I don't have time for such luxuries.'

Now that his mind was set on a course of action, Gallinus was sweeping aside all opposition to his plans, as if they were chaff before the storm winds.

'I am, of course, forced to continue with the mourning period that is still left to me at my own home, so it is probably best that your marriage take place here at the Villa Poppinidii. I am certain that Gallia and Julanna will be cheered at the prospect of planning a wedding celebration. Ladies love such distractions.'

Artorex wasn't so confident. Gallia was no blushing maiden, having proved that her small body hid a very large heart. And Julanna had learned through tragedy that duty ruled a woman's life, not entertainment.

In the event, Gallia cried a great deal when Gallinus informed her of his decision. She didn't know precisely why she wept, whether out of joy or terror, but she knew that Artorex was a man of honour and her children would stand tall in their world. She understood, too, deep in her inner self, that Artorex was destined for a noble future.

And so the tangled fates of Artorex and Gallia were sealed with the *sponsalia*, the formal betrothal. Although the *confarrato*, or sacred marriage, was not the norm in these far lands, the offspring of Gallicus ate barley cakes at their wedding feasts to show that they were wed for life. Joy might come for Artorex and Gallia, and strength, but a dark legacy had been born with the passing of the pestilence and now it waited for time to call it forth.

CHAPTER IX

THE IDYLL

In the last weeks of winter, Artorex wed Gallia of the House of Gallus with all the pomp and splendour that Ector could muster as a provincial lord. The time wasn't propitious, for all good citizens of Roman blood married during the warm and fecund month of June when Juno, the goddess who guarded all girls, was at her strongest. But circumstances called for haste, a decision that suited none of the women of the villa, who bemoaned the absence of flowers in this inauspicious time. Snow had come to the lands around Aquae Sulis in unaccustomed flurries and the fires in the hypocaust had to be kept stoked so that the floors and walls could warm their guests.

Grunn, the cook, at the head of an army of kitchen maids, cooked and basted, boiled and candied, fried and roasted, until the villa was one long succession of succulent smells. Even Caius, mindful of his debt to Artorex, and now thoroughly nervous of his foster-brother, ordered wood cut for great iron braziers to warm the rooms. Old Frith was bursting with pride, and in her strange, barbarian fashion, went out into the forest where the ice on the trees cracked and growled as if the wood itself was in pain.

When she had dragged home her booty of fallen boughs, she decorated the lintels of the rooms with holly, festooned cheerfully with its red berries. She found old, long-dried logs from fragrant trees, and ordered the manservants to drag them home to sweeten the wood that burned in the braziers.

On one of her travels, she found one curiously shaped knob of wood that she polished with oil until the small thing glowed in the reflected light, and then she pierced the timber with an awl so a narrow silken cord could pass through it.

On the night before the wedding feast, she visited the bride.

'My lady?' Frith called softly, as she scratched at Gallia's door. 'My lady, have you a moment for old Frith?'

'Come in, Frith, and welcome,' Gallia cried, and sat up in her warm bed.

Her hair was still very short, but Frith could see that the tumbled curls suited the young woman far better than the tortured coifs of great ladies.

'You would ease old Frith's heart if you would wear this talisman when you are wed,' Frith said, and pressed the little piece of wood into Gallia's hands.

'It looks like a small pregnant woman,' Gallia marvelled. 'It is so smooth and warm in my hand. What wood is this?'

'It's made from a knot of hazel tree, little one. The Druids forbid us, on pain of death, to cut the hazel for it is a holy tree. But I found this fragment on the earth, so it is a bride gift to you from the tree itself. It'll keep you safe and make your children strong.'

Gallia lifted an elegant, golden amulet that hung round her neck.

'My mother placed this *bulla* round my neck when I was born, to protect me from evil until I was a woman grown. Mother has been dead since I was ten, so she can no longer remove this amulet on the night before my wedding, as is custom. You'd honour me, Frith, if you would remove the *bulla* of my mother and replace it with your amulet.'

Frith's old head dropped, and a few tears snaked down her weathered cheeks.

'Aye, mistress. I'd be honoured to stand in place of your mother. Bend your head, sweet Gallia.'

As Gallia obeyed, Frith tied the simple cord round her neck and the amulet fell into the warm cleft between Gallia's breasts.

'I thank you, Frith. This is a gift fit for a queen, and I promise to keep it always.'

Frith would have left Gallia to her rest, but the girl asked her to stay for she was too excited to sleep.

'Where are you from, Frith? Your eyes and hair are different from the colouring of the Celts, and there is something about you . . . something . . .' Gallia struggled for words.

'Alien, my lady?' Frith smiled, with only a touch of irony.

'Yes, although that word is very harsh for one as devoted to the Poppinidii family as you are.'

'My lady!' Frith exclaimed. 'The Villa Poppinidii owns me, body and soul. Didn't you know?'

Gallia was quite shocked. In many ways, Frith was more of a domestic despot than Ector.

'Yes, mistress. My sweet Livinia's father, Livius, purchased me when I was a child. They say I was found as an infant in the floating shell of a boat after a great storm off the Isle of Vectis in the south. Where I lived, or where my family came from, was a mystery, for I was alone in a battered, barbarian ship. Had I grown with dark hair, perhaps I would not have ended up on the slave block, but my hair was white, little different from what it is now.'

Frith paused, before continuing.

'When I was about three years of age, I was sold to the Villa Poppinidii by traders from the north, when Livius was still a young man. I raised his only child, Livinia, and I buried her too. But I am still a barbarian, Mistress Gallia, and at times my ways are strange, for all that I was a babe when I was found.'

'Did you ever marry, Frith? Did you have children?'

'Of course, mistress,' Frith boasted. 'I wed a good Celt from the village – for all that I would not leave the villa to live with him. I bore seven living children for him.'

'Did they become slaves too?' Gallia asked with unintentional rudeness.

Fortunately, Frith was not offended.

'Mistress Livinia set me free years ago, with scrolls of manumission and all that the law requires. But I told her then, as I tell you now, that we should always master our own fate, and I chose to remain a slave at Villa Poppinidii. I bear no slave collar because Livinia wouldn't permit me to wear it again, but I remain a slave because I chose to burn my manumission. The villa has owned me for as long as I can remember. Everything I love is here; everyone I have ever cared for lies in this soil or works this land. I belong to the Villa Poppinidii. But Master Ector is also a slave, if you look closely at him. And so is my dear Artorex. And so, in time, will sweet Gallia also be a slave to our house.'

She smiled across at the young girl.

'Now, goodnight, my lady. For tomorrow you become wife to my beautiful Artorex.'

Gallia was wed in a white gown edged with golden thread that she had stitched herself during the years of her maidenhood. A wreath of wheat heads encircled her brow and matched the sheaf of grain that she carried as a plea to the gods for fecundity.

Under her wreath, Gallia's hair shone with cleanliness while, around her waist, Julanna had tied a complex belt called the Knot of Hercules. When Artorex untied this belt, Gallia would be his.

The bride had taken care with every detail of her appearance.

The wedding might have been arranged in haste, but Gallia would be as radiant as her happiness – and her mother's cosmetics casket – could make her. Wisely, she had used only a touch of stibium to define her brows and eyes, but she had chosen to paint her lids with malachite, knowing that the rich emerald would enliven her face. A little staining of her lips with cinnabar, coupled with a hint of perfume of jasmine and henna on her palms, the soles of her feet and her nails completed her toilette.

Bemused and ignorant, Artorex watched his bride as she floated towards him, her beauty incandescent in the light of the braziers.

In the absence of a priest, Ector officiated over the brief ceremony.

'*Quando tu Gaius, ego Gaia*,' Gallia whispered in the ancient promise to follow whenever, and wherever, her husband travelled. Although the vow was a formality, Artorex found it vastly moving, as if he now possessed something of great rarity that had chosen to belong to him.

The barley cake was eaten, and the feasting began.

Flushed with wine, Artorex had little time to consider his lot. Did he truly want a wife? He knew that he wanted to possess Gallia, but was that lustful desire the same thing as love? The questions went round and round in his brain until his wits were muddled and he surrendered to the pleasure of the moment.

Bemused, he stared fixedly at his new wife who lay beside him on the eating couch.

Yes, she was fair. Her hair was a black aureole around her small head. Her lips were ripe and full and even that long, narrow, Roman nose was delicate, with nostrils that even now seemed to flare a little. Artorex felt his body stir.

Her eyes stared back at him. He saw them as deep amber pools that showed every thought that swam like fish within their depths. While the poets extolled pale eyes as windows to the soul, Artorex knew to his own satisfaction that it was the darker eyes that had the power to entrap a man within their warm depths.

Against all custom and decency, and because he could not help himself, Artorex bent over and kissed Gallia's full lips. He was lost in something that is akin to love.

Ector thumped the laden table with his fist.

'The groom is eager to depart, my friends. He searches for food other than this feast we have laid before him.'

The guests laughed, even Caius, but with good nature.

'You break with tradition, my boy, but I remember what it was like to be young. I would be anxious to depart myself if I was newly wed to your beautiful bride.'

The guests laughed again, and both Gallia and Artorex blushed.

Gallia took Ector at his word. Rising to her feet, she led Artorex away to her chamber that had recently been prepared by Frith, so that dried rose petals perfumed every corner of the room and scented oils burned in the lamps. Artorex was almost carried away from all self-control by the heady cloud of perfume and the wines that he had consumed during the feasting.

Gallia giggled like a little girl as Artorex stripped off his tunic and then struggled to untie her belt. In the lamplight, his body was beautiful as he stood clothed only in his loincloth, and his skin shone with a deep amber glow. She reached up and unplaited his hair, which tumbled into long brass-coloured curls under her fingers. His body quivered under this simple, gentle touch and he would have reached for her had she not motioned for him to lie on her perfumed bed.

Bemused, and aroused, Artorex obeyed.

Gallia eased off her wedding raiment with studied slowness.

Her body was revealed for him alone. For the first time he saw her heavy white breasts, with pink nipples that seemed to beg for his mouth, and her tiny waist that flared into womanly hips bisected by a bush of curling black hair.

'Gallia!' Artorex called. 'Come to bed – immediately!'

'No, my lord.'

'No?' Artorex was startled.

'I must fulfil my wifely duties.'

'Uh!'

Artorex knew he sounded foolish, but such was his state of arousal that her teasing was making him inarticulate and mindless.

From a small glass container, Gallia poured oil into one palm and then began to caress her husband's body. Under her delicate touch, all his nerve endings screamed, so that he believed, at last, that if this period of pleasure was the penultimate before marriage was consummated, then he was fortunate indeed. His shoulders, chest, belly and thighs, even the tender places between his toes, all received his wife's ministrations, until his will crumbled completely, and he pulled Gallia down on to her back and entered her without further ceremony.

Her face grimaced in pain, but Artorex was beyond thought. He luxuriated in her body, in the garden of her breasts and the flowers in her hair. He tasted her mouth, until her body also warmed under his hands and lips, and neither husband nor wife felt the sleet at the shutters, nor heard the wind wailing in the roof of the stables. Lost in the mysteries of Aphrodite, Artorex rode his wife until their marriage was sealed in mutual pleasure.

For Artorex, his new wife was a never-ending mystery and a marvel. Virginal she had been, but Gallia was as sensual as her Roman ancestors and was an intelligent lover who gloried in physical sensation. As a handsome young man, Artorex had known many women, but sex had been fast and unencumbered by any accompanying commitment, so it had seemed as trivial as a sneeze, or like eating when he was hungry.

Every day, when his duties as steward were done, Artorex sought Gallia out, even if she was playing with little Livinia, or gossiping away the last of the winter with Julanna. And Gallia always obeyed her husband, for she was as eager as he was for the pleasures of the bed. Trivial stimulations, even the sight of a bare foot, could ignite his lust, so that each day passed like an Otherworld dream and the only reality was his Gallia, laughing earthily as she stroked his body; Gallia, biting his shoulder until the blood came; Gallia, crying out with her eyes blind in a passion that was her very own.

Gallia had much to occupy her days, besides the heady distractions of lovemaking. After the death of her mother, the wives of her many brothers has seen to her wifely education over the years and she was already hard at work on a length of wool designed to serve as a winter tunic for her husband. She also took pleasure in learning the more mundane tasks of cheese-making, preserving fruits and curing meat. She might never need to prepare the food her family consumed, but no provident Roman matron would leave servants to their own devices without supervision.

As spring advanced, Gallia knew that she was with child. She hugged her belly and smiled those secret smiles that every woman in the villa could read with complete accuracy.

Around her, Gallia saw that new life was insistent and paramount. The landscape was newly washed by the onset of spring into a tapestry of green and chocolate; young lambs, calves, foals and chickens stumbled, cavorted and tumbled over their gangly limbs; puppies and kittens squirmed into every free nest of straw in the stables and the wild birds were noisy in the alder trees as they protected their nests. The whole world was pregnant, like Gallia, and she gloried in her new condition.

Artorex remained in blissful ignorance until Gallia chose her own time to tell him of the wonders that would soon come into his world.

One night, he lay spent upon their bed, his flesh fast cooling as Gallia slid down into the hollow of his shoulder and whispered in his ear.

'Will you cease to love me, my dearest master, when my belly is too big for the pleasures of the bed? Or will you find a compliant maid, my stallion, and leave me to pine?'

'What . . .?'

As with all men, Artorex was made to sound and act like an idiot when a woman holds the reins of love.

'Your heard my words, my heart.' She smiled shyly. 'There are quite a few months left for us, of course, but I fear our time alone may soon be over.'

'You are with child!' Artorex exclaimed flatly.

In all honesty, he had no idea how he felt about this unexpected news.

Gallia pouted. 'You sowed the seed, Artorex, and now your child grows within me. But I am fearful that a son of your size may well nigh kill me.'

Artorex felt a warm surge of pride run from the soles of his feet to the crown of his head. He had sired a child. It grew, even now, under his hand. The wonder and mystery of it almost stopped his heart.

Artorex kissed his wife's mouth, her belly and her heart, and she could find no fault in her husband's reaction to the news.

Now, spurred on by circumstances, Artorex had reason to work.

In what time was free to him, he began to clear Ector's bridal gift and, once the site was bare, he marked the outline of a simple six-roomed villa. He couldn't afford the luxuries of the Villa Poppinidii, but he would build his own house with his own two hands if he must, so that his child would know its own roof.

Artorex was blissfully and joyously happy, for he had never known such true contentment. And when villagers and servants showed their affection by assisting him to flag the earth with split stone, build walls of wattle and mud and lay out gardens for the developing house, Artorex knew that such unalloyed joy was both a temptation and a challenge to the gods who control us all.

He roofed his house in the Celtic way, with plaited thatch and split stakes of wood, so that the steep pitch of the roof could provide storage space for water as well as shedding rain or snow. Gallia looked at his strange, hybrid efforts and was happy as only a woman near full term can be.

The house was shaped like a square but open at one end, except for thick-planked wooden entrance gates. The courtyard, or atrium, was cobbled with river stone except for a small alcove that served as Coal's stable. Artorex built the manger and stall himself from wood dragged from the forest and sawn over a pit.

Until their house was completed, he and Gallia shared his cramped quarters at the Villa Poppinidii. Julanna vowed that she did not want her friend ever to leave, but Gallia pointed out that she would only be a short walk away. In fact, the stone flue from a chimney that Artorex had cunningly copied from a northern design could be clearly seen from the villa.

'But you will have to work like a servant,' Julanna pouted.

'Only if I wish to do so.' Gallia laughed. 'I still have my maid and manservant, and Frith has asked Lord Ector if her great-grandson, Gareth, could be permitted to work for Artorex. Fortunately, when Frith makes a decision, nothing deflects her.'

As his house grew, so did Gallia, and Artorex began to fear for his wife's health, so large was the child within her belly.

But still his fortune held. When Gallia's waters broke, her labour began quietly. Her tiny frame seemed unable to bear the great rippling surges of the contractions but, within a surprisingly short time, Gallia was delivered of a fine, healthy girl child, with dark, bronze curls and amber eyes.

When he held the strong, squirming body in his arms for the first time, Artorex thought his heart would break with his love and fears for her. Now he knew how Gallia had felt when her family had died of the pestilence. Now he understood Julanna's nameless fears for her child. He swore to protect his Licia, for so he named her, for as long as he lived.

When the child was one week old, and autumn had turned the land into a carpet of gold and flame, Bregan, the blacksmith, came to the gates of the Villa Poppinidii with a cloth-wrapped gift for Artorex. Bregan refused an offer of food and drink, and wouldn't stay, for Artorex was supervising his workers in the south pastures.

'I've kept my promise. Tell Lord Artorex I made this gift with all the skills I possess.'

When Artorex returned from the fields that evening, Gallia gave him Bregan's gift. As he struggled with the twine binding, she stared at her young man of nearly twenty-two years, and her heart was full and grateful.

Within the wrapping was a swathe of fresh grass. Within the grass was a dagger.

The blade was well over fifteen inches in length, slightly curved and shining. It was an instrument of death. The edges were razor-sharp and a vicious point ensured that the dagger would be perfect for both thrusting and slashing.

But it was the pommel that left Artorex and his wife gasping with surprise.

Bregan was a fine blacksmith and no one could conjure blades for scythes and reaping hooks so well in all the villages in the vicinity of Aquae Sulis. But Bregan had nurtured a streak of artistry in his soul that had been unused in his agricultural trade, until now.

Somehow, Bregan had designed and constructed an iron dragon. This creature was nothing like the pretty, malevolent toy that Llanwith bore on his dagger, but was a creature of such might that it could have sprung from the iron veins of the mountains themselves. The beast's head and body formed a pommel that was scaled so that the grip was firm, with the snarling mouth of the dragon at the very end of the shaft. Its half-furled wings curved backwards and offered protective wings of metal for the hand that held it. The dragon's tail curled forward in a strange spiral to enter the dragon's mouth at the end of the pommel. The owner's hand was cradled in a fist of iron.

Fish skin was bound around the dragon's body on the hilt, providing a cushion for the owner's hand. The gaping jaws and ridged brow bone of the snarling head formed nasty, jagged teeth on the pommel, perfect for striking at close range. The hilt of the knife mimicked the scales of the great dragon beast, creating a dagger that was strange, alien and wonderful.

Bregan had made a weapon quite unlike the straight-handled Roman short swords, or even the longer Celtic blades that possessed such beautiful twining decoration. Here was a blade that was neither sword nor dagger, one constructed both to kill and to protect, so that its owner need not fear that a sudden slash from an enemy would sever his fingers or shake his grip. This dagger was a miracle of function and beauty.

Artorex was stunned and his jaw dropped, causing Gallia to accuse him of looking like one of her brother's fish.

'I refused several potential husbands because they looked like cods,' she laughed, but her eyes were drawn to the strange, deadly weapon.

'I've never seen such a knife,' Artorex marvelled. 'See? The dragon's wings protect my knuckles, while the tail protects my palm and fingers. Bregan has created a masterpiece.'

'You deserve it,' Gallia insisted loyally.

'No,' Artorex murmured. 'I've no totem, least of all the dragon. Men such as Prince Llanwith deserve the protection of this beast, but who am I to carry the Winged Worm of the Celtic Kings?'

'You're my husband. You're heroic and noble, and I'll not listen to your silliness. Do your hear, Licia? Your father pretends that he's just like other men – the dolt! We know, don't we, my little dragonlet.'

When Targo was shown the weapon for the first time, he stroked it with his calloused fingers as if it were the body of a woman.

'Bregan has laboured over this weapon for more than a year. He pondered the design for many a day, searching for a totem that would do you justice. He chose the dragon, at last, because the Roman legions carried it, and also because it is a creature born in fire. He has made you a weapon the like of which I have never seen, a counter-balance to the sword. It is without the reach, but it is deadly as it waits for an opening. Truly, I envy you this gift.'

The men of the villa marvelled at the design of the dragon knife and many men hefted it to feel its wonderful balance. Bregan's gift drew many other warriors to his forge in the years that followed, but no weapon he designed ever matched the odd beauty of this simple iron knife. Later, Artorex would be given weapons with pommels of gold, silver and electrum and set with gems of great worth, but Bregan's dragon of iron would never leave his side.

So is the stuff of legends made.

Still, Artorex's idyll of happiness endured. When another

spring came, full of promise, his house was finished and the small family made their way to their new home. Otherwise, little changed at the Villa Poppinidii. Gallia had larger duties in her daily life, but she still spent her free time with Julanna and occasionally Gallinus sent money, so her small home filled with the household items that all women hold dear.

By the time the seasons changed and winter had come again, Gallia was pregnant once more and Artorex believed his waking dream would last forever.

Then the three travellers returned, after the passage of three long years, and with them came the time for Artorex to move towards his destiny at last.

CHAPTER X

AT VENTA BELGARUM

The solstice was at hand, and the days were grey and grim when the three travellers next visited the Villa Poppinidii. It had been a harsh winter thus far, and the earth had been frozen into iron, while the nights were made fearful by the howling of wolves. Half a dozen hides were stretched and freezing on the fence of the horse paddock, and Gallia was stitching a collar of wolf fur for Artorex's woollen cloak. In a dim afternoon, the horsemen rode up the treacherous, icy path to the villa.

Their baggage, such as they carried on their weary horses, was placed in their usual rooms by the servants of the villa, while the three men were led to the baths to wash away the rigours of their cold journey.

Then, at the customary welcome feast, Artorex met his patrons once again.

Myrddion clasped his arm in a display of friendship between equals and Artorex was surprised to see how lightly the eleven years since they had first met rested on the ascetic face of the scholar. Myrddion's skin was unlined and was as smooth as the complexion of a youth, but the white streak in his hair was wider now, almost shocking in its silver contrast with the black hair that still fell in a thick mane to his shoulder blades.

Luka, on the other hand, had aged considerably since

Artorex last bade him farewell. His plaits were threaded with white and he was heavily bearded. Most noticeable, beside a torc of massy gold around his throat, was a band of that same ruddy metal worn across his forehead. Power and responsibility had settled into the deep creases that ran from each nostril to the corner of his mouth, and extra flesh now padded his lithe frame with the trappings of authority.

As for the ever-silent Llanwith pen Bryn, the seasons had taken their toll on him also. His hair was thinning, even as his beard was now beginning to curl upon his breast. A great disc of the eternal serpent devouring its tail held his cloak at the shoulder, and heavy golden arm rings adorned each wrist.

The three men wore their might like great cloaks, so that Artorex wondered how he had ever dared to speak aloud in the presence of these noble leaders.

'What news from the east?' Ector asked, as was his custom each time the travellers arrived at the villa. The three guests looked grave and, as was usual, it was Myrddion who bore the weight of imparting unwelcome news.

'The Saxons advance daily, swelled by more and more shiploads of warriors, so that even Londinium will fall if Uther doesn't find a way to slow their march.'

Ector was shocked. Londinium was the greatest of the Romanized Celtic cities and the centre of Britain's commerce. Such news could not be immediately absorbed, least of all believed.

But Luka bore news that was even more alarming.

'My father, king of the Brigante, fell in a minor skirmish across the great mountains near Cataractonium. I am now king, and my warriors hold the mountains safe – but barely.'

'Your loss is our loss, King Luka.' Ector spoke with genuine regret and amazement. That the barbarians had moved so fast, in only three seasons, seemed impossible to credit.

'With every attack, they destroy our buildings, only to rebuild again in their own fashion,' Llanwith added gruffly. 'Every temple of Rome or church of the Christian God is razed to the ground and, behind them, the barbarians leave only a path of death and carrion birds. The holy oaks are felled to provide the timbers that make their halls. Our world is slowly dying, my friend, even though, as my father's heir, I now hold the Marches strong. They will be the last to fall. I swear, while my hand can still wield a sword.'

'Sore news travels tardily to us, for we are far removed from the centres of commerce, my lord, and your words are hard to imagine,' Ector replied. 'But the Villa Poppinidii will do everything in its power to aid the High King, especially if it keeps the barbarians away from our own fields.'

'That's good, friend Ector, for we are called to Venta Belgarum in the south. We wish to take your steward, Artorex, with us, so he might see for himself what chaos is brought to the goodness of the land, and also to swear allegiance to the High King,' Myrddion stated. This was not a request, it was an order. His words were heavy with authority and left no room for protest.

Yet Artorex dared to question his instructions.

'My lords, I am newly married. I have a small daughter, and even now my wife quickens with another child. How can I leave them, husbandless and fatherless, in these perilous times?'

The three lords looked at each other and amazement and chagrin were written in equal measure on three sets of tightened lips.

'You're married?' Llanwith queried with amazement.

Artorex chose to be insulted, for Gallia's sake, if not for his own.

'Yes, my lord. I have wed Gallia of the House of Gallus.'

'This is preposterous!' Llanwith snapped and Artorex rose to his feet with his hand hovering near his dragon knife.

Myrddion, as always, eased the sudden tension that filled the dining room.

'A worthy wife, and a worthy family,' Myrddion murmured. 'As I recall, she's the young lady who was here on the Night of the Innocents.' He smiled at Artorex. 'Is she still scarred or was my handcraft good?'

'Your work on her wounds was excellent, Lord Myrddion. She had to cut the rest of her wonderful mane but her hair grew back soon enough and covered the wound.'

'So speaks the lover,' Luka muttered drily under his breath.

Ector broke into the conversation, for he recognized the rise in Artorex's slow but inexorable temper, and he could see the dangerous flattening in his foster-son's eyes.

'If Artorex is needed, then Artorex must go, and he can be assured that the Villa Poppinidii will care for his family as surely as if he were present. Caius and I can muddle our way through his duties during his absence.' He turned to Myrddion. 'I'm still not entirely sure, my friend, why you should need the boy so badly.'

'Artorex is a man, not a boy, and he is also a weapon,' Luka said imperiously. 'Have we not honed him to sharpness over these many years?'

Artorex was pale with anger. 'My lords, I am a person! I am myself! I am Artorex! If my master orders me to journey with you, then so be it. But I'm no man's tool, even if he is a king.'

All three visitors looked up at Artorex's haughty, angry face. They exchanged closed, knowing glances.

Luka nodded unwillingly in his direction. 'Perhaps my words had a sting that was not intended, Artorex. I was merely surprised by your change of circumstances.'

'You've been absent from the Villa Poppinidii for more than two years, my lords. How could my life not change during your absence? For, in truth, it doesn't wait upon your bidding.'

'Be silent, Artorex!' Ector ordered sharply, for he was becoming seriously alarmed by the words and manner of his foster-son. He was usually so equable of temper and so rational by nature that to see the rise of killing rage turn Artorex's eyes almost colourless and blank gave the old warrior a nasty twinge. 'You'll go to the Mistress Gallia and assure her that I'll be as a father to her during your absence. And you'll send word to Targo in the village. Gallia will sleep better if she knows that the old rogue will guard your back.'

'I'll abide by your advice, Master Ector.'

Artorex and Caius bowed and took their leave, but Artorex lagged behind and, as soon as Caius had disappeared down the colonnade, Artorex crept back to the doorway. He didn't hold with secrets that concerned him, even secrets held by the great ones of the west.

'Why did you allow the boy to marry?' Llanwith grumbled at Ector, as if the master had conspired with Artorex to wreck long-cherished plans.

'My friends, I don't understand your concern for the lad. The match was very good, and was well above what Artorex could normally expect to achieve.'

'Above his station?' Luka scoffed.

Ector stared at him in surprise.

And then, almost as if Llanwith guessed that ears listened, the voices became indistinct rumbles, and Artorex was left frustrated and angry – and feeling extremely foolish.

Gallia greeted the news of her husband's imminent departure with a hot flood of tears. Normally, she was not a woman prone to fits of weeping but to be deprived of her husband in the depths of a harsh winter and for no particular reason that he could explain, dismayed and frightened her.

Her moods had been mercurial since Licia's birth, and Frith

had counselled Artorex to be patient with her, for women sometimes acted strangely when they bore children. And so Artorex accepted her occasional mood swings and periods when she feared that all her happiness was doomed.

He privately agreed with Gallia's complaint on this occasion. Why his presence on the journey to the south was so important was a mystery to him. Why would his absence matter? Artorex made a valiant attempt to soothe Gallia's fears and passed on Ector's promises, but all she could envisage was bearing a child alone while her husband was deep in the south and riding into unknown dangers. She was certain that he would never return to her arms.

'I know that Ector's orders are hard to understand, my love, especially when he only accedes to the desires of the travellers. I don't wish to leave you, but perhaps I'll discover what threats might come to the gates of the Villa Poppinidii in time to avert them. I'll return, I swear to you, and I'll be as deeply in love with you as I am now. I care for our little Licia too much to extend my absence and, with luck, I'll return before the new babe is born.'

'And perhaps you won't.'

Gallia wept until Artorex kissed away her fears and took her to bed. There, as he stroked her warm little body and kissed her belly, where the swelling showed that the child grew, he felt the same tenderness that he had felt when Licia was born. For a short moment, as they moved together with the sensuousness and passion that Gallia always brought to their bed, Artorex was sickened by a fear that he might lose her.

Perhaps Gallia felt the same fear.

'You'll forget me when you see the ladies of the High King's court. My breasts are chewed by a babe and the purple marks of childbearing cover my hips and stomach,' she murmured wetly against his chest.

'I consider each mark to be a badge of honour, far more honourable than the scars of battle,' Artorex joked lightly. 'Truly, if the badges of childbearing were left on the bodies of men, there'd be no babes born at all. Besides, your breasts are beautiful, so how could I forget them? I think you're more likely to forget me, now that you are mistress of a house. You can have a dozen men as good as me, if not better.'

'I love you more than my life, Artorex,' Gallia said, smiling back at him. 'Now, I have no wish to sleep, my lord, since we will part tomorrow. You must remind me of all that I will miss in the long weeks to come.'

Artorex spent the next morning detailing the many necessary duties that must be handled if the Villa Poppinidii was to function like the well-ordered machine he had developed. During the discussion, Targo arrived, a sword and dagger at his side and an old Roman shield slung over his back. He was obviously eager to travel south with his most favoured pupil.

But Artorex was still troubled and sought out the faithful Frith to calm his growing dread. As usual, he found the slave woman in her accustomed warm corner of the kitchen, while maids bustled about her, packing provisions for his journey.

'I've been expecting you to visit me,' Frith said calmly. 'The world has come to Artorex, and he's afraid!'

'My fears aren't for myself, Mother Frith, but for Gallia, Licia and the child that will soon be born. I ask you to keep them safe. I'll sleep easier for knowing that your wise eyes are upon my family. I sense danger in the air. It smells of blood and, yes, I'm afraid!'

Frith clasped both his large hands in hers and he felt the strength of her character and purpose that even great old age could not dim. She smiled up at him with the same openness and trust that Livinia had given to him as she died. Artorex felt a surge of affection – of love – so complete and visceral that he considered, for a moment, how blessed he was. Strong, extraordinary women had nurtured him and he had accepted their affection for him without thought. Livinia was dead and she would never be able to know his gratitude and love for her. But Frith was still alive. Before he departed on a journey that might be dangerous, Artorex decided to tell the servant woman how important she was to him.

'But Artorex,' Frith said seriously when he had told her of his feelings, 'I always knew that you cared for me, even though you found it difficult to tell me your feelings. You can be assured that I'll keep your family safe, my dear. Aye. And Gareth will help me. The villa can spare me for a time, so your family will be within sight of these tired old eyes. Trust me, Artorex, for I swear I'll do as I have promised – until death takes me.'

'Death wouldn't dare to come near you, old Frith, for you've scared him witless your whole life,' Artorex joked. 'I'm comforted by your words, little mother.'

'Ah, my lad, I wish I'd been your mother. I always have!'

Frith chose to be silent concerning her own dread. The old woman felt something unfurl its dark wings and take flight from her withered breasts, something that had waited decades to take to the winds. She'd dreamed of crows for three consecutive nights and her brave words hid her unspoken thoughts.

I'll not let anything harm my boy, even if the gods have decided otherwise, she swore to herself as she hurried over the fields to Artorex's house. Perhaps I'm imagining horrors that don't exist – for who would threaten the peace of a provincial steward?

Still, Frith felt that Artorex's destiny was unfurling at last and even as she comforted Gallia with well-chosen platitudes, her arthritic fingers trembled with an incomprehensible anxiety.

So Artorex departed from the Villa Poppinidii and the

civilized world of Aquae Sulis for the first time in his memory. Although darkness had seeped into the weak daylight that struggled to light their journey, no fear of wolves or outcasts would shake the purpose of the travellers to ride all through that first long night. A rutted track would lead them south across the mountains to meet the Roman road that would carry them to Sorviodunum, and thence, by an easier route, to Venta Belgarum itself. Coal set his hooves dancing on the treacherous black ice of the road and the scent of snow filled the evening air.

'I'll see the Giant's Dance on my journey,' he marvelled. 'And I'll see the great plain where the strange stones lean drunkenly – the place where wights are said to steal away a man's reason.'

In some matters, Artorex was still a boy, so little of the world had he seen during his twenty-three years. The adventure of his journey was exciting, for all that he was already missing Gallia. Only thoughts of her, waif-like in her warmest cloak and clutching her squirming toddler to her breast, dampened his anticipation. His ordained place in life lay with the Villa Poppinidii, small as that place might be in the thinking of Celtic kings. His place in the world could never be Venta Belgarum, Sorviodunum or even Londinium itself.

In the darkness, lit only by a moon as bloated and as pale as the face of a drowned man, the horses picked their way cautiously through frozen mud. Luka pressed the small group onward, at a walk but without wasting time for rest or comfort. In the early morning, as the weak sun rose over the horizon to reveal a rough landscape of treacherous shale and glowering trees, Luka brought the party to a halt to allow the travellers a short period of sleep. The horses were hobbled so they could not escape yet could search out what dry grass might be found in this wild and unforgiving place.

'You may have four hours only for sleeping,' Luka warned.

'Time marches onwards, and our presence is awaited at Venta Belgarum.'

The earth was hard with frost, but Artorex was very weary after a day and two nights with little sleep. Yet, on the very brink of dreaming, his exhausted brain conjured up an image of his family. Already he was beginning to forget those fair and familiar faces, and tears leapt unbidden to moisten his sleepy eyes.

Only a moment seemed to pass before Targo nudged his ribs with his soft riding boot.

'It's time to eat, boy,' the old man said cheerfully and thrust a small bowl into Artorex's numb fingers. 'It's gruel, and it's hardly fit to eat, but I still recall how I enjoyed such meals.'

'You're nostalgic, you old faker!' Artorex waved a hand over the rising landscape, the silent valleys and the crows that called hoarsely from a stand of nearby pine trees. 'You actually love all of this. If I'd known that you took pleasure in this jaunt, I would have demanded payment from you before allowing you to come with me.'

'Master Ector gave me my marching orders, lad, and don't you forget it.' Targo smiled crookedly at the young man. 'He told me I was to guard your back – it was so plain that even I understood. But aye, I'll admit to you, boy, I love being on the road. I've missed it for near on fifteen years while I've been in Ector's service; there's nothing like the tang of wood smoke, danger and blood to make a man feel alive.'

As noon turned to afternoon in their steady climb up the low hills, even Artorex couldn't maintain his feelings of ill-use and resentment. The cold air flushed his face under his grey, wolf-pelt collar which he used to fashion a half cowl to cover his head and shoulders. Gallia had lined the hide with soft wool, and Artorex knew he cut an odd but not uncivilized figure. The boy inside him was fascinated by the circling hawks as they hunted for unwary rabbits, and the presence of rooks, ravens and huge black crows that seemed more numerous than in the softer landscape of Aquae Sulis.

'They always give me the horrors,' Targo said conversationally, nodding towards the carrion birds as he eased his horse next to Coal on a wider part of the track. 'The buggers will take the eyes out of a dead man's head as neat as can be. Actually, they aren't too fussy if the man isn't quite dead, either.'

'Thank you, friend Targo, for one more lesson on the pleasantries of the battlefield,' Artorex retorted sardonically. 'But I suppose even birds have to eat.'

'With them it's more than hunger – they're nature's way of cleaning up the mess, I suppose. I've fought in places where it was so hot, I thought my armour would burn my skin black – and those carrion eaters were there. I've fought in places where you piss ice – and they're still there, waiting to clean up the mess.'

'All things must live, Targo,' Myrddion called back to the old veteran without bothering to turn his head.

'I just don't want them to live on me,' Targo muttered, and tapped the side of his nose.

Artorex laughed out loud and disturbed the crows, which rose from the trees in a small cloud of black wings.

At Luka's urging, they rode as fast as the landscape and the condition of the horses would permit. Another day passed as the small troop climbed over the last of the low hills and approached a flat, grey-green expanse that stretched as far as the eye could see.

'The Great Plain,' Myrddion said. 'And over yonder, that's the Giant's Dance.'

Artorex could see that the Roman road on which they now travelled bypassed the Giant's Carol that was a familiar marker on the road to Sorviodunum. He also deduced that the road was designed to avoid the structure, for the Carol was a magical thing that was beyond rational explanation – even rational Roman understanding. There was no opportunity to closely examine the stone teeth with their great raised lintels but the gaping open circle seemed incomprehensible and menacing.

Artorex decided that the stone in his glade in the Old Wood was a brother to these rough-hewn, grey pillars, not tall in the winter light, but thick and mossy – and dreadful.

'What do you think of the Carol, Artorex?' Myrddion asked. 'My people believe that the Sun God spirited these stones across the Sea of Hibernicus from the Blessed Isles, and laid them out here, exactly as you see them now, to claim this land for his children forever.'

'It's a pretty tale, but do you believe it, my lord?' Artorex countered.

The older man laughed, openly and without guile. 'No, Artorex, I don't believe in magical stones that fly. Men built the Carol – and surely not Myrddion, the Lord of Light.'

'You were named for the Sun God, my lord?'

'Aye.' Then Myrddion sighed. 'I was given my name many years ago, and the words spoken over me froze me into the man you see before you, with neither living wife nor children. It is destined that only the exercise of power and influence will be my lot.'

Artorex's last view of the stone circles was of a brooding, grey landscape as they passed. Hamlets sent up plumes of smoke from holes in sod roofs, but the riders avoided all civilization. Even Sorviodunum was bypassed, although Artorex saw the palisades of its walls in the distance and wondered why wood was used to repel any threat of attack.

Fire burns and consumes wood, so why don't they use stone? he asked himself as he remembered his own house with its walls constructed of field rock and mud brick.

The end of their long journey was now approaching. The roads they travelled were well maintained and carried a heavy traffic of traders, bands of warriors and priests. Without exception, fellow itinerants gave Myrddion's party a wide berth, not only because they were recognized as men of power but also because the four men had a grim, purposeful mien.

'It seems that the world journeys to Venta Belgarum,' Luka said derisively. 'They call Uther Pendragon a failed and dying man but, when he calls, they come.'

'Who else is there to rule in such desperate times other than the High King?' Artorex asked, but his question was ignored.

Artorex was unshaven and dirty when they reached the low stone and wooden walls of Venta Belgarum. He was embarrassed by his wolf cloak and by the stubble on his face, for Venta Belgarum was the largest and most extraordinary city that Artorex had ever seen.

In reality, the thatched and sod-roofed cottages that clustered outside its walls had sprung up around a small Roman administrative centre that controlled the protected ports to the south that welcomed trade from Gaul and elsewhere in the Roman world. Inside the walls, the buildings were of wood construction and were plastered and decorated in the Roman style. The only exception was a small stone building perched on a rise at the centre of the city.

'What is that place, Myrddion?' Artorex asked, pointing to the strange, unwieldy structure.

'That's a temple dedicated to the Christian god and presided over by Branicus, the bishop. Uther Pendragon professes to be a Christian, especially since many highly born Romans have embraced the Jewish faith, so he keeps court at Venta Belgarum when he can, in order to be near his confessor.'

Artorex scratched reflectively at the stubble on his chin.

'Does the king rely on his gods or on his strong right arm?' he asked Luka, who stood beside him. 'And where does he reside if the strongest of these houses is used by his priest?'

'You ask many questions, Artorex,' Luka answered gravely. 'I know that Uther pays homage to the Christian god and to his confessor, for he believes his sins will be washed away by the Christ. And if you had waded in as much blood as Uther, you would also need spiritual comfort when Death peers over your shoulder.'

Artorex snorted in disbelief, for as far as he was concerned, praying was a sign of weakness if a man depended on it overmuch. Targo had taught him, as a boy and as a man, to trust firstly in himself.

'There is the hall where the High King resides.' Llanwith pointed towards a courtyard and a long building with shallow steps that elevated it above the mud of the roadway. The basic construction was of timber, and artisans had carved every exposed beam and wall, so that dragons, serpents and creatures of legend writhed upon every surface. The carving had been gilded and painted with such skill that the strange animals almost seemed to move and breathe. But Artorex grimaced as he looked beneath the splendour and recognized the decay in the fine structure, in its fading, rain-washed paintwork and its splitting decoration. The rot was barely noticeable as yet, but it was there, visible in the blackened beams in the forecourt where great braziers had been permitted to lick their flames and dark smoke into the ceilings.

Uther's Great Hall was splendid, gorgeous and dying.

The hour was late, and the party didn't have the luxury of time to bathe, so the small and rather odorous group handed their horses to stable workers and joined a growing crowd of supplicants in the forecourt. Artorex brushed at his clothing in a vain attempt to remove the worst of the mud and wondered at the perfumed sycophants who talked vivaciously in corners while beautiful women clustered with their menfolk like brightly painted butterflies. One woman's face, partly hidden by a heavy black cowl that covered her hair, seemed oddly familiar to the young man, but she passed Artorex without acknowledging him.

A servant hurried to Myrddion's shoulder and bowed low. He whispered hastily in Myrddion's ear and nodded towards huge, wooden doors that were decorated with winged serpents and birds with the faces of women – all covered with beaten metal.

'Uther summons us,' the scholar stated bluntly, turning to his friends. 'Now you will learn, Artorex, on what shoulders the fate of our world rests.'

Servants bowed and opened the brazen doors, permitting the five members of the party to pass through unhindered. Inside, huge Celtic warriors with long bound hair and torcs of various metals and decorations, as befitted their stations, formed a guard at the door. More men were standing behind the dais at the far end of the draughty hall. Even a roaring fire in a central stone pit couldn't heat the chill air, and Artorex was glad of his wolf pelt, for all that it made him seem to be first cousin to a barbarian. Fortunately, the ceiling was high; the thick grey smoke formed an overhead blanket that stained and obscured the painted serpents in the rafters.

Artorex looked up and spied a round hole cut into the ceiling to allow the smoke to escape, which it dismally failed to do.

This hall is primitive, he thought in amazement, remembering Ector's villa and its warm floors and cosy rooms.

Two shallow steps led to a dais above the level of the many warriors, Druids, priests and tribal aristocrats who huddled by the many smaller braziers inside the large, chilly room. On the dais sat a shrunken figure shrouded entirely in an over-robe of thick, luxuriant bear fur. The man's face was old, its sallow skin stretched thinly over massive bones. His mouth was cruel and the corners were turned up in a parody of a smile, even when his lips were at rest. The eyes in that vicious face were buried in heavy pouches, but Artorex could see the glint of steel-blue irises gazing at him, as inflexible as bluestone from the western mountains. This skeletal mask was the face of a man who still held the reins of power in his huge wasted hands that clutched the arms of his chair. The malice that ruled him was evident in the puckered full mouth and its empty, meaningless smile.

'Hail, Uther, High King of the Britons!' Myrddion paid homage to the man in a voice so ringing that it carried to the furthest corners of the Great Hall. Then he sank to his knees. 'I have come, Lord Uther, as you ordered.'

'Hail, Uther, High King and Liege Lord,' Luka and Llanwith repeated, also sinking to their knees.

Rather awkwardly, Artorex and Targo dropped to the hard, stone-flagged floor, unsure of their purpose in such exalted company.

Three women sat on silken cushions on the dais. Artorex observed them closely from under his lowered head and eyelashes, while Uther Pendragon called for a wine cup, arrogantly leaving his guests to kneel at his feet.

The oldest woman had long passed her fiftieth year, a very respectable age for a female, but her ruined beauty was a sad contrast to the complexions of the younger women who attended to her needs. She was dressed in various shades of blue and grey wools, including a finely woven shawl that half concealed the faded hair that had once been rich and nut-brown. Half hidden by drooping eyelids, her eyes were a clear, clean grey. The jewels at her throat, great cabochon sapphires and misshapen pearls, and the golden rings on every finger, even her thumbs, proclaimed her status.

For the first time, Artorex looked on the face of the fabled

Ygerne, wife of Uther Pendragon and widow of Gorlois, the Boar of Cornwall.

The two women who sat beside her, one on her left and one on the right, had a strong physical resemblance to Ygerne but lacked the Otherworld beauty that legend swore had driven Uther mad with desire in the days of his vigorous middle age. The older of the two females lowered her black cowl and Artorex was stunned to recognize the odd face of Morgan, itinerant fortune teller and beggar, now decked in gold chains over her sable robes. The woman on Ygerne's left was younger and softer than Morgan, and she seemed petulant at being forced to sit in the chill hall for hours. Like Ygerne, her hair was covered, signifying her wedded state, but she disdained her sister's black raiment. She wore an ermine-edged cloak of dusky crimson and her under-robe was a rich, clear yellow.

'Rise, my guests, rise!' Uther ordered as he sipped wine warmed with honey. 'Well, Myrddion, my sharpest eye in the east. What havoc do the Saxons bring to discomfort me now?'

'They bring fire and death, burned cities and ruined temples and churches.' Myrddion spoke slowly and with ponderous gravity, as if he could stir the High King to action by the power of his words alone. 'By spring, when the next wave comes, their foothold on our lands will be complete. I fear that we shall never drive them out, sire, if you do not choose to strike before they are within their own fortified walls.'

Uther ignored Myrddion and turned his reptilian eyes on the two kings who accompanied him.

'Welcome, friend Luka, King of the Brigante, and pen Bryn, King of the Ordovice. I bid you rest in my city, and know that I mourn with you for the deaths of your fathers. Yet, as I'm sure you agree, it's sometimes a good thing that old men eventually die – especially fathers!'

Myrddion had flushed when Uther ignored his words utterly, but now it was the turn of Luka and Llanwith to clench their fists and redden across their cheekbones at Uther's calculated insult.

'Never, my lord, for those who love their kin,' Llanwith answered, his body strung tight with repressed rage.

'And who are your other companions? They're a pretty duo of oddities – obviously the long and the short of it all.'

The courtiers in the hall responded to their king's rasping laughter with polite titters of their own, although Artorex's great size and Targo's small but tangible sense of menace were not the natural subjects of jokes. Artorex noticed that no guards smiled, for their wary eyes had scanned the pair as soon as they walked through the brazen doors and had immediately deemed them to be fellow warriors.

Myrddion beckoned Artorex and Targo forward. His dark eyes begged the young man to exercise caution.

'I have brought Artorex, foster-son of Lord Ector of the Villa Poppinidii at Aquae Sulis, a warrior. His companion is Targo, a Roman veteran and Artorex's personal guard.'

Uther's lips curled as he chewed upon a new jest at Artorex's expense. Artorex composed his features so that his grey eyes and chiselled face showed nothing of the thoughts passing through his brain.

'Remove that covering from your head and come closer. I wish to look at you.'

'Aye, my King,' Artorex replied and swept off the wolf-pelt cloak. He passed it carefully to Targo without permitting his flat eyes to leave Uther's face.

Artorex's extraordinary hair, plaited at the side but free to tumble and curl down his back, caught the reflection of the fires in a blaze of ruddy gold and blood-red. His great height allowed him to look directly into Uther's eyes.

As old blue irises met impenetrable grey, the air crackled and hissed with tension.

'Who was your father, boy? Or don't you know?' Uther grinned mirthlessly, with a sneer of contempt. 'What would I care for Aquae Sulis, or Ector of the Old Forest? Provincial Romans, lad! Provincial nobodies!'

No one laughed.

'I don't know my lineage, my King, but Lucius of Glastonbury must hold the secret of my birth. On his orders, I was sent to Master Ector as a babe and he has continued to pay red gold for my tutelage these twenty-three years.'

A small cry escaped from Ygerne's lips. Instantly, she covered her mouth with her hand while her faded eyes devoured Artorex's face and form.

Morgan smiled enigmatically at Uther Pendragon. She seemed oblivious of her mother's distress, while she fed off Uther's sudden gasp of consternation.

Uther was no dissembler. He sat rigidly, his beringed fingers gripping the wood of his chair arms with whitened knuckles.

'Where did you get that dagger, boy?' Uther pointed to the dragon knife on Artorex's left hip. His forefinger trembled, ever so slightly. 'I want to see it! Bring it to me – someone – anyone!' His voice rose to an old man's quaver.

Artorex drew out the long blade from its scabbard and handed it, hilt first, to a grey-haired warrior who approached from the King's right hand.

Once Uther had the knife in his grip, his fingers traced the iron dragon on its hilt, following the creature's spine along the tail and back to its wicked mouth.

'Who gave you leave to use *my* dragon?' Uther snapped, his eyes burning, malicious and vindictive within their pouches of wrinkled flesh.

227

Artorex was perplexed and for the first time he permitted his face to show his confusion.

'That isn't *your* dragon, my lord. A blacksmith from a village near to my home forged the knife for me. He believed he owed me a debt, and he copied its features from the Dracos Legion standard.'

Myrddion moved forward, his body taut with apprehension.

'Aquae Sulis remains very Roman, my king. The Dracos Legion left its mark upon the towns closest to Llanwith's lands, where the Romans built their forts. This dragon is Dracos of Rome, with some refinements. No insult was ever intended, my lord.'

A thin sheen of sweat covered Myrddion's face. Artorex had never seen him alarmed or disconcerted, and he felt his nerves twitch. Why was Myrddion so frightened? And why did this mad old tyrant play cruel games with his guests?

'Hmmff!' Uther grunted. Plainly, he wasn't mollified. He returned the knife to his guard who, in turn, placed it in Artorex's hands.

The old warrior chosen for the task examined every line of Artorex's face during this process. Then he honoured the younger man with the slightest hint of a bowed head.

'It's a fine weapon, young sir,' the guard said quietly.

Uther turned to Myrddion.

'Are you playing with me?' he snapped, while Artorex thought irreverently that the mouth of his king was like a pike's maw, filled with wicked teeth and rapacity. 'Why did you bring this lad to me, Myrddion? What are you plotting?'

'Sire, Lord Ector is a friend of the west, and he's a stalwart supporter of your Highness in all that you do. His ties to Aquae Sulis are strong and, where he leads, many of the common people will follow. Within his own small sphere, Artorex has performed many heroic deeds. At great personal risk, he destroyed a group of depraved child killers, and he is, arguably, the ablest warrior in the north-west. I brought him to Venta Belgarum to pay homage to you, and to offer his strong arm and cold logic to you for use against the Saxons.' He dropped to his knees and bowed his head in supplication. 'I wouldn't plot against the High King of Britain, sire. Ever! I have been your loyal servant for longer than I care to remember, and so I will always remain.'

'Enough, Myrddion, I can only tolerate so many compliments in one day.'

The old man gnawed on one yellowed nail and then smiled with malicious delight. As he formulated his plans, he almost gloated as he stared at Artorex's aureole of amber hair.

'We shall soon see whether your boast is true,' he giggled. His attention remained fixed on Artorex. 'Artorex? That is your name?'

'Yes, my lord.'

'Are you willing to undertake a small sporting contest against the best of my warriors? Or don't you trust your arm?'

'I'll do whatever you desire, my king, if it gives you pleasure,' Artorex replied evenly.

Uther heard Morgan laugh softly at his words. The sound was delicate and mocking, like the tinkling of silver bells.

'My suggestion amuses you, Morgan? Well! If that is so, perhaps you, your sister and your mother will watch the contest with me and be entertained.' The High King did not even trouble to glance at the women.

'I'll welcome it, my dearest stepfather,' Morgan replied, her face as reptilian as the mask of her king. 'Anything to break the tedium of endless speech.'

Uther made a dismissive motion with his hand and Myrddion gripped Artorex's elbow and pulled him backward bodily.

'Bow, boy!' he hissed and the five warriors backed away from the uncertain temper of their king.

As Uther turned his attention to some new petition, Ygerne swept away, almost at a run, her blue skirts swirling about her and loose tendrils of bound hair flying about her anguished face. Her daughters followed her at a more sedate pace while, behind them, a low hum of muffled conversation drew attention to her odd retreat.

The five men backed swiftly and silently out through the brazen doors and into the forecourt. Once those doors had closed on fresh meat for Uther's pleasure and malice, Artorex turned to the three travellers – as they would always remain in his mind.

'That madman is Uther Pendragon?' Artorex asked Luka, his face at last permitted to register his disgust.

'He's not a lunatic, Artorex. Our task would be far easier if he were. Uther was always a predator, so perhaps the cruelty in his nature was the quality that permitted him to assume the mantle of High King. But his internal fires have burned low. He's lost the will to take risks, so he vents his bloodlust and frustration on those nearest to him, including those who are faithful unto death.'

Luka explained the situation calmly and quietly, but Artorex saw that his hands twitched and clenched.

'He must die!' Llanwith hissed and the faces of his old friends blanched at his treasonous words.

'Don't say or think such treachery,' Myrddion ordered the western king. 'Not when we are so close to success. We walk between knife points here, but we have delivered a message to Uther. Perhaps the sorry impasse between the west and the Saxons will finally be broken if the High King is forced to march against our enemies.'

'You dream, old friend,' Llanwith grumbled as they

strode out into the cold night. 'Uther will only act when Artorex's head is delivered to him on a platter. And then he'll dance a jig rather than go to war. We're taking enormous risks, Myrddion.'

Perplexed, Artorex looked directly at Myrddion.

'Why do you continue to speak in riddles?' he protested. 'I don't understand. Why would Uther want me dead? And why does Llanwith hate our king with such passion?'

'With Llanwith's permission, and without going into detail as even the night wind has ears in Venta Belgarum, perhaps I can explain,' Myrddion began.

'I've no objection,' Llanwith rumbled testily.

'Uther didn't turn into a monster overnight,' Myrddion said softly to avoid any chance of being overheard. 'He was ever a difficult, capricious man, as his . . . punishment of Gorlois of Cornwall indicates.'

'I've no idea what you're talking about,' Artorex complained.

Myrddion sighed irritably. 'The older woman on the dais, Queen Ygerne, was once married to Gorlois, the Boar of Cornwall. Uther gazed on her face but once, and he lusted after her. He seduced her by trickery and when Gorlois objected, Uther sent him into a battle where the Boar was killed treacherously. Later, Ygerne quickened with child, so Uther took her as his wife. Those who knew Uther's secret believe that the child died in childbirth, leaving Uther without a legitimate heir. The other women sitting with Ygerne on the dais are Morgan and Morgause, the daughters of Gorlois.'

'I've met Morgan, although she was pretending to be a poor fortune teller at the time,' Artorex murmured. 'How does she feel about Uther?'

'Can't you tell?' Luka interrupted. 'She loathes him to the point of obsession so she conspires to stay as close to him as she can. Morgan is a beautiful woman, but I'd be afraid to be alone in the same room with her. She'd castrate a man as soon as look at him, and then expect him to be grateful for her gift.'

'Your language is colourful, Luka, but it doesn't explain why Llanwith and his king are at odds,' Myrddion retorted testily. 'The other vain bitch is Queen Morgause. She's married to Lot, the King of the Otadini, who rules the low lands north of the Wall. Lot may be fat, but he's a formidable fighter and an important ally of the west. With his marriage connections, he considers himself to be a claimant to Uther's throne. The children of Gorlois are dangerous women, so be warned, my young friend. You may be assured that I'll be expecting an explanation of how you became acquainted with Morgan.'

Myrddion paused.

'At the time of which we speak, Llanwith's late father was king of the Ordovice tribe. Like many good Celts, he disapproved of the fate that befell any Dumnonii warriors who refused to accept Uther's version of the death of King Gorlois. Uther created a credible lie, but many prominent men found it hard to believe that Gorlois was a traitor and deserved his sticky end. Consequently, Uther was angry with the Ordovice and his spite resulted in the death of Llanwith's uncle. Uther sent him to Camulodunum with a troop of hand-picked warriors. They were slaughtered by the Saxons.'

Artorex raised an eyebrow as he absorbed this information. How could Uther be at fault if Llanwith's kin had died in battle?

'I can tell that you don't understand the ruthless subtlety of your High King, Artorex,' Llanwith said in a voice that was quiet and calm. 'My uncle and his troop were all men who had angered Uther in some way and, somehow, the Saxons were warned of the foray. My father didn't believe in coincidences – and neither do I.'

Artorex was unable to find anything to say in either

sympathy or understanding. He stood and watched as the three travellers made their way out of the forecourt.

'I wish someone – anyone – would tell me what is going on,' Artorex exclaimed to the cold air and then stirred his long legs to join Myrddion, Llanwith and Luka, who were striding off into the afternoon darkness.

'I can't tell what the king requires of you,' Targo answered his pupil drily. 'But I do know that the old bugger doesn't like you overmuch. I thought we'd be put to the sword when he saw that knife of yours. One of the first things I learned in the legions was that a common soldier should stay as far as possible from them that gives the orders. It stands to reason that leaders such as Uther Pendragon have far deeper games to play than to care for the pawns who exist within their world.'

The deepening gloom was pervasive, but the snow clouds had fled at last. The stars appeared like white holes burned into the sable cloth of the skies and Artorex ached to think that Gallia and Licia could see those same stars from their snug villa. Around him, the stillness of silent walkways smelled of danger so that he set his feet on the cobbles carefully and lightly, his hand resting on the pommel of his sword.

Mud and filth collected in the corners of the city, as if a high tide had washed a detritus of rubbish through the alleyways when the citizens were asleep. The corpse of a dog, stiff-legged in rigor, lay frozen near a stone doorstep, and Artorex smelled the rank odour of raw sewerage that overlaid the even more nauseatingly sweet stink of death.

Artorex had come to Venta Belgarum and had discovered that it was further from home than he could ever have imagined.

CHAPTER XI

TRIAL OF STRENGTH

As the five men settled their weary bones in their rooms in the Wild Boar Inn, the apartments of Queen Ygerne were in unaccustomed disarray.

Ygerne had torn her sleeping room apart, tossing cushions, coverlets and boxes of perfumed wood into a great pile on the rush-matted floor. Her hair had come undone as she smashed and ripped her own treasures in an excess of anger and fear. Now she lay, curled up protectively on her wool-stuffed pallet, and wept bitter, scalding tears.

Morgan entered quietly, followed by a timid maidservant who began to clean up the mess.

'Is he trying to drive me mad?' Ygerne raised her tear-ravaged face to her daughter and gripped Morgan's hands tightly. 'What does he want of me?'

'Who, Mother?'

'Uther! God save my soul, does the man hate me so much that he finds suitable young men to taunt me? It would be easier to kill myself and be done with this farce.'

'No, Mother. Uther has no part in this particular game. He's as shocked as you are – and he's frightened, too. Myrddion Merlinus is the puppet-master this time and he bears you no grudge. He aims his barbs squarely at my so-dear stepfather, the High King.'

Morgan lifted Ygerne to her feet and held the weeping woman protectively in her arms. As much as she was able, Morgan softened her stern, handsome face and rocked her mother as if she were a child.

As Ygerne's sobs slowly died away, Morgan ordered the servant girl to straighten her mistress's sumptuous bed and then leave the room.

'I'd not be tempted to gossip about the queen's tears,' she added. 'Do you understand me, woman? If you should speak, then I'll be forced to silence your voice permanently.'

The maid fearfully opened and closed her mouth several times, but no sound came forth. Wide-eyed and almost tripping in her terror, she curtseyed awkwardly and backed out of the room.

'We can't be overheard now. Lie down, Mother, for you're overwrought and exhausted. You need to regain your strength.'

Morgan gently eased her mother out of her outer robes and coaxed her on to her carved sleeping couch. Ygerne clutched her daughter's hand in sudden panic and Morgan could feel the delicate bones that were as fragile as sticks of ivory, yet strong with desperation.

'What does Myrddion want of me?'

'Nothing, Mother. Now be still. That young man, Artorex, has no idea who you are. Nor will anyone else make the connection – unless you tell them.'

'But he can't be my son,' Ygerne wailed. 'Lucius swore to me that the babe died shortly after birth.'

How this sad woman wished that she had never set eyes on that cold, young face in the king's hall and yet, if he was her son, she wanted to soothe her fears by seeing him again – and yet again.

'He is your son, Mother. I know. I bade him cast the bones years ago and his birth was written in the patterns. He'll become King of the Britons – if the bones tell the truth.'

'But is he the seed of Uther or is he from Gorlois, my husband? I couldn't bear it if that monster had spawned himself in my body.'

'He's Uther's son! Could you not see, Mother? I didn't need the bones to tell me so. Did you not see his hair?'

Ygerne sighed, and a world of bitter regret and self-knowledge was in that sound.

'I lay with my husband and Uther spent his seed in my body. Either could have fathered the child, or so I told myself, when I quickened. But Uther's son will hate me for my desertion of him. Uther's son will require a reckoning. What will become of us?'

'Artorex isn't Uther. Uther always burns with heat until he consumes everyone and everything around him – even you, Mother. But Artorex is cold, like ice or iron. His mind is his sovereign, not his passions, and we may yet be glad for that mercy.' Morgan's voice was quite flat and toneless, as if the trials of the Great Hall had happened long before she was born.

'Then Uther will kill him,' Ygerne wailed. 'The King is much like Cronos, the Greek god who devoured his children. I can see the blood lust in his eyes.'

'He may try, Mother, but I tell you now that Artorex will not die easily. I know that Myrddion is playing a dangerous game – one that may bring salvation for the west.'

Morgan drew a fur coverlet over her mother's shoulders and stroked her faded hair, almost as if their roles had been reversed – as perhaps they were.

'Sleep, Mother. Tomorrow will bring troubles enough, but you must be careful to show no partiality for this young man or, truly, he'll be killed without cause by the High King.'

'Do you also hate Artorex, Morgan? If he is Uther's son, then he is the poisoned fruit that was born out of your father's murder.'

Morgan stood upright, and her eyes saw beyond the room,

perhaps beyond time and the imperishable stars themselves.

'I will always detest him, Mother, but it is not my place to lift my hand against him. The fates have already decided that another will bring him to ruin – a woman with yellow hair.'

Ygerne sighed again and Morgan stroked her hand as the chill wind moaned outside and keened through the corridors of Venta Belgarum like a pack of foraging wolves.

In the Wild Boar Inn, Artorex washed and scraped at the stubble on his chin with a sharp blade and longed for the calidarium and his battered strigil. Hunger made his stomach growl, yet the thought of food revolted him. Tonight, he decided, he would wring answers out of Myrddion, or he would leave this ugly, freezing place that was ruled by a mad, blood-soaked king.

At supper in a private room, Artorex seated himself on a bench in the Celtic fashion and presented his ultimatum to the three lords.

'Either someone explains what is going on or I'll ride for home at first light. I know that I owe you a great deal, including my education and my safe childhood at the Villa Poppinidii, but I'm heartily sick of being treated like a child.'

'But you won't be permitted to leave, Artorex,' Luka exclaimed impatiently. 'You've sworn to battle one of Uther's best warriors on the morrow.'

'I can do as I please, Luka. How many times must I tell you that I am no man's tool?'

'Very well, Artorex. Very well. I will explain what I can,' Myrddion said calmly, although Artorex could see that his narrow hands trembled slightly. Myrddion took a deep breath and spoke quietly, for the walls in Venta Belgarum had ears.

'Uther wasn't always the shell you saw today. He was once a fighting man of greater skill than any of us here and, perhaps, possessed even more talent than you, my young friend. I became his servant during my youth when he was still in his prime, and he used my intelligence and my knowledge of languages the way you use your knife. I rose high in the courts of the King, but now, in his old age, he trusts nothing and nobody, not even me.'

Artorex coughed awkwardly, because he could feel the hot regret behind the calculating eyes of his friend.

'Morgan, his stepdaughter, is a seer and a Druid priestess, and she's risen as high in that order as any woman can reach. Even as a child, she hated her stepfather and foretold that a child with russet hair would eclipse him. Uther was angry beyond reason and no well-born child with fair colouring was safe from his murderous retribution.'

Myrddion paused, and then continued.

'You are highly born, Artorex, as your name implies, but I cannot reveal your father's name to you; not even if you leave us and bring all our long years of work to nothing. You must accept that your father handed you to Lucius and eventual safety, for Lucius sent you far from Uther's court to keep you free from harm. We've watched over you for much of our lives, young man, and even though we fear and despise what Uther has become, we never planned to use you as a weapon against him. The High King has but little time to live, as you have seen.'

The wind shook the shutters of the room and slid its way along the cracks to wind its cold fingers through Artorex's hair.

'I know. He smells like carrion already.'

'You must be seen as a worthy warrior by the tribes and gain a name that reflects the skills that Targo has taught you, so that you can serve the people when the old king dies.'

'Perhaps you might even become High King yourself,' Llanwith rumbled.

'Don't jest, Llanwith. I lack the authority to become High King.'

'But there's no reason why you shouldn't use your hard-won skills to help Uther, if he resumes his war against the Saxons. If he doesn't go to war, or if he dies, you can fight to assist his successor. Most citizens have heard the prophecy of the russet-haired warrior so, should you succeed against Uther's champion, people will believe that a new hero has come and will ask the High King to renew the defence of our lands. How could such actions harm you? Or hurt your family?'

'It can't hurt my family but I'll be risking . . .' Artorex's words petered away.

'You've promised Uther that you will fight tomorrow. It may have been in a fit of pique but you made a vow to the High King,' Llanwith stated. 'He'll want to know how highly you value your word.'

'That's a low blow, Llanwith!' Artorex turned to face the Ordovice king. 'I've been manoeuvred into some kind of contest for reasons that aren't very sound.'

'Uther obviously has no liking for you,' Luka said. 'But a smart man would have been meek and compliant, regardless of how rude his sovereign was.'

'So now it's my fault that I've been coerced into armed combat. Please, Luka, I'll need a better reason than that to face Uther's man.'

'Uther's court is Celtic in its nature; but you've been raised with one foot on the Roman way and the other in tribal cultures,' Myrddion continued, his dark eyes full of fervour. 'But we now have need of the old Roman virtues.'

Luka took up the argument. 'We Celts are too passionate. Left to ourselves, we'd squabble and fight with each other, just as we did for untold generations before the Romans came. How else could the Romans have defeated us? Their strategy of divide and conquer worked perfectly.'

'The great Caesar picked us off, one by one,' Llanwith cut in roughly, in his usual curt fashion. 'The Saxons will do the same to the west if we don't have a strong hand to unite and guide us. But you may leave if such is your wish, Artorex. After all, like all Celts, you resent being told what to do. I, for one, won't stop you.'

'Very well,' Artorex growled in irritation. 'I won't leave. But Uther will order me to be killed tomorrow, in combat and before the people, if he truly wants me dead.'

'Are you strong, boy?' Luka asked grimly.

'Aye, lord. Strong enough,' Artorex replied.

'But are you fast, boy?' Llanwith continued.

'Aye, lord. Fast enough.'

'And do you know how to cheat, lad?' Targo added, his grin wide and mischievous.

'Yes, I know how to cheat, and to think, and to fight on ground of my own choosing, using either hand,' Artorex replied with an ironic grin.

'Then you won't die tomorrow,' Myrddion responded. 'You'll survive.'

Artorex smiled sardonically and began to eat a light meal under the watchful eyes of his elders. He drank fresh water instead of mead or ale and took care not to overfill his stomach, for he would need his body to be strong and faultless on the coming day. When he finished, the four men who had been his guardians for most of his life rose to their feet and ordered him to bed.

Targo was the only man to offer practical advice.

'You must clean, sharpen and oil your weapons at dawn tomorrow, Artorex. You saw the size of those Celtic brutes in Uther's Hall – no insult intended, gentlemen,' he apologized for the racial slur.

'None taken, friend Targo,' Llanwith rumbled.

'Do you want my shield? It is yours for the asking,' Targo offered.

'I've never cared overmuch for a shield, so I'll use my dagger and sword. If I lack the skills to avoid the reach of Uther's warrior, then I deserve to be defeated.'

'Remember—'

'One mistake and I'm dead,' Artorex finished for him.

But for the first time that night, Artorex's heart was light, for now he would, at least, be doing something he understood.

The morning was as cold as ever. After breaking the rime of ice in a bowl and washing himself as clean as possible, Artorex dressed in a leather jerkin over a woollen undershirt and encased his legs in soft leather trews.

Targo entered Artorex's room as he was contemplating his feet.

'Those boots you wear are heavy and likely to slip on the stones. But barefoot your feet will freeze and become numb, so the outcome will still be the same,' Targo said in his practical, hoarse croak.

He offered Artorex a pair of knitted woollen sleeves, the foot wear used by old men in the village as they dozed before the fire.

'Try wearing these sleeves instead of your boots. I believe you can fight in them for a time, bootless, as long as the ground isn't wet.'

'I'm not in my dotage yet, Targo,' Artorex protested.

'Try them,' Targo pressed.

Artorex slid the wool over his long feet and up to mid-calf and Targo lashed the leggings into place with narrow strips of leather.

'Try moving about in them,' the veteran ordered.

Artorex jumped and spun, parried and thrust in pantomime. To his surprise, his toes could grip the flags through the rough, knitted wool and the soles were not slick and likely to betray him. The socks were even quite warm.

'I told you I've fought in places where you could piss ice,' Targo laughed. 'We barbarians know a thing or two, especially about combat. If I'd known we were coming to this place, I'd have fashioned kid boots for you without a heavy sole. They would've given you extra traction, but these will do until we have the time to cobble together some better accoutrement for you.'

'My thanks, Targo.'

'Enough, boy. Llanwith has sent a cloak and Luka has sent a helmet – just an iron cap with cheek guards and a nosepiece, but it might save your thick skull,' Targo said with a smile. 'And Myrddion sends you these.'

From his cloak, Targo pulled out a pair of wristbands, each four fingers wide. They were made of iron, and the metal was embossed with the Winged Worm insignia of the Celtic Legion – its long, sinuous tail and small legs marked this dragon as a creature other than Dracos of Rome. Its wings spread as it rode on the curve of the metal.

'These will protect your wrists. They're not particularly heavy, and won't save you from an axe blow, but soldiers of the Legion learned that a wristband could deflect a sword blow.'

He smiled at his charge once more.

'I wish we had time to find you a mail shirt and a breastplate. You can bet your opponent will be protected by armour from head to foot.'

'Then I'll be lighter than Uther's man,' Artorex quipped, although he felt a shiver of alarm. 'I'll simply remember the Scythian woman and how fast she proved to be.'

'Your friends wish you luck, and they'll see you in the courtyard before Uther's Hall.'

'The High King has sent word then?'

'Aye. You meet his champion at noon.'

So little time! Artorex could see that the sun was high, for he had slept overlong after their hurried journey to Venta Belgarum. Targo had insisted that his charge sleep as long as his body needed, but now Artorex knew that he would have to hurry.

'Don't fuss, my boy, for the contest can't start without you,' Targo replied, as if reading Artorex's mind.

'But I've never fought in serious combat, Targo. I've never killed anyone in the heat of battle. How can you know I'll be able to defeat anyone, least of all a seasoned warrior?'

Targo chuckled in amusement at first, then he looked at the face of his young charge and realized that Artorex was serious. Targo was so accustomed to the physical talents of his pupil that he had forgotten his charge might find the coming combat an ordeal.

'To begin with, my boy, killing is a lot easier when you've been trained to do it. It's often automatic. Someone comes at you with a sodding great axe, so you kill him – or he buries the weapon in your brain. I'm not saying it's right, mind, but we warriors do what we're told. Besides, boy, you haven't been ordered to kill Uther's champion. You've just got to ensure that he doesn't kill you.'

Artorex nodded. Targo's explanation made good sense.

'As for your inexperience, you've got to start somewhere, and in front of the High King and a whole city is an excellent place for your first combat. You've practised daily for half your life, you know every move that I know, and you've been taught every dirty trick that I've ever seen. I'm an expert, lad. If it makes you feel better, you can treat this bout as just another practice and tell yourself that it's exactly the same as one of Lord Luka's tests.'

'Aye. Except that this warrior really will kill me.'

'Only if you can't find an edge.'

Artorex laughed sardonically. Targo, as always, had found the crux of his needs, and the large muscles in his shoulders started to feel relaxed and limber. He thought he should be terrified, but all he felt was a tightening in his gut as excitement began to surge through his blood.

Life is very strange, Artorex thought again, and began to prepare his weapons for the coming fight.

Artorex was the object of a surprising amount of curiosity from the moment he stepped outside the inn. Before he was even halfway to the field of combat, he realized that his test of strength was an excuse for a day of entertainment for the citizens of Venta Belgarum.

To his amazement, every street was crowded with tinkers, peasants selling all manner of fruit, vegetables and meat, and so many vendors of cooked food and drink that the young man's head spun with the noise and competing smiles. Many men tried to clap him on the back and girls gave him flowers, while some wags even shouted insults or educated him by quoting the odds being wagered on his imminent and painful death. The crowds, the din and the excitement rose up around him like a rather odiferous wave.

He arrived at the appointed place of combat accompanied by Targo and an entourage of hundreds of men and boys who pushed, shoved and fought those citizens who already had a good vantage point.

The large square courtyard before Uther's Hall was ringed with onlookers, curious to see the promised sport. The citizens of Venta Belgarum were only too aware of the strength and martial capacities of Uther's personal guard, so word had spread quickly of the giant youth from the provinces who would challenge Uther's selected champion. Curiosity, and the promise of blood, brought out those fortunate enough to find a place to stand.

Still more of the citizens clustered within the nearby houses whose roofs provided a view over the tallest heads. The square seemed full of tier after tier of rapacious, eager faces when Artorex entered the prepared arena.

The steps leading to the Hall's forecourt were bare, except for a cloth-of-gold pavilion and several braziers. There, the High King would sit, surrounded by his women and his guard.

The roar of a ram's horn announced the entrance of Uther and his retinue. As they moved slowly towards their seats, the multitude knelt in the street as one, while Uther's guards positioned themselves around the pavilion in a ring of drawn steel.

At a wave from the hand of the High King, the citizens of Venta Belgarum rose to their feet and a babble of voices swelled and surged through the densely packed crowd.

As Artorex knelt to remove his boots, Targo checked the lacings at his calves once again, and several seasoned warriors in the crowd laughed at his unconventional footwear. Artorex chose not to listen and blotted out everything to concentrate on the flagged stone surface of the fighting ring that had been circumscribed by lengths of rope. He practised falling into a fighting crouch with his sword and dagger drawn and ready for combat.

'Is your Artorex here, servant Myrddion?' Uther called – and the crowd grew silent at the insulting title. The whole world knew of Myrddion Merlinus, who had long been seer, physician and loyal adviser to the throne of the Britons.

Myrddion stepped out into the field of combat and bowed low to his liege lord.

'Myrddion Merlinus, my trusted steward, claims that this boy from the province of Aquae Sulis is the best warrior in the north-west,' Uther wheezed out to the crowd. 'Who here has heard of Artorex?'

'No one!' the crowd roared back, hugely amused by the mood of the High King. 'No one! No one! No one!'

'Our champion, Ban of Durnovaria, Firebrand of the West, will test the mettle of this Artorex.'

The ram's horn sounded once again and Ban stepped out of the King's Guard. He was a warrior of no more than thirty, with a face that was seamed by a scar crossing the cheekbone and nose where they could be seen under his green plumed helmet. He was large, and heavier in the body than Artorex, while his bare arms were adorned with Pictish blue tattoos in the same whorls and spirals that Artorex had seen on the stone in the Old Forest. Ban carried a shield, circular in shape, and with a great metal boss and spike in the centre. Artorex knew it would mean broken ribs or punctured lungs if he allowed Ban to penetrate his defences with that wicked fist of iron.

As Ban bowed to the High King, and then to the crowd, Targo whispered final instructions to Artorex as he stepped away from his pupil.

'Look for an edge, my boy,' Targo intoned. 'Every fighter has a flaw. And keep away from that damned shield.'

Ban's legs were shorter than his torso promised, and his long sword and shield must have been heavy. Even though Ban's arms were ridged with muscle and the tangle of veins that are only seen on superbly fit and strong men, he carried a slight belly under his leather battle tunic.

'Are you ready, Artorex?' Myrddion whispered.

Artorex stepped forward and unsheathed his short sword and long dagger. The weapons arced in the cold air with vicious little hisses as he swung his arms.

'Aye, Lord Merlinus!'

Turning towards the dais, he bowed low to the High King.

'Get on with it, then!' Uther ordered, swinging his old man's white plaits in irritation.

Ban approached his opponent at a run, his sword carving a

great slice through the freezing air. The crowd cheered in expectation of seeing Artorex split into two.

But Artorex was no longer there. Nimble in his unshod feet, he evaded the swinging blade easily and skipped away to Ban's left, slicing his dragon knife across the warrior's eyes.

It was only his lightning-fast reflexes that saved the over-confident Ban. His head reared back at the last second and the blow passed harmlessly across his helmet, sending up a small explosion of sparks as the blade struck metal.

The crowd roared their approval at the contact, but Artorex didn't hear them. He had blotted out everything and everybody but his adversary. He moved back to the right, his dragon blade probing, probing, while his right hand held his short sword close to his body, ready for an opportunity to thrust.

Ban moved like lightning, and Artorex parried the blow with his short sword and the dragon knife raised in a cross above his body. Before Ban could slam him with his shield, for such a move Artorex could clearly read in the warrior's eyes, Artorex disengaged and danced away, forcing Ban to turn once more in order to face his opponent.

'You're not bad, boy, but you really need a shield,' Ban hissed. 'It's going to be a pity to cut you up today – if you ever stand still and fight like a man.'

Artorex ignored the provocation and simply skipped away once again, then changed direction and hands in a blur of steel as he moved, nicking Ban just above the knee in a wicked slice. The dragon blade winked as its point reddened.

'Not good enough, boy,' Ban yelled and increased his efforts to take advantage of his longer reach. Every trick that Targo had taught him came into play, as Artorex parried, cut and thrust, all the time evading Ban's deadly sword cuts through the use of his agile feet.

'You talk too much, Ban,' Artorex replied conversationally

when the initial surge of effort had ended, and both men continued to feel their way over the uneven ground as they sought for an advantage.

Ban was brilliant in his way. His strength was legendary and he was totally fearless, for it had always been his dearest wish to die on the battlefield. He was agile for a big man and had the stamina of an ox but, after fifteen minutes of combat, both men were breathing heavily, while blood oozed steadily from the cut inflicted by Artorex.

Uther was growing restive. This callow youth should have been dispatched long before now and the king's feet were growing cold.

'Finish him, Ban!' the King screamed. 'Surely you can catch a provincial nobody.'

Artorex winked at Ban – and grinned.

The crowd, at least, were mesmerized by the equal battle, and large wagers were being laid on the fringes of the square.

Following a feint with his sword, Ban succeeded in thrusting his shield straight into the shoulder of Artorex. Only instinct saved the younger man from a killing blow from the spike; he managed to spin away and deflected the force of the shield by tumbling backwards with it. Still, his helmet was lost, knocked from his head, and Artorex's hair streamed out like a banner.

The crowd gasped.

A small cut leaked a trickle of blood from Artorex's hairline where the shield boss ought to have split his skull. But Ban had overreached himself to breach the defences of his opponent, and now the dragon knife slashed him across the sword arm . . . down to the bone.

Artorex quickly changed hands once again, slipped under Ban's guard, and swept his opponent's feet out from under him. Ban hit the cobbles with an audible thud, his shield arm falling away from his belly and leaving his throat exposed.

Artorex's short sword pressed deeply against Ban's pulsing throat artery.

'Strike hard, my friend, for it's a good day to die,' Ban said proudly.

'Yield, Ban!'

'I can't. Only my master can give me the order to surrender. And he won't do it.'

Artorex looked up at Uther, while holding Ban supine with his left foot on the warrior's upper arm.

'Well? Kill him, Artorex, or don't you have the taste for blood?' Uther ordered.

The crowd was utterly silent.

Uther's women sat like creatures of stone as they watched the drama unfold before them.

Ban was the only person who was truly alive at that moment, for there was a distinct probability that he was sucking in the last exhilarating moments of his life.

He didn't know if he was going to live or die.

'I'm here to kill Saxons for you, my liege, not my companions at arms,' Artorex shouted to Uther – and at the rabble – with his sword at Ban's throat. 'I ask that Ban should not die by my hand this day but that he should live to perish for a nobler cause.'

The crowd roared as Artorex stepped backwards and away from his erstwhile opponent.

The warrior eased himself slowly to his feet, picking up his fallen sword as he did so. 'Sire, I beg that you do not shame your champion, for he will kill a thousand Saxons for you, if you but ask.'

The crowd roared its approval once again. Ban waited for his master's orders, trying to grip his sword with his wounded arm.

'Very well,' Uther replied in great ill humour at the crowd's response. 'You may have your way – on this occasion.' He glared at his erstwhile champion. 'You are excused, Ban. This contest is over.'

Angry beyond measure, the High King and his retinue disappeared into the Great Hall, leaving Artorex to the acclamation of the crowd.

As Artorex snatched up his cloak and boots, the well-wishing citizenry surrounded him, especially those admirers who'd shown the foresight to place wagers on his strong right arm. His shoulders and arms were pummelled to aching rawness by congratulatory fists, and it took some effort for Targo to force his way through the press of bodies to lead his protégé away from the makeshift arena.

Throughout the cobbled streets, the name Artorex reverberated so loudly that even those few citizens who hadn't chosen to enjoy the contest were hearing much-embroidered tales of the amazing battle even before the young man reached the sanctuary of the Wild Boar Inn. The rough-cut, wooden building was soon bursting at the seams with a motley crowd of townsfolk, farmers, mercenaries and warriors, all of whom were shouting at the top of their lungs, drinking almost as much as they spilled and joking, laughing, gesticulating and gyrating in noisy re-creations of the epic battle.

Once there, Artorex would have drowned in free ale if Myrddion hadn't insisted on first dressing his wound. The threat of force became necessary to clear a path for Artorex to escape to the upper floor.

The story of Ban's conqueror sped through Venta Belgarum like wildfire. The young warrior was a veritable giant, yet he had the strength and agility of a fighting cat. And this young man rejected the Celtic shield for the dizzying protection of a spinning web of iron. And then, when victory was assured and Ban was at his mercy, Artorex was magnanimous and refused to shed Ban's blood needlessly. He had defied the orders of the

High King – and survived to tell the tale. With a Roman sword and a long knife, he had beaten the legendary Ban, the Firebrand of the West, and Lady Fortuna had protected his back at every turn.

More importantly, those few greybeards who had known Uther when he was a young man marvelled at how much this Artorex resembled the High King they remembered from his early manhood. Even Botha, the Captain of the King's Guard, had been shocked by the resemblance. Once seen, such hair could never be forgotten, for it was barbarian hair, sometimes called Caesar Red, although the legends suggested that the great Julian had a balding pate.

The old men sucked on their toothless gums, and wondered aloud what strange kin of Uther's could have come willingly to Venta Belgarum.

Targo mixed with the press of excited men, sipped ale slowly – and listened. The rumour-mongering was active and told that two of the more important tribal kings and the famed Myrddion Merlinus had brought Artorex to Venta Belgarum as their champion, and that he fought with all the skills of a Roman, a Celt, and a barbarian. Targo heard talk that Artorex even resembled Uther Pendragon, and might well have some kinship to the High King. The veteran's heart quailed to imagine the consequences if the High King should catch a whisper of such gossip.

When Targo meandered his way back to the narrow attic room he shared with Artorex, the warrior found his protégé stripped to the waist while Myrddion tended to his wound. Llanwith lounged on Artorex's pallet, but Luka was conspicuous by his absence.

'By all the gods, Artorex, you made money for me today,' was Targo's opening sally. 'If I'd known you were going to be so profitable, I'd have had you in the arena years ago.'

'I'm happy that somebody is pleased,' Artorex replied. 'Myrddion believes I should have killed Ban, and not drawn the ire of Uther.'

Myrddion continued to stitch a shallow slash on Artorex's forearm. He smiled indulgently.

'I merely suggested to Luka that the High King wouldn't be disposed to forgive your lesson in courtesy,' he stated. 'Personally, I was not the least surprised that you permitted Ban to live, but the fact that the crowd demanded it as well was unusual. That was a factor that I hadn't expected. Nor will Uther forgive you for your popularity with the masses.'

'Well, it's too late now,' Targo responded. 'All of Venta Belgarum has heard the name of Artorex. When I left the drunkards downstairs, you had assumed giant proportions – and you bore magic weapons.'

He paused momentarily.

'Incidentally, there is gossip that says you are either Uther's bastard child or you're some distant kin to him.'

Artorex looked shaken. 'I'm not, am I?'

'What?' Myrddion asked.

'Am I Uther's bastard son?'

'No, you're not his *bastard* son.' Myrddion's reply was definite. The silence dragged out achingly.

'Perhaps it's time we left Venta Belgarum for the good of our health,' Llanwith murmured from the edge of his bed. He seemed outwardly unconcerned, and casually kicked off his boots for comfort.

'We'll know what to do after Luka returns,' Myrddion replied, as he completed the last stitch in Artorex's wound. 'I've never known how he does it, but kitchen maids feel compelled to whisper juicy titbits of gossip into Luka's little pink ears.'

✠ ✠ ✠

Uther sensed that his final destiny was fast approaching. He knew that age was about to defeat the iron fist of his mind. His skin was thin and its papery surface bruised and bled easily. His bones supported neither flesh nor muscle beneath his wrinkled skin, and he realized his remaining vitality was slowly rotting from deep inside his body. His chest pained him, his ankles and feet were swollen to twice their natural size and they were blue and cold to the touch.

Uther wasn't afraid of physical death, and he had few regrets about how he had achieved his ends during a long and bloody life – except for the seduction of Ygerne. All things considered, her amazing beauty had not been worth the scandals, the trouble and the tears she had showered over him in the many years since he had first seduced her and stolen her from her first husband, Gorlois of Cornwall.

And now, when he should have been entitled to lay down the sword, draw peace from his confessor and live out his last days in a semblance of comfort, Ygerne had sent him a nasty and dangerous tool of revenge.

Artorex! Even the name, with its unambiguously regal *Rex*, was an insult to Uther's rule. He should have smothered the brat himself when Ygerne's midwife shoved the tiny, whining bundle into his arms. At the time, he feared that Ygerne had borne one last child to her dead spouse, a son who might one day claim Uther's throne to settle the blood debt he was owed.

But he, Uther Pendragon, would never surrender his crown so easily.

'Lucius! That sodding, pious bastard!' Uther swore pungently, describing the Bishop of Glastonbury in soldier's terms.

Lucius of Glastonbury had taken up the squalling infant and had sworn to Uther that he would never see the brat again. At the time of Ygerne's travails, Uther hadn't yet recognized the grasping power of the Church of the Christus – but he understood its ambitions now. The troublesome brat had been grown to manhood in a faraway place, safe from Uther's arm, and had been raised more as a Roman than a Celt – as was that Satan-spawn, Lucius. The boy had been trained from birth to be a weapon against Uther Pendragon, led by the trusted Myrddion Merlinus, who had plotted against him and guided his enemy's path to manhood.

Uther fumed impotently and hurled his silver cup feebly against the wall, where it rolled pitifully in the red lees of wine. How like spilled blood the wine appeared. He could no longer remember a tenth of the men he had killed, but the Boar of Cornwall's face had never left him, waking or sleeping. After all, that filthy cow, Morgan, never allowed him to forget whose child she was, and how his wife, her mother, would never truly love him for the treacherous crimes he had committed in the name of lust.

'Damn the bitch!'

He should have had her strangled – but he desperately needed her skills with herbs and magic spells.

And now, the brat had come to Uther's Hall and had dared to lock eyes with his liege lord. He should have died at the hands of Ban, but the High King's champion had been outwitted by the tactics of Myrddion. Uther had watched as the eyes of his faithful servant Botha had measured the young man; he was certain that Botha recognized the father in the son.

Perhaps other men were speculating on Artorex's parentage at this very moment.

'Botha!'

Uther had been the king of the Atrebates when Botha had first sworn allegiance to him. Botha was a young, red-headed warrior of the Trinovantes tribe, from Camulodunum beside the Litus Saxonicus. He had fled from his tribe, his city and his family because of a woman, having killed his cousin in combat over her adultery. A blood price pursued him, and Botha was as landless and as friendless as any man can be.

Uther had met Botha on a windswept, dreary plain beyond the swamps of Venta Icenorum. The Saxons had pillaged a church and killed its priests in an orgy of ferocity, and Uther had answered the call of the Catuvellauni tribe who hurried to root out the barbarians. The Saxons had been harder to prise from the land than lice from bedding, and many Celts had bled into the cold, winter earth.

Uther had fought with his men, as was his custom, and had swept aside the Saxon battleaxes with his huge sword as if they were mere willow wands. Only a partly frozen trail of blood and brain matter had betrayed his feet, and he had eventually slipped under the weapons of his enemies.

Then Botha had appeared out of the press of warriors, straddling the King's body with his strong, golden legs, and used his sword and shield in a wicked, glittering wall of death. Uther had managed to scramble to his feet and kill a Saxon who was about to behead Botha from behind. And so they had fought on back to back, until the barbarians had been slaughtered.

In his youth, Botha had been a genius in the pure art of killing, but he'd also been a man with a core of decency that lent his trade a certain dignity and beauty. He had sworn his oath of allegiance to Uther in the old way, with his neck beneath the King's heel, signifying fealty for life, and Uther had taken a grim pleasure in the devotion of such a powerful, vital creature. In truth, the High King had never really appreciated Botha as a man until his own arm had grown weak and unpredictable, because he had always considered his most trusted servant as little more than a good dog.

Botha had survived the cruel passage of years with more vigour than his liege lord, and some blackness in Uther resented the ageing strength of his servant.

Still, for all his envy, Uther trusted no one living the way he depended on Botha.

The High King couldn't comfort himself with the possibility that Artorex was a pretender. Uther had seen his hair and remembered his own plaits, and the difficulty of keeping his red-gold curls in order. Ygerne had called it barbarian hair. She'd loved his hair – at least when he still had warm blood flowing through his veins.

Memory can be a cruel taunt, and Uther had earned its pangs.

He shouted querulously for his manservant and ordered that Botha should join him immediately, regardless of the hour. Of all the men who walked in the sunlight of the Celts, Botha alone would obey him without question. Uther would send Artorex, Merlinus and the traitor kings to die at Anderida at the hands of the Saxons, just as he had sent Ygerne's husband to certain death years before. The bastard would become a dead hero and Uther would be suitably mournful at the loss of such promise and patriotism.

Uther's rheumy eyes hardened.

For now, he had a more pressing problem, and only Botha could be trusted to solve it.

'Botha dared to bow his head to that upstart,' the High King muttered, as he sucked on his withered lips like a toothless old woman. He smiled secretively, and the air in his bedchamber seemed to leach away with his malice and cunning.

Botha would solve his dilemma because the warrior was a man of unimpeachable honour. When they were both young men and Uther had yet to win the gold crown of kingship, he had learned the measure of Botha. Uther remembered the crunch of a rib cage when he had buried his blade in a barbarian chest. The Saxon had gaped stupidly as Uther twisted the huge sword up into his heart – and saved Botha's life.

Although forty years had passed, Botha still remembered who owned his life. He could recall the blood, slime and mud and how he had wept when Uther took him into his guard. He'd sworn to serve his master and, through all the long and bloody years that had followed, Botha remained true to his ancient oath.

And he would obey now.

For Uther's misbegotten by blow must be expunged utterly! Uther's light must never be allowed to wane, even if the west must fall, so that his memory would be shielded in the glory of the legend. The Villa Poppinidii had nurtured Artorex as boy and man, so the villa, Ector and all within it must be destroyed and burned to the ground.

Uther had no compunction in ordering such a cowardly and petty act, for kings stand above honour and their most trivial desires are attained with simple orders. Kings are above the laws of man – and the gods.

Cat-footed, Botha entered Uther's chamber. His shadow was huge and menacing in the last darkness before the coming of dawn.

'Are you faithful to me unto death, Botha? And to me alone?' Uther asked the grey-headed warrior, with a mouth suddenly gone as dry as grave dust.

'I swore an oath to you, my King, that I would never serve another man while breath remained in my body. That oath cannot be broken, except by death.' Botha's face was sad, as if he knew already he was about to be used as a pure instrument in an impure cause. His noble, lined brow was frowning and his red-bearded jaw was clenched, as if in pain. The eyes of the warrior, as unclouded and as direct as those of the youth he had once been, looked inward at some invisible, unbearable truth.

Uther almost pulled away from his murderous grip upon the future, and he almost took pity on the one soul in the whole world who had given him unqualified love. But Uther had drunk the cup of raw power for far too long, and even the faithful Botha must play his part in the High King's memorial.

'What news of this Artorex?' Uther demanded.

One way or another, Botha heard everything that happened in Venta Belgarum.

'King Luka has been dallying with the serving maids, hunting out news. I gave him your orders personally – so Myrddion now knows his fate.' He smiled at his king. 'Luka drank more than was his intention, seeing no harm in the plump little pigeon who is my eyes and ears in the kitchens. Luka was imprudent in his bed talk with Eilyn, and he spoke of Artorex, of a daughter and another babe who quickens in the womb of his wife.'

'Damnation!' Uther swore expressively.

Already there were heirs presumptive squabbling for his throne before he was even laid out on his deathbed. Soldiers may die in battle, but Uther could not depend on chance and the vagaries of childbirth to rid him of further claimants to his throne.

'The children of Artorex must die – and the dam – and all those souls who dwell within the walls of the Villa Poppinidii must perish with them. This is your duty to me, Botha. You must obey for the security of my kingdom.'

Uther offered Botha no explanation or justification for the wanton murder of innocents. Kings don't explain, especially to those souls who are hand-fasted to them for life.

Botha nodded, just once, and Uther felt a momentary pang of grief as if he had broken a good sword over his knee.

'Take only trusted men, use whomever you must, but don't fail me. And ensure that no one lives to gossip that Uther has killed innocents. Disguise yourself as you see fit.'

Botha nodded, and Uther could see the shame leaking from the eyes of the old warrior.

'Go, Botha, and order my confessor to attend me at once,' Uther whispered.

Such business shouldn't be spoken aloud in the halls of the High King and, even now, Uther felt his heart stutter in his chest as if a huge fist clutched it and squeezed.

'My lord is ill,' Botha protested. 'Permit me to send for Morgan.'

'Bring me my confessor, Botha. Then carry out your orders,' Uther commanded, turning his face away from the one man he trusted. In truth, he couldn't face Botha's wounded eyes.

As the sound of Botha's boots faded into silent darkness, Uther slowed his breathing with an effort and contemplated the action he'd set in motion. Many men and women had died for the west, and many more would bleed to hold such a small island kingdom within their hands.

The light from an oil lamp slanted across the bedcovers and lit the King's profile with what he knew to be the cruel truth. He was as he had always been, a raptor in a cage of pigeons, with little thought for the weaker souls who lived and died at his command.

'So why do I feel so cold and alone?' Uther demanded of the silent air. 'Send me my confessor!'

His feeble wail was like the thin cry of crows seeking carrion.

As his confessor shuffled through the doorway on unwilling feet, Uther saw Morgan, like a storm crow herself, standing directly behind his priest. The lamplight caught the delicate bones of her face so that, for a moment, a skull stared back at him with the fire of the wick burning in empty sockets.

Uther blinked. Morgan was herself again, beautiful and cold as carved alabaster.

She clutched an amulet round her throat and locked her eyes with his. And she smiled. ✝ ✝ ✝

Artorex would have preferred to be alone. The inevitable plummet of his spirit after the heat of battle had left him feeling lonely and confused. A bare week ago, he had been happy and at peace with his lot in life. Now the rabble called his name, but he dare not set foot outside his room, and his life could be forfeit to the High King of the Britons, for no particular reason apart from Uther's spitefulness.

Luka returned to the inn a little before midnight. Llanwith had fallen asleep on Artorex's pallet and the small room shook with his stentorian snores. Artorex was seated cross-legged on the floor, wrapped in his cloak and obstinately cleaning his weapons, while Targo was asleep in an untidy mound of clothes and sinewy muscle across the entrance to the room. Characteristically, Myrddion had vanished some hours earlier.

Luka's entrance was noisy and embarrassing.

He had spent the evening drinking rough Gallic wine with his informants among the High King's retinue. As he entered the dimly lit room, Luka tripped over the inert body of Targo and crashed to the floor, waking a startled Llanwith in the process.

The Ordovice was on his feet, sword drawn, in an instant.

Artorex continued to hone his dagger.

Like a magician, Myrddion appeared in the doorway and helped the sprawled Luka to his feet. With a muffled hiccup and a slurred apology, the warrior fished around in his cloak and, with a drunken flourish, drew out a crumpled scroll. He giggled.

'Our orders have arrived from the High King, Myrddion. Uther has decided that we should raise a small troop and attack the Saxon fort at Anderida.'

He executed a drunken bow and would have fallen flat on his face had Llanwith not jerked him upright by his leather jerkin.

'Anderida?' Myrddion was actually shocked by Luka's news.

'That marsh-infested hellhole? It's almost directly across the straits of the Litus Saxonicum. Has Uther gone utterly mad?'

Llanwith pen Bryn began to laugh. It came out as a long, raucous guffaw that seemed to start at his toes and rose slowly and ever more loudly until his mirth made the icy shutters appear to quiver.

'What causes your amusement, Llanwith?' Myrddion asked with exquisite, dangerous courtesy. 'That flea pit has been in Saxon hands for twenty years. Gods, it was one of the first towns to fall to the barbarian kings, and you can spit across the straits of the Saxon Sea from there.'

'I know, Myrddion,' Llanwith hiccuped through a succession of suppressed giggles. 'Uther's outmanoeuvred us! We're off to Anderida, and precious few of us will return if the High King and the Saxons have their way.'

'Precisely!' Luka said with owlish seriousness.

Myrddion snatched the crumpled scroll and read its contents quickly.

'Uther suggests that if we are so eager to stop the Saxon menace, then we should push them back into the ocean. We are permitted to raise a troop, if any sensible warrior chooses to commit suicide with us. And he insists that Artorex must lead the attack personally, for he is now Uther's champion of the west.'

'He's outplayed us, Myrddion. Damn me, but he must have been a great tactician when he was young!'

Llanwith appeared to be genuinely impressed by Uther's acumen. Myrddion saw no humour in the situation and scowled at both of his friends and reminded Llanwith that his uncle had been a victim of the same ploy. The Ordovice king sobered instantly.

'He's trapped your queen, Myrddion,' Luka agreed, as he collapsed on to Artorex's bed with Llanwith. 'And we didn't even know we were playing a chess game.'

Myrddion glared at Luka and then viciously kicked at the wall, his teeth bared in furious irritation.

'One other matter has come to my attention. The old devil's body servant told me that Uther has only a month or two to live. Mind you, the idiot has been saying the same thing for years.'

Myrddion paced back and forth, while Luka fell asleep and Targo mumbled something incomprehensible about an old soldier needing his rest. He stumbled off to Llanwith's room to use a vacant bed.

'I'll join you,' Artorex snapped, his patience well worn by the events of the day. 'If I'm going to die then it's best I be well-rested when I do.'

Artorex fell asleep on a flea-infested pallet in a dirty attic somewhere in the back streets of Venta Belgarum and dreamed that he lay with his Gallia. Elsewhere, on a bed richly covered with fine wool and smooth linen in the palace of the High King, Uther Pendragon struggled to stay wakeful lest his sleep be troubled by a persistent nightmare of a huge sword that had once belonged to him. Now, no matter how hard he tried, his wasted muscles couldn't lift the vast blade.

Of the two, father and son, Artorex slept more easily, although he sensed that he could soon go to the shadows – and before his allotted time. As he lay in his wife's warm arms in the web of his dreams, he heard a voice call out of the darkness so loudly that the whole world seemed to shudder from the sound. 'Fortune smiles at last! Behold her wheel turns to raise you high. Beware, Artorex, Fortuna's fool.'

But Artorex smiled in his sleep as his dream wife kissed him. For who can fear a goddess when love holds tight to the heart?

CHAPTER XII

TO DIE IN ANDERIDA

Ignorant of Uther's unholy intentions for the Villa Poppinidii, Myrddion faced a day of strenuous mental and physical effort. The call to arms was being shouted from the High King's forecourt and some fools would answer out of a simple desire for excitement and adventure.

Word ran through the narrow streets of the city. Through alehouses, meeting houses and crossroads, the call to arms moved swiftly and set the imaginations of the citizens afire. But the young bloods that sought glory must be convinced to remain in safety in Venta Belgarum, for novices had no place in the storming of a fortress such as Anderida where they would be a hindrance rather than an advantage. In this deadly game that was being played to spite the scheming of Uther Pendragon, numbers didn't count. Skill and cunning were far more important.

To add to his woes, Myrddion must convince the most talented of his supporters to throw their lives away in the first skirmish of a series of battles that would lead, hopefully, to their country's salvation. They would die as pawns in the affairs of greater men and Myrddion's conscience had yet to find the exact words to persuade them.

'A grey day,' he sighed broodingly. 'But we're not dead yet, as Targo is so fond of repeating.'

Nor did Myrddion wish to die himself.

It was plain to him that Uther was prepared to sacrifice his chief counsellor and two stalwart and loyal kings because he envied the potential strength of his own son. Llanwith, Luka and Myrddion weren't expected to return, but the real target was Artorex.

Myrddion brooded.

'Uther Pendragon will destroy the stability of the west to protect a crown that he believes is his forever. At least two tribes hang in the balance, great and loyal tribes, but Uther would tear the fabric of his pact with the kings to ribbons to retain – what? Is it the hunger of a diseased mind? Is it the savagery that grows in the head when the arm grows weak? I'll never understand what drives the man!'

Grey, sullen skies outside the inn mirrored Myrddion's mood, while scudding cloud came from the sea and was torn to shreds by winds that the human eye couldn't see.

Rooks called and sleet threatened.

'We agree that Uther must be stopped, yet we must still win Anderida for him. But how can we achieve this impossible task?'

Targo was engaged in the process of preparing Artorex to face the stares and curiosity of the townsfolk by cleaning his charge's leathers and brushing the mud from the wolfskin cloak. He served his pupil willingly, for he realized that Artorex was reaping the rewards of many years of practice and training, and was developing the mien of a commander. It was a role taken up by the young man unwillingly, perhaps, but Targo couldn't fail to recognize the burgeoning signs of authority demonstrated by his protégé.

Targo had never knowingly sired a son of his own, so he had never felt a sense of loss at the lack of children at his hearth. Artorex was his child of choice, because Targo had moulded the warrior streak in the young man and had watched his pupil prove his worth in combat with mixed feelings of fear and pride. For Targo, a soldier never lessened his stature by serving of his free will and only became a slave when he surrendered to his enemies.

Artorex woke to a grim day of dripping eaves and drizzling, half-frozen rain, with the familiar sound of Targo's tuneless whistling in his ears. If the boy in Artorex was confused, the man in him was optimistic. A mere day earlier, he had awoken to the knowledge of his impending death, but he still lived and breathed. Today, the muster for a suicidal raid on an entrenched enemy would begin, but Anderida was far away and Lady Fortuna alone would choose the time when Artorex would meet his destiny.

'It is a good day, Targo,' he greeted the older man. 'You need not clean my kit – we are friends and fellow soldiers. That is, if you are not offended that I speak of myself as your equal.'

'You talk nonsense at times, boy,' Targo retorted gruffly, but with affection. 'And who, in days to come, will remember old Targo? No, I'll answer for you – no one! But I've a feeling in my water that they'll remember you.'

'I'd rather be at home with Gallia, my friend,' Artorex replied sadly, as he stretched his long legs.

'You should tell that children's tale to someone who believes you, Artorex. I *know* that a part of you enjoys the scent of the coming battle.'

'Where is everyone?' Artorex changed the subject, knowing that he was no match for Targo's sharp eyes.

'They've eaten, dressed and gone,' Targo responded economically.

'Oh.'

Targo could tell that Artorex was disappointed, so he took pity on the younger man.

'Get up, get yourself dressed and we'll convince some of

these sheep to die with the great Artorex. Myrddion has estimated a force of no more than one hundred good warriors is needed but, in my opinion, even that number is excessive. It'd be better to have forty seasoned warriors than three hundred young boys.'

Artorex swung his long legs out from under a cover of moth-eaten fur.

'I don't even know where Anderida is,' he stated in all honesty.

'I've never heard of it myself but it must be situated on the south-east coast somewhere,' Targo replied. 'And I can guarantee it won't be pleasant or Uther wouldn't have chosen it for your death, my young hero.'

Artorex threw an empty wooden cup at the older man. Targo caught it neatly and spun it in his hand.

'You're reading my mind, boy. It's time for a drink.'

After a hurried bowl of porridge and several rather withered apples, Targo and Artorex faced the miserable weather outside the inn. Under the shelter of the wolf cape, Artorex managed to avoid most of the rain, but a dozen steps had him spattered with mud.

'This rain is the soldier's friend,' Targo explained drily, eyeing his ruined handiwork on Artorex's kit with the patience of long experience. 'The commanders stick to their tents when rain comes to the battlefield, so mud takes the edge from everyone.'

'The only detail about Anderida that Myrddion bothered to share with us was that it's near a swamp. I predict that mud won't be our friend.'

'Hell, boy! You know how to make an old man feel better.' Targo laughed boyishly.

'But even mud can be an edge, especially if our enemy believes we'd never flounder through it to achieve our objective.'

Targo stared hard at Artorex. His eyes were narrowed, and very bright.

'You may have an idea there, boy. You could be right.'

Artorex's fame had spread quickly, and well-wishers slowed their passage through the narrow streets. An hour of damp wandering through the town finally led the pair to Myrddion and Llanwith in a very disreputable drinking house outside the gates of Venta Belgarum, where they were selecting warriors for what Llanwith was calling a 'little hunting expedition.'

When Artorex saw the motley bunch his two friends had collected, he suspected that Llanwith and Myrddion had lost their minds.

Of course, Luka had vanished once more.

The appearance of the group of warriors drinking at a rough trestle table was unprepossessing. Myrddion appeared to have chosen the roughest and filthiest warriors he could find. Scarred, tattooed and ragged in hair and clothing, the men shared only one characteristic – their weapons were impeccably clean and shining.

Targo cheerfully greeted the Scum, as he called them, and immediately seemed right at home. After a few moments of conversation with them, the old veteran invited Artorex to meet some of the grinning and unrepentantly dirty troop of warriors.

'You sons-of-whores have claimed that you want to meet Artorex – and here he is,' Targo shouted above the din of the warriors who were talking loudly in small groups. 'To you men, he is Captain Artorex and he is your commander. I won't be introducing you pretties to the captain for the moment because he won't remember your names. But now that you've joined our impossibles, you'll need to smarten up a bit.'

Artorex endured a round of backslapping, and soon became aware that many of the men had gambled on his right arm in his contest with Ban.

'Why?' Artorex asked one small, thickset man with repulsive features.

'It stands to reason, Captain. My name's Pinhead, by the way. Your gear's good. It's not pretty but it's good. And you move real well. You didn't need a shield, although I don't fancy distance fighting or going up against arrows without one.' He grinned amiably at Artorex, and winked with his single eye. 'And most important, you didn't give a damn about what was going on around you. You kept your eye where it belonged – on your enemy.'

'And you're very pretty!' A tall Celt with an evil squint smiled and blew a kiss in the direction of Artorex.

Without a moment's thought, Artorex backhanded the hulking brute across the face with sufficient force to knock him to the ground.

The Celt came to his feet with blinding speed. Artorex expected the man would draw his sword, but he merely shook his shaggy head and grinned sheepishly.

Pinhead sniggered. 'Always the big mouth, Rufus. It's a wonder you're still alive. You're lucky the captain only gave you a little kiss back.'

'Beg pardon, Captain,' Rufus apologized simply and, when Artorex nodded, he returned to his ale.

'This one here is Odin, Captain,' Targo said slyly of another huge warrior. 'It's not his real name but none of these pretties have been able to work out who he is. He's a Jute.'

Artorex's eyes passed over the man. Odin was so tall, even in his bare feet, that Artorex had to look upward to study his face. The Jute was fully clad in furs and Artorex had difficulty recognizing where hair ended and pelt began. Under a simple helmet, the man's long mane was nearly white, while his beard, which was extraordinary in length and thickness, spread out in a red spray over his barrel chest. The warrior bore an axe threaded through a loop on the right side of his belt and an extremely long, and inhumanly heavy sword in a beaten scabbard on his left.

'Now, this one's a really pretty warrior,' Targo told the troop, and everyone laughed.

Odin began to speak rapidly in a language Artorex couldn't even hope to understand, apart from recognizing one word, Thor, uttered with reverence.

Then, to Artorex's complete embarrassment, Odin knelt and placed Artorex's foot upon his neck.

'Don't pay no mind to Odin, Captain,' Pinhead explained. 'He's swearing one of his barbarian oaths – he seems to have taken a liking to you. He was most impressed with your little battle yesterday.'

'How did a Jute find his way to Venta Belgarum?' Artorex asked, through a deepening blush of embarrassment. He pulled his foot away from Odin's huge hands.

'Well, it wasn't by choice,' Pinhead explained. 'He was running from a troop of Saxon vermin outside Londinium – and I mean running. Seems he'd upset them somehow. Five to one seemed an unsporting way to fight, so Rufus and I equalized the odds. Then we found we couldn't get rid of him.'

'The only thing we understood was that he was making a blood oath,' Rufus said. 'He seemed to think his life belonged to us.'

'Oh, and he kept going on about Odin, so the name stuck,' Pinhead explained in tandem with his friend.

'He fights well, though,' Rufus added conversationally. 'What he does with that axe fair gives me the dreads. You could say goodbye to any Saxons we meet if you had forty of Odin.'

'Then I'm pleased that he's taken a liking to me,' Artorex responded, raising Odin to his feet and taking out his dragon knife. Artorex thrust the hilt of the dagger towards Odin, while retaining his grip on the blade in a gesture of friendship. It was a dangerous game, for the Jute could have severed Artorex's fingers just by pulling the blade free. Instead, as Artorex had hoped, Odin simply placed his hand upon the knife hilt and repeated his earlier blood oath.

A commotion at the door drew Targo's attention.

'By the bare breasts of Mother Juno, it's Ban,' he muttered.

Unconcerned at the stir he was causing, and with a brief nod to Artorex, Ban strode over to Myrddion and spoke quickly and quietly to him. The two men grasped each other's wrists briefly, as if a pact had been sealed.

Then Ban swaggered out, as easily and as casually as when he had arrived.

Artorex sheathed his knife and joined Myrddion and Llanwith.

'Fortuna is with us, Artorex. She certainly smiles on you,' Llanwith chuckled.

'Ban told me that he wishes to assist us in our expedition. He, and his entire personal guard, have offered to ride with us. He believes himself to be in your debt.'

Artorex shook his plaits in perplexity. Ban was a nobleman and a warrior, the master of vast lands, men and great wealth. Artorex repaid every debt and remembered every kindness offered to him, but he was surprised when men such as Ban behaved similarly. Caius, Severinus and the rest of their intimates had shown no sense of duty that Artorex could ever discern. Nor did Uther Pendragon prize honour overmuch, to judge by his actions.

'How many men do we have in our combined force, Myrddion?' Artorex asked.

'Including Targo's scum, we have sixty seasoned warriors, and I believe that number will be more than sufficient. In a surprise attack, and with luck, we have the numbers to win. If we fail in our task, then Uther's forces are not greatly weakened. As we have no friends to assist us on our expedition, we shall have to live off the land and forage as we travel. Our party is not too large, so we should be able to maintain some element of surprise.'

Artorex nodded his agreement; Myrddion's tactical appreciation was sound.

Myrddion beckoned to Targo to gain his attention. The warrior looked up from his ale cup and ambled over to where the two men were standing.

'Yes, my lord?' the veteran asked, all attention under his shield of soldierly indifference.

'Your men must be up and mounted at dawn,' Myrddion said. 'You're now their leader, though even your talents mightn't be sufficient to discipline that rabble. Artorex is the Captain of our force, and he'll determine all questions of leadership. For the moment, you may tell your beauties that there'll be no more drinking this night.'

'They'll just love that,' Targo snickered. 'But they'll obey. You have my word on it.'

'And you'd best find a horse for that barbarian – a very large horse,' Llanwith called after him.

'If we have sixty men, our force should be divided into three cadres of twenty,' Artorex decided. 'Targo will command his troop, while Ban commands his choice of twenty of his best men. Llanwith should take whoever is left.' He smiled at Llanwith. 'I'm sorry, my friend. You must do with them what you can.'

Llanwith grinned at Artorex's rueful expression. 'Men are men. Whoever they are, and whatever gods they serve, they'll obey.'

'Luka will act as your forward scout,' Myrddion said, 'and will remain ahead of the force when you are on the march. He has a talent for subterfuge, he understands the Saxon tongue and we'll need to utilize every tactical advantage open to us.'

'What of you, lord?' Artorex asked. 'If any man should lead this expedition, it should be you.'

Myrddion grimaced. 'I'm not a fighting man,' he stated unequivocally. 'I am a strategist, so I never developed the skills of combat. I'm a manipulator and a scholar, but I'm not a master of men. My purpose on our expedition will be as a mentor, a healer and an adviser – for those are duties that I do best. You four will lead the raid, with Artorex in overall command, exactly as Uther demands. If Artorex falls, it'll be Llanwith's task to return here with the survivors.'

Luka did not return to the Wild Boar Inn until the afternoon sun was low on the winter horizon. The rain had cleared to a light drizzle, but Luka was soaking and chilled to the bone.

Worse still, his eyes were hooded and he couldn't quite meet Artorex's speculative gaze.

'What news, Luka?' asked Llanwith. 'While you've been out enjoying yourself, we've recruited our entire troop.' He poured some warmed wine for his friend.

'Uther has been with his confessor since dawn. He won't see his queen, and refuses to suffer the ministrations of Morgan. The High King's court prepares itself for his death.'

'And?'

'Morgan is happy.'

'Only the death of Uther and all he stands for would give that bitch joy,' Myrddion said vindictively.

'I agree. There is one detail of concern – but the little Eilyn, my eyes and ears in the Great Hall, could be wrong.'

'Spit it out then, Luka,' said Llanwith with a smile. 'How bad could kitchen gossip be? Our situation can't get any worse than it already is.'

Something in Luka's face made Llanwith pause and his easy grin quickly melted away.

'Botha and twenty seasoned warriors left Venta Belgarum just after dawn. They rode to the west, in the direction of Sorviodunum.'

Myrddion frowned. 'I don't see—'.

'Before departing, Botha freed his slaves and he gave twenty pieces of red gold to Eilyn as a bride price,' Luka went on. 'It seems that the man is her uncle, and she believes he has no intention of returning from this particular raid.'

'There's more to this tale, isn't there, Luka?' Artorex interrupted. He felt a chill surge through his body until it raised the blond hair on his arms. Every sense was shouting alarm.

Artorex captured Luka's impassive eyes with his own steely gaze. Will clashed against will, and Luka was the first to break eye contact.

'Where does Botha go? He wouldn't leave Uther's side except on the orders of the High King.'

'Botha avoided telling Eilyn any details of his mission or his destination. But she told me that he was profoundly disturbed by the orders he'd been given.'

A single, awful thought left Artorex gasping and sick with urgency.

'Uther wouldn't lift a hand against Ector, would he?' he said, aghast. 'Not even the High King would dare to alienate Roman Britain. No! . . . It can't be! . . . I must return to the villa!'

'You can't leave, Artorex,' Luka cried out. 'I've done all that is possible. I've sent two fast couriers by separate routes to the Villa Poppinidii as soon as I heard of Botha's departure. I took this precaution, just in case.' He paused. 'You can do nothing to change the course of events that has already been set in motion, even if you returned to the Villa Poppinidii now. You are at least one day, probably more, behind Botha. I'm afraid we have no choice, for we are obliged to continue with our plans and ride with our Impossibles to Anderida.'

Luka squeezed Artorex's shoulders to console the younger man, but Artorex thrust his arms away violently. Luka's face seemed magnified and Artorex was unable to tell if the emotions it wore were self-interest, pity or panic.

'If Uther has sent Botha and his warriors to the Villa Poppinidii, you'd be too late now to help them, even if you rode until Coal's heart burst,' Luka begged. 'You must trust that my couriers arrive in time to warn Ector and your family.'

'Still, I must ride back to the villa, even if I should be too late,' Artorex repeated, and began to collect his roll of travelling furs. 'If any harm was done to my family, I'd never live with the shame.'

'You speak nonsense, boy!' Llanwith snapped. 'Uther's crazed hatreds can't be laid at your door. He's the architect of any wickedness that occurs in this place, and he alone must accept the blame. Besides, aren't we trying to guess at Uther's intentions? The road that leads to Sorviodunum winds on to many places that lie within the domains of the High King, and Botha could have been sent to any of these locations. What could Uther gain by sending his guard to the Villa Poppinidii?'

Luka averted his eyes; only Llanwith heard his sudden indrawn hiss of apprehension.

'Nevertheless, I intend to return to the Villa Poppinidii immediately, regardless of your explanations,' Artorex repeated, his mouth set in stony determination.

The three travellers looked at each other, their faces aghast with the possibility of total failure in their mission and the unravelling of all their carefully constructed plans.

'Uther will call you a coward and he'll have you killed as a traitor,' Myrddion pleaded. 'If you desert your command, he'll raze the Villa Poppinidii to the ground as punishment for your treachery and Ector will be declared an outlaw. Your warriors – and your friends – will die as well. He'll determine that all of us are unfit to live.'

'Nevertheless, my duty lies at the Villa Poppinidii with my

family', Artorex murmured with certainty. 'I regret any harm that might come to you but I've no choice.'

As he bent to gather up his weapons, something came at Artorex from beyond his peripheral vision. Before he could turn away, his head exploded and his knees collapsed under him.

Targo looked down at his fallen master, and shook his bruised fingers where they had been trapped around the knife hilt that had stunned Artorex.

'You great ones amaze me. You talk and you talk! This boy would have left here and returned all that distance to his family, while you were still thinking up noble phrases to keep him from harm. So old Targo has to knock the boy senseless to stop him from throwing his life away. I love that boy, and I'll probably die for him, but I'm damned if I can see why Uther hates him so much.'

Luka and Llanwith lifted Artorex gently and moved his flaccid body to a pile of furs in the corner of the room. Luka checked his breathing and Llanwith covered him with another heavy fur. Meanwhile, Myrddion gripped Targo's arm and forced the old warrior to listen to him.

'I know you're angry, Targo,' Myrddion whispered to the soldier. 'I can understand that you might think we've failed Artorex in some way, but it's time that you learned the whole story of the boy.' He paused to control his thoughts.

'Artorex is Uther's first and only living son, born of Ygerne's body after a hasty marriage. Following the birth, Uther issued orders that the babe was to be taken to Bishop Lucius of Glastonbury, who was to arrange for the child to be exposed to the elements and allowed to die. Lucius lacked the stomach or the immorality to kill infants, even on Uther's orders, so he sent the child as far from Uther's influence as he could, to Lord Ector and a Roman way of life. The good priest then spent many hundreds of hours on his knees, as he prayed to his god for guidance after defying the wishes of his king.'

'But you assured Artorex that he was no kin to Uther,' Targo protested.

'I didn't lie to the boy. I told the boy that he wasn't a *bastard* son for, beyond all argument, he's Uther's *legitimate* son. How could I warn the boy of the perils of his bloodline? He'd have revealed that knowledge to Uther – by a look, a gesture, or even a careless word. And then that madman would have killed him out of hand.' Myrddion stared at his hands. His face was downcast with shame. 'I had no choice. It is the land and the common people who matter.'

Targo made a sharp exclamation of disgust. 'Does Ector know what manner of child he has fostered for Lucius? Did he realize the danger that his kin would face when he allowed the child to enter his house?'

'No. It was nearly twelve years before Lucius confessed the details of his involvement in Uther's evil scheme to me. And the bishop didn't know if Artorex had Gorlois for a sire or Uther Pendragon. Nor did we, until we first saw him. Gods, I almost bowed to him when he was twelve and had scabs on his knees. Since then, our sole aim has been to keep the boy safe, for Artorex is our only hope if we are to oppose the inexorable advance by the Saxon hordes. Our intention must be to unite the tribes under Artorex's banner so they'll fight as one body.'

'No wonder you objected to Artorex's marriage,' Targo muttered. 'The Celtic kings wouldn't welcome a queen with a Roman lineage.'

'Poor Gallia,' said Luka. 'But I swear I had no inkling that Eilyn was kin to Botha when I was bedding her.'

Three pairs of eyes swivelled towards Luka with dawning horror.

'Did you tell that bitch that Artorex was married – and that he was a father?' Myrddion asked, amazed by Luka's stupidity.

'Yes, I did,' Luka confessed, his eyes downcast. 'She spoke of Artorex and described him as a handsome man. Without thinking, I told her that he was already taken by another woman. We were each making use of the other, and I'd drunk far too much wine trying to gain what information was to be had,' Luka pleaded. 'I only learned of Botha's movements because of Eilyn. How could I predict that a drunken slip of the tongue would lead to Uther gaining such dangerous knowledge of the Villa Poppinidii?'

'I can't believe that you were so thoughtless and stupid, Luka!'

Myrddion's gaze was hard, and Luka quailed under his friend's accusing stare. When he chose, the gentle Myrddion could be as terrifying as Uther Pendragon.

'Hades take all tyrants!' Myrddion cursed, and kicked at Artorex's pack. 'My apologies, Luka. You couldn't expect to know they were kin but I wish you'd been more circumspect.'

'Aye. The fault is mine. And also the shame, if any harm should befall little Gallia.'

Luka looked so downcast that even Targo lacked the heart to belabour him further.

'So, what can we do now?' Llanwith asked pugnaciously. He pointed at Artorex's unconscious form. 'The lad won't trust us again – and I don't blame him.'

'We can't do anything. We must let chance rule, for all our decisions have been made and we are committed to them,' Myrddion answered sadly.

'I hope you realize that the boy might never forgive us for what we've done tonight?' Targo whispered, his eyes sad and stark.

'I know, Targo. I understand the implications of what has occurred,' Myrddion replied distantly. 'But the fate of the west is greater than any single man or group of men. And little Gallia must now take her chances – as we do.'

When Artorex eventually awoke, he had a blinding headache, a heaving stomach and couldn't remember at first where he was. Then his memory of the events of the night, and the possibility that Botha meant to harm his family, returned to terrify him. He sat up abruptly and fumbled for his weapons.

Targo sat with his back to the door with a drawn sword over his knees.

'It's too late now, boy. Whatever may happen at the Villa Poppinidii – if that is Botha's destination – will have been set in motion many hours past. You are now far too late, so dress yourself, for today we ride to Anderida.'

Targo looked at his erstwhile pupil with a face pained by the unblinking, hating eyes that glared back at him.

'Why have you done this evil to me, Targo? Is Villa Poppinidii not your home also?'

'Don't taunt me, boy. I'd knock you senseless again if it would save you from stupidity.'

'Then don't speak to me at all,' Artorex snarled, as cold fury rose in his pale eyes. 'Leave my presence! Immediately!'

'No, boy. You may hate me if you want but I'll not leave you.' Targo chose his words carefully. 'You will ride to Anderida with your Scum, for they'll never be held loyal if you can't master yourself. Your foster-father has vowed to keep Gallia safe, as did Frith, and they'll not break their oaths to you lightly. You may kill me if you wish, or even order me to kill myself, I'll obey your commands. But your destiny is to become a great leader of the Britons, and your fate won't permit you to cast aside the future of the west for a hundred wives or a thousand children. Decisions made for self are the flawed actions of a petty Uther Pendragon.'

'Why, Targo? Why does he hate me so much?'

'Uther can't bear the thought that *anyone* could be a great warrior or a gifted leader to rival him. He's maniacal, and so set on preserving his reputation that he's prepared to cut off his nose to spite his face.'

'He may fear me but I'm no threat to him. May the vile old monster die in agony if he harms my family for no reason.'

'If need be, I'll personally see that he screams in extremity,' Targo promised. 'But, for now, you must wash your face, dress yourself and present yourself to your command. Many of your men will die for you in the days ahead.'

And so Artorex was forced to reconcile himself to his first great sacrifice. Against all his finer instincts, his love for his family and his wish to protect his home, cold reason washed over his passions through a quiet, inner voice that assured him that Targo's words were true.

Yet, as he accepted his fate, something in Artorex's soul withered. He realized that, even if Gallia and little Licia were safe and well and even if the villa remained undamaged, he'd made a conscious, personal choice – one that he could never forget, least of all forgive.

Anderida wasn't particularly far from Venta Belgarum as the crow flies, but the attacking force had no obvious and convenient route to their destination.

According to Myrddion's maps and local knowledge of the terrain gained from his spies, Artorex had four possible choices of approach to reach his destination. Unfortunately, his choices narrowed if he hoped to achieve any element of surprise in the campaign they were about to undertake.

The first of these choices was to take the easy coastal route, but Artorex soon concluded that the lack of cover from vegetation, the flatness of the land and the chalky cliffs that edged the sea made discovery of the attacking force a certainty.

The Saxons would be warned of the approach of Artorex's force long before they'd come within sight of Anderida. The small force would be caught between the mountains and the sea, and would be crushed by the Saxons.

The second and third routes were equally impractical. They would take the force through thickly forested chains of hill country that led to secure areas overlooking their destination. Unfortunately, each of these routes ended in stout gates leading to the fortress.

The fourth, and final, choice was to ride through a sodden, lightly forested valley that led to deep marshes. This treacherous and treeless waste protected the western approaches to the garrison.

Artorex understood that the easiest route was suicidal, and this option must be rejected out of hand. Further, passage through the high ground would be extremely difficult, except for accomplished horsemen such as those led by Ban and Llanwith. Similarly, the marshes could only be traversed on foot and then only by warriors with limited supplies and arms to slow them down.

To further complicate their choices, Luka explained that Saxon raiding parties regularly foraged out from the fortress of Anderida, for it was strategically situated on the edge of the narrow coastal plain that led to Noviomagus, Portus Adurni and thence to Uther's winter capital, Venta Belgarum. The Britons had long described the Saxons as wolves. They struck fast and viciously in small packs, and killed every living thing that stood against them. Then they retired to Anderida where they lived in complete safely, with the sea at their backs and treacherous swamps protecting their northern flanks.

As Artorex's force rode out of Venta Belgarum, a silent crowd gathered to watch the volunteers as they passed, for rumours had sped through the streets of their impending departure. Even the multiple-storeyed wooden buildings seemed to lean inward out of curiosity as the troop rode towards the main gate that led out of the city.

Artorex was still impressed by the size of Venta Belgarum, so even the fears he held for the safety of his family and his sullen rage couldn't entirely override his awe at the size of the crowds clustered on every vantage point to watch them pass.

Targo's men had already fashioned an impudent banner, a crude strip of old white cloth on which one of their number had daubed a red dragon rampant. This rag had been mounted on a pole, probably stolen, and was now gripped in Pinhead's gloved paw.

Ban's men rode under an embroidered banner of an iron fist clutching a burning branch. Their body leather shone with bronze discs and their faces displayed the competent demeanour of professional soldiery. The crowd cheered and Ban raised his clenched fist in both an acknowledgement and a salute.

There was little difference between the men of Ban's troop and those of Llanwith's cavalry, except that pen Bryn's standard bore a green crouching dragon with its wings spread in attack. Llanwith chose to ignore the crowds who threw flowers for the cavalry to ride over. Women ran forward to thrust small gifts at the warriors and Artorex was embarrassed when an old woman pressed a narrow length of ribbon into his hands. He would have returned the gift, but she vanished into the crowd.

'Why are the people so interested in our expedition?' Artorex asked Targo.

'Anderida and its Saxon hordes scare the people of the south so badly that anyone who tries to relieve them of this menace has their gratitude. Wear the old woman's ribbon and remember how much our attack means to ordinary people.'

'I feel like a fraud,' Artorex replied, but he tied the short length of scarlet ribbon round his wrist. 'I'm not certain that I want to be here – and I'm far more interested in my family than I am in the common people.'

'Then try to pretend,' Targo snapped, his eyes fixed on the road ahead.

During the first night, the men were ordered to keep fires to the barest minimum and muffle the hooves of their hobbled horses with strips of cloth. Saxons could be behind any tree and Luka remained their only advance warning of any impending ambush.

The Brigante king rejoined the troop in the grey light of a watery dawn.

'The terrain ahead is nasty, friends. The coast route offers damn all cover, but the mountain routes appear to be slow and hard going for men and horses alike.'

'What of the valley route?' Artorex asked.

'There's some cover, but not much.' Luka smiled thinly. 'The marshes, though, provide an effective bar to our passage.'

'But the marshes aren't totally impassable, are they?' Artorex persisted.

'No. But the wooden palisade of the fortress overlooks some of the marshland. And there are acres of water, reeds and the sucking mud. There's no way out if you get caught in the mud without assistance.'

'Do they guard the marsh approaches?' Artorex hammered away, to the irritation of both Luka and Ban.

Myrddion's eyes gleamed. 'There isn't even a gate on that side, Artorex. Why would there be? Who's going to crawl out of a swamp and scale their walls?'

'I will, and so will the scum! It's the most direct route, although it seems painfully slow. The Saxons don't expect an attack from that direction and their defences will be concentrated on the entrances to their fortress.'

'True,' Llanwith agreed cautiously. 'But the cost to our numbers as we try to climb the ramparts will be wicked if our men are on foot – or if they are detected before we are ready to launch our attack.'

Artorex gripped a piece of twig and roughly scraped a drawing of the garrison and the surrounding terrain on the muddy earth.

'If Ban's group of twenty cavalry can be directed along the ridges to the north, they should be able to evade detection on that route,' Artorex explained sparely. 'And there are fewer men and horses to slow their movement across the rough terrain. This group should be positioned to carry out their attack through the northern gate.'

The other men nodded.

'If Llanwith's troop takes the southern route, and keeps to the cover of the ridgelines, they should be able to avoid detection from the coast. They'll carry out their attack on the southern gate.'

'I agree with your assessment, and I'm happy to carry out my allotted task,' Llanwith nodded.

'If we could gain entrance through both the northern and southern gates at night, or in the early dawn, we'll cause havoc,' Ban stated. 'But unless those gates are opened, we're a spent force before we even start. Our timing must be perfect.' He grinned at the other leaders as a frisson of excitement showed through his guarded eyes. 'But if the third group could emerge from the swamps in darkness, using stealth to climb the palisade with grappling hooks, they could open the gates before the Saxons are aware of what is happening. We could have the advantage of total surprise over our enemy.'

'Exactly!' Artorex smiled.

'Unfortunately, the size of our force is limited so I doubt that we have the numbers to successfully implement this plan,' Ban continued regretfully.

'But the Saxons have no horses,' Artorex pointed out. 'In addition to the Scum, we will have forty mounted cavalrymen attacking in the early morning darkness with the advantage of surprise. If we are successful, we will rain down fire from our arrows on their quarters until the fortress is ablaze. Our weakest link is that some of our warriors must attack the palisades on foot. If they fail, we all die!'

Artorex challenged the other men.

'Do you have any reservations? Speak now, for I am but a novice at warfare and I will defer to wiser heads than mine.'

'I have no better plan,' Ban replied, with a white grin. 'We all have to die sometime, so I will take my troops to the north. They are skilled riders and are experienced in battle.'

'And I will take the southern route for much the same reasons,' Llanwith volunteered with a wicked grin.

'The Scum will take the direct route under the orders of Targo,' Artorex said bluntly. 'It'll suit them, as little discipline is needed – just rat cunning, close fighting and some nasty dispositions.'

'One final matter remains. We have to be close to our destination by dusk within three days so we can assume our attack positions in darkness.'

'Oh, joy!' replied Llanwith with a mocking laugh. 'I love to charge at impregnable gates when I can't see the rabbit holes.'

'But we can build some nice little fires inside once we are ready to attack, because wood burns well, my friends,' Ban stated. 'Especially if we add a little melted fat and some pitch.'

'It will take the slowest of the groups at least three days of travel to get into position,' Artorex continued. 'Once Llanwith and Ban reach their rendezvous points, they must remain there, undiscovered, until Luka can confirm the positions of the other two groups. Luka will advise you of the timing needed to co-ordinate your movements. He'll then join us on the ramparts of

Anderida.' Artorex gazed at the faces of his commanders. 'Is there any matter we have not considered?'

All the leaders shook their heads.

Myrddion examined the expectant faces of the assembled group. 'Then you've made your decisions, my friends.' He looked up at the pale, ashen sky. 'There will be no sun today. This rain will continue, so we must move quickly along our separate routes while there is cover and concealment. We must strip the wagon that carries our kit and provisions, and carry only those weapons that we need for the attack. When we resume our march, each group will act independently until we rejoin at Anderida.'

He smiled at his young protégé.

'I wish you good fortune, Artorex. For you'll need it.'

Silent, grim men rode out of their bivouac to the north and to the south in their order of march, while Targo's scoundrels followed the forested tracks of watercourses and kept to chains of oak coppices that had sprung out of the ground, long before even Uther was a lad.

Artorex recounted the plan to Targo, so the veteran could relay their role in the coming action to the Scum. To Artorex's surprise, the men preferred the back door approach, for it gave them the best odds until they were actually in place on the ramparts.

These ragged men knew how to fight. In fact, most of these mercenaries had no other skills and their best abilities came to the fore in narrow, tricky places where their cunning and ruthlessness gave them an edge.

They're the perfect weapon for the swamp and the palisades, Artorex reminded himself and tried desperately to wipe Gallia and Licia from his mind, just as he had struggled to forget that many of his men, verminous as they were, would die because of him in this audacious attack.

The Scum didn't complain when they were refused fires at night for they understood that no sensible commander would betray their presence to an enemy. Nor did they disapprove of travelling mostly in the darkness and sleeping for just a few hours of daylight under mounds of leaves or alongside fallen logs.

'One campaign is much the same as any other,' Targo told Artorex as they bunked down in light forest for their first period of rest. 'These men have fought across the Roman world, so they know the privations of soldiering. Just as long as they get their spoils at the end of the battle, they won't care about mud, swamp or cold steel. They have simple priorities.'

Gradually, the campsite became silent.

'I'm sorry, Artorex.' Targo's voice was ragged and Artorex wondered if Targo had wept under the cover of darkness and a thick coverlet of leaves.

'Never mind, old man. At least you were motivated by affection for me.' Artorex was surprised by the bitterness in his own voice. 'The three travellers view me as a means to save their own world.'

'No, lad. You're wrong. Myrddion, for one, would do anything – *anything* – to lift this burden from you. Yes, you're a necessity to their plans – but they love you. I've watched them closely, because I also didn't want to be used in the grand plans of other men. But you must acquit them of this sin.'

Silence fell, and Artorex wondered if his old mentor had fallen asleep.

'I needn't have worried, Targo, before I fought Ban at Venta Belgarum.'

Artorex heard the rustle of dried leaves, as if a ghostly wind stirred through the mounds of dried grasses.

'About what?' came a thready whisper.

'Whether I'd have the balls to kill another man. Uther has

given me incentive, and I believe only blood will make me feel better. Someone is certain to die and, as I can't kill Uther, I'll have to kill Saxons instead.'

'Be careful, boy. Death is serious – and it's permanent.'

'I'm my father's son, aren't I? What's a few Saxons more or less?'

Deep in his mound of leaves, Targo would have wept, if he knew how.

A few hours later, the troop was moving forward at their best speed, although their stomachs were pinched with hunger. Better to carry weapons that preserved life rather than food. The Scum would eat and drink when they had taken Anderida and the fortress was theirs.

Targo had become quite fond of his rag-tag troop and knew the names of every warrior under his command. Of them all, only Odin gave Targo the 'wierdies', as he called it.

'That hulking mass of hair and muscle is absolutely silent once he climbs off a horse and is afoot. I swear that he disappears into the landscape so well that you could walk over him. The first you'd know of him was when he cut off your balls.' Targo glanced across at Odin who was ahead of the troop among the trees. 'Gods, Artorex, his feet are bare! And he doesn't seem to give a damn about how cold it gets.'

'I'm glad we face the Saxons and not the Jutlanders, if his countrymen are all like Odin,' Artorex replied mildly as they rode slowly on muffled hooves through the lightly falling snow.

'I can't tell the difference between any of the barbarians,' Targo complained. 'They're all built like walking mountains.'

'That's why Caesar left them to hack each other to pieces on the other side of the River Rhenus.'

After two hard days of travel, the tree cover thinned away to nothing but bare, snow-dusted folds of brown wasteland. The hobbled horses were left to forage within the remains of the tree cover, while the men took to their own legs. Where the land provided no cover, the warriors crawled on hands and knees.

Targo drove the men hard, for they must find cover before night came drifting over the eastern horizon. They must lope on, though their legs ached and their hands were blue with cold.

Targo spoke little to Artorex, fearing to intrude into that calm, impenetrable place where his master had retreated. As he pushed his old legs to follow Artorex's mile-devouring stride, he cringed when he thought of the lad's bitterness and anxiety. If thoughts of revenge keep him safe from the Saxons and that bastard, Uther Pendragon, then so be it. Perhaps we have worried for nothing, he mused.

But Targo had a soldier's prickling in his palms and a hunter's instinct for men like himself. Botha had probably gone to his death, for Uther's captain had indicated that he didn't plan to return to Venta Belgarum. The task he'd been given could well have been dishonourable. If so, everything old Targo loved had probably been destroyed – and he'd done nothing to prevent the disaster.

And the marshes were now before the Scum, and Anderida beckoned with its siren call of invincibility.

CHAPTER XIII

CARRION CRY

In far-off Villa Poppinidii, some hours before Artorex had defined his reckless plan to attack Anderida, Ector and Caius were supervising the training of their crop of yearlings in the horse paddock. As they watched one of the young colts being introduced to the bridle, a house servant pointed to the long roadway that led up to the villa.

A stumbling horse, seemingly of its own accord, was plodding slowly up the track, carefully avoiding its dangling reins as it picked its way carefully through the ruts.

Ector gave swift orders, and a house servant ran towards the beast. Ector and Caius followed at a more sedate pace, in deference to the older man's stiff joints.

When the servant began to lead the faltering horse towards them, Caius and Ector made out a figure that had slumped across the horse with his arms bound together around its neck. Blood stained the defined muscles of the horse's chest, and ran down the right leg of the beast from a deep wound in the man's side.

Somehow, the wounded man had managed to bind his neck scarf into a thick pad to slow the bleeding. He had then lashed his wrists together with part of his undershirt in case he lost consciousness, and had set the horse upon a course towards the villa.

Both men were sickened as they imagined the pain the young warrior must have endured to secure himself upon the back of the stallion.

'He'd have died of exposure if he'd fallen from his horse in this icy weather,' Ector said softly. 'Still, he's only alive now because his blood has congealed in his wounds before they drained him utterly. He's near death – and I'll be surprised if he survives.'

Ector scanned the long road carefully in the direction from which the rider had come.

'Everything seems as it should be but I wish I could be sure,' Ector warned his son. 'I smell trouble in the wind.'

'Perhaps our workers should remain at the villa tonight,' Caius suggested. 'I, too, sense that strange eyes are watching us. I'd sleep more soundly knowing that extra men were close at hand in the barn if we should have need of them'

'Issue the orders then, son. At best, they'll sleep snugly in the stables. At worst, we may need their help if there are Saxon raiders abroad.'

Nothing stirred.

Nothing moved.

Even the birds were silent, and Ector felt a shiver of apprehension in his belly. A scent of snow was in the cold wind and he knew he should deliver the wounded man to the care of the women in the villa as soon as possible, but his palms itched as if a trap closed around him.

Ector realized with a tiny frisson of recognition that he was afraid.

Caius took the reins of the horse and dispatched the servant to carry a hurried message to the headman of the village warning him to send the women and children to the forest in case of attack and requesting able-bodied men to assist with the defence of the villa.

Father and son then encouraged the exhausted horse to make one last effort to carry the strange rider to the warmth of the villa.

Gallia was resting in her own warm bed, having been wracked by fits of nausea that caused her stomach to reject all food. That morning, satisfied that her mistress was not seriously ill, old Frith had brought Licia to the villa to prevent the curious child from disturbing her mother with her childish prattle. Frith's healing talents would now be needed.

As always, Julanna welcomed the presence of Licia who played quite happily with her own little Livinia, so Frith hurried to a spare storeroom where the wounded stranger had been laid out on a pallet. Frith bathed the gaping wound in the young warrior's side with hot water and clean towels. She observed, with disappointment, that pearl-pink loops of bowel were visible to the naked eye and were clearly damaged. The wound already had a slightly rank odour, so the old woman deduced that her ministrations would come to naught. Still, she stitched and bathed the wound before binding it tightly. She sat with the boy, for he was little more than sixteen, throughout the long afternoon.

In all that time, he spoke not a single, lucid word.

True to his promise, Caius kept the field workers at the villa after they had completed their normal daily toil. Fortunately, most of these men had been trained for the villa's defence by Targo, so they were familiar with the swords, daggers, bows and axes held in the villa's armoury. Rather than sleeping in the servant's quarters, they planned to stand guard in the storehouses close to the villa.

Caius was also grateful to welcome a number of other men sent by the headman of the village. While lacking conventional weaponry, all the volunteers carried hoes, reaping hooks or other evil-looking farm implements. These men were sworn to the unwritten pact that existed between the Villa Poppinidii and their own homes.

For those souls who lived in these lands, any threat to one person was a threat to all. Besides, these villagers were almost in a festive mood for, after all, there are worse ways to spend a cold winter's evening than in a billet in a warm barn with brewed ale to drink and a rich stew to devour.

The Villa Poppinidii had been built in the Roman tradition, with thick, earth-packed walls that offered scarcely a single egress for an enemy. Heavy wooden gates sealed off the villa proper, and clean light and air came via the gardened, open atrium that lay within the long rectangle of the villa's structure. A colonnade surrounded this atrium and rooms opened directly on to the long, tiled corridor. The villa was almost impregnable.

But gates can be broken, and no place is totally secure. Cross-ventilation was provided from both long sides of the rectangular structure of the villa by a series of shuttered slits, half a man in height and an arm span in width, that helped to mitigate the summer heat. Here lay the villa's weakness. That one such shutter should lie in the storeroom where the wounded man now lay was to be expected. That Julanna should choose to sleep in the chamber with the other shutter was a quirk caused by her dislike of enclosed spaces. Ector determined that these two rooms, and the central gate, must be guarded at all cost.

The villa was surrounded by outbuildings, including stables, piggeries, the servants' quarters, an apple press, storage rooms and a cold room set in the ground, all of which were placed like chickens around the skirts of the villa. With the horse paddocks on the western side of the villa, there was little cover that could hide an enemy, but the apple, pear and lemon orchards could conceal an army approaching from the east.

Ector chose to keep his farm workers and the volunteers from the village within the horse barn and the granaries as a reserve for those defenders who were in the main part of the villa. From this outside vantage point, they could fall upon any foolish souls who assaulted the gates in a frontal attack. The villa's women were barricaded into the servants' building, the *rustica*, for safety.

As night fell, and flurries of snow began to fall, Frith decided to return to Gallia's house, leaving a tired Licia to sleep with Julanna at the villa. But her patient needed nursing and care, so she informed Caius that Gareth would return to the villa and take her place, having learned the use of simples from his great-grandmother. The lad was sworn to protect Licia with his life, if need be, so not only would he guard one of the weakest spots in the villa, but he'd also assist Caius, if needed.

Before Frith made her slow way to Artorex's villa, Ector stopped her and voiced some serious concerns.

'The Villa Poppinidii can be readily defended, Frith, but Artorex's house is isolated. If the Saxon raiders are unfamiliar with the villa, perhaps Gallia and her servants will not be detected, but I'd prefer that they were with us behind our thick walls.'

Frith sensed dark wings hovering over her. Danger threatened, she knew.

'I agree, Master Ector. I will persuade my lady to seek shelter here.'

'I am relieved, Frith. Indeed I am.'

As Frith hurried towards Artorex's snug little home, her barbarian superstition warned her that the air with filled with black wings and the thickets with staring eyes.

The house servants had already bolted the gates and Frith had to pound upon the panels to gain entry. Once inside, Frith hurried to Gallia's bedchamber where her mistress was lying, wan and tired. Her pregnancy had only reached the fifth month, but her child was unusually large and was sapping Gallia's strength. Besides, the mistress had been subject to fits of black depression since the birth of little Licia, when Gallia wept for her lost kinfolk and swore that she would be better dead. Artorex and Ector had tried to comfort her when her dark moods came upon her, but she could only bear Frith to be near her. Even little Licia became an irritant, and Gallia would cry inconsolably that her daughter would fare better without her.

'Gallia!' Frith murmured. 'Wake up, Gallia! Lord Ector believes that a Saxon attack is imminent and wants us to go to the villa for protection.'

Gallia opened her sleepy eyes. 'We've never had trouble with Saxons before, Frith, and our house is remote from the villa. I'm so weary, I'd rather remain here where I can rest.'

'I know you're tired, my precious, but we must go. Let old Frith help you into warm furs and we'll leave this house. If you're too weary to walk, your manservant can carry you.'

'I dreamed of Artorex as I slept, Frith. He's riding into danger – and I know he's going to die.' A small tear glistened on Gallia's cheek.

'No, sweetheart! No! He won't die, I promise.'

Gallia shook her head like a broken wooden doll. 'He's in danger, Frith. I saw him in a dreadful swamp, surrounded by corpse fires.'

Frith tried to shatter Gallia's fey mood with any means at her disposal. The slave gripped her mistress's hand and shivered at the icy coldness of her flesh.

'All the more reason to keep yourself and your babe safe,' Frith replied, trying to warm Gallia's hands between her own palms. 'He'd want to ensure that you were protected.'

'There's no point, dear Frith. Licia is safe and I'm certain we'll not be found here on the edge of the forest. I'm quite prepared to let fate take its course. I don't want to leave – so I won't, no matter what you say. Go, dear Frith. Please, I just want to sleep.' Gallia's small mouth was set in a mulish pout.

'Please, Gallia!' Frith persisted. 'Don't be obstinate! This house is difficult to defend, so we must leave. If you don't want to think of your own safety, then consider your servants and your unborn child!'

'It's far too late, Frith. Let the servants go to the villa if they wish. The Saxons will be watching us anyway, if they are here, and they'll see us if we attempt to reach safety. They'd intercept us on the track. Whatever the gods decide will happen, whether I'm at the villa or here, in my own home. As long as Licia survives, nothing else matters.'

Gallia turned her face to the wall and fell into a light doze. Frith wanted to scream at her and shake her shoulders until her mistress acted sensibly.

But the barbarian slave knew, through her ancient, alien blood, that Gallia had sensed a change in the tenor of her world. When the three travellers came, she felt the patterns move and alter. Something dark was impelling Gallia to act foolishly, but Frith had no idea how to force her mistress to her senses.

'Heaven help us,' Frith thought aloud. 'We will all die!'

Not for a moment did the old slave consider leaving her charge, although her heart fluttered in her withered chest as if it would leap out of her rib cage.

Gallia's personal servants also refused to return to the villa, or even to venture into the Old Forest for safety.

Gareth was also proving difficult. Frith was forced to spend many minutes persuading him to leave Lady Gallia and return to the villa to protect Licia.

Gareth had grown into a strong youth who was utterly devoted to Artorex and his family. While he wasn't particularly tall, Gareth's appearance was imposing because of the strength of his bone structure, the unusual blondness of his hair and his quick intelligence. Like Frith, he had a streak of creative sensitivity that gave him an acute sense of beauty; like Frith, he was stubborn to a fault, and was impossible to move once his mind was set – as it now was.

'If I were a Saxon, I'd attack this house first,' he hissed, to avoid alarming the house servants. 'You need at least one other man here to protect the house.'

'Someone must protect Licia in the main building,' Frith pleaded. 'Who else but you, my grandson? I'll not fail my oath, and nor should you.'

Only an appeal to Gareth's sense of duty could have forced the young man to return to the villa proper. Frith kissed his firm, sun-reddened cheek, tousled his lovely hair and blessed the lad, for he was leaving her to protect her beloved Licia. Frith's heart told her that she'd never see her great-grandson again.

Fortune favours the brave, but it especially protects those who are prepared.

At a little before midnight, the villa was attacked by Botha and his trained warriors.

The total force, less than twenty men, came with stealth, creeping from the orchard through the shallow, newly fallen snow like blots of spilled ink on the white scroll of the earth. Carefully, with muffled weapons, they encircled the main building, while Botha sent three young men to destroy the distant cottage on the far side of the fields that had been found by his scouts in the late afternoon.

Ignorant of Gallia's peril, Gareth was closeted with the wounded courier who had, by now, lapsed into a coma. The youth half-sensed the approach of Botha's warriors, although he only heard a mere scrape of metal against stone, but all his faculties were immediately alert. Through the bolted shutters, he saw fur-cloaked men moving stealthily in the moonlight. Two of the men were carrying blazing torches.

'Awaken!' Gareth screamed. 'Awaken! We're under attack.'

And then, after latching the storeroom door, he raced to the great bronze gong in the colonnade with its large hammer that had been provided to warn the occupants of the house of impending threat. As the metal sent out its deep knell of warning, Ector awoke with an oath.

The alarm had not been struck since starving wolves had attacked the villa some twenty-five years earlier. Ector felt the old fires of battle stir in his thinning blood.

'Awake!' Gareth continued to scream from the colonnade as the attackers began to batter at the shutters and the main entry door to the villa. Caius and Ector had slept fully dressed, with weapons beside their beds, and they now ordered the house slaves to danger spots inside the villa while they protected the right colonnade themselves.

Ignoring his instructions, Gareth abandoned his patient to his fate and scurried to Julanna's apartments. He was determined that he would defend Licia with his life if need be.

He found Julanna clutching the two children to her shivering body as an iron pommel beat against the wooden shutters. The face of the mistress was as pale as parchment, and she cried thinly in fear. Gareth sent all three females into the small, windowless room that linked Julanna's apartments with her husband's sleeping chamber.

'Keep the bars secure on the doors, no matter what you hear,' Gareth ordered, a long knife made by Bregan in one hand. 'And you must keep the children silent – for my sake.'

Gareth didn't know that four of the attackers were already dead, killed from behind by the village recruits as they tried to break in through the narrow front doors of the villa.

He didn't hear the bloody death rattle as his patient's throat was cut when the villa's defences were breached through the window of the recently vacated storeroom. Nor did he realize that Ector and Caius, supported by the house servants, were already engaged in desperate combat in the colonnade.

He was certain, however, that every attacker who entered the windows of Julanna's chamber would die.

Gareth easily killed the first intruder, as the warrior was pressed against the wall, half inside and half outside the slit in the window, in an ungainly attempt to clamber through. With speed on his side, Gareth cut the warrior's throat with one carefully measured slash, before stepping backward to avoid the jet of arterial blood that arced across the room.

Fortunately for Gareth, the second intruder slipped on the spilt blood as he leapt through the breach, so Gareth was able to blind the intruder with another quick slash of his knife across the man's eyes. This warrior, bleeding profusely, roared in mingled pain and rage, and struck out with his sword in the confined space, but Gareth dispatched him easily with a wicked knife thrust from behind.

Gingerly, Gareth peered out of the broken shutter. This side of the house was now free of attackers, but he could clearly hear the sound of vicious fighting from across the atrium.

'Keep the door barred, and remain here until I return,' Gareth ordered through the door that should keep Julanna and the children relatively secure.

When she disobeyed him, he thrust a discarded sword into her shaking hands. Her eyes widened when she saw that the boy was covered in fresh blood. Then, her hands steadied as she hefted the heavy weapon, and Gareth registered a new hardening in the eyes of his mistress.

'Don't let the children into the bedchamber. Latch that door,' Gareth roared, before he sped away across the atrium on naked feet that left a bloody trail behind him on the mosaic floor.

Four huge warriors were forcing Ector and Caius to retreat inexorably towards the locked entry doors when Gareth ran up behind the attackers. The bodies of four house servants lay on the tiles where they had fallen after being cut down like ripe grain. Caught between the intruders and the metal-bound entrance, father and son had little chance of survival.

From behind, Gareth hamstrung the warrior closest to him with one quick slash. The man screamed and fell to the ground, while the warrior in close combat with Caius dropped his concentration, and his sword arm, for one brief, lethal moment.

It was enough.

Trained by Targo, Caius understood the value of the edge when fighting at close quarters. He slashed at the warrior's sword arm, now exposed, and the forearm was sliced to the bone.

Mercilessly, Caius stabbed his enemy through the neck without a flicker of compunction.

The other two attackers were now caught between the three defenders. Hemmed in by the narrow colonnade, the two warriors fought until they were cut to pieces.

The surviving warrior was still trying to regain his footing with a useless leg when Gareth knocked him senseless with his sword hilt.

Simultaneously, a villager with a slight head wound stumbled up to the locked wooden gate and began to pound on the timber with a blacksmith's hammer.

'Master Artorex's house!' He screamed through the timbers. 'It's burning!'

Gareth unbolted the gate, and Bregan tumbled into the open entryway. The blacksmith was repaying his debt to the Villa Poppinidii.

'Are any of these curs outside the villa still alive?' Ector roared, his bloodstained sword dripping in one hand.

'No, my lord, we seem to have hunted them all down but Master Artorex's house is burning from end to end.'

'Mistress Gallia is still in there!' Gareth shrieked, and began to run.

'Wait, boy,' Caius yelled after him. 'Wait! The gods alone know how many more of those animals are still alive out there.'

'Go with him, Caius,' Ector ordered. 'Try to save Gallia if you can. Bregan and I can manage here – can't we, old fellow?'

Caius ran at his best speed, but he was less nimble than the stable boy. By the time he was within sight of his foster-brother's house, he could see that speed was useless.

Lit by the leaping flames, Gareth stood in the small courtyard with bloody arms upraised, screaming anguish and defiance at the uncaring night sky. He had found old Frith at the side of the house, stabbed through the body many times when she had thrown herself over Gallia to protect the young woman after all escape had proved hopeless.

Gallia's throat was cut down to the spine.

At the open gateway, Caius found Artorex's servants, hacked to pieces as they defended their mistress. One of the enemy warriors lay dead some little way off from the bodies of Frith and Gallia. A metal hairpin had been driven through one eye, deep into the man's brain.

Caius recognized that familiar pin with a pang.

'See, Gareth? Frith has gone to glory with her enemy,' he shouted over the roar of the flames. 'She drove a needle into his brain.'

But I've failed in my oath, Gareth thought inconsolably – and Caius feared the boy would cast himself into the flames.

'Does Licia still live?' Caius shouted, as he tried to pull the boy back from the crumbling structure of the house.

'Aye. She lives. She's with Julanna and her babe,' Gareth remembered and allowed himself to be drawn away a few steps backward.

'Then you should be guarding her,' Caius ordered savagely. 'That was your duty.'

Unwillingly, as if his eyes refused to leave the staring, empty face of Gallia, Gareth backed away, his feet slipping on the icy surface. He paused and returned to the small tragic bodies. With his knife, he cut an amulet from Gallia's ruined throat, and then bowed in one final act of reverence.

After a last glance back at the tragic scene, he ran in the direction of the villa to make good his pledge.

Caius drew his hands over the death mask of the beautiful young woman. Her puzzled expression disappeared as he closed her eyelids.

'Poor, harmless and joyous Gallia,' he murmured to the flames.

Caius shivered.

He knew instinctively that many men would perish when Artorex discovered the fate of his wife and unborn child, and many worlds would burn to ashes before the steward could be deflected from his revenge for these senseless acts of murder. Caius's fertile brain scrambled to invent an excuse for his negligence in leaving Gallia outside the villa proper where she could not be protected. Regardless of their wishes, Frith and Gallia should have been forced to sleep under the protection of the villa's defenders.

And the same stars that looked down on Gallia's body, still cradling her unborn child in her belly, were also smiling down on Artorex as he continued with his Scum towards Anderida. For such is always the fate of those few people whom Fortuna raises high on her terrible wheel of chance.

Even as night became day, the ravens, crows and rooks were

gathering at the Villa Poppinidii. Already, the smell of carrion tainted the winter wind.

Hamstrung by the blade of Gareth, Botha did not deign to scream, even when Caius cut off his fingers, one by one. A maddened Julanna sliced him unspeakably with a kitchen knife with ruthless, female cruelty, but still the old warrior gritted his teeth and uttered only his name, as if that admission were guilt enough.

Nor did he utter a word of explanation or defence for his actions, even at the point when Ector took pity on his tortured body and beheaded the old warrior with his own sword.

Uther's most loyal servant joined his fellow warriors in an untidy, bloody pile in the snow of the horse paddock.

These animals were Celtic warriors, Ector thought, his thinning hair awry and his eyes blurred with tears, as the field hands bore the bodies of the villa's dead to be washed and prepared for cremation. How could Celts kill Celts? And slaughter innocent women? And innocent children?

How will I justify our failure to Artorex? Caius thought, with a flutter in his belly. He will be beyond rage.

He kicked at a fallen warrior's bloody face with his booted foot and enjoyed the crunch of bone under his heel.

Let the birds feast on their eyes before their burning, Gareth thought viciously, as he spat on Botha's emptied face. Let them go sightless to the Shadows.

And the crows came.

CHAPTER XIV

OUT OF THE MARSH FIRES

Artorex stared laconically at the expanse of marshland, punctuated by a number of odd stunted trees that reached almost to the edge of the palisades of Anderida. The last flags of light gave him few clues on how to locate a path through the wasteland, so he beckoned Targo to his side.

'What do you know about swamps?' Artorex asked curtly. Time was no friend on this night, for the scum must cross the wasteland before midnight. Soon, Luka would bring confirmation that the other troops were in position to commence the attack.

'It's less than I'd like but as much as I need,' Targo answered drily. 'The only safe way is to move slowly, in single file, testing the ground as we go. It'll take us most of the night before we are across it.'

'Damnation!' Artorex swore. 'Spending a day exposed at the foot of the palisades is a crazy risk. We have to move faster.'

'I can try using Odin as the lead scout. He's supposed to live where swamps are commonplace and his weight will find the sucking mud faster than either you or me,' Targo suggested guilelessly.

'I sometimes think you consider him expendable,' Artorex drawled softly with a grimace that could have been a smile.

'However, I agree with you. He's the best possible choice – so Odin leads us out. We start immediately.' He paused. 'Tell them to daub themselves with mud. You too. It'll save our skin from the insects. And ensure that the men protect their weapons at all cost, for they'll soon need them.'

'Aye, lord.'

Targo melted away like a grey ghost.

When the darkness seemed absolute, tiny fires flared up in the distance, multicoloured and hideous. Artorex remembered the legends of lost souls that called to the living to follow them into the maze of water and mud until they were doomed.

'Marsh gas,' Targo explained softly, but Artorex saw him clutch his amulet tightly for luck. 'Fire without heat.'

On elbows and bellies, or bent double, the scum crawled through tussocks of sharp-bladed grass and pools of icy water, following Odin as he made his way through the swamp. The Jute seemed perfectly at home in the sodden landscape. When he signalled a route that bypassed a patch of deceptively firm ground, Pinhead threw a rock at it and watched nervously as the earth sucked the light object in before returning immediately to a semblance of innocence and solidity.

Pinhead shuddered and scuttled around the margins of the sucking earth, cursing under his breath.

Artorex need not have ordered his men to coat themselves in mud.

Within minutes, the whole troop looked like unholy creatures of folklore that had risen from the swamps to kill off unwary villagers.

'Let's hope the Saxons are superstitious,' Artorex spat as he crawled on sore elbows and knees as quickly as he could, while ignoring the eerie beacons of flame that came and went like wraiths.

The Scum had been moving quietly through the swamp for

several hours, listening to the distant sounds of carousing men within the fortress, when silence gradually began to settle over the blackness of the night. Sleet and rain still threatened and patches of dense cloud often obscured the moonlight. A light drizzle was falling as they moved like heaving tussocks of mud and grass through the rank, wet landscape.

Then Odin rose to his feet, bent low to examine the earth and began to move with greater confidence in a zigzag pattern through the morass. Signalling with a thin whistle resembling that of a night bird, Targo ordered his men to follow in the tracks of their guide.

Now, as the pace picked up, the palisade loomed in front of the troop. The Saxons had cut down tall trees, stripped them of branches and sharpened the trunks into great points. Lashed together and sunk deeply into the muddy earth, this wall was an effective barrier to all but the most determined enemy.

'Pass the word to your men that no one must speak, for any reason, even if a marsh snake bites them on the arse,' Artorex ordered Targo in a whisper.

A further hour of bent backs, careful steps and the start of cold rain saw the whole troop huddled at the base of the palisade.

'Are Ban and Llanwith in position?' Targo whispered in Artorex's ear.

His master shrugged.

Artorex had lost all sense of time, but the moon was lowering in the sky when Luka slithered out of the swamp like a dark serpent.

'Well met, Artorex,' he grinned, his white teeth the only visible feature in his muddy, grease-blackened face. 'Ban and Llanwith await your pleasure.'

'Then we must hope the Saxons sleep deeply,' Artorex hissed back. 'For they will hear us at work if the palisade up there is guarded.'

Targo rose up from behind a tussock. 'You're late, Lord Luka. The moon is going down.'

'And so are you. Your Scum are none too fleet in the mud.'

'Shut up, both of you. Don't speak unless it's necessary,' Artorex ordered in a whisper.

He looked up towards the palisade towering above them. 'How many grappling hooks do we have?' he hissed to his sergeant. Mentally, he blessed Myrddion's foresight and knowledge of Anderida.

'Four, sir,' Targo responded.

Five men apiece, Artorex thought.

'Right. We go over the wall now, Targo. You and Odin go up first with one group. I'll lead the second, and Luka will lead the third. You can select someone else to lead the fourth group. With luck, we'll all be on the ramparts before the Saxons know we're abroad.'

'There'll be guards for certain. The Saxons aren't stupid,' Targo whispered back.

'Perhaps. But Uther hasn't made any offensive probes against Anderida for years, so there's a fair chance they've become overconfident. In any event, if there are sentries, we'll have to remove them – by any means possible.' Artorex glanced back towards his men. 'Send Pinhead to me.'

Pinhead crawled to Artorex's side. He looked infinitely muddier, nastier and more dangerous than usual.

'Do you have your bow, Pinhead?'

'Aye, for what it's been worth so far,' the warrior replied with a grin. 'I've also lugged a good supply of arrows along, and some burning fat in case we need flame arrows.'

'Excellent, friend. When the Scum are on the ramparts, set fire to one of your flame arrows and send it high into the air. This signal over the swamps will tell our friends to the north and the south that they can commence their attack on the gates.'

Pinhead nodded. 'I thought you'd want to use fire so I've already prepared the arrows.'

'I'll tell you when to loose the first barb. If Llanwith and Ban can't join with us in a coordinated attack, we just have to improvise.'

As they spoke, men clutched tightly to their amulets, and Artorex could see their lips moving in soundless prayers or promises. The Scum knew that many men would die and so, in their own separate ways, they made their peace with their gods. Only Odin held aloof, a grappling hook attached to a length of rope dangling in one ham-like hand.

When Artorex, Rufus and Luka had chosen their own grappling hooks and checked that their ropes were secure, Artorex gave a brief signal, and Odin's hook flew through the air high above the palisade. He pulled on the rope with the full weight of his body, and the grappling hook held.

Immediately, and with astonishing grace for such a giant, Odin began to climb.

Artorex, Rufus and Luka cast their hooks as one. Rufus swore as his hook fell free but, fortunately, it snagged on some unseen obstruction on the ramparts.

Silently, the troop began their climb.

Odin and Targo were already dim shapes in the shadows, and were creeping silently towards a brazier near the north gate as Artorex swung his aching body over the wall. The sight of a giant and a stunted old warrior hunting together should have been ludicrous, but Artorex smiled with satisfaction as the quickly moving shapes were blocked out from the light of the braziers.

The short figure of Targo padded silently back towards Artorex, while Odin disappeared into the darkness.

Both men would have headed towards another brazier, dimly visible through the damp mist of rain at the south gate, but

Targo mimed a throat-cutting action and the shambling Rufus disappeared like a ghost into the fine drizzle.

One by one, the last of the Scum landed, light-footed and undetected, on the ramparts.

A sweet sappy scent of newly-sawn timber rose in the rain, a comforting smell that was alien to the dark task ahead. Artorex dispatched two groups of six warriors with the sole task of securing the north and south gates for the entry of the attacking horsemen, while four bowmen with a plentiful supply of arrows were positioned at strategic points on the ramparts to support the attack.

With his small force in position and ready to attack, Pinhead joined Artorex high above the Great Hall of the Saxons, surrounded by its attendant sod huts.

'You have the warning arrow safe and dry? And ready to fire?' Artorex hissed.

Pinhead nodded.

'Then light it and let it fly – come what may.'

Pinhead grinned through blackened teeth, and freed a short bow from an oilcloth wrapping, and strung it effortlessly. A bundle of arrows wrapped in very dirty cloth soon followed, and Pinhead was obliged to use his whole body to protect them from the thin mist of rain. He gripped the first arrow shaft in his disreputable teeth.

A tinderbox was produced from somewhere on his verminous body, and Artorex marvelled at the natural skill with which Pinhead struck the flint against stone. The noise did not travel far in the still, fog-shrouded night, and Artorex trusted to his luck and the lightly-falling rain to mask any sounds. Again and again, Pinhead worked the flint until a few weak flames leapt up and he thrust the arrowhead into the feeble conflagration.

What Pinhead had used to fuel his signal arrow, Artorex had

no desire to know, but the cloth caught fire immediately, even in the light rain. Pinhead inserted the arrow into his bow, pulled back on the gut string and the signal soared high into the air, trailing fire, until it dropped away into the swamp.

Then, just as Artorex thought that he had avoided the worst possible outcome – immediate detection – a long ululating cry went up from the south gate and Artorex knew that Rufus had failed to kill the sentries silently. The scream was cut off as it reached an inhumanly high note, but the damage was already done.

Warriors in various stages of undress boiled out of the sod and reed huts and from the entrance to the Great Hall. Their long, unbound hair streamed out in the firelight which suddenly rose to reveal the flattened earth below the ramparts.

The Saxons seemed to cast impossibly long shadows as they poured from the doorways like ants. Most were naked and they appeared fearsome with huge swords and axes that they swung with manic eagerness.

Gods, there are too many of them, Artorex thought to himself, as a bolt fired from Pinhead's bow sped past his ear. A Saxon warrior, wearing only a fur cape and a fierce grin, fell before he reached the ladders leading up to the ramparts.

The Scum sped towards the gates as they fought toe to toe with the Saxons to gain every foot of advantage. Smaller but faster, they fought savagely with the knowledge that they would die horribly if the gates remained obstinately closed.

But twenty men, even rat-cunning veterans of a hundred campaigns, could not hope to defeat over one hundred Saxons, not counting their women, who fought even more viciously than the men.

A horn echoed through the steadying rain from the north, echoed by the brazen cry of its mate to the south. Artorex scarcely had time to recognize the sudden drumming of hooves out of the forest to the north before the Saxons were upon him. Pinhead fired arrow after arrow while Artorex protected the smaller man from attack. Every dirty trick that Targo had ever taught him in his youth was employed, as Artorex lashed out against unprotected body parts so he could bring the dragon blade across suddenly undefended throats.

In the narrow confines of the ramparts, Artorex had his edge, but Pinhead was almost out of arrows and still the Saxons swarmed towards them. Artorex attempted to move forward in the direction of the southern gate that had borne the brunt of the fighting so far, with Pinhead using the last of his arrows as his shield. The pace was pitifully slow.

Artorex had never experienced the true carnage of battle. Targo had tried to prepare his pupil for difficult ground that was slick with blood and spilled entrails, but nothing his tutor had described prepared him for the smell. Even over the rain, the hot reek of blood steamed like brass and clogged the back of his throat. The smell of vomit, urine, pierced bowels and the rank stench of frightened, sweating men created a terrible stew of odours that made Artorex's gorge rise. All he could see was the face of the man before him as he cut, parried and slashed, until that face fell away and another took its place.

A long bull roar rose over the howls, curses and screams of desperate fighting men.

Odin.

The gods themselves seemed to answer as a rumble of thunder appeared to shake the sodden earth. Then Artorex realized that horses were within the confines of the fortress, crushing friend and foe alike, and the mailed fist of Ban rose over the troop like a green flame.

'Artorex!' Pinhead screamed as he raced up the ladder to the top of the parapet. 'Artorex!'

Both Saxons and Celts looked up, for the small man had tied

Artorex's dragon flag to his bow like a makeshift banner, and in the flaming thatch of sod huts, hissing in the rain, the beast seemed alive and malevolent. The Saxons at the north gate fell back in superstitious dread until Ban's horsemen hunted them down.

But the battle was still balanced on a knife edge.

Twenty cavalry and the remnants of the Scum were still outnumbered three to one by the Saxon defenders, and Ban's forward momentum started to waver.

At the northern gate, Odin still swung his axe in a wicked parabola of reddened steel, as he protected Ban's flank with the small detachment of scum that had been sent to join him.

But at the southern gate only a few warriors fought on, hopelessly outnumbered, against a swell of yellow-haired Saxons.

'We must get Llanwith in through the southern gate or we will be slaughtered,' Artorex shouted over the screams of dying men.

Ignoring the feeble movements of the wounded, he leapt through the mêlée of horses, his sword and dagger dancing in a crisp interplay of movement that allowed him to continue the momentum of his headlong rush.

At the southern gate, the dead were heaped in a grisly half wall around Luka and four of the Scum who fought back to back, and were now, with every blow, being forced nearer to the closed wooden gate.

'To me! To me!' Artorex roared.

Targo looked up, his sword still held protectively over his body.

Two powerful slashes felled two Saxons before him, and Artorex forced a bloody passage through the press of enemy and confronted them alongside his Scum. Beside him, his men were bleeding from many wounds and Artorex could tell that they were almost spent.

Eight Saxons were pressing forward towards their prey.

'Open the gates! Open the gates – now!' Artorex screamed, as he slashed at the press of warriors before him.

At first, the enemy warriors seemed to seriously outnumber the Scum, even allowing for Artorex's arrival at the gate. But all he needed was a few seconds' respite, time for Targo to remove the massive plank that was proving to be such a major obstacle to achieving their objectives.

He killed one Saxon with his sword, piercing the pagan's throat with the dragon blade and neglecting to even watch the man fall.

Oblivious to everything other than the groaning protests of the great timbers as the bar on the gate slowly rose, Artorex fought on at the head of his men.

And then, as quickly as it had started, the gate was open and the battle was over.

Llanwith pen Bryn cantered his troop into this bloodstained charnel house and, caught between two troops of cavalry, the Saxons began to give way.

They fought to the last man and woman, but they were outmanoeuvred and outmuscled by the weight and power of the horsemen, leaving the Britons to develop a crucial edge over the battle-weary Saxons.

Eventually, exhausted and driven before their Great Hall, the remaining Saxons died in a fusillade of arrows. Every wounded Saxon was mercilessly put to the sword.

And Anderida was won.

The cost was fearsome and, once his blood had cooled, Artorex experienced the full horror of comforting those of his men who were mortally wounded and about to die for their cause.

Artorex looked at his shaking, bloodstained hands, and repressed a shudder of revulsion. How many men had he killed?

Targo had been correct. A well-trained warrior moves instinctively, his body following patterns that were almost unconscious. Other than the smell, Artorex had scarcely felt a moment of disgust but, then, he hadn't really thought of the men who came at him as being fully human.

It was now time to fulfil his duty to the dying.

Inside the Great Hall, where the Saxon chieftain had fought until he was pierced with many arrows, Myrddion tended to the wounds of the surviving impossibles. There, with needle and catgut, and potions made from poppy juice, Myrddion attended to the living and eased the passing of the dying.

And wherever Myrddion went, Artorex followed to give a word of cheer, the promise of a share of the plunder and to hear the last words of the dying. He swore to each man that his kin would hear of his noble ending; he vowed that wives would receive the portion of coin that should have been theirs and he held back useless tears so that he shouldn't shame the sacrifices given by these brave men.

Llanwith sought him out during this grim duty.

'Targo won't rest his wounds until his Scum have picked the bones of Anderida clean. They were promised spoils, and spoils they'll have, except for a one-tenth share to the High King, a one-tenth share for you, and a one-tenth share distributed between the captains.'

'The men may take my share,' Artorex sighed. 'I'll not profit with a single piece of gold from any man's death.'

'Don't allow your foolish scruples to override your common sense, my young hero,' Llanwith replied scornfully. 'How will you raise an army without funds? How will you dress, feed and arm your warriors? Or do you plan to send the last of the Scum back where they came from? To starve, or to beg.'

Artorex managed to look both confused and mulish, and Llanwith remembered that the young man was barely out of his youth. He'd just fought his first battle, and was still learning the heavy responsibility that came with command. Only Targo and six of the Scum remained alive, and all carried wounds.

'Targo is your man, and he'll do all that is necessary. Now come, for Ban is dying.'

'Ban?' Artorex gasped. 'Ban? How? He was on his horse. How did the Saxons catch him unawares?'

'Ban was always a little mad, Artorex. He took risks, and he pressed his luck. Myrddion believes that he wanted to prove his worth after being defeated by a stripling such as yourself.' Llanwith paused. 'I saw him as he charged the shield bearers that were guarding the Saxon chieftain. None could have doubted his intention – but one of the Saxon women gutted his horse and it fell. Ban was at their mercy.'

'So his men loosed their arrows on his killers and, in so doing, they robbed those Saxons of a warrior's death,' Artorex guessed, with the satisfaction of a victor.

'Exactly, my boy. War isn't fair, and there's little enough glory to go around. We must be grateful for the gifts that men like Ban bring when they pay us the honour of riding with us.'

Myrddion had ensured that Ban was as comfortable as possible on a nest of discarded furs, but even Artorex's untutored eye could see that the wounded man was near to death. The worst of the blood from sword cuts to the body had been staunched, but Ban's torso was literally held together by his own armour.

A lesser man would already be dead, Artorex thought sadly.

He schooled his face into some semblance of a smile.

'Still abed, Ban? Don't you realize you've won us a great victory? Your banner stands before the Great Hall of the Saxons even as we speak. It is our personal tribute to your service.'

'You have difficulty lying, Artorex, for all your skill with a sword,' Ban whispered wryly, each word forced from his filling lungs with great pain. Bubbles of blood were forming at his mouth, so one of his warriors wiped them away gently with a clean cloth.

'You must listen, Artorex, to the words of a man who is now one of your few, true friends. The High King will kill you, if he is able. But before Uther Pendragon becomes worm food himself, many false men will vie for the privilege of betraying you. You must remember this . . . and beware.'

The warrior's eyes were filming over, and only with the greatest of effort did Ban force back death for a few brief moments.

'My orders were to kill you during the attack,' he gasped. 'I couldn't . . . I must know . . . that my death has some . . . purpose . . . take the throne.'

'I am not meant to be a king,' Artorex stated.

'Answer . . . me fairly,' Ban demanded with all his old fire. 'My eyes are as good as those . . . of Uther. Uther . . . your sire.'

His words struck Artorex like body blows.

'If the kingship should be offered, I will take it.' Artorex's voice was firm, but his eyes were moving restlessly as they hunted for escape. 'I swear this to you on the lives of those who died at Anderida.'

Artorex told himself that he was swearing a harmless lie, and he smiled down at Ban with something akin to fondness.

'I'll remember your lesson, my friend,' he said softly. 'So fly to the heights, Firebrand of the West, to set the abode of heroes ablaze with your coming.'

'My . . . brother!'

And so Ban died, simply and quietly.

As one, the remainder of Ban's guards swore their allegiance to Artorex until death, for where their master had chosen to serve, so too would they.

And, as they swore their oaths, the young man pondered the

depth of human frailty. Ban's basic integrity had stopped him from killing Artorex, even though a promise to Uther Pendragon should have made him a murderer.

Uther was always certain that he would win this game, whether by chance or by treachery, Artorex thought sadly as he bent over the warrior and kissed his bloody lips. The High King underestimated Ban's basic decency but I, for all of my days, will always remember this man as a true warrior.

He rose to his feet and turned his attention back to Targo.

'We leave none of our dead to the carrion,' Artorex ordered. 'No matter how lowly, not one of our comrades shall be defiled. Their bodies shall be burned and their ashes collected in the finest golden box in Anderida. The only exception is Ban, whose body shall be returned to Venta Belgarum with us for burial. He shall receive full honours.'

And the warriors marvelled at the beauty and hawk-like cruelty of Artorex's face. As he ordered, so was it done.

All too soon, Artorex was forced to commence his preparations for the return of his command to Venta Belgarum and Uther's court. The Saxons possessed wagons built to be drawn by great oxen, and one of these ponderous carts was piled high with weapons, gilded crosses and chalices that had been looted by the Saxons from churches in the East. Even the sod huts were small treasure troves that turned up furs, jewels and adornments of gold, electrum, brass and bronze.

Many of the Saxon children had escaped into the wild woods, but those who could be found were tied within one of the wagons, to be taken as house slaves in a world that was brutal, even to the innocent.

In the other wagons, those wounded Britons who couldn't ride were gently placed on to thick straw pallets. Myrddion would ride with them, and would tend them as best he could.

All that remained was for a small detachment to be sent to

collect the horses left by Targo's scum near the approaches to the swamps. These beasts, along with all the Saxon animals that could be found, would follow the wagons along the easier coastal road back to Venta Belgarum.

Only Llanwith, Luka and Artorex remained behind as the cavalcade moved out.

'And now we burn Anderida to the ground,' Artorex said grimly. 'Until only ash remains.'

'The Saxons will return, Artorex,' Luka replied patiently. 'You know as well as I do that the Saxons own this coast, and they'll rebuild Anderida, just as it was before.'

'Then we'll burn it again, and again – a hundred times, if need be.'

'The Saxons may have something to say about that,' Llanwith grinned, and Artorex flushed hotly.

'Yet, you are right, Artorex,' Luka said with grim logic. 'Any delay to the Saxon advance is better than nothing, and Anderida holds several hundred Saxon corpses who won't breed again, and neither will they kill our brothers in the west. So let's burn the fortress down, so that those Saxons who are forced to rebuild the structure will understand that we intend to fight for our lands, come what may.'

And so, the fires were set. At first, the logs smouldered and smoked, but finally the fire took hold. The timber buildings, along with the corpses of the defenders, were consumed in the flames.

Long after Artorex and the impossibles were out of sight of the fortress of Anderida, they could see the great column of black smoke staining the grey noon sky. It marked the first frail victory by the warriors of the west.

The cavalcade arrived at Portus Adurni after two slow days of travel, taken in easy stages for the sake of the wounded. Artorex led his small command towards the stone-walled village above the harbour, where ships still plied a brisk trade with Gaul and beyond. The townspeople looked on in amazement as the column slowly wound its way up the Roman road.

To all the questions thrown at the warriors as they set up camp for the night, only one message was passed on to the population.

'Artorex has taken the fortress at Anderida. The Saxons were put to the sword and they died, to the last man and woman.'

Small gilt boxes were brought forth. They were filled with the ashes of both Scum and warrior, all mingled in death.

'And these are the ashes of our fellow heroes, who came to Anderida to prove that their oaths of allegiance were true. They died for the land, for their King and for Artorex, the Warrior of the West.'

The townsfolk speculated on how such a small troop of warriors, so battle-worn in their attire, could attack and overcome a fortress such as Anderida. They stared, wide-eyed, at the contents of the two groaning wagons that moved with them, and marvelled at the fat-tailed sheep and milking cows as they were herded into the pens of Portus Adurni and turned into gold and silver coins. Man turned to man, each wondering who, or what, this Artorex might be and whether the old days of glory might have come to the west once again.

Word and rumour spread faster than the slow-moving cavalcade could travel, so where small villages clustered near the Roman road, folk came out to stare, to cheer and to throw green branches over the chill roadways lest horses and oxen should slip on the black ice. Young children sucked their thumbs and stared up with wide eyes at the dour, grim-faced men as they passed, their destination of Venta Belgarum fixed firmly in their minds. Maidens sighed at their first sighting of the russet hair of Artorex, uncombed as it was, and at his wintry features that were so brave and so fair. Old men recalled the heroes of their youth and compared Artorex with a young Pendragon, come back to succour his people in their time of peril.

So the story became legend, and the glory ran like Greek fire through the snow-shrouded hills.

Artorex rode at the head of the column with his troop commanders alongside him. Odin walked, as silently and as steadfastly as ever, his eyes always searching for any threat in the lines of trees that ran parallel to the road. Rufus had died at the southern gate, but Pinhead still lived, although he sported a new and even uglier wound across his cheek that had severed part of one ear. The four other remaining members of the Scum took great pride in their status as the last heroes of an impossible assault on an overwhelming enemy, and Artorex had little difficulty in imagining how the story would grow with the telling. Already, he was embarrassed at how villagers bowed their heads or tugged their forelocks as he rode past, for he knew that Odin had turned the tide of the battle when all seemed lost, that Targo had saved the situation at the southern gate and that the irrepressible Ban had brought the conflict to its ultimate conclusion.

'The plan was yours, Artorex, and the final responsibility was yours,' Myrddion lectured him, a day's march from Venta Belgarum. 'You, too, could have died on the ramparts with your men. You are the figurehead, the Warrior of the West, whether you like it or not. And you alone must face Uther's fury when we return to his court.'

'Aye, but I don't wish to take what credit is due to others.'

'You can be sure, lad, that no one is likely to face the vicious wrath of Uther other than you,' Targo told him solemnly.

Even the Scum laughed.

And so, with their deeds already being sung in the inns of Venta Belgarum, Artorex's expedition returned to the High

King's city on the first day of the spring thaw. The church bells pealed their approach, warriors and townsfolk lined the muddy streets, while eager hands helped to unload the wounded into the care of the priests. Many of the townsfolk cursed their bad fortune in not courting death with the impossibles, and they looked up at Artorex with eyes that were awe-filled and envious.

Rumour had travelled fast from the coastal settlements that Artorex had won a great victory at Anderida and was returning to Venta Belgarum, so it was inevitable that a swift messenger from Pontus Adurni brought the news to the High King that Artorex and his band of warriors were less that two days' march away from his court.

Morgan brought the messenger to Uther in person. Her eyes were alive with malice although her marble-cold face was contained.

'Lord King, Artorex bids you all homage and all honour. He has taken Anderida and has left the Saxons to feed the crows, exactly as you demanded.'

Uther's breath drew in sharply, causing his whole, wasted frame to snake inward under the weight of his robes, almost as if he protected his belly from a stab wound.

'Don't speak that name to me,' he ordered querulously. 'Artorex is dead! No one could take Anderida!'

'Your confessor has told you tales of the Jewish King David, has he not?' Morgan smiled delicately. 'And he will have told you of how the great King lusted after another man's wife, the divine Bethsheba. King David sent Bethsheba's husband out to die, just as you sent Artorex to fight and perish in your service.' She glared her hatred at Uther. 'It's too sad for you, Stepfather, that a ruse you once used so successfully didn't work nearly so effectively on the second occasion.'

Morgan's light, girlish laughter was hideous within the King's previously silent rooms. His confessor turned his wide, frightened eyes towards the face of his monarch. On receiving no response, he slipped from the apartment lest he should hear words spoken that would consign him to the strangler's rope.

The eyes of the old King narrowed with cunning.

'Ban hasn't failed me. The Firebrand is loyal until death!'

'You have such fickle hopes, my lord', Morgan retorted. 'I must inform you that the body of Ban is lashed to the back of his horse and that he is one of the honourable dead of Anderida. Even as we speak, Artorex rides to Venta Belgarum in triumph, with the sound of the people's cheers ringing in his ears. If you still wish his death, you must find another fool to wield his sword on your behalf.'

'The whelp will never rule in my stead. He will never cast me down as High King of the Britons – and he will soon be forgotten by my people.'

'It's too late, Lord Uther. Far too late. You alone have turned this youth into a hero of the people. Yes, you alone have done this foolish thing. He came to Venta Belgarum as a nameless and deedless young nobody, and you've turned him into the greatest warrior of the Celtic people.'

Morgan knelt before her King and looked up into his rheumy, malicious eyes. Her small pink tongue explored her upper lip and stroked a small gap in her teeth.

'How my father would laugh. How Gorlois smiles on the other side of the veil as he waits for you to join him. Hail, Uther Pendragon, the High King, who will be remembered only as the cur who sired the saviour of the Britons.'

'Do not speak such filth to me.' Uther blocked his ears with both age-spotted hands. 'I can have you strangled – and perhaps I will, if you aim your poison at me. Be silent, or you will shriek your last breath away.'

'How could you cling to life for just a little longer if I were dead?' Morgan crooned. 'And how could you plot against

Artorex if you are worm food? I alone can keep you breathing beyond your time, which is something your confessor and his foolish, fruitless prayers can't do.' She smiled once more. 'And when your eyes close at last, a long line of your dead will be waiting to meet you.'

Morgan poured a small quantity of white powder into Uther's half-drained wine cup, where it hissed and bubbled ominously.

'A stimulant, my lord.' She held the goblet out to her step-father. 'Artorex comes to greet you – whether you wish it or not.'

Uther took the proffered potion and gulped it eagerly. Only spite, hubris and Morgan's powders could keep the blood circulating through his ancient, tired heart.

'You hate him worse than me, you viper,' he whispered as the stimulant cleared his brain.

'Aye, lord, but here's the oddity of it – I love him too,' Morgan replied, her eyes void of all emotion.

'Then God help the cub, for you'll skin him while you caress him.'

Morgan left her King to his endless, circling thoughts. On the stone threshold, conscious of the cold seeping through her thin slippers, she looked back over her shoulder towards the wicked old man and his dreams of immortality.

What a poisoned pair we are, Uther, she thought ruefully. Perhaps what we seek will only be won because we have become pawns in the destiny of Artorex, the boy – who has now become Artorex, the man.'

She shrugged away her thoughts, because the habits of hatred were too deeply ingrained in her nature to be weakened by the demands of history.

Morgan, eldest girl child of Gorlois, the long-dead Boar of the Dumnonii tribe, slipped away from the King's apartments like a whisper of acrid smoke on the breeze.

CHAPTER XV

ENDINGS AND BEGINNINGS

Artorex waited with Myrddion, Luka and Llanwith in the forecourt of the Great Hall. Dressed now in the best finery that the Saxons of Anderida had to offer, including a great cloak of white wolf pelts bound at the shoulder with a dragon pin in bronze, he was an imposing and regal figure. Targo had insisted he do honour to the Scum by wearing the torc of the Saxon chieftain, a massive neck-piece of pure red-gold, in the form of the winged worm-like dragon of the northern barbarians. The young man's hair was combed and loose, except for plaits that left his wide brow free, and his winter tunic beneath the barbaric cloak was of fine Roman wool.

Odin stood behind him, bearing a great wooden box.

The Jutlander had been bathed and barbered, not without some heathen protests, but now master and servant towered over the other courtiers outside the Great Hall, while many covert glances were aimed at the impassive faces that stared straight ahead towards the carved and verdigris-encrusted entrance doors.

'The High King keeps us waiting to put us in our place,' Luka hissed, while maintaining his soldierly bearing.

'The desperate act of an impotent man,' Llanwith agreed, with contempt.

'Yet Uther was once a great king and a gifted leader of men, my boy,' Myrddion murmured. 'It's important for you to remember this lesson.'

Artorex chose not to reply.

He stood mute, for not long after he arrived at Venta Belgarum, Caius had joined him after a furious ride from the Villa Poppinidii.

The preceding night had been fine and cloudless, white stars visible at last. After seeing to the welfare of his men, Artorex had returned to the Wild Boar Inn where the drinkers' voices had been stilled by the changes wrought in the raw young man during his trial by combat.

In his room under the eaves, Artorex had prayed to Mithras, to the Christian Jesus and to the Celtic Duan de Dartha to protect his family. But even as he intoned the intercessions to all the gods that he knew, he could feel a heavy weight pressing on his chest.

The arrival of Caius was no surprise.

His foster-brother was travel-weary and mud-stained, his dark hair awry and his impeccable clothing marked by the headlong pace of his journey. With new eyes, Artorex saw a thin stain of dried blood on Caius's cloak that was almost concealed by mud, and Artorex realized dispassionately that the other man could not quite meet his unwavering stare.

His foster-brother was afraid.

Caius told his tragic story simply and sparely, hoping to shield this new, wholly alien stranger from the worst excesses of sorrow.

'Ector mounted a great funeral pyre for Gallia, Frith and your servants. They have gone to the gods in glory together, just as they lived in life,' Caius explained slowly.

Artorex merely nodded.

The silence dragged out painfully.

'Our father mourns with you, and he holds little Licia as close as his own grandchild. Gareth guards her day and night – and his sorrow knows no bounds.'

At last he looked Artorex directly in the eye.

'Gareth has sent this talisman that he took from Gallia's body. Frith made it, and Gallia wore it, so Gareth believes that it is meant to be in your care. It is a final gift from two women who have played an important part in your life, so I pass it on to you.'

Artorex took the small pregnant form and caressed its swollen belly with his thumbs. He should cast it away lest grief overwhelm him, but the warm fragment of hazel felt so smooth and so full of love that, eventually, he decided to keep it. He folded his hands over the amulet and nodded his head in thanks.

Later, much later, Artorex would wear the tiny figure on a golden chain round his neck so that it would lie over his heart.

Caius felt decidedly uncomfortable and burst into hasty speech.

'The vermin who killed her are dead. We burned their bodies, and scattered their ashes to the winds so their souls would be lost forever. But first, we let the carrion eat their fill.'

Something of Caius's old cruelty had returned to his eyes as he told his tale, and Artorex thought, irrelevantly, that here was a tool fit for his use if ever he had such an ugly need.

Like father, like son, Artorex thought coldly, for he had finally reasoned out his kinship to Uther and his importance in the scheme of Myrddion's plans.

He felt as though tainted blood was running through his veins and yearned fervently for the opportunity to be alone with his grief.

'Only one of the assassins survived the battle, so we did everything in our power to ensure he revealed the reason for the attack on the villa,' Caius added. 'He was hamstrung by Gareth inside the villa, and couldn't move, except to crawl on the earth like a snake. Julanna applied her own ministrations in an attempt to extract information from the man by slicing his body in those places where the nerves are closest to the skin. I would never have believed my wife could act as she did.' Caius shook his head at the memory, for the young man was lost in the no-man's land between admiration for his spouse and the sudden fear that strikes when a harmless pet is found to have turned into a rabid animal.

He sighed.

'All we managed to extract from him was his name – Botha. He did not try to hide his identity, or mitigate his actions, regardless of torture.'

'In his own way, then, he was an honourable and loyal man,' Artorex said reflectively.

'He died hard, my brother. Ector and Julanna saw to his suffering, for I find I have had my fill of inflicting pain. Other than saying his name, or to pray to his gods, or to beg the pardon of the house, he said no other word. His ashes were scattered in the fields.'

'Thank you, Caius. It is my wish that you attend me in the morning when I visit the High King,' Artorex replied distantly. 'We live in strange times, brother, when women are the pawns of power, and I find that your great mother knew that one day I'd have need of you. I bound myself to you with my promise to Livinia and I'll always remember that promise.'

When Caius eventually found a spare sleeping pallet, still caked with dirt from his travels, he marvelled that the tender flesh of the boy he had called Lump had become the fully grown, cold and confident leader of seasoned warriors, some of whom he had just spoken to.

I never knew him at all, Caius wondered with a sense of unease. This new Artorex makes my blood run cold.

In the morning Caius washed carefully in the Roman

manner, dressed and armed himself as a Roman nobleman and joined Artorex and his friends in the forecourt of the High King.

Caius carefully seized the opportunity to mend his reputation with his foster-brother and the three travellers. Coldly, and with an eye to the main chance, Ector's son began to tie his fate inexorably to the destiny of Artorex. He blessed his mother, for she had recognized the quality in her foster-son and had bound him to her family through an oath.

Only Targo, as faithful and as intuitive as always, had entered Artorex's small room during the night. He came late in the evening and found his master wracked by voiceless tears as he clutched Gallia's amulet to his lips.

Long was Artorex's grief, and deep, for all its silence; Targo could do little except offer a soldier's company to a fellow soul who was in torment. When Artorex had wept all the tears his eyes could shed and had fallen into a restless sleep filled with blood and murder, Targo stayed on watch, his heart breaking from the memories of little Gallia and her lost, evanescent joy.

Artorex never wept again. In the long years that followed, he would know hideous loss but never again would he weep so honestly and so free of shame.

As he had done in the past, Uther underestimated the ultimate effect of his discourtesy to Artorex. The soldierly mien of Artorex and the oddity of several tribal kings and a Roman nobleman left cooling their heels in the forecourt was natural fuel for gossip, and the rumours did little credit to the High King. Artorex and his companions never complained. Silently, they stood at attention when other men would have wearied. Eventually, the High King realized his foolishness for, after two long hours, the brazen doors were opened and Artorex was summoned into Uther's presence.

The man who entered, flanked by Caius and Llanwith on one side, and Luka and Myrddion on the other, was no longer a youth but a man. His face was unlined and his hair as golden-red as ever, but his features had settled into an expression of measured authority, unencumbered by passion or wild emotion. His eyes glittered in his face, and they were unreadable, direct and beyond fear. The courtiers and priests who were present in the throne room shrank from his presence, for Artorex was the true king among them, relegating Uther to little more than a shrunken, ancient mummy, a shadow of his former self.

'I have brought you Anderida, as demanded, my liege.' Artorex's voice filled the furthest corners of the room. 'I bring you greetings from Ban, Firebrand of the West, who joined the glorious dead at the siege of the Great Hall of the Saxons. I bear the spoils of the Christian churches of the south-east as your portion and I ask your lordship's permission to wage war against the Saxons wherever they may be!'

Artorex raised one hand, and Odin advanced, bearing a great chest. At the foot of the dais, he bowed his head, opened the heavy, brass-bound lid and exposed the golden relics of the Christian churches that had been looted by the Saxon hordes. The gasping admiration of the court washed over him in waves.

Odin backed away to stand directly behind his master.

Uther did not deign to gaze upon the heaped religious treasures.

'Ask? Ask? You're not asking! You're demanding! What right do you have to instruct your king in the niceties of warfare?' Uther looked contemptuously around the court as if inviting laughter, but the room remained unnaturally silent.

Myrddion stepped forward fearlessly.

'My lord, Artorex is the true hero of Anderida, your leader who captured the impregnable fortress. He is the truest of warriors who fights in your name – and your name only. He is the Warrior of the West!'

Uther snorted as Myrddion stepped back.

Llanwith took his place.

'Artorex determined our strategies, planned our victories and personally caused the destruction of many Saxons. They burned like logs of wood in your brazier. He is the supreme Warrior of the West.'

Llanwith stepped back into position.

When Luka took his friend's place, he grinned at the assembled courtiers with a smile that held little amusement.

'My lord, Artorex alone holds the trust of all men, whether high or low, who know him. He alone can stand in your stead as your supreme warrior, now that age has brought your sword hand low. He has borne the burden of the death of our warriors bravely, and he has proved himself to be the Warrior of the West.'

Uther paled, and the crowd stirred like dry leaves in an autumn wind.

Finally, Caius took Luka's place and Uther peered at the unknown man, wrapped in a toga and armed with a Roman short sword.

'My liege, Artorex is the hope of the helpless, the bearer of burdens and the last Dux Bellorum. He is the Warrior of the West – regardless of the fact that he is my brother.'

Consternation filled the hall, and voices rose, twittering like birds or calling like gulls towards the blackened ceiling. Uther impatiently raised his hand and silence fell over the court.

'Who is this Roman?' he demanded.

'Caius is the son of Ector, guardian of the Villa Poppinidii and the Old Forest of Aquae Sulis,' Artorex stated in a loud, clear voice. 'His mother was Livinia, the last of the pure Poppinidii line, and he is my foster-brother. He brings you greetings from Botha, who remained true to his vows unto his death.'

Artorex's face was cold, unemotional and grim. The mention

of Botha, captain of Uther's guard, caused the audience to whisper and speculate, while Artorex waited to spring the trap.

Uther was dumbstruck. His grey face became pasty and his hands and mouth trembled as if in the grip of palsy. No one in that cheerless, imposing room could fail to notice that the King had been struck a body blow. His twisted, ivory fingers clenched and unclenched on his bony knees and Caius thought the old man would faint with shock.

So that's the way of it, Caius thought calculatingly. Uther wants Artorex dead. I wonder why.

The High King's guards, who were unaware of Botha's mission, were startled at the mention of their captain's name, while the faces of Myrddion, Llanwith and Luka were frozen in amazement. Only Caius and Artorex remained outwardly unmoved.

'The Villa Poppinidii stands strong, and continues to control the route to Aqua Sulis. No Saxon will pass while Ector, or I, draw breath,' Caius swore. 'And no flames, no treachery, and no murder in the dead of night will breach its ancient walls.'

If any man knew and understood that every word spoken was charged with a silken threat, then none dared to give any sign of that knowledge. Caius felt a wave of exultation course through his blood, for Uther seemed to reel and shake as if from a seizure.

Ygerne stiffened and Morgause simply gaped. Morgan smiled vaguely – and played with her knucklebones.

But Uther knew. He realized that his scheme had failed and that Artorex was leaping above his tragedy like a phoenix rising out of its own ashes. Aghast, Uther finally understood that Botha's raid had strengthened Artorex's position and, in the process, he had lost his most loyal servant. Now, surrounded by enemies and the merely curious, the High King seemed to deflate from within.

'You may do what you will – and we thank you,' Uther whispered in a voice that was as thready as the wind that slid through the cracks in the door.

And then, anti-climactically, the audience was over.

But Uther Pendragon, victor of so many battles, was not yet finished. Beyond doubt, the young man was from his loins, but the knowledge gave the old monster no pleasure. All Uther still possessed was pride, now grown hugely into hubris, and he swore that not even his own son would live to rule in his stead. Better that Celtic Britain fall into ruin than for his fame to be eclipsed.

To that end, the High King set his sharp mind and his iron will to develop his strategies.

For many hours, Uther schemed in his web like the spider he had become, until he eventually determined to send his sword and his crown to the Bishop of Venta Belgarum, thereby charging the Church with the selection of his successor. Uther trusted to the jealousies and fears that divided Christian from pagan to keep his throne free from the iron fist of Artorex.

In her sumptuous room, surrounded by fine cloth, jewellery and Roman glassware, Ygerne decided that Venta Belgarum would never be her home again. Her daughters were twisted and embittered by her bad choices, and to watch Morgan's cruelties and the vanities of Morgause prolonged Ygerne's pain. She'd return to Tintagel as soon as she could, leaving all the fripperies of her position behind her. Myrddion would know what to do. He'd been the architect of her fall from grace, albeit unwillingly, so he should be inveigled into helping her escape from her gilded, uncomfortable cage.

Uther would scarcely notice her absence.

Queen Ygerne stared into her silver mirror. Her grey eyes, so different from her son's cold orbs, softened as she remembered her father's face, like – yet unlike – Artorex. Uther may have stamped his bloodlines on the young man in hair and body, but the boy's firm jaw and those colourless eyes belonged to her father.

In the Great Hall, those grey eyes had looked at, and over her, without any recognition. Why should he care for her? Had she fought for him when he was too small to fight for himself? She had not. Had she taken the honourable course when she discovered Uther's plot to trick her into his bed? No. She never even thought to open her veins. And hadn't she stayed with her monster husband for decades, when common morality suggested that she should have left?

For the first time in many years, Queen Ygerne laughed freely. Uther was embarked upon a fruitless struggle with his only son that would poison the last years of his life. Beyond doubt, Uther would fail. Her father had been a warrior beyond peer and Uther had been the greatest tactician of Celtic Britain. So what would Artorex, the culmination of them both, achieve?

'More than you, Uther. More than you!'

Four weeks after his audience with the High King, Artorex returned to the Villa Poppinidii with the core of the Impossibles at his back. He would have travelled during the first week after his return from Anderida, but he was obliged to make provision for the wounds of his men, and Venta Belgarum was unwilling to let their hero go. Also, to his shame, a corner of Artorex's heart feared to face his daughter and the decisions that he'd made for her future.

The spring thaw had begun and the earth was sodden with seeping water that fed the bulbs, flowers and weeds as they thrust their green heads through the moist farm soil. The Villa Poppinidii was at its best with the peach and pear trees laden with blossoms, buttercups growing in yellow drifts in the fields while newborn calves, foals and lambs frolicked in the long grasses.

Artorex could smell the rich, heady aroma of life beginning again as spring embraced the land once more.

'Winter has passed, so joy and happiness can return,' Artorex said softly to Ector as the two men gazed over the fertile fields. 'All that death and waste was for such a petty thing – a crown that is as dead as stone. This place was all I ever wanted, so why did the three travellers ever come to change the natural way of things?'

As always, Targo and Odin stood behind him, grim guardians who watched Artorex's back at all times. They would have turned away from their master's grief, but Ector was standing beside Artorex and Odin trusted no one.

'Who can say why men are such cruel, brutal creatures, my son?' Ector replied thoughtfully as one hand stroked his foster-son's broad shoulders. 'It's the women who civilize and the men who destroy. I think often of my Livinia and her gardens, and of little Gallia as she found beauty at the edge of the forest in places where we see only usefulness.'

'Aye,' Artorex answered simply.

He gazed fondly at Ector and struggled to put his thoughts into words.

'I will go to Gallia's house soon but, before I do, there is a request I must make of you,' the young man said gently as he fixed his gaze urgently on the older man. 'It is a matter of importance to me, and I will ask you to swear your oath on the Villa Poppinidii and the memory of our Mistress Livinia that you will keep your word on this matter.'

'Ah, young man, what have they done to you in the south that you can doubt me? You, more than any other person, should know that I'd do anything you ask of me, if I could. I don't need to swear my oath, but I'll accede to your wishes. I swear my oath on Livinia's ashes, on this good earth and on the love that keeps me here where the world is quiet and pure.'

Ector's face was old now and was seamed by wrinkles, but he was still as strong as an old oak and the years stood lightly on his balding head and huge shoulders.

'Licia cannot continue to be my child.'

Artorex's voice was empty of grief, or filled with it, depending on the sensitivity of the listener.

'I have been told that I am the legitimate son of Uther Pendragon, the last child of a warrior line whose blood has been poisoned by greed and corruption through many generations. I won't expose Licia to ambitious men who'd exploit her to achieve their own ends.'

Then he sighed with all the regret that any true man can feel for the loss of his loved ones. He gazed around the fields and the mists of morning.

'I want you to adopt Licia as your daughter. In these fields, she can grow tall and strong under your influence, just as I did. It is the best solution I can devise to ensure that she learns to live and laugh like her mother.'

'But the Gallus family knows the truth of Licia's birth,' Ector protested.

'Gallia's family is much smaller now and her kin are very proud,' Artorex responded. 'They'll follow your advice. Gallinus will understand the risks involved to his niece. Think, Father. She's the granddaughter of Uther Pendragon, and she's the niece of Morgan and Morgause, two truly frightening creatures. If Morgan knew that Licia still lived, she wouldn't hesitate to snatch her away in an instant to teach her perversities. Can I permit such a fate for my little Licia?'

'No!' Ector replied forcefully.

'If it be known in the future that she is my daughter, the Villa Poppinidii will become a magnet for the greedy, the violent and those men who'd want to father a son on her, even if rape was the only option. To such creatures, the grandson of Artorex would be a huge prize, and I wouldn't wish such a fate upon her.'

'Never!' the old man hissed. 'And I would die to prevent it.'

'Then you must take her into your family. If such an arrangement would be acceptable to you, I would ask that I be permitted to become her foster-uncle so I can see her when duty permits. She is very young, and I'm certain she will forget me in time.' Artorex's face was infinitely sad. 'I've never asked so much of any man as I now ask of you, Father. She'll have a bride price of great worth, and the Villa Poppinidii will be safe, at least for the duration of my life. Gareth will see to everything else.'

'I want nothing for this duty,' Ector stated unequivocally. 'For there's no gold or land that can have half the worth of my children.' He gazed into the face of Artorex. 'Caius will be silent?'

'Aye. Caius and I have reached an understanding,' Artorex replied. 'His fate is tied to mine, and will always be so.'

'Well, I'm damned if I understand him,' Ector said with some humour – and father and foster-son laughed ironically.

Later, Artorex strode across the fields, his shadows in place behind him, until he came to the burned earth where he'd known such joy. The timber of the framework was now ash, but the burned stone of the walls and the jagged foundations pointed to love that had been real, but was now lost forever. Already the tendrils of wisteria shoots, tougher than Artorex could imagine, struggled with the ivy to gain a foothold on the stone.

Absently, Artorex bent over to pull out a succulent weed growing between the flagged stones of the courtyard. Odin followed his master's lead, so the weeds were soon gone and the tomb of Gallia and Frith, for such this place now was, was cleansed of the parasitic plants.

'My greatest wish is that you should plant flowers around and among the ruins of my house,' Artorex told Gareth that night. 'Roses, spring blossoms and the deep strong roots of alder and hazel should flourish there, because a garden in Gallia's memory is the only object of real worth that I can give to the baby Licia.'

Gareth knelt before his master and swore to serve Artorex as long as he lived, without question.

'The Garden of Gallia shall be beautiful, for I will tend to it as you require. But I crave my lord's permission to grow herbs and simples as well, and the ordinary daisies and poppies that Frith loved.'

'There's no need to ask, Gareth.' Artorex smiled at the youth. 'You may raise a memorial to Frith, my mother of the heart. I will send gold to pay for its construction.'

'I'll do as you ask, my lord. If you agree to come with me tomorrow, I'll show you what I want to do.'

And so, in the morning, Artorex found himself back at the place where his journey had begun, in his glade in the Old Forest where the weak light of spring reached downwards to split the darkness.

The stone had not changed, nor had its powerful, eerie carvings. Artorex sensed that he was in the presence of something holy that was as alien to him as the ways of women.

Even Odin sensed the mystic presence and abased himself before the stone.

'I ask a boon that I might keep this stone under my protection, Lord Artorex,' Gareth explained while pointing at the carving. 'Gallia and Frith came here almost every day, for it was a place where they felt contentment and were at peace with the world. Gallia said she felt close to you when she was here, and Frith told me the stone was sacred to women and was as old as the world. She ground her herbs in the cup on its spine.' He smiled shyly at Artorex. 'She told me that blood had defiled the stone in times long past, but that her woman's magic had destroyed the demons that lived within it.'

'Then you may move the stone where you will. Ector will give you whatever men you need to position the stone in its new place of rest. Perhaps you might lay it in the forecourt of the ruins so that a pond forms around it and water might drain from the cup when the rains fall.'

Artorex sighed, for in the past he'd only ever imagined a flow of fresh, sacrificial blood in its holy cup. He hadn't discerned any other use for the ancient relic.

'Perhaps, water flowers might make it an object of beauty rather than a symbol of death.'

During the coming months, Artorex, his scum and those warriors who flocked to his banner rode through the mountain chain like an armed whirlwind. No Saxon dared to walk on soil that Artorex deemed to be sacred to the cause of the west. No Norseman dared to cut a single tree in the forests that Artorex claimed as his own. And no man was left to breathe who stood against the dying Uther in his dusty Great Hall. The last Dux Bellorum became the Warden of the Britons, and his fame grew.

On those few, brief occasions when quiet settled on the borders, Artorex returned to the Villa Poppinidii. There, he played with a small blonde girl whom he called Licia, who was accompanied always by her constant shadow, the pale-haired Gareth.

Ector's remaining hair also whitened, but the old man gained a whole new lease of life when Caius rode off to war as one of Artorex's captains. Ector was often heard to say that Lucius's gift of a foster-son was the greatest piece of luck in his long and fortunate life.

No house rose on the foundations of the old house where

Gallia and Frith had died. Only flowers were allowed to live there, blooms that were cared for by Gareth who promised that no one would trouble Licia's peace with tales of a warrior father. Artorex came to love her as an uncle should, on the surface at least. And if he wept for the loss of his daughter to preserve her safety, then only Targo knew. And Targo never told.

The sun rose and fell on the Villa Poppinidii as it had done for hundreds of years, and Gallia rested in a golden urn set in a niche in the ruined walls of her house. Regardless of the worth of her last resting place, no hand would dare to touch the Dux Bellorum's garden or its contents. Eventually, even to the faithful Artorex, she became a dream, and then the faint memory of a dream, and time washed her away in the great actions of powerful men.

But the garden bloomed on the defiled earth where so much of her Artorex had died. The cup in the stone filled with clean water and washed away the memory of old evils. And Frith's spirit danced in the wild daisies that grew in great white masses, intertwined with blood-red poppies like the heart's blood she had shed for love.

For one year, Artorex pushed his great strength to the limit, living in the saddle and gathering around his core of surviving Impossibles a large force of young and eager warriors. The nobility, the villages and the last Celtic-Roman settlements all sent their best sons to ride with Artorex, the Warrior of the West, and the few Saxon toeholds in the north-west of the British lands were forced back into the mountains or the Wash, like mud cleansed from Artorex's feet.

Icy purpose drove him. When the west became a secure bastion, Artorex made camp in the mountains, in the old fortresses, creating a string of guardian towers to watch the encroaching Saxon menace that lay just over the borders.

During this time, Venta Belgarum never saw his face. He told himself that his hatred for Uther was so deep that he could not trust himself to allow the ancient, dying King to live. He tried to convince that coldest part of himself that his neglect of the source of all British power was also to protect Targo, who had sworn an oath to avenge Gallia's murder.

But Artorex knew, in a sickened corner of his soul, that he couldn't bear to see his own self in all of Uther's ruin and cruelty. So he rode, fought and pushed the Celtic edge to the limit – through the power of Celtic horsemanship.

At the end of winter, Myrddion found Artorex in a windswept bivouac. The young man was brooding over maps drawn on soft, rolled cowhide as he planned his next campaign against the Saxon underbelly.

'Don't you have a smile for an old friend, Artorex?' Myrddion murmured from the entrance to the simple mud and wattle hut.

Artorex raised his head to meet the dark eyes of Myrddion.

'You're always welcome, Myrddion, oldest of teachers.' Artorex's mouth twisted a little in irony, and Myrddion felt a wrench in his heart for his pupil's lost innocence.

Artorex swept furs, discarded maps and an old and dirty wooden plate off a stool in the centre of the room.

'Sit, my friend, and ignore my distraction, for I'm tired and heartsick at what must be done this spring. How goes Venta Belgarum?'

'The city is quiet, like a warrior waiting for the call to battle. Uther bunkers in his city like a dying spider, but he's caught in Morgan's machinations rather than his own. Beware of her, Artorex, for she hates all things that are Uther's – and you are his greatest legacy. She'll do you greater harm, if she can, than simply keeping that old monster alive with her vile concoctions.'

Artorex's lips twisted bitterly. 'Life was infinitely simpler when I had no blood kin.'

'Your mother has returned to a convent near Tintagel,

regardless of the whispers that her absence has caused. She has become a penitent and rumour says she has taken a vow of silence. She whips her body to save her soul.'

Artorex merely raised his eyebrows.

'Don't you care, boy? You've lost a wife in a foul murder, but Ygerne lost her husband through trickery – and then her child was taken from her. She believed you were dead for countless years, and she has finally fled from the man who wronged her so deeply.' Myrddion shook his head slowly. 'Don't you feel curiosity, at the very least, about her motives in marrying Uther?' Myrddion was showing signs of impatience, and Artorex turned away from the older man's concerned scrutiny.

'I find it difficult to care what penances a spoiled queen belatedly offers to her god. In my heart, my mothers were Frith and Livinia, one a Saxon and the other Roman. And both were fine, upright women who had no guile or cowardice in their natures.'

'You're overly harsh, Artorex, for Ygerne was a tragic victim. I was the one who helped Uther deceive the fairest woman of the Britons – another sin upon my conscience. My only justification is that it was important to our cause that she should give birth to Uther's successor. You may judge me if you must, but save some pity for a frail woman who has suffered far more cruelly than you have.'

Artorex snorted.

'Allow me to speak, Artorex,' Myrddion demanded. 'Ygerne was a famed woman. She was a beauty, but she was also able to read and write, to sing like a nightingale and was so good of heart that her physical charms were the least of her talents. Men loved her on sight and longed to earn her smiles, but her heart was fixed upon her husband, Gorlois, the Boar of Cornwall. He was an ally of Uther Pendragon.

'At a feast, Uther met the fabled Ygerne. I remember that

night, for so much misery stemmed from a simple meal. He saw her, he wanted her and he sickened to have her. Waking and sleeping, Ygerne filled his thoughts so that Uther neglected his duties. Nothing I said deflected him and no other woman slaked his desire.

'Well you might laugh, Artorex, but you're not past forty, as was Uther. And the man had fallen in love for the first time in his life. Uther had enjoyed any woman he wanted in the past, but now he had found a paragon whom he couldn't have, and his obsession almost cost him his reason.

'Yes, I eventually found a way to trick Ygerne so that she welcomed Uther into Tintagel and she lay with him as her husband. What could Ygerne do when she discovered the ruse? Uther raped her once she proved unwilling and planted you in her womb. Yes, I watched as he sent Gorlois into a suicidal battle. And I watched as he made the outcome certain by declaring that the Duke of Cornwall was a traitor and had him killed. Can you imagine how Ygerne felt when she saw her husband's beloved head raised on a pike over the gates of Venta Belgarum?'

'She could have arranged her own death,' Artorex interrupted brutally.

'She'd already quickened at the time of which we speak, and she thought the child came from the seed of Gorlois. She couldn't take her own life! She had two daughters, and Uther had used them as hostages to take the queen to his bed and ensure her compliance. I ask you, Artorex, what would you have done?'

Artorex reddened along his high cheekbones at his mentor's implied criticism.

'My name may still be Artorex, but I'm no longer the boy who bore that name,' the young man stated matter-of-factly. 'Unfortunately, the happy life that Artorex knew and loved is long dead. Regardless of the sins she endured, Ygerne still has nothing to do with me, although I'll acquit her of the flaws of vanity and cowardice. I accept that Uther has turned many innocents into sinners.'

'You're angry, and you're hurt to the heart, my boy. I wouldn't have had you suffer, as you well know. In this instance, you've been required to sacrifice something of yourself for the sake of the common good.'

Artorex drank deeply from his wooden wine cup, and then spat the lees on to the sod floor. He raised his eyes to his friend and smiled in the old, trusting way while, outside, a chill wind rattled the stiff cowhide covering at the door lintel and stirred his loosened hair.

'I hope you'll forgive me, friend Myrddion. I feel lost and only Saxon deaths seem to imbue me with purpose. I'll think on your words and, if I decide to make my peace with Ygerne, then I'll do so. Regardless of my decision, I'll always be grateful for your guidance and advice.'

They clasped hands as they stood inside the warm room and, wisely, determined to avoid painful subjects.

'How does Caius?' Myrddion asked curiously. 'I still find myself wondering about that young man, for those incidents at the Villa Severinii still haunt me.'

Artorex grimaced a little in memory.

'Does he make a suitable horse captain?'

'He does well enough, and his tactical ability demonstrates a certain ferocity. I need him, despite my reservations about his lack of judgement, because he hates the Saxons even more than you or I. Sometimes, I don't believe that he sees them as human beings but, rather, as wild animals. I believe that Caius is one of those men who enjoys warfare and who are at their best in times of violence. But enough of Caius! What brings you to this godforsaken place?'

'This and that, Artorex. I've sent several good men into the heart of the Saxon east to bring me intelligence. They risk their lives to keep us both aware of Saxon intentions.' Myrddion's face was sad. 'These men often die for us, and they are unhallowed and unsung. Like you, I often feel their shades clustering around me, so I regret the desperate need which forces me to order such brave men into enemy settlements. But they – and we – serve as we must, for it is only the land that matters.'

Myrddion paced the small, conical room, refusing wine in favour of water, and for all that his advancing middle age was whitening his hair at last, his tortured face reflected all the bewildered pity of a boy.

'Even as we speak, I am awaiting news from my best servant, Gruffydd, a peasant who grew up with the Saxons as a slave. His skill with the language has kept him safe for many years. I hope that Gruffydd will give you the disposition of the Saxon advance, for the east is now completely theirs.'

He peered at Artorex through the gloom with a concerned expression on his smooth, still-youthful face.

'I fear we will be driven out into the lands far to the west, Artorex, and all the civilization that Romans and Celts have built will be burned to the ground.'

'Not while I live.'

'Nor I, Artorex,' Myrddion replied. 'But now we play a waiting game, for Uther lives on, against all nature. The tribes are divided and Morgause has many sons. When the High King does die, as must soon happen, claimants to the throne will rise like nettles to seize power for themselves, and the old alliances will be cast aside like straws in the wind.'

'I have no desire to fill Uther's shoes, for the duties of the Dux Bellorum are onerous enough for me,' Artorex replied honestly.

'My boy, there are no claimants to the throne who would

dare to let you live. You must have a care, Artorex. You can trust no man except those who are tied to you by bonds that cannot be broken. You must understand that the lips of those who aspire to greatness may smile, but the serpent in their hearts can be impossible to recognize.'

Artorex rose to his full height, so that the tall, willowy form of Myrddion was forced to look up into his eyes.

'And what of you, old friend? Would you betray me for the land?'

'I could lie and say that my love for you outstrips all other duties, but I won't burden my soul any further. If you bring blood and death to our people, then I'll be forced to choose against you. But I swear by the love I hold for you, as the son I never sired, that I will never use Licia as I've used you.'

Artorex nodded gravely.

Although he did not realize the importance of his words, Myrddion had passed Artorex's greatest test. He had spoken the purest truth.

The young man offered Myrddion his sword arm, and the two men embraced.

'Thank you for your honesty, my old friend. I expected no less from you but I had to ask those ugly questions. You can blame my tainted blood for my coldness and my suspicious nature.'

'Tainted? Oh, no, my lord. You are what Uther should have been but wasn't. For you have a love for those people who are the strong spine of our lands. Uther always used his warriors without a qualm for the cost, but you care for the men who die for our cause. You are your mother's child.'

'But which mother would that be, Myrddion? That's the question that haunts me.'

'Perhaps you belong to all of them. Have you considered that possibility? Livinia's sense of duty, Frith's courage and Ygerne's steadfastness have all helped to shape you, so who can say which woman is your true mother?'

Artorex shrugged.

'You'll find your way, my lord, because you must. But for now you must point me to a warm bed because I must be gone by morning.'

That night, Targo noted that Artorex smiled more easily and the cares that had bowed his shoulders seemed to have lifted a little.

'That Myrddion is a clever devil,' he told a half-comprehending Odin. 'But, whether Artorex knows it or not, he is the master's true edge.'

Wisely, Odin said nothing. But when Myrddion's shadow touched him, he clutched his amulet to his chest for luck.

CHAPTER XVI

THE UNBORN CHILD

Gruffydd arrived late at the burning village, having ridden his lathered horse almost to death during the long ride from Venonae. Covered in mud from the swamps of the Wash and with his temper frayed from hours in the saddle nursing his exhausted horse, he was coldly angry to discover that the small settlement had already been put to the sword.

The village of Durobrivae had only one stone building, a remnant of the old Roman garrison. The years had weathered the stone and neglect had permitted lichen to cover the façade with a brilliant display of greens, silver and the occasional flash of rust-red. The rest of the town was raised on heavy wooden piers, for a river ran beside Durobrivae, while the Wash was notorious for its floods and swamps.

Gruffydd's nose twitched with distaste. Innocent villagers and Jutland warriors alike had been killed, many burned in their homes, for they had feared to venture forth into the rain of arrows ordered by the captain of the Celtic troop. The attack had been brilliant in its way, for it spared many soldiers from the dangers of hand-to-hand fighting, but Gruffydd was a man of the Marshes and he scorned such safe carnage.

The stink of blood and roasted flesh was everywhere. Groups of men were sitting at their ease, a few plucking chickens for roasting and others, with soot-covered hands and faces, had been busy plundering the dead. Gruffydd felt his gorge rise.

As he dismounted from his horse, a dark-haired young man in a brass breastplate moved forward carrying a Roman helmet. His indolent manner and fine features marked him immediately as Lord Caius, foster-brother to the Dux Bellorum of the West, the invincible Artorex.

'Well met, friend,' Caius greeted him cautiously, as he casually tossed his helmet to a waiting youth. He commenced cleaning his Roman sword with a bloody rag, but Gruffydd was not deceived.

The black eyes of the troop leader were alive with curiosity and something else that Gruffydd could not quite recognize.

'You must be Captain Caius,' Gruffydd stated. 'I bring orders for you from Lord Artorex.'

Caius nodded with an inborn elegance that was at odds with his bloody gauntlets and the brain matter he was cleaning from his sword.

'You are summoned to Venonae, my lord,' Gruffydd began. 'I have been sent to gather in the wolf packs that harry our enemies in the Wash. Lord Artorex has information that he wishes to impart to all his commanders.'

Caius looked about the blackened remains of the village with genuine regret.

'Is there no one left for our warriors to kill?' Gruffydd asked sardonically.

Caius ignored him. 'When does my brother require my presence?' He asked indolently, his eyes seemingly busy with the cleaning of his armour.

'Three days hence, my lord. Yours is the last troop I have had to search out, although rumour had it that Durobrivae was about to be attacked by your troop.'

'Durobrivae is destroyed – at least around the edges,' Caius muttered with amusement.

Some of the soldiers within earshot looked up from their various tasks and snickered, or grinned, in acknowledgement.

'You may eat with us, messenger. As soon as darkness falls, we will ride to meet with my foster-brother.'

'My thanks, Lord Caius,' Gruffydd replied with a respectful lowering of his head.

The warriors lounging nearby groaned their displeasure in the manner of all soldiers, but Gruffydd had no doubts of the affection they seemed to hold in their hearts for Caius. The messenger was aware of Caius's reputation for cruelty and cunning but, while he approved of the way the young man could generate loyalty in those he commanded, he could never approve of the callous way that Caius encouraged his men to strip bodies of their wealth, and casually consign even infant children to the flames.

Gruffydd had accepted Caius's offer of food with both civility and caution, for Myrddion had warned him of Caius's dangerous temper that came to the fore when he was crossed.

Unpredictable as always and, having won Gruffydd's acceptance of their relative roles, Caius changed his plans.

'The snow's coming.' Caius looked skywards. 'So the sooner we're on our way, the easier the journey will be. I'm sorry, messenger, but I've decided not to wait.'

He began to stride towards the small knots of cavalrymen.

'On your feet, you idle curs. We're off to meet with the Dux Bellorum. Take only what you can carry easily for we depart immediately!'

The unfortunate Signus, one of the warriors, had been in the process of cutting a sheep's throat. His arms were covered in blood to the elbows but, obediently, he thrust the corpse away from him without further argument.

Gruffydd noted that all of these warriors obeyed Caius instantly – and all held a respectful affection for their commander. The Roman officer appeared to be a contradiction in terms.

'Will you join us for the journey, Gruffydd?'

'Nay, my lord,' Gruffydd replied. 'My horse needs resting. But you may expect to see me at Venonae with Myrddion, my master.'

'That storm crow! Very well. We'll meet again soon.'

Turning to his sergeants, he barked out his orders for the troop.

'Ulf, find my brother's messenger a bowl of food and fodder for his horse, and then get your arse moving. I intend to be long gone when the snow starts to fall.'

Snow was actually falling in thick blankets before the troop mounted quietly and vanished away into the darkening light.

Gruffydd was finally alone with the dead.

The snow mercifully blanketed the bodies of warriors, most of whom had been hacked to pieces where they fell. Ever the planner, Caius had ordered his men to collect their spent arrows and weaponry, but it seemed to Gruffydd that the bodies of the enemy warriors had been needlessly desecrated. The gaping wounds in their bodies could only have been inflicted on men already prone upon the earth, while their women were curled into foetal balls with their throats cut and their eyes staring wildly at the grey sky.

When he peered inside the shells of the huts, he found even his strong, battle-hardened gorge rising in his throat. Blackened bodies clutched even more terribly burned children, their ages and sexes burned away with their hair and clothes, so that sooty finger bones seemed to summon him to them with the rictus of flame.

'The crows will feed well on these Saxons,' Gruffydd

murmured to himself. 'Perhaps Caius intends this brutality as a warning.'

But, in the secret parts of his brain, Gruffydd knew that he would be watching Artorex's foster-brother very, very closely from this time onward.

One fact was certain. Gruffydd could not sleep and rest his horse in this charnel house for the five or six hours needed to recover their strength. He must be gone long before dawn, and even if it meant sleeping in the snow, he must clean the stink of death from his nostrils.

His horse whickered its discontent and shied away from the bloody carcass of the dead sheep. Even in the growing darkness and the light snow, Gruffydd saw a beaten path leading away from the village and guessed that it led to water. Perhaps he could wash the stink from his hands in a running stream, no matter how cold the water might be.

Immediately, he noticed that booted feet had made deep indentations in the muddy path. Gruffydd felt sick once again when he discovered a smaller footprint, partially covered by a grown man's spoor. At least two people had passed this way towards the river, so his instincts screamed at him to choose another route to find shelter and water. But curiosity was ever Gruffydd's weakness. His thirst to know the best or the worst of human nature had made him the most able of Myrddion's agents.

The shallows at the edge of the river were thick with dead weeds and flower heads. Willows dipped over the water which already had a thin, perilous skin of ice. Were it not for blood trails on the dead grass stems, the river bank would have been chilly and beautiful in its stark simplicity. Near a huge, half-dead willow, Gruffydd's horse shied and rolled its eyes whitely in fear.

After he had tethered his mount to a sapling, Gruffydd dropped on to all fours and crawled under the spreading cavern of the willow's branches. A powerful smell of blood, urine and faeces, and something else indefinable, almost drove him back into the open air. The darkness in this makeshift cavern was almost impenetrable but, as Gruffydd's eyes adjusted to the gloom, he could make out a huddled figure leaning against the scabrous trunk of the ancient tree.

The body before him was of a young and very fair girl. Even laced with rivulets of blood, her hair was a translucent wave of blond-white. Her face was pale and free of blemish except for the wide, staring eyes that were an intense blue, even in the dim light. They were filmed over with agony and horror.

The ground beneath her was soaked with blood.

Gruffydd sighed and raised the cloth of her skirts that had already been pulled up to her knees. He recoiled in disgust.

She had been raped, of that there was no doubt, for semen and blood stained her thighs. But Gruffydd could see that there was a great slash in her pregnant belly, for the distended, fair skin was now flaccid and empty. Even the dangling, liver-coloured cord had been cut through, and he noticed with horror that her hands had been sliced to the bone as she fought to save the life of her unborn child, even as her own life force ebbed. Gruffydd could imagine her running as fast as her swollen belly would allow before she was caught by a soldier and dragged into this dark place where no one, except for the gods, could see her shameful death.

Gruffydd also noticed that her blood was still wet.

She had bled to death – and recently.

Sickened, Gruffydd backed out of the charnel house under the willow tree. Her child was undoubtedly dead and well beyond his aid. He thought of his wife and sons at Venta Silurum, safe from attack and rapine, and thanked god that Artorex did not sanction such gruesome deeds. The Dux

Bellorum had but one weakness in Gruffydd's eyes, and that was his unaccountable trust in Caius.

Gruffydd began to walk his horse upstream to move away from this tainted tomb, but a cry, as thin and frail as a newborn kitten's, caused him to halt. His ears strained to find its origin.

There! He heard the cry again. Somewhere beyond the willow and its grisly occupant, the whimper of a child could be faintly heard.

'It can't be alive. No child could live in this cold.'

But the feeble, failing cries drew him behind the tree to a place where the reeds were choked in ice. He discovered the babe caught in the withered grasses.

Careful not to fracture the ice, Gruffydd scooped up the child, saw that the cord had not been knotted off and used a strip of leather from his hair to tie the stump of umbilical cord where it joined the tiny belly. The child was blue with cold, but perfect, so Gruffydd could only surmise that the thick, dead grasses and reeds had offered some warmth and shelter, sufficient to keep a girl child with a strong life force alive for a brief time. She was beautiful and must have been close to full term, marred only by a great bruise around her right ankle where a man's hand had swung her and then tossed her among the dead flowers.

Gruffydd seethed. He swore to himself that an animal who would commit deeds such as had been carried out in this desolate place deserved to die, while the child should live to know that the murderer had followed her mother to Tartarus.

But first, Gruffydd must save the child from freezing to death for, even though he placed her inside his tunic against his heart, he could feel her life force weakening.

Upstream, Gruffydd fetched dry sticks and made a fire, a risk in enemy territory, but he had no doubt he could pass himself off as a Saxon who had found the ruins of Durobrivae, and now sought to save the life of an orphaned child. He foraged in the ruined village to discover any rags, lengths of cloth or pots that had been overlooked, but the troop had been extremely thorough in their pillaging.

His eyes turned to the dead sheep. At least its wasted corpse might now serve a useful purpose.

Quickly and efficiently, Gruffydd skinned the beast. Speed was necessary so the task was not carried out as neatly as he would have liked, but the fleece would make a good swaddling cloth till the babe was warmed sufficiently to survive. Then, with silent apologies to the dead woman, he retrieved a length of her dress that wasn't stiffening with her blood to help with the cleansing of the child.

Casting one last look at the remains of the young woman, he noticed a curiously-designed bronze pin that had been used to hold back her hair. The rapist had obviously missed it in his haste. Gruffydd knew that every child deserved some trifle that would remind her of her birthright and a mother whose name she would never know, so he thrust the small item of jewellery into his belt pouch.

The fire was burning strongly by the time he returned, and his simple pannikin quickly heated the cold water from the stream. As he washed away the evidence of birth, the baby's flesh slowly warmed and a little pink took the place of the ominous blue colouring. Even the birth sac must have helped to save the life of the child, Gruffydd decided.

He wrapped her in the length of cloth and then covered her entirely with the fleece, the bloody side outward.

'It's a blood-soaked beginning for you, my girl, and it will be all for nothing if I can't find you some milk.'

The hide of the sheep's carcass was sticky and rank against Gruffydd's skin as he returned the child to the inside of his shirt. The babe had been crying weakly, but the beating of his heart offered comfort and she seemed to doze in the warmth of his body.

The cow byres were empty and partially burned. A dead calf lay stiffening pathetically, its tender flesh blistered and its hindquarters hacked at by knives.

Sickened anew, Gruffydd turned away and walked deeper into the marshes where paths criss-crossed the swampy ground, his ears straining for the distinctive sound of a cow bell.

Eventually, he heard the familiar, tinny peal he sought and, light-footed, he followed the sound until he found a brindled cow bellowing in distress. Her udders were swollen and distended and Gruffydd knew that her calf was dead.

He stroked the babe with its silken head against his breast.

'You are lucky, my child, lucky beyond the counting of mortal men,' he muttered to himself. 'For now you have food.'

He led the cow back to the river bank, taking care to avoid the cow byre and the swelling body of the calf. Her eyes were soft and desperate, but the cow permitted him to milk her, filling his pannikin once more.

By using a strip of fine cloth from his tunic, Gruffydd dribbled milk into the tiny rosebud mouth.

This process was not a success, for the child had no idea how to swallow. Gruffydd tried again, this time soaking the cloth in milk and placing it in her mouth.

The child sucked.

The process of feeding the babe was long and cumbersome, but eventually she gave a great burp and closed her midnight-blue eyes.

Hours had been devoted to feeding the child, during which time his horse had foraged for grass and broken the ice to drink at the water's edge. Night was waning when he was finally on his way, encumbered by the cow, for he must take the babe's source of nourishment with him.

Never had a journey seemed so long. The child's wrappings needed regular washing, and Gruffydd was forced to sacrifice his best tunics to keep her clean. At the same time, her feeding seemed to take forever and he soon devised a way to feed the child while on the move, even on horseback, once the cow had yielded its supply of milk.

In fact, to keep the cow healthy, Gruffydd found himself drinking more milk than he had ever deemed necessary in his entire life. Even his horse partook of the supply and then looked at its master with affronted, scornful eyes.

As Gruffydd slowly continued with his journey, the odd hamlet he deliberately visited was happy to exchange a pail of milk for clothing more suited to a baby. He could have sold the cow a dozen times over, but although she slowed his journey, Gruffydd could not afford to leave the beast behind.

Eventually, to the laughter of the townsfolk, Gruffydd arrived at Venonae, three days late, and trailing a cow behind him. The fortress was built of grey stone on the highest peak of a range of hills and its slit windows overlooked the undulating, wooded country that stretched away towards the east like a great green coverlet.

When he was ushered into Myrddion's presence, the master was not amused.

'The audience is already over, Gruffydd – and I was blind to the situation in the east,' Myrddion snarled. 'What possessed you to take so long? And why a cow?'

Gruffydd began to give a detailed explanation of the discovery of the babe, but was immediately interrupted by his master.

'Do you realize that Uther Pendragon is dead? The High King has been with the shades of his ancestors for nearly three months. Typically, Morgan's been tardy in her tidings. The peace forged by Uther is broken, and the jostling for the throne has already begun.'

'Oh, shite!' Gruffydd could think of nothing more intelligent to say. He realized the security and safety of the west had been torn away in those few words.

'Morgan has just informed Artorex of the situation, with some pleasure, and he then called in his captains for a discussion to determine what strategy would now be adopted by his warriors. I was blind and deaf at the meeting because my best agent – you – was conspicuously absent. I've no idea what Artorex has decided to do – and Venonae is in the eye of the storm.'

He glared at the unfortunate Gruffydd.

'Of one thing we can be sure. We can have no doubt that Morgan, bitch that she is, is enjoying herself hugely. And, no doubt, Morgause's eldest son, Gawayne, is already seeking the location of the symbols of Uther's kingship – his sword and his crown.'

The years had been kind to Myrddion Merlinus, although his forehead now wore a deep frown. His face was burnt brown from many journeys, and his thin features were as handsome as ever, although he was now well past forty years and had never felt the need to take a wife. Many women watched him covertly, admiring his slim, elegant body and his ready wit, but he passed through their butterfly-like clusters with mild and disinterested smiles. The most snide and proud of the rejected maidens would have labelled him as a lover of boys, but there had never been even a whisper of interest on Myrddion's part for this type of sexual pleasure. Certainly, the young effeminates followed him as unsuccessfully as the maidens.

To Gruffydd, Myrddion was an engima. His master was rarely angry, for he always kept his emotions in check. It was Gruffydd's opinion that Myrddion loved only three people. These were his friends, Llanwith, Luka and, above all, Lord Artorex. As Gruffydd often told his plump wife, Ganeth, men such as Myrddion came rarely to this world, and they were not bound by the lusts and dreams of smaller men.

Husband and wife agreed that Myrddion was more to be pitied than feared.

Now, under Myrddion's cold gaze, and in a daze over the rapid changes occurring in the west, Gruffydd told of Caius's attack on Durobrivae and what he had found there.

Nor did he spare Caius in the telling.

'It was a slaughter, my lord, for the defenders were mostly farmers and the townsfolk were so confident in its unimportance that it was barely defended. It was simply an agricultural centre, and it was hardly worth our attention. The killing of women and children will not endear us to the Saxons either, although I believe that most of those settlers in Durobrivae were actually Jutes. It was bad, my lord, very bad.'

Gruffydd paused and looked directly into Myrddion's eyes.

'I don't care for the way Caius likes to inflict pain. He seems to enjoy it too much for my liking.'

'He always did', Myrddion murmured under his breath. But his cruelty sometimes serves our purposes. You'd do well, Gruffydd, to give Caius a wide berth, for he has a streak of viciousness under his charm and I'd be hard put to save you if you openly offended him.'

The baby awoke, wriggled her limbs and began to cry lustily.

Myrddion's eyebrows rose, but he said nothing as Gruffydd drew the child forth in its fleece-lined wrappings.

'Ah! That accounts for the smell.'

Gruffydd looked offended at Myrddion's words, so the older man hurried to explain himself.

'The untanned fleece of a sheep has a distinct aroma about it.'

Gruffydd explained his protection of the child, the presence of the cow and the reason for the tardiness of his arrival at the gathering.

Myrddion's mouth grimaced at the description of the mutilated woman, and he agreed that Caius should find, and punish, the offender. He knew that such brutalities weren't the way of the Celts and wouldn't be tolerated by the Dux Bellorum.

'I'll speak to Artorex myself,' Myrddion promised. 'But what do you plan to do with the child? Your use to me as an agent would hardly be effective with a baby in your arms.'

'Someone will surely take pity on the little mite,' Gruffydd said. 'She's a fighter, I can assure you. Any other infant would have died immediately from shock. Whoever she is, she deserves the chance to live.'

'Very well. If she means so much to you, you can take her to my cook. She's a good woman who will find a wet nurse for the babe.'

'Thank you, my lord.'

'Don't thank me. My instinct tells me the child is going to be a nuisance.'

Gruffydd was soon lost in the stone fortress of Venonae that crowned the hilltop and was surrounded by the familiar sod and thatch huts of the common folk. Uncontrolled additions to the buildings had taken place over recent years, most usually in wood, so corridors seemed to go nowhere in particular and the arrow slits in the original garrison let in insufficient light in the dead of winter.

Asking directions of hurrying servants only served to confuse Gruffydd more thoroughly, until he stopped to speak to a dark-cloaked woman in the doorway of what appeared to be a solarium.

'What is your business in the bower of women?' she demanded imperiously.

Stuttering, Gruffydd explained Myrddion's orders and the woman dropped her cowl so he could see her chilly, lovely face.

'My Lady Morgan, I beg your pardon for intruding,' Gruffydd

apologized, his voice quaking slightly with fear. Morgan was a noted witch-woman, so few could meet her blue-black eyes directly.

'A child,' she said softly.

Her hand dropped on to the silky head and the babe's eyes opened to stare deeply into Morgan's face.

'And she is a Jute, unless I miss my guess. Does she have a name?'

'None, my lady. All I could think to call her was Willow, but that seemed ghoulish, since her mother was murdered under one such tree.'

Morgan stared deeply into the child's clear, blue eyes. The baby should have been too young to focus properly, but Gruffydd knew, in the deepest recesses of his superstitious mind, that she saw and understood Morgan for what she was.

'Ah, how strong she is. She is born for a great destiny, this little soul, for she will steal away the mind of the kingdom. Long will they sing tales of the beautiful Nimue!'

Gruffydd wanted to cross himself, or grip his amulet in fear because, like all sensible Celts, he had one foot in the Christian church and one with the Druids. All he managed to do was to break out into a cold sweat.

'Remember, Myrddion's man, that Morgan has given her the name of Nimue, the Serpent Child,' she told Gruffydd imperiously. She smiled mischievously at the terrified man. 'And now I shall show you to your master's kitchens.'

Gruffydd was certain his heart would stop with terror as he carried the baby in the wake of the black-clad witch. Princess she might be, but no man dared to lay a finger upon her marble-cold flesh and no man gazed upon her beauty with lust – only terror. Some women swore she was over forty, but her skin still retained the bloom and texture of youth that had been frozen by an unnatural frost many years before.

Now that he had seen her for himself, Gruffydd believed that even the most fanciful tales about Morgan were probably true.

At the doorway leading into the kitchens, Morgan turned to Gruffydd and stared deeply into his eyes.

'As you love your master, I charge you to keep this baby safe. As you love Artorex, I charge you to give her affection. For this little snakeling could be dangerous if she feels unloved.'

'I swear, my lady!' Gruffydd replied earnestly.

He would have promised anything to avert the evil humour he saw in her eyes.

'Hold to your word, Myrddion's man, for I will be watching.'

And then she was gone.

Normally, Gruffydd loved kitchens. The large hearths with their black cauldrons of stew, haunches of meat on spits that sizzled fat into the fire, the smell of fresh bread and the bustle of women and boys as they busied themselves in the mysterious ways of food preparation always filled him with comfort.

His eyes searched through the bustle for the woman who controlled this well-organized confusion, a task quickly achieved when the person he sought tapped him hard on the chest with a wooden spoon.

'What are you doing here, dolt?'

'I am sorry to disturb your peace, Mother, but I bring orders from Master Myrddion.'

'Oh, you do, do you?' the plump, slab-faced peasant stated bluntly.

Gruffydd knew better than to answer.

'Well, I'm busy. What does Master Myrddion want of me – besides his fine supper?'

Once again, Gruffydd drew the child out of his tunic and little Nimue kicked and cried as she was removed from the comfort of his beating heart.

The mistress cook, Gallwyn, stared at the child as if it had suddenly grown two heads.

'A baby? Does Lord Myrddion wish it cooked on a bed of greens?' The woman snickered, and her busy minions grinned at her joke.

'The little thing was cut out of her mother's dying body by one of our warriors and was tossed away like rubbish from your kitchens. I've brought a good milk cow to feed her, but my Lord Myrddion believes you have the power to find a wet nurse to care for her.'

Gallwyn examined the baby closely, while Nimue looked back at her with her strange clear eyes and gurgled contentedly. Gallwyn tutted when she noticed the yellow bruising around her tiny ankle and even Gruffydd could see that the child was already entwining herself around the heart of the plump cook.

'Perce!' Gallwyn shouted, and a youth with a face flushed from the heat of the fire leapt to do his mistress's bidding.

'That fat cow, Eleanor, has birthed again,' Gallwyn said. 'Fetch her. She may be one of Lord Llanwith's women but she's a serving maid, for all that.'

Perce nipped out of the kitchen as if the Saxons were on his heels.

'He wants to be a warrior,' she explained portentously, her large breasts quivering under her robe and apron. 'Fat chance, I say, but these be strange times. Does the babe have a name?'

'I became lost finding your kitchens and the Lady Morgan showed me to your door. She told me that the child was to be called Nimue. She said that the babe was a little serpentling.'

Gallwyn crossed herself, while the kitchen maids stared at Nimue as if the babe was poisonous. Aware that he might have damned the baby out of hand, Gruffydd hurried to explain how he'd found her and described how the baby had stared down the basilisk eyes of Morgan herself.

'Well, my darling. That makes a big difference to me.' Gallwyn took her in her arms and held her up to the light. 'Nimue has a pretty sound, and I'd prefer not to risk Morgan's anger by choosing some other name.' She turned back to Gruffydd. 'You can leave her with me, young man. I'll see her right.'

Gruffydd was profuse in his thanks, for a huge weight had been lifted from his shoulders. He had almost reached the door, and a quick escape, when he remembered the bronze hairpin.

'Her mother was wearing this pin in her hair when I found her body, and her murderer missed looting it.' Gruffydd smiled apologetically. 'Every child should have some keepsake to remind them of their mother, but this hair pin was all I could find.'

The bronze was shaped into two winged serpents, coiled around each other in a curious pattern. The tines of the pin could well have been needle-sharp claws.

Gallwyn shuddered a little as the pin lay in her hand. Like many women of the north, a streak of knowing ran through her, and she sensed there was power in the bronze adornment.

'I'll protect it for her, and I swear it will be hers when she has enough hair to wear it. You're a good man, Gruffydd, so you may come to my kitchens at any time and in any place my Lord Myrddion sees fit to send us. I'll find you some sweet bread and a little roast venison.' She winked impishly. 'This is just between us, do you see?'

'Aye, Mother. I thank you, for I have grown fond of the little creature.'

And then, with a fresh swagger in his step, Gruffydd strode forth to find a decent shirt and leggings. If he knew Lord Artorex, he would soon be summoned into the presence of the Warrior of the West, so a bath might be a sensible course of action.

Gruffydd grinned reflectively. 'A spy, an infant and a cow. I must have looked a sight when I returned. Ah, well. Venonae will have more pressing rumours to chew over now that Uther Pendragon is dead.' Even as he stripped off his filthy clothing and luxuriated in the old Roman baths, Nimue was closing her baby fists on Perce's fingers. As Gallwyn watched indulgently from the shadows, the child spun her charming smile into a web of affection. Gallwyn was captured.

CHAPTER XVII

BLOOD PRICE

The next two days passed slowly, while Gruffydd cooled his heels at Venonae. Ten years of riding the frontiers in the sweet aloneness of the landscape, laced with the frisson of imminent danger, had made him unfit for the life of a courtier. Gruffydd was uncomfortable living with those warriors who harassed the Saxons, lest he should find himself seated next to one of Caius's curs. He knew that all conversation would be devoted to weaponry, the sacking of villages and the usual complaints by the soldiery. He was more at home in the stables or the kitchens, places where Nimue lay on a bed of furs and kicked her tiny legs and cooed at him when he lifted her into his arms.

Gruffydd noticed, with pleasure, that the babe was already a firm favourite in the bustle and din below the quiet corridors of power. Kitchen maids always found time to pick her up while they basted meat or stirred stew, while even the gruff old Gallwyn referred to the babe as 'pretty one'. The old cook had even insisted that the ancient priest of Venonae bless her with the Christian holy water.

'Just to be safe, mind!'

The child had already put on weight, as her wet nurse fed her without complaint.

The only cloud on Gruffydd's horizon occurred on the third

day, when he found Nimue missing from her fur bed in the corner of the kitchens.

'That Morgan has taken the babe to her chambers,' Gallwyn complained when he asked after the babe. 'She swept in like she always does – and said she'd return the child shortly.'

Gallwyn wasn't happy, and nor, for that matter, was Gruffydd. Where Morgan meddled, trouble followed.

'Lord Artorex is too kind to that witch,' Gallwyn whispered, crossing herself as she spoke. 'He'd lock her in her father's fortress at Tintagel and throw away the key if he had any sense.'

A maidservant returned the child while Gruffydd was eating an impromptu meal on the long kitchen table. The child was fretful and whimpering when she was handed to Gallwyn and all the kitchen staff eyed the blushing servant girl with dislike.

'Well, it wasn't my doing!' the girl whined, and beat a hasty retreat. 'I'll be back for her tomorrow.'

Gallwyn inspected the child and gave a hiss of superstitious dread when she saw the beginnings of a black tattoo around the child's bruised ankle.

'Did you ever,' she exclaimed to the rafters of the kitchen. 'It's a good thing I took her to the priest when I did.'

A drawing of a serpent's head was beautifully and clearly defined on the child's delicate skin. On her fair, baby flesh, the pattern was an abomination.

'That Morgan!' the cook snapped. 'She does as she pleases and counts no cost.'

'Quiet, old mother! The walls have ears and Morgan is a fearsome enemy. Don't you remember what happened to Uther?'

Gallwyn bit down on her lip. Every person in Venonae had heard tales of the illness of Uther Pendragon, High King of the

Britons, and how he would have died raving and alone in Venta Belgarum if not for the expert ministrations of his stepdaughter.

'When will Lord Artorex become High King, Gruffydd? Have you heard ought from Lord Myrddion's table?'

'Hush, woman! Are you mad? I may work for the great ones but there are a dozen men queuing to claim the seat of Uther's power. I've no wish to die for another man's ambition.'

Gallwyn looked around the kitchen with an eye that was skilled at finding the smallest fault. No servant dared to eavesdrop on her conversations but Gruffydd had a natural distrust of all persons other than Myrddion. And sometimes, in the darkest parts of the night, he even wondered about the motives of his secretive master.

'I've heard rumours that Uther's sword has vanished,' Gruffydd said softly. 'And until it's found by a rightful claimant, there'll be no High King to rule the west. As Dux Bellorum, our master is safe because he holds the mountains against the barbarians and harries their villages and garrisons. Artorex gives them no peace and no chance to set down deep roots, so even the most envious and vicious kinglet knows that his safety relies on the iron fist of Artorex. But Artorex himself must soon make up his mind what he is to do.'

'But nothing is forever, Gruffydd. Sooner or later, a king will rise and try to wrest power using Uther's sword.'

'If they can find it,' Gruffydd replied.

Gallwyn's voice dropped to a whisper. 'I heard in the markets that King Lot of the Otadini looks higher than his mountain retreat. He is married to Lady Morgause, Uther's stepdaughter, when all is said and done.'

'Lot is a fat fool!' Gruffydd snapped. 'Someone will cut his bulbous nose off for him if he dares to poke it into the south.'

'Morgan has stated that she will support Artorex's claim,' Gallwyn responded. 'She professes to hate him, so why does she keep herself so close, if not to aid King Lot and her sister, Morgause?'

Gruffydd was bored with rumours of plots, weary of Venonae and cynical of the conundrums of power. In this city where the Dux Bellorum's eyes forever wandered to the four points of the compass, even cooks became enmeshed in the plots of the great ones.

When he finally spoke, it was an honest warning.

'You should concentrate on your ovens and your cauldrons, Gallwyn. If you want the advice of a simple man who must hear secrets beyond his liking, then you should mind what you say and what you ask. There are few true friends in Venonae, and even fewer honest men. You may ignore me if you wish, but I've a liking for you, gibble-gabble that you are, and I've no heart to watch you roasted in your own ovens.'

Gallwyn covered her mouth with her hands and her eyes fairly leapt from her head. But, for all his good advice, she continued to listen to gossip in the marketplace and, when Gruffydd asked for information, she repeated the rumours, even though she occasionally imagined that the flames were already licking at her skin.

On the third day, after the noon meal, Gruffydd was summoned to Lord Myrddion's library. He barely had time to plait his wild, carrot-red hair before the messenger was hurrying him to the appointed meeting place.

Out of habit, Gruffydd slipped through the door on soundless feet. The library was lined with stone and lacked even a single window, so that jars of oil must burn both day and night and the air within the confines of the room was sultry and stuffy with smoke. Without a hearth, it was cold, and Gruffydd could not imagine why a man of Lord Myrddion's distinction and sophistication would spend so much time in a chilly, dimly lit dungeon of a room.

Of course, Myrddion knew that no one could hear what words were spoken within these four impenetrable walls.

On recognizing the dignity of the three men who were seated at a heavy table, Gruffydd dropped to one knee and bowed his head low. He had met the three travellers on regular occasions, so he knew of the prestige that each held in his own right. King Llanwith of the Ordovice had shrunk a little with middle age but power still radiated from his bearded face and hawk-like eyes. The smaller, neater King Luka of the Brigante retained the volatility of his youth, but now his rashness and turbulence of nature had been tempered by the cares and discipline of kingship. Both kings seemed ill at ease. Only Lord Myrddion appeared calm and good-humoured as he lounged in his hard-backed chair.

Peering up from beneath his lowered brows, Gruffydd could see that the table was burdened by a large and rather battered chart traced on fine doeskin.

Booted heels entered the room from the door behind Gruffydd, and the agent heard the great latch drop into place. As Myrddion, Llanwith and Luka rose and bowed their heads in respect, Gruffydd stayed in his position of full obeisance. The tall figure of Artorex swept past him, so that Gruffydd caught a glimpse of long, blond-red hair that fell well below the wide shoulder blades.

Gruffydd bowed even more deeply from his kneeling position on the floor of the room.

'Get up, man!' the compelling voice of Artorex boomed in the enclosed space.

Turning to Myrddion, he smiled at his friend before nodding a greeting to Llanwith and Luka.

'Why do you insist we meet in this ice-box of a room?' Artorex asked of Myrddion as he threw himself into the only comfortable chair. 'I know you have a passion for secrecy but I freeze half to death every time I enter this room.'

So this is Artorex, Gruffydd thought reverently as he scrambled to his feet.

Artorex poured a goblet of wine. The kings seated themselves at a wave of his hand and Artorex grinned at them with open affection.

Here is a man to love – and to die for, Gruffydd thought to himself, for he, too, was caught in the spell of the young leader's open, white smile.

As if he read Gruffydd's thoughts, Artorex turned to face Myrddion's agent, taking in the red hair, the hide cloak and the barbarian boots with a quick measuring glance.

'So this is your spy, Myrddion. Introduce us, my friend.'

'This man is Gruffydd, of Venta Silurum.' Myrddion smiled. 'He does have the look of a barbarian about him, doesn't he? And he has the most remarkable gift for languages. But Gruffydd is Celt through and through, and I trust him in all matters.'

Gruffydd found himself colouring in embarrassment at the unexpected praise from his master.

'My lord,' Gruffydd responded. He would have bowed again but Artorex ordered him to stop such nonsense.

'Any man who travels the dangerous paths you tread has no need to bow to me,' Artorex said softly. 'What news of the east? And don't tell me what you think I want to hear. The truth, please, Gruffydd.'

The spy sucked in a lungful of smoky air. The truth. How did one tell the powerful ones of this world the complete truth – and live to tell the truth at a later time?

Artorex's grey eyes bored into his. Gruffydd was convinced the Dux Bellorum could read his mind.

'The truth, please, Gruffydd,' Artorex repeated softly.

'Lord, the wolf packs we send out harry the garrisons and the villages, and this strategy works in that the Saxon fields are burned and we cause havoc. We'll bring famine to some villages in the east this winter. But these barbarians are not like you, or Lord Myrddion, or any peasant in the west. These warriors were born in cruel lands where starvation is a constant bedfellow. We give them no respite, but they haven't retreated.'

Even Myrddion was now staring at Gruffydd with hard, interested eyes. Spies reported what they saw but few were asked for an honest opinion of what they believed to be true.

'And why do they not retreat, friend Gruffydd? Are the winters in these isles so mild that they can survive in the deepest snow?'

Gruffydd laughed shortly. Then, covered with confusion, he apologized profusely.

'The truth, Gruffydd,' Artorex reminded him.

'They can't retreat, lord, for their blood stains the land. Only a blood price will wash away the deaths that have already been given up to the west. The Saxons are a warrior race, and they despise our weakness when we attack only helpless villages. Should the Saxons, the Jutes, and the northerners unite under one commander, we won't defeat them.'

'You are convinced of this?' Artorex asked flatly.

'Aye, my lord. Even now, one powerful king is gathering his forces against you out of Camulodunum. If he should ignite the warriors of the south and the north, we would have to fight along the length of the mountains to save your forces in the west.'

Artorex stretched his neck muscles and flexed his fingers.

Gruffydd noticed, abstractedly, that his leader's hands were free of rings. His face was grave, but his eyes were alive with a cold intelligence.

'And who is this ambitious king?'

'I have only heard the name of their new leader, I haven't seen him. He is called Oakheart. It is whispered by the common people that they look to him to stop the rapine in the east.'

Artorex sighed deeply and shrugged in the direction of his three friends.

'What can we do, my friends? We can raid their garrisons and slow their advance, but in doing so we feed their rage and entrench them further. I won't consider retreat, and I won't relinquish one inch of western soil, so we have an impasse beyond my intellect to break.'

Myrddion's face was a chiaroscuro mask, half brightly lit by a lamp and the other half plunged into darkness.

'You fight the Saxons with one hand tied behind your back,' Myrddion stated in a matter-of-fact voice. 'Only a High King can rally the tribes, and only a High King has the stature to keep the princelings from each other's throats. This Oakheart will have us all as food for the kites unless you take up Uther's sword.'

Artorex leapt abruptly to his feet and began to pace. He strode up and down the small, stone room, his face set like a fine, unlined bronze statue.

'And how am I to take what is hidden?' Artorex replied. 'For Uther's sword is well concealed from me even if I decided to claim it.'

'You can leave the search to me, Artorex,' Myrddion stated confidently. 'I only ask that you agree to use the sword to unite the tribes if I should find it.'

'But I have no wish to acknowledge Uther Pendragon as my father. I'm sickened by the actions of that vicious old monster, and I desire nothing that was his.'

'Swords can be reforged, my friend,' Llanwith rumbled quietly in his deep voice.

'Swords are only symbols, Artorex, and nothing more,' Luka added. 'Even so, they are powerful forces that can strike fear and awe into the hearts of friend or foe, so their usefulness should never be underestimated.'

By now, Gruffydd wished that he was far away in the warm kitchens where he could neither see the Dux Bellorum as a troubled man nor hear secret plans that could cause his head to be separated from his body.

Artorex turned his flat, grey eyes towards Gruffydd. The spy suddenly recalled a shark he had once seen that had been caught in the village fishing nets. Even as it bit at the spears that impaled it, and even as it suffocated on dry land, its flat grey eyes continued to hold the same nothingness that now filled the eyes of the Dux Bellorum.

Gruffydd shuddered inwardly.

'You, at least, have spoken the truth as you believe it to be. I am in your debt, Gruffydd. If you have need of anything, then you may ask, and it shall be given to you.'

Gruffydd's mouth was dry and he was forced to hawk to loosen his tongue. Of all the luxuries he could request for himself and his family, only one desire surfaced from the deepest roots of his Celtic heart. He had no hesitation in making his request.

'I want the head of the beast who left the child Nimue to die.'

All the men in that small, dangerous room were silent.

Then Artorex found his voice.

'Who is Nimue?'

'She's an infant, my lord. I found her at Durobrivae, a small farming village that was put to the sword a week ago. The child's mother, who was on the point of giving birth, had been raped and used without mercy. Later, the baby had been hacked from the young girl's womb and the tiny body was thrown on to the banks of the river. I discovered the babe and determined to save her if I could. The life of an infant barbarian is less than nothing in the scheme of things, but a Celt committed the abomination on her mother, a young girl who should never have been left to die in agony. By now, the Jutes will have found her body, so they will hate us all the more fiercely for our depravity. I saved the babe – and it now lives in your kitchens. It is my desire that the child will grow to adulthood in the Celtic way, and will believe in our way of life. This child can be the living symbol you spoke of, Lord Luka, but the responsibility for the sin of her premature birth is inescapably ours.'

Artorex's head reared back and twin flames ignited the grey depths of his eyes.

'Are you telling me that this young woman had her babe cut out of her living flesh? Tell me slowly what you know, and leave nothing out.' Artorex's face was a study in cold fury, and Gruffydd's courage almost deserted him. He was alarmed, for this aspect of Artorex was unfamiliar to him.

Myrddion could have explained to Gruffydd that Nimue's birth awoke dormant memories of Gallia's fate and the cowardly murder of two defenceless women. The rigidity of the Dux Bellorum's body caused the spymaster to clench his fist under the table and to pray that Gruffydd kept his wits about him.

With growing repugnance, Artorex absorbed the full, harrowing tale. Like a tongue must probe a broken tooth, so the Dux Bellorum continued to ask pointed questions that revealed the depth of depravity and callousness of the perpetrator of the crime. In his recitation, Gruffydd didn't spare the sensitivity of his Celtic audience for he decided that Artorex was a man who valued truth, however unpalatable.

'The head of the warrior who committed this atrocity will be served up to you, Gruffydd,' Artorex said softly. 'Like you, I've no taste for the murder of helpless women or children. Is there anything you desire, or need, for yourself ?'

'I ask for nothing but the safety and well-being of our people, my lord.'

'Good man!' Artorex grinned for the first time in some minutes, and Gruffydd discovered that he could breathe again.

'The guilty man is a member of Caius's troop,' Myrddion said blandly.

Luka and Llanwith exchanged meaningful glances, and Artorex raised one eyebrow.

'Lord Caius is innocent of the murder, my lord,' Gruffydd said quickly.

'How do you come to that conclusion?' Artorex asked shortly. He stared at Gruffydd with emotionless eyes.

'Lord Caius wasn't saturated in blood, my lord,' Gruffydd replied economically.

'Good!'

Suddenly, the mood in the room lightened, as if a heavy weight had been lifted.

'Well, if that is so, then Caius shall enjoy the pleasure of delivering the cur up to me,' Artorex decided. 'My word has been given. Luka will carry the happy tidings to Caius. A public execution may serve as a warning to the more zealous of our warriors.'

'There'll be some resentment among the troops,' Myrddion began, but Artorex waved away his protest.

'We'll contrast the life of an innocent infant against the life of a fully grown man. And we'll let the mood of our people decide whether our cause is just.'

'Like King Solomon of olden times, we will be cutting the baby in half,' Luka said in admiration. 'What real man would place the life of a rapist and a murderer above the safety of a child, regardless of whether the infant should be Jute, Saxon or Celt?'

'Then we'd best keep the babe's foot covered,' Gruffydd muttered softly.

Four heads swivelled in his direction, and four pairs of eyes looked at him for an explanation.

'Is there more to this tale, Gruffydd?' Artorex asked softly.

'The Lady Morgan saw the babe when I first brought her to Venonae. She made a prophecy over the babe and even gave it a name – Nimue. I didn't approve, Lord Myrddion, but what was I to do? I couldn't gainsay Lady Morgan.'

'But there has been more, hasn't there, Gruffydd?' Artorex stared at him with his flat, unyielding eyes.

'As I explained, I discovered that Nimue had been ripped from her mother's womb and thrown into the reeds by one of her legs. The bruises on her leg were ample evidence of that. Today, the Lady Morgan took the child to her quarters and she ...'. Gruffydd's voice trailed off.

'Out with it!' Myrddion's voice was angry; the entire group knew that Myrddion's hatred of Morgan was implacable.

'She has begun to place her symbol on the injured ankle, and has commenced placing a tattoo of the head of a snake on the child's leg.'

'Shite!' exclaimed Llanwith inelegantly. 'She intends to mark the child as a pagan.'

'That would end her usefulness as a symbol.' Luka swore pungently.

'Nimue has been christened and blessed already by the Christian priests, my lord,' Gruffydd exclaimed, for he imagined that Nimue could be harmed because of the pagan mark on her fair flesh.

'You've given me a brilliant idea, Llanwith, my friend.' Myrddion grinned wickedly. 'A good tattooist could easily turn a drawing of a snake into the winged serpent – or the dragon. Especially if the first drawing hasn't been completed.'

'The tattoo is incomplete, my lord,' Gruffydd said through dry lips.

Myrddion turned to Artorex. 'Perhaps, then, you could order the babe to be marked as your own. If you put the Dracos mark upon her baby flesh, she will become a true symbol, one that you can appropriate for your own uses. This child can be used as a force to unify our people, and she would be living proof that we aren't barbarians.' Myrddion's expression was that of a satisfied tomcat.

Artorex laughed at the self-satisfied smirk on Myrddion's face. 'You love to tweak Morgan's nose, Myrddion,' he said. 'One day she might grab you by the balls and then you'll speak with the voice of a girl.'

'And one day the sky might fall – but that day is still far off.'

Artorex made his decision. 'I'll send Targo to collect little Nimue in an hour,' he stated. 'She'll not be harmed and will suffer only a little discomfort. By sunrise she'll be marked as the protégé of the Dux Bellorum.' His cold eyes warmed as he turned to Gruffydd once again. 'You'll forget all that you've heard in this room, Gruffydd. Nothing we've said must pass your lips.'

'I'm not suicidal, my lord,' Gruffydd replied dourly.

Artorex clapped him on the back and laughed. 'I like you, Gruffydd, I really do. And I'll not forget you, or your little Nimue!'

Lord save me, Gruffydd thought to himself, for to be known to Artorex could become a mixed blessing.

Gruffydd hastened to the kitchens. The hearth was a pile of hot coals, for the fire was not permitted to die entirely, while a sleepy boy was there to tend it during the night.

Nimue lay with Gallwyn on a pallet in an alcove that was separated from the kitchens by a fine woven curtain of striped wool.

'Gallwyn? Wake up, woman! Lord Artorex is sending someone for the child Nimue. Wake up!'

Gallwyn's tousled head appeared around the side of the curtain. She may have been asleep, and was still drowsy, but her eyes were sharp and alarmed.

'What are you at, Gruffydd, waking decent women in their beds? What would Lord Artorex want with little Nimue?'

'To undo what Lady Morgan has begun. You must arise from your bed, Gallwyn, for if I know Artorex's speed, his man is halfway here already.'

The conversation had been hissed, for neither Gallwyn nor Gruffydd cared to waken the kitchen staff who slept with their meagre possessions on the floors of the common room.

'I'm coming! I'm coming! Can't an old woman have even an hour of sleep?' Gallwyn complained behind her curtain.

'You can tell that to the Dux Bellorum,' Gruffydd snorted.

The two friends barely had time to wash the babe and change her wrappings before two warriors entered the kitchen. The men were complete opposites. The older of the two was a small, bandy-legged ancient with a sharp eye, some nasty scars and a short Roman sword. The second man was a giant Jutlander who was tall and blond, except for his red-gold beard. The taller man remained silent.

'I'm Targo. You're expecting us?' the smaller man said, and Gruffydd knew that this soldier walked in Artorex's shadows; these men were the Dux Bellorum's personal bodyguards.

'This here lump is Odin.' Targo gave a gap-toothed grin. 'He doesn't say much but he's as gentle as a lamb, aren't you, friend?'

'Gallwyn mothers the child Nimue, and she is chief cook for Lord Myrddion. I am Gruffydd, Lord Myrddion's man,' Gruffydd replied, somewhat awkwardly.

'Mistress!' Both men nodded to Gallwyn, who bridled slightly with pleasure.

Targo turned back to Gruffydd. 'I've heard tell of you, good sir. Artorex says you're a man to watch. He likes you, so we've been told to take an interest and ensure you're kept safe.'

'My thanks to Lord Artorex,' Gruffydd managed to reply through a tightening throat.

'So this is the infant? Aye, she's a beauty.' Targo clucked over the little bundle. 'Give her to Odin, mistress. He's got big hams of hands but he's gentle-like and won't harm her. By the time he's finished with his tattoos, Morgan will be . . . er . . . cut out, so to speak.'

'Good,' Gallwyn replied brusquely, and placed the sleeping child into Odin's huge arms. The giant looked down at the child and seemed to soften in face and form as he smelled the child's milky sweetness.

'She's a . . . a sea-wife!' he said in a voice that was rusty with disuse.

'Whatever you say, Odin.' Targo replied. 'But she will be as Lord Artorex commands.'

'She will be a . . . wise woman.' Odin struggled for the words.

'So much the better if she is to be marked as Lord Artorex's protégé,' Targo replied.

Targo noticed a kitchen boy who had suddenly woken to find the large room full of wonders.

'You,' he commanded the boy gently. 'Back to your sleep.'

The boy's expression was the same as a startled rabbit caught in a circle of light. The whites of his eyes were completely visible.

'You get back to sleep, Perce,' Gallwyn said softly and pointed in the direction of the sleeping room. 'You're just having a dream so off with you, and I'll watch the fire for you.'

Perce vanished behind the striped curtain, and Gallwyn turned back to her visitors.

'I expect you to take care of Nimue or you'll have me to answer to,' she said in a valiant return to her usual acerbic manner.

'We'll be back before dawn, mistress.'

Targo grabbed Gallwyn's ample buttock with one hand and gave her a resounding kiss on the lips.

Before Gallwyn could regain her voice, the warriors and little Nimue were gone. The night air, stirring through the swing of the leather curtain, caused the coals on the hearth to flare into sudden life.

‡ ‡ ‡

Gruffydd and Gallwyn took turns to sit up through the long and chilly night. Honey in warm water sustained them and, at times, they talked quietly of family matters and the simple pleasures of life in their home villages. Gallwyn could see the man that lay behind the mask of the spy, and recognized his deep love for his family and his homeland. She empathized with the sacrifices he had made by leaving a world he loved so he could preserve it for the future.

In turn, Gruffydd discovered that Gallwyn ruled a small kingdom in much the same way that Artorex cared for a larger one. Her abrasive manner hid an exceptionally kind heart, one that often bled for her charges when they were afflicted by the small exigencies of life.

Two hours before dawn, Odin returned with a very fretful Nimue. She whimpered and refused to be comforted, even when Gallwyn's soft finger rubbed honey against her baby gums.

Gallwyn stared fixedly at Odin and snorted reproachfully.

'This child has been hurt,' she said sharply.

'Yes. The tattooing took many hours . . . care was taken . . . but she was hurt,' he replied sadly.

Gallwyn swept back the cloth that covered the child. A superb tattoo of a serpent dragon encircled the tiny ankle, its wings spreading up the tiny calf of the babe. The flesh was angry and red, and had been smeared with a thick salve.

Odin mutely offered a wooden box with a tightly fitting lid that, presumably, held more of the remedy. One huge hand gently supported the child's head.

'She is a serpentling. A little magic woman.' The descriptions were offered like a prayer, unlike Morgan's malicious tones, although the words used were almost identical. Gruffydd felt a chill that had nothing to do with the giant Jute, or the small, fretful girl child.

'She belongs to Artorex now – or perhaps he belongs to her,' Gruffydd said. 'I am not certain which is which.'

Both Gruffydd and Gallwyn examined the child's tattoo.

A skilled hand had reshaped Morgan's reptilian form. The mighty northern dragon was incongruous on the child's body but Gruffydd could see that the dragon would grow in power as the child aged. With an eldritch life of its own, the black scales and the vivid red eyeball of the beast would glow against the white flesh of an adult woman.

'I'll wager that Odin, or whatever he calls himself, finished that tattoo himself. And I can easily believe that such detailed work has taken most of the night. Poor little Nimue! She must live into this mark. Damnation to Lady Morgan for starting this whole sorry process.'

Gruffydd felt a burning resentment against the witch, and wished heartily that his path had never strayed into her bower.

He spat on the hearth.

Gallwyn grinned impishly. A rather odd expression had appeared on her plain, broad features. 'I can't wait to see Lady Morgan's reaction when she sees that tattoo, for it is finished beyond her power to change it. She'll fair fly into a rage.'

'I have no desire to be turned into an insect or poisoned – I wouldn't put anything beyond that creature. You should heed my warnings, Gallwyn, and not tweak the witch's tail. Nimue will have need of you, and I will be gone in two days.'

'But you'll be back?'

Gruffydd laughed. 'Aye. Artorex has promised me the head of a truly evil man, so you can be certain of my return.'

Gruffydd was closeted with Myrddion when Morgan sent her servant to collect Nimue, after the fasting of the night had been broken.

Gallwyn asked the servant to report to her mistress that Lord

Artorex himself had already ordered the tattoo to be finished.

The servant girl paled in fear. 'How am I to tell my mistress?'

'I'd tell her very carefully.' Gallwyn grinned with dry good humour.

Gallwyn was not surprised when the servant girl returned within minutes with a message that she should bring the child to Lady Morgan's rooms.

The cook considered refusing the instruction, but Gruffydd's warnings prevailed. After pausing to give swift orders to the kitchen staff, she picked up the sleeping child, furs and all, and followed Morgan's servant to a hexagonal wooden structure built just beyond the smooth stone walls of the Venonae fortress.

Gallwyn was awed and a little frightened by the strange, exotic chamber into which she was ushered. Heavy fabrics covered the walls, and arcane symbols were painted on the floor. Jars filled with unspeakable things filled five shelves on one stone wall, and Gallwyn marvelled that the containers were made of precious glass. She was glad that she couldn't see what lay within those repulsive phials.

Morgan sat at the very centre of the room, with a band of hide across her forehead. Gallwyn shuddered when she realized that the hide seemed too delicate for cow or sheep hide, and had a finely grained texture. It was fragile, just like human skin. Her blunt, woman's sensibilities were revolted by the thought.

'Show me the child, woman!' Morgan ordered.

Gallwyn obeyed, her hands trembling uncontrollably.

Morgan examined the tattoo – and hissed.

'Go!' she commanded.

Crossing herself as the good Bishop of Venta Belgarum had taught her, Gallwyn went as fast as her chubby legs could carry her.

Morgan pulled the hide band over her closed eyes and

commenced swaying to a muttered chant that she whispered under her breath. Faster and faster she swayed, until her black hair lashed her pale face.

Then, as abruptly as she had begun, Morgan froze and all movement was stilled. The only sound in that exotic, wooden room was the witch's laboured breathing.

'Artorex thought to bind me,' she whispered. 'But he has bound himself – for the little Nimue will be the cause of his greatest loss.'

She smiled, and her lips were as moist and as seductive as those of a young woman.

Then her eyes opened with a sudden realization.

'But she also binds me to Artorex, for his dragon has now swallowed my serpent.'

Her pale face whitened until it resembled a fleshless skull of bone.

'I'll remain silent until my chance arrives. I waited on Uther these many years for his day of reckoning to come, so I can wait on his bastard son as well. Artorex is no greater than his father was before him.'

With this comforting thought, she reclined upon her furs and closed her tired eyes to drift into sleep.

But Morgan's dreams were filled with scenes of blood and death – and a pale, white woman wearing a necklace of silver water and moonlight who laughed at her. Before the woman, shrouded figures appeared, bearing harps, crosses, hammers and chisels. As one, the figures turned their backs on Morgan to face the woman in white. She continued to laugh until her mirth stopped the witch's heart.

Morgan screamed in her sleep.

CHAPTER XVIII

A CHILD'S RECKONING

Gruffydd was ordered to return to the Wash to move amongst the Saxons and Jutes, and to become a familiar face in one of the towns so that he could regularly come and go without causing suspicion. Prudently, once Gruffydd had safely departed, Artorex called for Caius to join him that same evening.

'Artorex!' Caius greeted his brother jovially as he was welcomed at Artorex's plain evening meal of meat and flat bread. 'How may I help you? I haven't seen you for over a month.'

'Does Ector continue in good health?' Artorex asked mildly.

'I received word not two days ago. He has pains in the joints but, otherwise, seems set to outlive even Targo, who is older than time itself. Julanna has presented me with another daughter and Ector's foster-child, Licia, is very well and growing like a colt. She is all arms and legs.'

Artorex winced a little at Caius's mention of his daughter but returned briskly to the matter at hand.

'You have done very well in your operations against the barbarians, Caius. Excellent, in fact. Your family must be proud of the leader you have become – and I won't forget your efforts in the years to come.'

Caius smiled complacently. But, having sweetened the cup, Artorex was now about to force his foster-brother to drink gall.

'However, I have a matter to discuss with you that touches on the honour of our cause and your personal reputation. My council, from whom I take advice, is concerned about some instances of unnecessary brutality that have come to their attention. So vile are the claims made to the council that any continuation of these practices might defeat the very principles for which we are fighting. We are concerned that if we are more barbaric than the barbarians, then we will unite their tribes into one force that will be almost impossible to defeat. Burned villages and the death of simple villagers is, regrettably, a part of war, but I have heard tell of actions at Durobrivae that are unnacceptable.'

'At Durobrivae? Little untoward happened in that flea hole. We expected a garrison – and found only a few warriors. Spit it out, brother, if the matter is so grave.'

Artorex formed a steeple with his fingers and stared directly into the black eyes of Caius, eyes that were so like the colour of those of Livinia, his mother. For her sake, and to honour his promise to the dying woman, Artorex chose his next words with exquisite care.

'I have been made aware that a woman was raped beside the river at Durobrivae. It's not a matter of great moment during the course of a campaign, I know, but this woman was about to give birth. One of your men cut the child out of the woman's living belly, severed the cord, and then threw the baby into the river.'

Caius made a small expression of disgust.

'I share your concern, Artorex. But there's little that I can do about lamentable bad taste on the part of one of my warriors. These men are not particularly scrupulous in their personal habits.'

Artorex suppressed his distaste for his foster-brother's lack of concern.

'The child was saved and is under my care in the kitchens.

She is now my vassal, Caius. Her rescuer has requested the head of the murderer, and I have agreed to his request. We are concerned that such behaviour could spread through the ranks until we become worse than the barbarians whom we would oppose. I've decided that an example will be made of this particular warrior who, as you say, has had the lamentable bad taste to be caught out.'

Artorex's voice had a sharp edge, and Caius studied his foster-brother's face in alarm.

'The mother of that child was a Gallia to some person,' Artorex added.

The statement caused Caius to drop his haughty eyes in embarrassment, and to silently curse the murderer, whoever he was. The fool had brought the anger of Artorex down on Caius's head.

Caius was more than a little affronted, although Artorex had attached no personal blame to him. Caius understood that Artorex expected him to make an example of the culprit when he was eventually found, but he also understood his troop and he felt certain that the offender would never admit to the crime. Time would pass and other urgencies would send Artorex off in other directions. Caius had only to stall his investigation until circumstances deflected Artorex's will. With luck, the rapist would never be punished for his actions.

'Of course, my brother,' Caius answered silkily. 'You shall have my full cooperation. I'll order the sergeants to make a diligent search for the offender.'

Artorex smiled, although it stopped well short of his eyes.

'I expect a report from you within three days. Your men will remain on guard duty until that time.'

'Of course, Artorex,' Caius responded with equal blandness.

He smiled across at Artorex and changed the subject

adroitly. 'I have received a note for you from the Villa Poppinidii. Should you wish me to send a reply, you have only to ask.'

As Caius strode away after depositing a sealed piece of rough vellum on Artorex's campaign desk, the Dux Bellorum reflected on how little he could trust the judgement and behaviour of his foster-brother. While Caius was a brave man in battle, and a clever commander, his occasional taste for violence could never quite be slaked, making him an enigma to most of the captains who served alongside him. Caius could pretend to be the noble Roman for years at a stretch, but once power was placed in his hands, he seemed to revert to his dark, sinister and secret nature. Unfortunately, he knew that Artorex had a living daughter, a secret that gave him a measure of protection.

One day, brother or not, Artorex knew he would have to remedy the problem of his foster-brother.

The Dux Bellorum turned the sealed scroll over and over in his fine, well-shaped hands. Who had he become that he could contemplate the sanctions he was considering against Caius? Since Gallia's death, he'd hardened his heart to all manner of atrocities and knew that his tiny, civilized wife would have been horrified that her husband could make such dreadful decisions with so little feeling.

But Gallia was dead, and he'd never see her again this side of Hades. The princelings and the common people had never heard her name and, in any event, would probably have disapproved of a pure Roman wife for their Dux Bellorum.

I doubt that you'd still love me if you were alive, my Gallia, he thought, with a pang of self-pity. In fact, I can't even recall your face.

It's odd, he thought. I can see her mouth as clearly as if she was still alive. If I put my mind to it, I can remember the texture of her skin and the shape of her face. I can even recall those almond-shaped eyes that could snap and glitter with excitement. I can remember all the individual parts of her face but, no matter how hard I try, I can't seem to put them together.

Artorex felt a surge of sadness rather than grief – the kind of sadness that comes after the initial pain of loss has gone. Gallia was dead, cold ash. She had been dead for such a short time, and yet his mind had already begun to expunge her memory.

But Artorex could remember the flowers that were nurtured around the odd little villa that he had built with his own hands. He would probably remain prouder of that small achievement than the salvation of the kingdom, if that goal were ever to be reached. He recalled again the scorched roses and the cracked stones of his fallen house with a dim regret.

Artorex opened the scroll by breaking the waxen seal.

Well, boy, all is as ever at Villa Poppinidii, and the flowers and bulbs have been planted at Gallia's grave as you requested, although a ruin seems an odd monument. Once the winter thaw comes, her resting place will be as pretty as ever.

Licia is now nearly three. How quickly time travels when you are as old as I am! She follows Gareth like a puppy and he dotes on her like a parent.

He can be depended upon to keep the girl safe. At any road, she takes no notice of what I say, rather like a lump of a boy that I remember all too well.

I am always grateful for the love and care Gareth has given to our family, and I am determined that one day he will make his own mark on the world.

We hear of your deeds, even in quiet Aquae Sulis, and I cannot help but think my dear Livinia would have been so proud, with both of her sons fighting for the land. If you come home in the summer, we will feast like the old days. But I won't ask you to wait at table.

Ector, Master of Villa Poppinidii, and your proud Father

Such letters always made Artorex yearn for the peace and permanency of the life he had enjoyed in his youth; he knew that his future was now inextricably entwined with the past acts of Uther Pendragon – and there was no help for it. Even now, he was avoiding decisions that had been made for him by birth and fate.

With a knife and a polishing stone, he removed every trace of the words on the vellum as he always did. Too many eyes and ears watched and listened for the Dux Bellorum's weaknesses. He never wrote to Ector and the old man understood his reasons, but even as the old Artorex slipped away, the new Artorex wished fervently that his destiny had allowed him to remain a humble steward at the Villa Poppinidii.

Three days passed, and Caius reported to Artorex that no one purported to know anything of the woman under the willow. He hinted that, perhaps, she may have been a victim of Saxon barbarity.

Artorex held his peace and waited.

Gruffydd returned to Venonae the following day, at a time when the icy ground was turning to slush and the first shoots of spring appeared on the trees around the city walls.

He brought grave news.

'Oakheart's name is Katigern. He is the grandson of Vortigern, a king who won a foothold in the south-west some forty years ago,' he reported to Myrddion.

'I remember Vortigern well,' Myrddion murmured. 'He believed he could sacrifice me to stopper up a natural spring – of all things – when I was only a small boy. I revealed a demonic prophecy to him that he seemed to expect, and I was fortunate to escape the long reach of his arm. Uther Pendragon drove his sons out of our lands many years ago.' He frowned deeply and toyed with a small fruit knife on his table. 'We will have problems with this Oakheart. I judged Vortigern to be a kingly man and he was exceptionally clever – except for some stupid superstitions. What type of man is his grandson?'

'He's vigorous, ambitious and is fair of speech, my lord,' Gruffydd responded. 'He's extremely capable and dangerous. I discovered that he has allied himself with Otha, the Saxon princeling. Together they intend to destroy our world.'

'With such a pedigree, the man could prove to be dangerous.'

Myrddion was worried. Normally, his thoughts wouldn't be so evident but, on this occasion, his brow was furrowed and his dark eyes appeared uneasy. Gruffydd could plainly see that his master was disturbed. Local gossip was full of Artorex's inaction – and a belief was growing that the Dux Bellorum was permitting the throne to slip through his fingers. Myrddion had begun his search for the relics of Uther's reign, but Artorex's attitude was a source of concern. The young man's manner was reticent and he was stubbornly uncooperative.

'Vortigern, and his sons Katigern Major and Vortimer, were more than half-Briton so, as High King, Vortigern wasn't much different from the Romans when they lorded it over us. But his bitch queen was Saxon to the bone and her legacy showed in the sons that Vortigern bred off her. Katigern Minor might be young, but he has become what his grandfather never was – more Saxon than Celt.'

'Aye, lord. He claims his grandfather was High King in the west in years gone by, and that he has the right of blood for all the wrongs that Uther inflicted on his descendants. His birthright gives legitimacy to the Saxon invasion and he claims to speak for those remnants of Vortigern's people who still live in the high mountains in the west – both Saxon and Celt.'

'Of course. I'd do the same if I were in his boots. It's unfortunate that atrocities such as the one that occurred at Durobrivae happen – they feed the growing flames.' Myrddion sighed deeply. 'I wish our barbarians were simple pillagers and destroyers – as they once were.'

Gruffydd stood impassively in his ragged Saxon garb.

'Off with you, Gruffydd.' Myrddion smiled. 'You'd best bathe and dress so that the garrison doesn't decide you are a Saxon – and turn you into a pincushion.'

'No chance of that, my lord.' Gruffydd grinned and departed.

Later, Myrddion spent several hours with Artorex, but the weight of his fears were far from lifted. However, he was able to assure Gruffydd that a full parade of all troops that were in bivouac outside Venonae would take place on the morrow. No absences or excuses were to be permitted. Artorex had tired of the endless excuses made by Caius.

This man was born to be the king of the Britons, Myrddion thought proudly, after Artorex had issued his instructions. Caius will not enjoy Artorex's method of finding the culprit and apportioning blame. Nor, for that matter, will the rest of our warriors, for they will initially see the murder of one woman as insignificant. Still, the Dux Bellorum must be seen to be fair in all matters relating to discipline.

Myrddion sighed a little as he recalled the tender and considerate youth that Artorex had once been.

Gruffydd would be present at the parade.

'I require you, personally, to bring Gallwyn and the child Nimue to the exercise yard outside the gates of Venonae,' Myrddion told him. 'The infant will be shown to the people who attend our entertainment.'

'Aye, my lord,' Gruffydd replied, and hastened to inform Gallwyn of her part in the day's activities.

Word soon spread like wildfire through the garrison, village and bivouacs that Artorex wished to speak to all good Celts. An hour before Artorex's scheduled arrival, the meeting place held a sea of faces and the event was beginning to develop a festive air. Artorex's warriors had thoroughly prepared themselves and their horses for the occasion and were a splendid spectacle for the townsfolk to marvel at, even though a chill wind blew.

Flanked by Myrddion and his vassal kings, Artorex arrived in full state, the wolf cloak now full length and splendidly barbarous over his Roman breastplate and helmet. His great height, his amazing hair and his stern demeanour were sufficiently powerful to silence the crowd, but when he divested himself of his weapons and his helmet, placing them in the arms of Targo and Odin, the crowd drew in their breath with excitement.

This would be a momentous day, for even the witch, Morgan, clad in her crow-black clothes, was standing on a vantage point overlooking the crowd. Many eyes were turned surreptitiously towards her still form and each person prayed that her eyes wouldn't alight upon their face.

'I have heard that her looks can kill,' one old besom said to another in superstitious dread and secret enjoyment.

'The High King turned up his toes when she gazed at him,' her friend added.

Shortly thereafter, the brazen roar of battle horns silenced the crowd.

Artorex stepped up on to a raised dais over which his battle standard flew, snapping viciously in the cold wind. He turned to survey the horse troops and their captains.

As was his strategy, Artorex offered praise for the fields of Saxon grain that had been burned black, the granaries that had been plundered and the trade routes that had been disrupted.

The troops smiled at their leader's approval, although like good soldiers they held to their positions in the ranks.

Then Artorex explained the emergence of Katigern Oakheart, Saxon to the bone, but born and nourished in Britain. He added that Katigern had claimed a tenuous legitimacy to supremacy over the west. The townsfolk and soldiers roared their anger and defiance while Artorex smiled openly, although his eyes were very cold.

'But great trouble afflicts us all, my loyal men of the west. How can I speak of the charges laid against us to men such as you, men who demonstrate their bravery and loyalty every day in pursuit of our freedom? How can I permit your efforts to be tarnished when the Saxons accuse you of wanton bloodlust and depravity? At first, I could not believe that these rumours were true. That is, until I discovered for myself that, indeed, these tales were not lies. Some of your brethren have flouted their vows, my noble soldiers. They have killed for sport – not for necessity.'

A great roar of denial rose to disturb the crows and rooks that gathered on the walls of the stone garrison. For one short, prophetic moment, the air was alive with black and shining wings.

'Bring forth the infant known as Nimue,' Artorex demanded.

Gallwyn had begged, borrowed and, it must be said, stolen what finery she could. The babe was all but invisible beneath her wrappings of furs. She mounted the dais, bowing almost to the raw wooden planks in homage, and then stood to face the horse soldiers.

'Show the child to the men,' Artorex demanded, and Caius felt his knees turn to jelly.

Gallwyn lifted the naked baby high above the neat lines of men, and the infant whimpered a little at the sudden chill upon her skin. But then she smiled, and her rounded limbs and extreme fairness reflected her natural beauty.

By now, Nimue's tattoo had mostly healed – and the symbol was clear to see upon her right leg and ankle.

'It is for innocents such as this babe that we fight. We die to preserve the old ways of honour and duty. To maintain peace for children such as this little one, we brave the snows of winter and leave our widows to weep in their loneliness. We risk everything we have so that such children might grow in beauty and safety. We are the champions of the west, not ragged barbarians who burn churches, rape women and split infants asunder with our axes.'

The whole crowd roared their approval. Artorex held them in the palm of his hand.

He took Nimue from Gallwyn's hands and wrapped her again in her furs, leaving only her right leg exposed to the air. Hundreds of eyes watched his every move.

'The bruises have faded under my mark. This child is no longer the bloody, blue creature found in frozen reeds. She was nigh dead from exposure.'

The crowd was utterly silent.

'One of you betrays the west, and this mongrel dog sullies the names of our great dead. Let me tell you of Nimue's birth and then *you* shall judge what I should do.'

Clever! Gallwyn thought to herself.

'Good man!' Myrddion whispered under his breath.

'Mithras save me!' Caius mouthed, while taking care that he shouldn't be heard. His Roman face remained impassive.

'The child's mother was a woman from the village of Durobrivae, a nothing place in the marshes. Our troop came to this place deep in enemy territory, ably led by my foster-brother, Lord Caius. The soldiers did their work, distasteful as it might be, and burned the granaries, the fields and the village itself, for such is the way of warfare. Nor do I begrudge them what spoils they took in my name.'

Artorex grinned fleetingly, establishing an immediate rapport with the warriors.

'Much that was taken was ours anyway, stolen by marauders. Yes, there were villagers who were put to the sword, and there were women, too, who died, for such measures are sometimes necessary when Saxon women fight like men.'

Many heads nodded in agreement, as Artorex continued in the perfect stillness of their complete attention.

'But Nimue's nameless mother was near to birthing. She had no weapon, other than her great belly and her beauty. She ran towards the river, and an old willow tree, to what she hoped would be safety.'

The silence was intense, a living thing composed of the indrawn breath of over a hundred citizens.

'She was wrong!' Artorex roared.

A sigh ran through the crowd, especially from the women. In Artorex's mind, the vision of Gallia, also heavily pregnant, rose up spectrally to nod her assent at her husband's words.

'One of our men saw her flee into her sanctuary – but *man* is not a word I choose to use when I speak of him, for to do so insults all warriors and citizens of decency and honour. He pursued her, followed her into the safety of the willow branches and then, free from prying eyes, he raped her.'

A few women and some of the men remembered the fate of their own kin, and tears ran unchecked down their cheeks.

'But such horrors happen, do they not? Terrible, unmanly, secret horrors that we do not care to pull out into the light of day. Such is war.'

Fewer men nodded in assent this time, while their companions looked sideways at them with the stirrings of dislike.

'But this man wasn't finished with the fair young woman under the branches of the hanging willow. No, not nearly. Hard as it would be, she could have survived her rape and borne her child, suckled Nimue at a mother's breast and lived with the nightmares of the willow tree as her daughter grew tall. That woman might yet have found some reason in this child to live on.'

The whole crowd was now mute with awful imaginings. That the child was here meant that her mother was dead. They pictured the victim with her throat cut or her heart pierced, and felt a little squeamish – just as Artorex intended they should.

'I cannot tell you why this man – this Celt – this one of us – carried out this abomination. I can't really bear to think upon his actions, for they step far beyond what you and I would consider to be the rules of warfare.'

Soldiers now stared at their feet, as they recalled the litany of their own hate crimes. Their own deeds in battle, small and great, flew like stinging wasps through their consciences.

'This cur cut this young woman with his knife. He split her belly open like ripe fruit and hacked at the open wound while she screamed and tried to fight him off. He put his hands into her womb and ripped the unborn child from her body while she still lived.'

A rumble rose from the crowd, soft, but full of disgust and loathing.

Artorex barely paused for breath.

'He cut the infant's cord with his knife, for he had plans for this tiny, perfect little thing. Aye. And this mother still fought, even as her blood gushed forth until the earth was red with it. Her hands were cut to the bone where she gripped his knife, for she feared that he would commit further unspeakable acts upon the body of her daughter.'

You clever, clever man, Myrddion thought silently. The rape of babes isn't acceptable in any society. To hint at it is enough to sicken any rational person.

'But he didn't rape the infant. Not him. Perhaps he was not man enough, or beast enough, for such a deed. He left the mother to bleed to death under the willow tree, safe from prying eyes.'

Artorex paused to determine the effect of the tale on his audience.

'This man gorged himself on suffering,' he roared.

He lifted Nimue's tiny body high into the air with one giant hand.

'He took this child by her fragile ankle, whirled her round his head and tossed her towards the river, a river that was covered in winter ice.'

The growl of the crowd was now louder, like the start of a heavy thunderstorm that builds and builds in intensity until it blackens the sky.

'The gods saw what was done, and perhaps they wept in pity for what had occurred that day. The dried rushes on the banks of the river cushioned Nimue's fall and protected her. Only an impossible chance sent a good man who was fortunate enough to find her, a babe whose ankle was black with bruises and whose skin was blue with cold. She was meant to live, this little one, as a symbol of what our Celtic peoples can become if we degenerate into Saxon ways. Yet, I have heard from our spies that even the Saxons were sickened by the actions of this beast whose victim bled to death in agony.'

Now the crowd roared its disapproval.

'Are we such beasts? Is this the way we make war?'

He held Nimue high once again.

'Should I dash this child's brains out now, so that she will not grow up to be a Jute or Saxon whore?'

'No! No! No!' the crowd roared in unison.

'And what should I do with such a man as this desecrator? I, the Dux Bellorum, ask you what the punishment should be?'

'Death! Death! Death!' The chant echoed through the assembled populace as soldiers and townsfolk alike shouted as one.

Artorex remained silent, and handed the babe to Gallwyn. The cook wrapped her in her warm furs, and held her to her withered breasts.

'But I can't tell you who this man is. And neither can Lord Caius, who's been unable to extract the answer from his troop. His warriors protect this beast – for at least one warrior must be aware of his identity. The poor girl's blood must have covered him from head to toe.'

A number of the warriors from Caius's troop paled, concerned at the anger of the assembled throng.

'Hear me!' Artorex ordered. 'I am the Dux Bellorum, and I scorn to shed innocent blood! I've thought long on this matter, and I've asked myself what the great ones would have done.'

The crowd was silent to a man.

'There, in the words of the immortal Caesar, was my answer.'

The crowd remained mute as they waited for his decision.

'The troop of my brother, Caius, is thirty in number, and they shall be decimated until the murderer stands forth or his brothers deliver him to justice.'

The crowd began to stir.

'May I have your permission to invoke the old punishment of the legions? Do we decimate?'

Gradually, slowly at first, and then growing in power, the crowd roared their approval.

'Decimate! Decimate! Decimate!'

A secret part of Artorex felt ill at the thought of the punishment he was proposing while the vengeful, bitter part of him sang for the pure justice of it.

The troop was isolated and divided randomly into three groups of ten men each, while Caius watched impotently. He schooled his face to show no emotion as each man in the ten was forced to draw straws. The man with the shortest straw in each group, gibbering with fear, was placed inside a circle formed by the other nine warriors.

'Are you the man?' Artorex asked each of the three condemned men. 'Do you know who he is?'

Desperately, the victims denied the charge in turn, including all knowledge of the incident. Perhaps they still hoped for mercy.

The crowd held its breath.

'I am the Dux Bellorum. Any guilt associated with what is about to occur will be mine, and mine alone.'

He paused.

'The nine must kill the tenth. They may use their hands, their spear shafts, or the pommels of their swords. No metal or sharpened weapons may be used.'

He paused once more.

'And those who will not carry out these orders will join their brothers within the killing circle until they agree to hand over the murderer of the innocent.'

Artorex waited and watched.

Perhaps these warriors feel that my threat is a bluff, he thought as he watched the three condemned men. Or perhaps they hope for intercession from the crowd. But Artorex knew that the thrill of bloody spectacle gripped the assembly.

'You will begin,' he roared.

The sound of wood, fists and even stone on flesh was sickening; Artorex felt every blow.

The three warriors took a long time to die.

'Now, will any man in the troop speak out?' Artorex waited. 'No? Then we begin again, this time with eight!'

The decimation was sickening, for its coldness gave added horror to the justice that it symbolized.

Finally, when Artorex asked the question for the third time, one of the warriors walked to the foot of the dais and lifted a tear-streaked face to look deeply into the grey eyes of Artorex.

'I suspect the murderer to be Gwynn ap Owyn, my lord. He is my sister's husband. I have no proof, but he was covered in blood to the shoulders when he returned to the campfire at Durobrivae. He wouldn't say where he'd been, and just gave me a wink. Forgive me, lord! I kept silent for the sake of my sister and her children.'

'Return to your group,' Artorex ordered. 'You will receive a just punishment at my discretion for your failure to impart this information at an earlier opportunity.'

He gazed over the assembled warriors.

'Gwynn ap Owyn! You will stand forth.'

No one moved, but suddenly two veterans in the troop turned and began to drag forward a large, middle-aged man.

The warrior immediately began to snivel and beg.

'Do not protest your innocence to me or I will personally cut your tongue from your head. You are no Celt, for you allowed six of your brothers to die for your crimes. You do not deserve to live.'

Artorex looked at the ashen face of Caius among his warriors.

'Lord Caius, you will personally hang this man who has brought dishonour upon your troop, then you will cut off his stinking head and send it to my rooms. You will throw his carcass to the dogs – if they will eat such carrion. Then you will bury your innocent warriors with all due respect, for they died as good Celts – and they didn't beg, like this cowardly animal. Reparation will be made to their families for their loss, although gold is not worth the life of a good man. We are Celts! We don't make war on innocents, and we don't betray the justice of our cause.'

One by one, each member of the troop spat on the weeping face of Gwynn ap Owyn, and the warriors dragged him away.

Once more, Artorex looked down sorrowfully at the assemblage.

'The duty of maintaining the honour of the Britons is a responsibility that weighs on all warriors. But the very survival of the west demands that our actions reflect the glory of our cause. I am ashamed that a creature such as Gwynn ap Owyn has soiled the reputations of his companions and of us all through his cowardice and brutality.'

Artorex looked directly at Caius, to ensure that his brother understood the full import of his words. Then Caius escaped to follow the Dux Bellorum's orders and salvage his honour in the eyes of his men.

'We are nothing if we do not hold to honourable and ancient ways that exemplify our history. Saxon men are our enemies, not their women and children. We fight for home and hearth and the glories of our past, not for the thrill of bloodshed. Let it be understood from this time onwards that no blame for the six innocent men who died today will be attached to any soul here. I take it upon myself, for I am the Dux Bellorum.'

Artorex's sadness, his patriotism and his charm had the crowd roaring his name as he made his way back to the garrison. His heart was heavy as he ordered Targo to ensure that red gold should be sent to six innocent widows and that good land should be deeded to their sons.

That little tactic worked well, didn't it? a small part of Artorex's consciousness whispered wickedly. Perhaps it's time to send Myrddion back to Venta Belgarum.

CHAPTER XIX

UTHER'S LEGACY

Myrddion Merlinus understood his own nature far too well. He accepted that he was born to be a strategist, the right hand of great men, and a coldness in his nature ensured that his intellect always ruled his emotions. There was no hardship in replacing a wife and children with the actualities of power, for his sexual drive was easily slaked.

If the truth were told, Myrddion loved plots and books far more than any living, breathing creature. Horses were mere transport and a dog was a slobbering nuisance. Books and scrolls never failed, while they never desired anything in return. He had friends, including Llanwith and Luka, but these two men only understood the edges of his agile mind. One day, they would die and he'd weep – he who hadn't shed a tear in nearly forty years.

Fortunate is the man who has such self-control for, without love, there can be no pain and no sense of loss. His preternatural youth was born out of his even temper and the great walls he had built around his heart. Even Artorex, Myrddion's personal creation, was often just a means to an end. Myrddion recalled how, at the decimation, he had felt pride in Artorex's cleverness and fixity of purpose, without truly recognizing at the time the connection between the death of Gallia and of the woman who had been killed under the willow tree. Now, in the darkness of the night, Myrddion felt a thickness in his throat and an unaccustomed prickle in his eyes as he thought of Artorex's words to the crowd. Myrddion winced as he recognized the pain that the young man must have felt as he lifted small Nimue high, acknowledging an orphaned child, while his own Licia would never know her father.

'You're becoming old and maudlin, Myrddion,' he told the lamp flame. 'You'll soon be fit for nothing but hoary old stories around a warm fire.'

But Myrddion's knife-sharp brain knew that he lied. His path through life was set and his allegiances had been given long ago. There was no path for him other than to be what the gods, or demons, had decreed for him, so thoughts of suffering must be shoved aside.

He turned to the tangible problem at hand.

'The sword. We must find the sword. Without a High King to counter Katigern Oakheart, we're finished. And Artorex cannot become High King without that sodding sword.'

Myrddion had puzzled and teased his brain over Uther's final spite for nearly a year and a half. Morgan was not privy to all of Uther's secrets. She had held great sway over that terrible old despot, but theirs was a relationship based on hatred and need. Myrddion had no doubt that Morgan kept Uther alive well past his appointed time, not out of compassion, but so the old monster might suffer as he watched his natural son eclipse him. Had Morgan possessed the sword, it would already be in the acquisitive fingers of King Lot, for Lot's wife was, after all, her dim-witted sister, Morgause. Morgan had been shrivelled with hatred when Uther expedited the death of her father, and she would gladly destroy the kingdom using King Lot, rather than allow Artorex to succeed to the throne.

'Ah! Old loves and old hatreds,' Myrddion told the flame, his only confidante. 'I'd pity Morgan if she didn't hate quite so hard. Uther deserved every second of pain she gave him, but Artorex bears no guilt for the crimes of the High King. Morgan has blighted her life for a curdled justice.'

No, the sword was as lost to Morgan as it was to everyone else.

When Uther was near to death, and even his servants were fearful of entering his apartments in Venta Belgarum, Myrddion came to believe that Uther had entrusted the sword and crown to Bishop Branicus, Uther's personal confessor. He'd asked the venerable man outright if Uther had given him the symbols of kingship, and could still recall the bishop's stern and seemingly honest reply.

'I don't have either crown or sword, Lord Myrddion. If I had them in Venta Belgarum, I would give them to you.'

The old bishop had passed away only one month after his obstinate master. Another priest, a younger man, had replaced Branicus and the trail was now cold. Myrddion knew and understood the ways of priests, so he could have sworn that the old bishop hadn't told a direct lie.

'But did he tell the complete truth?' Myrddion asked the flame. 'The Church of the Christus is a world of its own, and power is the mortar that holds it together. Did he tell the truth?'

Myrddion selected a piece of raw chalk and wrote the bishop's words on his table top. Then, his senses straining, he measured the weight of every word used by the old bishop.

'The bishop spoke to me as a man, flame, and not as a priest. He said, *I do not have*, he did not say *the Church does not have*.' So the Church probably did hold the sacred objects, but not at Venta Belgarum. The priest had been careful to name that city and deny that the crown and sword were there. The bishop didn't lie, he simply didn't reveal all of his knowledge.

Myrddion remembered that Branicus had been half-Roman, but he was also part Spanish, a man who understood the frontiers and the terrible cost of barbarian invasion. He probably would have preferred to give up the sword and the crown, but he had not. Why?

'Because Uther had bound him to an oath. Of course! The old fox made the bishop swear that Artorex would not receive the symbols of power from his hands. The bishop knew that I would eventually come to him when Uther was on his deathbed. He recognized that he would be obligated either to break his vow or damn the safety of Christian Britain. The Saxons have no love for the Christian god. Branicus must also have known that he, too, was sickening. What would he do? What would I do?'

The candle didn't answer, but it flickered in encouragement.

'If Branicus didn't lie to me directly, he indicated that he sent the objects away to somewhere safe. But where have they been sent? There are no clues for me in his words.'

Myrddion struggled to follow the bishop's dilemma. No one, not even a man of God, could have listened to Uther's confessions without distaste. The bishop was privy to all of Uther's gruesome secrets, but he'd taken them to the grave as the rules of his church demanded. But did he want the relics to be found?

'Yes, flame! That dour old man has told me so in his own words. He'd have given them to me were it not for the oath he gave to Uther Pendragon and the sanctity of the confessional.'

Myrddion was bone-deep weary. He had unravelled the edges of the bishop's reasoning but only rest and further contemplation would solve the puzzle.

After wiping away the chalk words with his sleeve, Myrddion retired to his bed, but his sleep was troubled by dreams of a willow tree, its ancient branches trailing down to the water of a deep and silent lake. He attempted to enter its confusion of branches but the tree itself barred his way.

Gruffydd had received a rough hide sack that held the head of the vicious Gwynn ap Owyn. He lacked the heart to view those coarse features so instead he decided to return the gruesome trophy to Durobrivae in the care of trusted confederates. They were instructed to mount the head on a stake before the willow tree as a tangible message of Celtic justice.

He felt that Nimue had been amply avenged.

'Should she be told of her birth when she is older?' Gallwyn asked him. 'The tale might cause her pain, but someone else will certainly inform her of the fate of her birth mother one day.'

'Of course she must be told,' Gruffydd retorted. 'But we should wait until she can fully understand, and we should give the girl her mother's hairpin at that time. Let us hope that she becomes a Celt before that day and has ceased to be a Jutlander.'

'The blood price you asked for her has surely been paid,' Gallwyn murmured nervously.

'Aye. But Nimue is under Artorex's protection, so I fear for her safety in the years ahead. He has set his seal upon her and she may grow to resent what it represents.'

'I'll do my best to guide her along the paths she must travel, Gruffydd, for I've a good few years left before I'm done. I'll raise her right.'

'At any road, Lord Myrddion has sent word that he and I will ride to Venta Belgarum tomorrow. He is planning Artorex's strategies, so we must prepare for his next campaign.'

Gallwyn gave a brief shudder. 'I always hated Venta Belgarum. Uther was like a thin, white slug, and his slime was everywhere. Take care, my friend, for there are rumours among the common folk that Lord Artorex must declare himself High King if he is to fight off this Katigern creature. If he waits too long, a pretender could steal his crown.'

'That's the whole trouble,' Gruffydd responded dourly. 'At the moment, he doesn't know where to find the crown, or even if it still exists.'

In hundreds of other rooms throughout the kingdoms, innumerable men dreamed of the sword, the crown and the legacy of Uther Pendragon. Some of these men were honest at heart, while some were almost wholly devoured by lust for power. Some were noble and others were vicious opportunists, for the sword of Uther Pendragon had a lustre and allure that did not depend upon its gems and its blade. The sword was the key to the kingdom, and the crown was a mark of the favour of the old gods.

In the frozen north, King Lot was desperate to find Uther's sword. He and his family had excellent claims to the throne through his marriage, while his eldest son, Gawayne, was even more likely to win the crowd's acclaim, for he was a handsome young man with more than his share of natural charm. More importantly, Gawayne was mad for glory and had begged his father to allow him to serve in Artorex's army.

Artorex had been nonplussed by Prince Gawayne's open admiration and his total inability to lie. Quixotically, he had sent Gawayne to lead the garrison at Venta Belgarum in the full knowledge that Gawayne would have been urged by both parents to search out Uther's sword. He had gambled that Myrddion's best guesses were right and that Uther had hidden the sword elsewhere. Gawayne had indeed searched assiduously for the sword, but it had remained stubbornly elusive.

At first, as Dux Bellorum, Artorex had been unfettered by the absence of the symbols of power, for he was the war chieftain and that role was more powerful than the inherited status of the tribal kings. The Dux Bellorum could demand troops from the tribes and was solely responsible for the shape and outcome of the war.

Artorex was already a king in all but name.

But Gruffydd knew with certainty that Katigern Oakheart had a legitimate claim to the throne of the High King of the Britons through his grandfather. Gruffydd also understood that Vortigern himself would not have approved of the wanton destruction that the barbarians had brought to the east. The White Dragon, a creature of ice and cold, came as predicted and it had spread its wings over the land of the Britons and killed them with its frozen breath.

It remains to be seen if the Red Dragon of Artorex can withstand such an onslaught, Gruffydd thought. The Saxons fear prophecies even more than we do, while Katigern knows our history. He'll do anything in his power to hinder Myrddion's search for the sword of Uther Pendragon.

Venta Belgarum was Celt and would remain so until the whole kingdom turned to dust. The High Kings had been crowned in its church, where once a sacred tree had flourished in the days of Druid ascendancy. Venta Belgarum was not the heart of Britain, but it was the blood of the body.

The city was unchanged from Uther's time, because Artorex kept a strong garrison to combat the Saxons who had refortified the coastline near Anderida. Artorex had chosen Gawayne as leader after seeing the young redhead in battle, as icy and as controlled as Myrddion himself. But off the battlefields, the boy had roguish charm, rash passions and a natural bent for leadership so, in the teeth of objections from Llanwith and Luka, Venta Belgarum had eventually become Gawayne's charge.

Thus far, Artorex had found no cause to regret his choice. Gawayne may have been subject to his parent's ambitions, but he was a loyal Celt with a ferocious desire for victory.

When Myrddion and Gruffydd arrived in Venta Belgarum,

after several gruelling days on horseback, Gawayne was quick to welcome his visitors. After the usual bowing, scraping and detailed reports, the two men were permitted to rest before preparing for the night's feasting. Gawayne was determined to impress his noble visitor with his hospitality and planned a night of enforced carousing for his guests.

So, instead of resting, master and servant made use of the afternoon to visit Uther's erstwhile apartments.

'These rooms have been tightly sealed since the death of Uther, my Lord,' Gruffydd reported. 'To be honest, the servants are terrified of this part of the palace and would refuse to clean it anyway, so we can expect clouds of dust once we are inside.'

'I'm certain the relics aren't here but I wish to understand the bishop a little better. It may help me discover what he chose to do with his difficult inheritance.'

Privately, Gruffydd believed that Myrddion was indulging in superstitious nonsense, but his master was very nearly always right when he assessed a situation.

Gruffydd took a long, iron key and inserted it into the great doors to Uther's private apartments.

The door fittings protested as rusty metal hinges ground against equally rusty supports. The doors seemed jammed, although only six months had elapsed since the entrance was sealed, and both Myrddion and Gruffydd had to use their best efforts to force open the great oak planks. Uther's servants had obviously neglected his apartments during the period before his death.

With a groaning and a splintering, the doors finally gave way.

'The stench in this room is foul,' Myrddion exclaimed. 'I smell the works of Morgan here.'

I smell something long dead, Gruffydd thought irreverently.

A mantle of dust lay thinly on every surface, and Myrddion

drew his finger through a cobweb that masked the entry to Uther's bedchamber.

'There's something evil resting here,' Myrddion shuddered. 'I can feel it.'

The great bed with its thick coverlet of fur had been neatly made. On one side, to the right, a cushioned stool was placed so the bishop could hear Uther's confessions. Every corner of the room was hazy with dust motes, a patina of neglect and a miasma of sickness.

But the white furs on the bed had been ruined forever by the remains of a large crow with outstretched wings that was pinned to the bed by long nails. Its skeletal body and empty eye sockets still seemed to shriek with life. With distaste, Myrddion realized that the torn wing feathers around the nails holding its carcass to the bed indicated that the bird had been alive when it was fixed in place. It had been left to starve to death – or to be devoured alive by the rats.

'What is that, lord?' Gruffydd whispered, pointing towards a cloth-covered shape across the great window of the bedchamber.

So vast was Uther's prestige that his window had been constructed of small pieces of imported glass, so that no chill should find entry and attack his old bones. Gruffydd knew the window existed, but now it was completely shrouded by a dusty length of black wool.

'Pull that blanket down and let in some light,' Myrddion ordered.

Gruffydd approached the black cloth.

He gripped the fabric, and pulled – and almost screamed with shock.

The corpse of a woman had been nailed to the window frame by her spread-eagled hands and feet so that her remains formed an obscene cross. The rats had left evidence of their presence on the dried corpse and Gruffydd was revolted by this proof of Morgan's malignancy. Transfixed by the grim scene, Gruffydd realized that the stains on the floor, and a gaping wound in the throat, indicated that the woman had been dead or dying when she had been nailed into position.

'What sickness is this abomination, lord?' Gruffydd asked in a whisper.

'It's nothing to do with her Druid teachings, and it's nothing Christian. But it's all Morgan. I believe she intended to keep Uther's spirit locked within this chamber forever. She placed the woman to guard the window and used the crow as the vessel for his soul. Then she attempted to have the apartments sealed off for a long, long time.'

'She's a strange woman, master. And her hatred is appalling.'

'Pitiful is a better description of Morgan,' Myrddion replied. 'She needs to believe that she can still control Uther's body and spirit even after his death. How unutterably sad.'

'Sad?' Gruffydd spat, and then crossed himself. 'The woman is demented.'

'Morgan has probably been crazed for years. She has buried every natural desire in order to take her revenge on Uther during the many years she remained with him. But this! It's so petty – and such a dreadful waste.'

'Well, I'm not going to spare any sympathy for the witch.' Gruffydd was affronted by the barbarity of Morgan's actions. 'If anyone should be staked out like this, it's Morgan.'

'No. Morgan is more to be pitied. Even with Uther dead and gone, she cannot give up her hatred. But staring at these old crimes does not serve our purpose.'

Myrddion looked across the corpse at the superstitious face of Gruffydd, and then issued his instructions.

'Leave this unhallowed place and find servants, and a warrior or two. I want these apartments completely refitted for the High

King when he comes to Venta Belgarum. Every stick of furniture, every piece of cloth, every fur and every trace of the presence of Uther and Morgan is to be burned.' He gazed around the dust-filled room. 'And you must find a priest to pray for this girl's soul and give her a decent burning.'

Gruffydd hurried off to obey his master's wishes, glad to be released from the mouldering room that was still full of implacable hatred.

Myrddion knelt upon the dusty stool beside the bed and rested his forearms, as if in prayer, close to where Uther's head must have lain. This was the position where Uther's priest had spent many hours, even years, listening to Uther's confessions throughout the period of his slow decay. Here, in the final days, the bishop would have given extreme unction to the dying Uther, even though he was close to death himself.

Myrddion was no Christian, but he had considerable knowledge of the Roman sect. He understood that the unfortunate Branicus, in his piety, must have crushed his natural feelings for years. In Myrddion's imagination, the final confession of Uther Pendragon must have been grotesque.

How often had the bishop knelt here? If the embroidered stool was any guide, a pair of knees had flattened the plumpness of the stuffing. How many hours had the bishop listened to the savage ravings of a decadent old tyrant as he struggled to bring that unrepentant soul to his God? Uther would not have parted with his sword and his crown during the final stages of his illness, fearing that Morgan would lay her henna-tipped claws upon his symbols of kingship. Lot as High King would have been nearly as bad as Artorex, for Uther loathed Morgause nearly as much as her sister.

No, Uther would have hidden the sword and the crown when Artorex became the Warrior of the West. Seen from Uther's point of view, what other choice did he have? His body was betraying him, Botha was dead and Artorex was beloved by the people.

No, the sword and the crown were long gone by the time Uther reconciled himself to the certainty of approaching death.

Myrddion knelt and tried to imagine the filth that had poured into the ears of the bishop. He tried to understand how Branicus must have felt when he had taken these ritual objects that were so soiled and degraded with lust, murder and ambition.

Accompanied by two warriors and four terrified menservants, Gruffydd knocked quietly on the door before entering. But, engrossed, Myrddion didn't hear him.

The grisly remains of the once virginal girl were removed from the window, while Myrddion continued his reflection. And, when the crow was gingerly pulled up as a mere tangle of black feathers and stick-like chewed bones, Myrddion's concentration was so deep that he didn't even acknowledge the presence of servants in the room.

He was far away inside the mind of the long-dead bishop.

As the servants tiptoed around him, glancing fearfully at his still, white face and tightly closed eyes, Myrddion was thinking. When he suddenly opened his eyes, they blazed with a new understanding. One of the servants squealed like a frightened pig when Myrddion suddenly leapt to his feet, ignoring his cramped leg muscles.

He picked up the prayer stool and thrust it into the arms of the servant.

'Take this confessional stool to the new bishop at his church. Tell him that it is a gift from me. You will further inform him that his predecessor, a good and holy man, used this prayer stool while he interceded with God for the soul of his master, Uther Pendragon. And you will also tell him that Branicus's stool deserves great honour.'

The servant scuttled away to carry out Myrddion's bidding, while Gruffydd doubted that the poor man would remember even a sentence of Myrddion's words.

The room was ruthlessly dismantled, and lest the servants were tempted to steal Uther's possessions, Myrddion explained that Morgan had cursed all items of value within the apartments. Because he was deemed to be so strange and so magical, his words were believed, causing the servants to flinch every time they touched an object with their bare hands.

One servant brought a jewelled box to Myrddion and placed it gingerly into his hands, after which he carefully cleaned his own hands on his dusty tunic.

The box was fine pearwood, inlaid with shell, with a rough pearl mounted as a knob on the lid.

Myrddion opened the pretty container. Gold chains, a pair of fine golden earrings set with garnets and a number of thumb and finger rings filled the pearwood box to the lid. At first, Myrddion was undecided what to do with Uther's jewels. His first impulse was to order the jewellery destroyed, but he decided to retain the box and have the gems reset, if necessary, as they were probably the property of whoever next became High King. He knew of a skilled Jew in Venta Belgarum who could be entrusted with the task of remaking Uther's trifles.

As he sorted through the chains and rings, Myrddion had a dreadful thought. One heavy neck chain was stamped with the symbol of a boar, obviously the property of Gorlois of Cornwall.

These trifles are trophies of those victims whom Uther betrayed, Myrddion thought to himself. Perhaps they should never see the light of day again.

Leaving the cleaning to those instructed to complete the task, Myrddion and Gruffydd returned to their rooms. Gruffydd was longing for ale, but he accompanied his master

M · K · HUME

with resignation. He noted that Myrddion was excited and his mood seemed decidedly edgy and eager, but when Gruffydd tried to ask what ailed him, Myrddion put his finger to his lips in a signal to remain silent.

'I'm tired, and I'm heartily sick of horrors,' Myrddion replied with his mouth, while his fingers moved in the sign language of the trained spy that said, 'There may be others listening here. We must wait.'

'Of course, my lord. Do we ride tomorrow?'

'It's unlikely, Gruffydd, so it doesn't really matter if I oversleep in the morning. We'll remain here for two more days,' Myrddion's mouth said blandly, while the sign language from his fingers told Gruffydd that they would be leaving at dawn.

'Of course, my lord,' Gruffydd replied with admirable ambiguity. 'I live to serve you.'

Gruffydd spent the evening in the company of a group of Gawayne's warriors as their honoured guest, for his hosts knew that Myrddion was a man of legend from one end of Britain to the other. Although Gruffydd recognized no direct threat in the questions they asked concerning his master, he was aware that Gawayne was the eldest son of Morgause and King Lot, who was an aspirant for the throne of the High King. Gruffydd tried to spill as much as he drank, but his head was pounding and his senses were swimming by the time he eventually took himself off to his pallet.

After drinking copious amounts of water to clear his head, Gruffydd felt a little better. To Gawayne's minions, he had simply been Myrddion's trusted servant, for his status as a spy was a well-kept secret that even Gawayne had not discovered. As he fought to clear his fuzzy thoughts, Gruffydd longed to be outside the stone walls and the narrow streets of Venta Belgarum that were so full of secrets. He needed the wilderness and the clean air of the mountains to clear his lungs of the stench of these Celts who were so ruthless in their pursuit of power and glory.

'The sooner we're out of here the better,' Gruffydd muttered to himself.

He checked his pack and made sure that it was ready for their imminent departure. Some instinct caused him to scatter a few items of soiled clothing around the floor of the room, and then he fell into a light doze.

A few hours before dawn, Gruffydd woke soundlessly, as was his talent, as the door to his chamber was slowly eased open. Two confident warriors looked into the darkened apartment with complete ease.

Gruffydd feigned a loud and drunken snore.

'This one won't waken, and nor will his master,' one of the warriors rasped. 'If there's anything that can be found in this flea trap, then Myrddion Merlinus will do it for us. And, if not, we'll follow them wherever they might go.'

'Keep your voice down, Grimm. Myrddion hasn't stayed alive for so long because he's lucky. Our master underestimates these men, for I think they're on a fishing expedition. It's best that we watch and wait.'

'Well, our friend Gruffydd won't see the light of day before noon,' Grimm sneered.

'Perhaps,' his friend replied, and the two men eased their way out of Gruffydd's tiny cubicle.

So that's the way the wind blows, Gruffydd thought. It's a good thing we'll be gone in a few hours.

Myrddion and Gruffydd were mounted and at the closed gates of Venta Belgarum before the break of dawn. Gruffydd woke the gatekeeper by pounding on his door until the man stirred. He staggered out in his undershirt and opened the smaller door within the gate so that the horses and their riders could pass through.

'You may thank your master Gawayne for his hospitality, but I must return to Venonae on the orders of Artorex, the Dux Bellorum', Myrddion told him.

The sleepy man nodded, but Myrddion still required that the doorkeeper repeat the message.

Then master and man were away.

At first, they took the Roman road that would eventually lead to Venonae, but then Fortuna smiled on Myrddion, as she had a habit of doing, and they came across the tracks of a trading wagon and its guards.

'We'll get off the road now. Ride only on the scree or the rock where our path is hidden, for we travel elsewhere on this day', Myrddion ordered.

'Would it be impudent of this simple servant to ask our destination?'

In Gruffydd's defence, he had a vile headache.

'We are just outside Calleva Atrebatum, and the road that leads north to Venonae. We shall leave the road shortly, and once we are assured we are not being followed we will travel by the most direct route to Sorviodunum.'

Myrddion actually laughed at the face that Gruffydd pulled.

'Ah, Gruffydd, my friend. I owe a good part of the intelligence I receive to your efforts and, even now, I should have you prowling around Venta Icenorum or Camulodunum – if my present need for your service wasn't so urgent. You know the perils we face, so you must forgive me if I expect you to listen to my problems as we ride.'

'My thanks, master', Gruffydd answered, his voice sharp with irony. 'You'll get me killed yet with your plots and plans.'

'Gruffydd, we need the sword of Uther Pendragon. The crown would be a nice addition, but the sword is vital to our cause.'

'Granted, my lord.' Gruffydd shifted uneasily on his horse

blanket. 'Nothing else will unite the west, for even the most lowly slave knows the worth of the sword. But why Sorviodunum?' State secrets of this magnitude made Gruffydd nervous.

'I began to feel the edges of Branicus's mind in that grotesque room. I'm certain now that Uther Pendragon gave the bishop the two symbols as a safeguard against claimants to the throne.' Myrddion paused. 'But the bishop knew that the crown and sword had been tainted with decades of innocent blood, and his hands must have trembled when he touched them. His skin must have crawled when he hid them under his priestly robes as he left Uther's apartments, for they were defiled by Uther's mind and touch.'

Gruffydd nodded his agreement.

'My assessment of the bishop rests on my belief that he was a man of piety and honesty. He would have sent these wicked objects of power and greed to a place where they could be safely hidden – and cleansed.'

'At Sorviodunum?' Gruffydd snorted. 'There's nothing holy for Christians at that place. Quite the opposite, in fact, with the Giant's Dance nearby.'

He had followed his master's reasoning up to this point, but now he was completely bemused.

'Think, Gruffydd. What is the most sacred place in Britain?'

Gruffydd looked blankly at his lord.

'It is the place where the Holy Christus is supposed to have walked. And the place where Josephus of Arimathea is purported to have planted a piece of the crown of thorns used in killing the Holy Christus in Jerusalem.'

In sudden understanding, Gruffydd grinned at his master.

'Glastonbury, my lord. Aye. Glastonbury, the Isle of Apples. A place sacred to the Britons long before the Christian priests came to tempt us away from the old ways and the Druid groves. Glastonbury is doubly sanctified.'

'And Lucius, the Bishop of Glastonbury, is a man who is capable of keeping secrets. He sent Artorex to Ector in the north and even I didn't know the boy's whereabouts until he was twelve years of age.'

Gruffydd thought hard and scratched his red beard. 'But surely other claimants to the throne could follow the same reasoning that you have travelled, master. And the sword and crown are still missing.'

'It's a puzzle, isn't it? But I swear the solution lies at Glastonbury.'

'Well, then I suppose we ride to the holy of holies', Gruffydd replied, his voice laden with melancholy. 'I believe we have nothing better to do.'

'Pray that we are not too late', Myrddion added. 'The wolves are snapping at our heels now, for Gawayne is his mother's son.'

'Aye, but he's not terribly bright − for which we should be grateful', Gruffydd said.

Myrddion only grunted and cast his eyes skyward. Rain was scudding in, and the blue skies of the spring morning were transformed by fattening grey thunderheads. The trees were already greening, and wildflowers grew in secluded hollows. Even the lichen on the fallen oaks seemed bright and fair, regardless of the threatening sky.

I'm certain of the course I must take, Myrddion thought as they turned their horses towards Sorviodunum. But first, I must find where the sword is hidden.

As always, only the crows stirred in the deep woods as they called to each other like portents and mourners.

CHAPTER XX

GLASTONBURY

If Britain laid any claims to ancient sanctity, it was here in the marshes surrounding Glastonbury Tor and the stone church that was erected when Christianity first crossed the narrow seas to civilize the isles of Britain. But, in earlier, far earlier times, the merchant Josephus, a Jew, was rumoured to have traded in this land. When his master, the Undead Jesus, rose from Josephus' own tomb, the merchant came to Glastonbury, bearing the lance that pierced the side of the Christ as well as the simple wooden cup that had been used at the Last Supper.

True or not, Christianity took easy root in the old groves of Glastonbury where a spring poured red water that was the colour of fresh blood, although Myrddion knew that this phenomenon was only caused by the iron content in the water.

In these days, it was a small, often-ignored, religious centre, but Glastonbury still held enormous power for all men of belief, whether they were pagan or Christian. Glastonbury Tor was mounted through a stone keep that some men still called the Virgin's Teat. Others referred to it in whispers and called it by older, far darker names.

Noble titles were immaterial at the Glastonbury monastery and Myrddion knew that the Bishop of Venta Belgarum must have consulted with Lucius, the master of this ancient place, on innumerable occasions. By birth, both clerics were of Latin origin and both were washed up in an alien land. Would the goodly Lucius have refused to shrive the keys to Uther's kingdom?

No!

Myrddion knew that Lucius had arranged for Artorex to be raised in the far-off Villa Poppinidii. He had also ensured that the young man would be educated, in case Mother Church needed the boy's services at some future place and time. The bishop would never put relics at any risk if there were even a frail chance that the true king might eventually need them.

The spring thaw had left the fields, streams and marshes of Glastonbury filled with shimmering stretches of water. From above, Glastonbury was an island, its waters aglitter like the scales of a great fish, and its tor, a finger of rock and earth, pointed towards heaven, even though only an earthen causeway linked its base with the church and its village. Gruffydd swore that he had not seen such soft green beauty in all of Britain, nor breathed air so sweet and clean, except in the tall mountains of his lost youth.

Entry of armed men to the Isle of Apples seemed a sacrilege. Centuries before, the Romans avoided its emerald fields, an oddity in itself, although a road ran through it. As Dux Bellorum, Artorex had ordered that Glastonbury should be free of all trespass. The tribes obeyed, but unwillingly for, like the Giant's Dance, it was a prize worth coveting. Its fertile fields, its ruddy-faced priests and its villagers who were clean and well-fed reflected the success of the religious community. Yet there was something strange and exotic about Glastonbury that stirred the hardest heart, while reminding the most cynical warrior that beauty and truth still existed somewhere in their world.

Christian or pagan, some deity had blessed Glastonbury.

Myrddion and Gruffydd were treated to a warm welcome by

the priesthood and penitents who comprised the church community. Gruffydd never truly learned to tell the difference between the various orders, for the lip service he paid to the faith was like a tunic over his essentially pagan flesh. Still, the men of the Church at Glastonbury seemed untroubled by his obvious ignorance of their ways. The two visitors were fed sweet bread and new milk, good cheese, and crisp apples from last year's store, until they felt as if they had eaten a feast of great splendour.

In a simple withy and sod hut, with undressed stone on the floor, and at a table of rough pine, worn smooth by many hands over years unmeasured, the two men were served water in brown-glazed jugs and beakers, and believed the taste was finer than the best imported Falernian wine. With a certain regret, Myrddion broke this quiet idyll.

'We've come for an audience with Lucius', Myrddion said to one of the priests at their table. 'I met him many years ago, so he will remember my name. I am Myrddion Merlinus and this is my servant, Gruffydd of Venta Silurum. Our quest is urgent, else we would not repay your generosity with brusqueness.'

'As always, Myrddion, your tongue is honey-sweet', a voice said from behind the two visitors. 'Well met, my friend.' A plainly garbed priest in the same rough woollen robe as his fellows placed a water jug on the table and sat with easy grace.

Gruffydd's eyes nearly popped out of his head.

'Your friend seems amazed that I would serve you myself, and wear the same robes as my fellow priests. The world is truly a place of vanity and shame, so I choose to dress and act as did my Lord when he washed the feet of his disciples and broke bread for them. Not all the gold in Britain can change a man's heart, nor ease it when times become hard. Uther came to learn that all his power and wealth meant nothing in the end. I, my friends, am far happier than Uther would ever have been.'

'This fair-spoken man is Lucius, Bishop of Glastonbury, Gruffydd, so please close your mouth,' Myrddion said, not unkindly. 'You look like a gaffed fish.'

'Well met, friend Gruffydd. You must be a good man if you travel with Myrddion, regardless of the god you serve. You will always be welcome at holy Glastonbury.'

'Thank you, my lord,' Gruffydd stammered, feeling like a child not yet free of its mother's care.

'There's no need to stand on ceremony with me, Gruffydd. To you, as to all souls who live here, I am simply Lucius.' The priest smiled and Gruffydd finally dared to examine the aged man who sat so easily at the table.

Lucius was very old; the knuckles of his hands were testaments to the joint pains that come after many years of living. His palms were calloused, as if he still worked manually, but his body was unstooped. The large bones of his body spoke of a broad, strong frame in his youth, although he was not tall of stature.

Lucius's face carried unmistakable authority. He had once had black hair, but his tonsured locks were now capped with a fringe of silver. A hawk-like Roman nose, intelligent black eyes, and a whitened scar that ran across his sun-bronzed forehead like the circlet of a king dominated the bishop's face.

Lucius noticed Gruffydd's careful regard and gently touched the slightly puckered cicatrix.

'This is my personal crown of thorns. I was a soldier once, a boy soldier, and I was tempted by dreams of glory. My name is all I retained after a sword cut took away my wits and my lust for blood. I served in the legions, I believe, as a tribune in Gaul, but when I recovered, I was quite, quite mad.

'Somehow, I found my way to this holy place. God took pity on me, and the priests nursed me, ignored my ravings and loved me. The very air of Glastonbury blew away the haze in my brain and allowed space within my heart for the Holy Child to enter. I am now what the priests have made of me, a servant of God, and each day I make penance for the lives I took and the blood I wantonly shed during my youth.'

Gruffydd knew little of holiness, pagan or Christian, but he recognized the sanctity of Lucius and bowed his shaggy head.

'Bless me, Father, for I am not Christian. I, too, have shed much blood and will shed more before I die. Perhaps the hand of Lucius will help a little when my soul is judged.'

Lucius rose and moved gracefully round the table and placed a forefinger in Gruffydd's beaker of water. He inscribed the sign of the Cross upon Gruffydd's forehead.

'You are a good man, my friend, regardless of what gods you serve. The Lord knows the worth of good men in this terrible world, so he will not hold your bloodletting against you if you fight for a just cause. I read in your eyes that you do not kill wantonly, or with hatred. I see, too, that you save whom you can, so you may accept an old man's intercession and blessing, although God knows you already.'

He smiled once more at Myrddion. 'But your master grows impatient.'

Myrddion was irritable, as he always was when faced by any matter that could not be explained by intellect. If he were honest, he would also have admitted that he was envious of Gruffydd's ability to accept what could not be rationalized.

Lucius touched Myrddion's long black hair gently as he moved back to his rough stool.

'I'd also give you my blessings, my son, if you so desired. The comfort and blessing that I promised to Gruffydd belongs as much to you as it does to him.'

'My thanks, Lucius, but I will leave my soul to its ultimate fate. What concerns me is the here and the now,' Myrddion replied tetchily. 'What have you heard of the barbarian wars?'

'Less than nothing, my friend. Little from the outside world touches Glastonbury, and nor should it. But I deduce from your manner that the war goes badly.'

Myrddion tapped the table with his long, eloquent fingers. 'Badly? Disastrously, would be a better description.' He grimaced. 'Artorex holds the west firmly but he isn't protected on his flanks. It's becoming more important each day that the Dux Bellorum becomes High King of the Britons, or else he cannot defeat Katigern Oakheart, the new leader of the Saxons. Katigern is the grandson of Vortigern, of infamous memory.'

'I remember Vortigern well. He was a king who was controlled by lust, and was quite willing to cast away his people for the sake of his yellow-haired Saxon woman. I believe he even tried to have you killed back in those times when the superstitious folk said you were the offspring of a demon.'

'Yes.' Myrddion's reply was curt.

'A grandson of Vortigern would be a formidable enemy, especially if the grandfather had taken the Saxon woman to wife before he was murdered. Yes, I can see why you are so concerned, my son.' Lucius seemed as untroubled as ever.

'I need Uther's sword. And I need the crown of the High King. Only these objects can force the tribes to acknowledge Artorex's right to lead Britain away from barbarism. The leaders know full well that he is Uther's son but too many of them want the trappings of power for themselves. The person who holds the sword and the crown holds the throne.' Myrddion was uncharacteristically tense. Gruffydd eyed his master's usually inscrutable face with alarm

'Don't upset yourself needlessly, friend Myrddion. The sword and the crown are safely held at Glastonbury.'

'Where?' Myrddion fired back at Lucius.

'I cannot tell you,' Lucius replied evenly.

Myrddion swore with particular venom, and many of the priests crossed themselves at his language. Lucius remained utterly calm.

'Only a true claimant to the throne of the High King of the Britons may find the sword and the crown. And that claimant must find the relics in person, for themselves. You, my friend, are not that man.'

Myrddion beat the table with his closed fist. 'If I bring Artorex to Glastonbury, every fortune hunter in Britain will be hot on his heels. The fate of the west will then become a matter of chance.'

'My boy, you're weary and disillusioned by years of plots and counter-plots. Like you, I also believe that Artorex is the one true claimant who, with your help, will find his birthright. Let the others come if they wish, but God alone will choose who will rule throughout these black days. You, Myrddion, must leave the outcome of this quest to a higher power.'

'You give me no choice,' he replied. 'You wouldn't reveal the hiding place to any person, even under torture. Branicus chose wisely when he entrusted the relics to your care.'

Lucius permitted himself a smile. 'Branicus was a far braver man than I could ever be,' he explained. 'I didn't have the task of hearing Uther's confessions, nor did I have to devote my last years to a moral struggle with a man whose mind and soul were diseased. When Branicus entrusted the relics to me, I saw that he was drained of all spirit except for his unshakeable faith in the justice of God.'

Myrddion winced. 'I knelt on Branicus's stool at Venta Belgarum and, even after the passage of some time, I could still feel the fear generated by the High King,' he admitted. 'I also felt the same self-loathing that Branicus experienced. I'm no novice in the service of Uther Pendragon, and I can still smell the blood that lies on my hands in his service.'

'Yours are the feelings of a poor abused servant, my friend. In fact, Uther Pendragon was judged for his sins at the time of his death. Our God will not be mocked, and the only true repentance is one that is heartfelt, or it is worse than nothing. You must judge yourself for your own sins, not those of your dead master.' Then Lucius bent and kissed Myrddion's forehead.

Myrddion blushed to the roots of his hair, but Lucius simply continued as if nothing had happened.

'Uther's sword has been completely reforged. The metal was clean within but blood had corrupted the pommel and its skin. It was beyond saving. Aye, I know it seemed clean and shining, but there were innumerable faults within it. The hilt is waiting to be made anew.'

'Fetch the pearwood box in my bags, Gruffydd,' Myrddion ordered brusquely.

With the assistance of a priest, Gruffydd hurried to where the horses were now stabled. He easily found Myrddion's worn travel bags, and extracted Uther's pearwood box.

On his return, Myrddion passed the box to Lucius.

'Could this gold and these gems be used to form a hilt and guard like no other, one fit for the sword of a High King?'

'Prayer can cleanse anything. I am aware that many of these objects were stolen.'

Lucius lifted the heavy earrings with their garnet stones and stared into their sanguine depths.

'These baubles hung in Ygerne's ears when she gave birth to Artorex,' the priest acknowledged. 'And she was wearing them when Uther first saw her, when Gorlois still breathed. Yes, prayer will cleanse these trinkets.'

Myrddion stared at the lamp flame as if communing with a friend. At last he looked up.

'We will ride to Venonae tomorrow. And Artorex will return with us, even if Hades should block my path.'

Lucius rose and made an almost invisible sign to the priests.

'You shall remain here this night, my sons. You will be provided with blankets and the fire staves off any wayward chill while you sleep. Be at peace, friend Myrddion, for my heart tells me that one day you will find what you need, and what you truly desire above all other things. I hope you remember my friendship at that time, my son, for I fear I will be long in my grave before that great day comes to you.' He smiled at his guests. 'And now, I wish a good night to all, and may you have dreams of joy and love.'

After Lucius and the priests had gone, both men made themselves comfortable before the dying fire. Gruffydd stared at the woven ceiling, packed with sod for warmth and obscured by a thick cloud of wood smoke, and considered the wondrous old man he had met that night. Rarely do spies sleep well and rarely do they act on impulse. Gruffydd should have been embarrassed that he sought forgiveness from a Christian priest, but his heart felt free and light, while his mind was filled with the faces of those men, women and children whose lives he had saved rather than the broken bodies of others whom he'd been forced to kill. As he slipped into a pleasant dream of his own wife and family, he blessed the old bishop and the master who had forced him to journey to the Isle of Apples.

Myrddion's thoughts were neither so happy nor so content. When faced by the penetrating Roman eyes of Lucius, Myrddion had been forced to confront his weaknesses anew. He had become comfortable with his emotional sterility and was inclined to consider Lucius a benevolent madman when the priest had spoken of Myrddion's future happiness.

But Lucius was touched by goodness, Myrddion knew. He could feel the warmth that radiated from the old man like the heat from new-baked bread. Myrddion almost believed in

Lucius's sanctity and, for the sceptical, cynical Myrddion, that thready belief in natural goodness was a great tribute to the character of the priest.

Nor was Myrddion truly angry at the decisions made by Lucius. He had hoped that the bishop would lay the sword and crown in his eager hands, in recognition that he would not be tempted by the power invested in them. But his intellect told him that Lucius was correct in his understanding of the tribes. Artorex must find the symbols of his kingship himself, and so be beyond reproach as High King of the Britons.

Eventually, when he fell into a deep sleep, he dreamed again of the willow tree, only now it transformed itself into a milk-skinned woman with silver hair and beguiling eyes, a temptress who beckoned him into her leafy arms.

By dawn, Myrddion and Gruffydd had eaten, packed their saddlebags with nourishing Glastonbury bread and were already on the road. They rode as fast as their horses would allow, sleeping in snatches and avoiding all settlements and villages. Frequently, Myrddion blessed the long-dead Romans who had criss-crossed the country with perfectly straight paths and wide thoroughfares that permitted travellers to devour the miles from departure point to destination in the shortest possible time.

On several occasions, the two men were forced to hide in deep woods when detachments of Celtic horsemen passed by.

'Why do we hide, master?' Gruffydd asked. 'We are not at war with the tribes.'

'They will know soon enough what we are about but I wish to give Artorex any advantage I can, even if we must skulk in the shadows when friends pass us by. Anyway, it is often difficult to truly winnow friend from foe. Can you always spot the difference, Gruffydd?'

'Now that you come to speak of it . . '. Gruffydd's voice trailed off.

He asked no more questions and the two men rode on, the days unreeling like thread on a spindle.

An unseasonal storm raged over Venonae when Myrddion and his companion finally returned. The black night sky, which was continually split by lightning, caused the townsfolk and warriors to huddle in their shelters, for they feared the anger of the gods.

However, Myrddion was in good humour as he was ushered into the presence of Artorex.

'Well met, my lord. I go to my study. Perhaps you will agree to join me presently, once we have freshened and donned new clothing?'

Artorex was weary, but he realized from Myrddion's manner that secrets waited to be shared. He consumed a light meal of bread and cheese and then dismissed his guard.

For once, the pyrotechnics in the dark heavens made Myrddion's windowless room far more comfortable than usual. The fierce lightning strikes, so rare in these mountains, seemed to shudder through the bones of the fortress, demonstrating a natural power that no king or army or string of fortresses could match.

As usual, Llanwith pen Bryn and Luka were present in the windowless room, having heard of the return of their friend. Gruffydd served wine to the assembled group, although he, too, was very tired and saddle-sore.

'What news, Myrddion, that you keep me from my bed? First you vanish so thoroughly from Venta Belgarum that poor Gawayne becomes sick with worry. And now you return during a driving storm. At this rate, the people will believe you are the storm bird.'

The kings laughed politely at Artorex's jest, but Myrddion did not bother to join them.

'I hope you are not too exhausted to ride with me to the Isle of Apples at Glastonbury – within the hour.'

'I've no intention of taking to Coal's back in this inclement weather. Contrary to the beliefs of my warriors, I like being warm and dry.'

Artorex was prepared to hold by his statement. He had spent half the day in the saddle, and the other half deploying troops along a critically strained defensive line.

'You must come now, Artorex, for it's imperative that you collect your sword and crown from Lucius. The bishop holds both safe at Glastonbury, but he will not give them to me or to any other man in the kingdom. As Uther's legitimate heir, you are the only person destined to discover them, although all-comers are entitled to carry out their own search if they wish to do so. By now, half the kingdom will be guessing that I have found Uther's relics, so I'm determined that you shall go, even if I have to drag you to Glastonbury.'

Artorex's face flushed with anger.

'In case you haven't noticed, Myrddion, I'm capable of making my own decisions.'

'You are the High King by birthright, Artorex, but if you grow careless and ignore the urgency of our task, you may find yourself bending the knee to King Lot or to some other pretender – immediately before he cuts your throats. Would Lot save the west, or would he skulk in safety behind Hadrian's Wall as Uther did at Venta Belgarum? Think, Artorex! You must travel to Glastonbury, for all our sakes. Even Gawayne is not so thick that he won't arrive at the correct conclusion eventually.'

Artorex longed to refuse the demands that Myrddion was making, for the thought of possessing Uther's crown and sword made him ill with loathing. The blood of Gallia stained these relics of power and Artorex knew that he could never forgive his father as long as he drew breath.

But Artorex also understood that he was no longer a simple man of flesh and blood who could consider his own future in isolation. The needs of his followers were far more important than his own desires. Ban's dying demand of him often came stalking into his mind, reminding him that the future of the Celts depended on his facing Katigern Oakheart on an equal footing.

The logical part of Artorex's brain had known for weeks that he must seek out the relics in person. For even as one hand flinched from the symbols of power, the other itched to hold them closely to his breast.

I am my father's son, he thought sadly, while an inner voice whispered in his ear that power was the ultimate means of doing good.

Those words are lies. Gallia would have known that this argument belongs to the Dark Ones, and that power, taken and desired for good reasons, can eventually twist the soul.

But what choice do you have? his other self answered quickly.

None! he replied silently for, above all things, Artorex had trained himself to be a realist. Only Gallia had seen the passion and the poetry within him – but that idyll was long dead.

'Very well. I'm ready to claim these trappings of rule and will accept your demands', Artorex finally agreed aloud. 'But first I intend to organize a captain to take my place during my absence. The Saxons are beginning to stir now that spring has arrived'. He sighed deeply and ran his hands through his tousled hair.

'No. That's not wise, Artorex', Myrddion argued. 'You'll give an advantage to your enemies if you bring anyone outside this circle into your confidence'. Myrddion was uncharacteristically abrupt but Artorex was ready to defy the older man's strength of will. The air within the stuffy room crackled with the first clash of conflicting purposes.

'I'd be prepared to act as your captain during your absence,' Llanwith volunteered. 'I hate to miss the fun, but Luka generally gets the shite work, so it's my turn to remain and face the music. Be assured that I'll do my best to ensure that Venonae remains safe during your absence.'

Both Myrddion and Artorex sighed inwardly, for this offer allowed them to step across a mental chasm that had been opening at their feet.

'That is generous of you,' Luka quipped. 'I'm usually left out – just because I've gained a little weight.'

As Luka was still reed-thin, except for a small paunch around the waist, this sally was an old joke. Myrddion didn't bother to smile.

'We waste time, Artorex, for we should leave within the hour. And we should attempt to make our journey inconspicuous, if that is possible.'

'He's bossy tonight, isn't he?' Artorex asked of no one in particular.

'Gruffydd, my loyal servant, I'm afraid that I must also ask you to join us on this journey,' Myrddion added. 'I know that you've been in the saddle for near to two weeks now, but someone may trip you up if you remain here, and you could inadvertently reveal our destination.'

'Lord ...' Gruffydd's voice trailed off. He was thoroughly offended at the suggestion.

'Or they could put you, or your family, to the torture. Few men can survive physical agony silently. You know that.'

Gruffydd felt ill at the thought of Morgan questioning him. Those eyes! The woman had watched, uncaring, as a young girl had been crucified at Uther's window. What would she care for him if he fell under her power?

'Aye, you're right, my lord.'

Myrddion gazed around the assembled group. 'Then we

depart in one hour. We'd best leave this room separately and meet outside the gates.'

And so Artorex, in company with Myrddion, Gruffydd and Luka, was forced to sneak silently out of his own stronghold.

A sleepy stable boy saw Myrddion and a cloaked man leave late that night, and the next morning, the child noticed that Coal was gone. Inevitably, the whole garrison soon knew that Artorex was wandering with Myrddion while Llanwith had assumed command of the garrison.

Morgan ground her teeth in rage, but there was still hope. She knew that Gawayne was vigilant, and even Artorex couldn't hide forever.

Myrddion drove his already exhausted companions with the urgency of a man who knows that wolves are hot on his trail.

As they were.

Gawayne, master of the High King's city of Venta Belgarum and the eldest son of King Lot, was sent word of Artorex's departure by a horseman who near killed his beast in his frantic haste to deliver his message. Morgan left nothing to chance.

Caught up in a family curse that he had never exactly understood, Gawayne reacted like a well-trained hound. His warriors were soon searching for Artorex and his three attendants.

Unlike Artorex and Myrddion, Gawayne paid scant attention to the health and welfare of the horses used by his warriors. He appreciated the urgency of his mission and spurred his troop on to greater efforts.

Gawayne guessed that Coal would be the weakness in Artorex's efforts to avoid detection. The stallion was a showy animal and left a clear trail of villager attention, so Gawayne simply followed the horse's spoor through villages along a route that eventually pointed directly to the Isle of Apples and Glastonbury.

Artorex's party arrived at the monastery a mere hour ahead of Gawayne.

'Hail, Artorex!' Lucius greeted the Dux Bellorum and his companions with his usual courtesy and calm countenance. 'You have grown tall – you resemble your father.'

The Dux Bellorum repressed a shudder of disgust at the comparison. 'Spare me such a fate, good Lucius. Were it not for the peril to the west, I would never seek any object that came from Uther's tainted legacy.'

Lucius pressed the young man on the shoulder with his gnarled old hands.

'Your face and your hair are his, Artorex, as is your stature. But your soul is your own, to mould as you choose. The sword you seek is only a weapon and you have the power to shape it, and to use it, as you choose. A crown? What is a crown but precious metal and gems? Who remembers that the evil Vortigern wore it in days gone by, and that he welcomed the first Saxons who arrived on our shores as his friends? You may follow your own destiny but you must display the courage and the strength to mould it as your heart dictates.'

'Are you now prepared to help us, Lucius?' Myrddion demanded. 'For other claimants pursue our little band.'

'I will tell Artorex what I will tell all other claimants. God, and God alone, will determine who is to become the High King of the Britons. However, I am pleased to say that you are the first to seek the relics.'

Lucius smiled kindly and proceeded to describe the hiding places of sword and crown in rather bad verse.

> I am sheathed in stone,
> but my blade is ever stout.
> No hand but a rightful king's
> will draw me out.

Air and darkness
are my hidden shroud.
Look for me where the spires
touch the dreaming cloud.

'There. I have now revealed the resting place of the sword to you.' Lucius seemed pleased at his obscure doggerel.

'My thanks, Lucius,' Myrddion responded with thinly veiled sarcasm. 'Could you please repeat the rhyme? Your skills as a priest far surpass those you have just displayed as a poet.'

Lucius shrugged amicably. Smiling, he repeated the rhyme once more, while Myrddion committed it to his formidable memory.

'And the crown?' Luka asked.

Uther's crown is what it seems.
It does not hide its golden gleams.
Seek where Uther made it so,
For its hiding place a king will know.

'Ugh!' Luka growled. 'That rhyme is even worse than the first. It says nothing! How can we find something that has been so successfully hidden for so long when the clues you give are laughable?'

'Do you say that I am a cheat?' Lucius eyed Luka directly, his Roman gaze stern and unamused. The sudden chill in the old man's voice, coupled with his authoritative air, ensured that Luka's eyes were the first to fall.

'No, I don't think that you cheat, my lord,' Luka muttered softly. 'But you could give us just a hint of a chance.'

'And then I would need to reward those warriors who are galloping towards us, even as we speak, with the same clues.' Lucius pointed towards a flicker of light reflecting from shields and body armour as the approaching warriors moved out of the eastern woods into the sunlight.

'We'd best be at it then, Myrddion,' Artorex decided. 'At least Lot's boy is a cloth wit – and we should be grateful that he's the one who leads our pursuers.'

Myrddion found a stray piece of raw chalk in his tunic pocket and scrawled the doggerel on the wall of a rough wooden stable.

All four men stood back and stared fixedly at the words, as if they could be forced to give up their secrets by determination alone.

'The sword is *sheathed in stone*,' Myrddion murmured. 'And the use of the word *spires* suggests that it could be in the chapel.'

He turned to Luka.

'You'd best check the church tower – and do it before Gawayne is close enough to see what you're doing,' he ordered.

'Don't forget that the sword has no hilt or guard,' Gruffydd reminded Myrddion. 'So we're looking for a small piece of metal tang.'

Luka trotted off as Myrddion nodded his thanks to Gruffydd.

'As for the crown, I cannot make head nor tail of the priest's meaning,' Myrddion muttered, pacing nervously as he considered the problem.

'It's hidden where it can't be seen, yet it's in plain view. Lucius hasn't suggested that it might be buried so that rules out a hiding place inside the walls,' Gruffydd offered, thumping the sod walls with his fist.

'And the floors must also be excluded. That'll save us a good deal of search time,' Artorex exclaimed. 'The key line is *where Uther made it so*. What did Uther do to affect the crown? As far as I'm concerned, he made the crown a symbol of murder. He stained it with blood.'

'Of course! The Bleeding Pool of Glastonbury,' Myrddion

muttered. Artorex looked at him, the excitement of the hunt obvious in the eyes of his old friend.

'The Bleeding Pool?' Artorex asked, and both men ran to find it. Gruffydd brought up the rear.

Neither Artorex nor Myrddion knew exactly where they were going, but the ever-practical Gruffydd simply asked one of the priests for directions.

Behind them, Lucius was already bidding a courteous welcome to Gawayne and his exhausted escort.

The Bleeding Pool was a natural underground reservoir, a result of the marshes and limestone formations that surrounded this cup of earth, crossed and recrossed as it was by ditches and streams in the mysterious ways of nature. Once Myrddion, Artorex and Gruffydd had negotiated the set of roughly-cut steps leading down into a series of tunnels, they were plunged into darkness.

In the entrance, Gruffydd discovered a torch that was already soaked in pitch waiting on one wall. He immediately struck fire from his flint box and the cavern erupted into a ruddy sea of light.

The pool was small and still, except where the stalactites hanging from the roof above dripped gore-hued droplets into the waters below. Ripples shivered the surface, disguising the depth.

The Bleeding Pool was well named, for the waters gleamed with a viscous hue that was reminiscent of old, thick blood.

Artorex was essentially a man of action. Once committed to a task, he set his sights firmly on his goal.

Fearlessly, he waded out into the shallows.

Oddly, he initially expected that the water would have the consistency and warmth of blood. But it was icy cold and, when he cupped it in his hands, he found it was clear and clean.

Artorex was fascinated by this optical illusion for, in the light of the flaming torch, he could swear that he was bathing in gore.

'Take your time, Artorex,' Myrddion advised. 'You must start at the edge and feel for the crown with your hands and feet as you go.'

'Shouldn't we help him?' Gruffydd asked his master.

'Artorex must find Uther's relics for himself. That is the task that has been set by Lucius, and we must abide by it. In that way he will never need to speak false to any warrior, villager or noble. You are our witness, for these are great events that transpire around us.'

Gruffydd paled.

Meanwhile, Artorex was patiently sifting his way through the impenetrable waters. The natural amphitheatre was silent, except for the murmur of water from the roof. The cold was beginning to numb his fingers when Artorex suddenly felt an underwater obstruction with one foot.

Despite his natural loathing for the waters in which he now waded, Artorex was excited by the boyish hunt for hidden treasure. He negotiated his way blindly over the smooth stones until his fingers eventually found a hard object wrapped in coarse fabric.

Exultantly, he heaved its unexpected weight to the surface.

As he waded out of the pool, Artorex ripped the sodden, stained homespun wool away from the concealed circlet. For a moment, the massive band of red gold seemed a part of the Bleeding Pool itself, especially as huge garnets were set at regular intervals around the rim of the embossed gold. The stones winked at him like the little red eyes of a dragonlet.

'Guard this trinket for me, Myrddion, for our task is but half finished.'

Myrddion slung the heavy crown over one arm at the elbow, covered it with his cloak and gave his other hand to Artorex, helping him out of the chill waters.

'I can hear raised voices,' Myrddion announced cheerfully. 'One of them belongs to Luka, our argumentative friend. Perhaps we should rescue him from Gawayne's temper, which is none too stable at best.'

Neither Artorex, nor even the sharp-eared Gruffydd had heard a sound.

By the time they climbed back to the surface and reached the light, Luka was visible in the distance as he attempted to bar Gawayne's entrance into the small stone chapel. The younger man was already flushed with anger and, remembering Gawayne's maddened rages, Artorex roared out to Luka to allow the troop from Venta Belgarum to pass unhindered.

Luka smiled at Gawayne with deceptive sweetness, stepped aside and whispered softly, 'Later, my young princeling. We – you and I – will speak again when this business is finished.'

Then he joined his friends.

'What of the church spire?' Artorex asked quickly.

'If Lucius hid it in the church, it's too well concealed for my eyes. Besides, there's no spire, and I've got an ache in my neck from staring at all the ceilings. Most are made of wood, anyway.' Luka was a little out of breath. 'I think I'm growing old.'

'Then hold what breath you can, and don't babble,' Myrddion replied drily. 'The only other stone building is on the tor.'

'Oh, shite! And it's uphill all the way.'

Artorex and his companions had a head start on Gawayne, who was somewhere within the chapel, but the tor was distant and its keep was at the very top of the conical hill.

'Do we ride?' Gruffydd asked pragmatically. 'Or do we run?'

'We run,' Artorex ordered. 'By the time we return for the horses, Gawayne will have discovered that the sword must be on the tor. He may beat us to the keep anyway.'

Artorex's assessment was correct. The four men had only climbed half the distance to the summit of the tor when a commotion broke out behind them. Gruffydd snatched a quick glance to their rear as his companions toiled onwards. He noted that Gawayne and three of his warriors had jostled their way out of the stone chapel and were now mounting their horses. With the best will in the world, the companions couldn't outrun Gawayne in the race to reach the tower.

Artorex and Myrddion, breathing heavily from their exertions, were struggling up the last few yards of the hill when Gawayne swept past them with a whoop of boyish glee.

It's all a game to him, Myrddion thought as his booted foot struggled to find purchase on the steep grassy slope. 'So we shall be beaten – right at the end.'

Gawayne dismounted from his horse and entered the tower at a run, while his warriors drew their swords and blocked the narrow entrance.

Their orders had been given, and their faces were set and grim.

Breathing heavily, Artorex reached the summit with Myrddion only a few steps behind.

The tower was a simple finger of cyclopean stones, set without mortar, in the very centre of a perfectly conical hill. Looking down the smooth slopes, Myrddion doubted that nature had cast up the regular shape of the embankments.

The maiden, he thought irreverently. We stand on her breast and the tower is her nipple.

A church may have stood below the tor, with all the trappings of Christianity that surrounded it, but something older waited here – and Myrddion embraced its patient silence.

The game was now in the lap of the gods, but Artorex did not intend to appear foolish in front of mere cavalry soldiers. He stood before the entrance, fighting to regain his breath, until his companions finally joined him.

'Step aside!' Artorex ordered the three warriors as he stood before them. 'I am the son of Uther Pendragon, and I am the Dux Bellorum. As your supreme commander, I give you a direct order on pain of death if you don't obey me. Your naked blades insult the sanctity of this holy place.'

'You're too late, Lord Artorex. Our master will have the sword by now,' one burly Celt gloated.

'Early or late, I've ordered you to step aside.' Artorex's voice was calm, untroubled and implacable. His grey eyes were utterly flat.

Luka moved his sword in its sheath with an audible hiss of metal, for he knew that Artorex's features had set into a deadly warning of impending force.

Gawayne's bodyguard shifted nervously.

Then, as if his path was unobstructed, Artorex strode directly towards the low entrance to the keep of the tor.

As one, the warriors stood aside.

'You! Gruffydd! You are my witness. Come!'

Why me? Gruffydd thought to himself, as he followed Artorex into the half-light of the tall stone finger of the keep.

Then he looked upwards.

'Ye gods! Those stairs! I'll never make it up there!'

But Artorex was bounding up the makeshift wooden steps with a boy's enthusiasm. Gruffydd had no choice but to follow his lord, although his lungs were on fire and his calf muscles were already jelly within his skin.

Up and up they rose, higher and higher, and Gruffydd feared to look down; no rail would protect him from a plunge to the stone floor that lay in wait, far below, if he should fall.

Artorex was looking determinedly upwards as he ran, for he could hear cries of frustration and the muffled sound of Gawayne's crude and imaginative swearing at the top of the stairway.

Artorex and Gruffydd emerged through a large, open hole in the flooring at the top of the steps. They found themselves in a circular space with a high, crudely constructed roof.

Gawayne looked over his shoulder at the two men as they clambered into the turret. His face was a study of mingled rage and chagrin.

Then, before they could join him inside the tower, he made one more leap towards the curving wall.

A tongue of metal protruded from the stone blocks of the tower.

It was the tang of a hilt-less sword.

Gawayne was a strong and well-built young man. Ygerne, Uther's queen, was his grandmother and the fair Morgause was his mother. His father, King Lot, now run to fat with advancing age, had been a large and burly man, but neither Gawayne nor his father stood near to six feet tall.

The tang was at least one foot beyond the reach of Gawayne.

Gruffydd understood why Gawayne was so red-faced and angry. To leap as this young man had done, while stretching his fingers to their maximum reach, risked plunging to certain death through the hole in the wooden floor.

But Gawayne could not reach the tang that was so tantalizingly close. He could almost touch the blade, but it remained just beyond his reach. And there was no object in the tower that could help him to overcome his lack of height.

During his short life, Gawayne had heard tales of the murder of Gorlois. His Aunt Morgan had told him, again and again, of the unfairness of all that had befallen the family and that the crown truly belonged to the descendants of the Boar of Cornwall. The young man firmly believed that the finding of Uther's sword was a blood debt that was owed to his kin.

But it remained a few inches beyond the reach of his questing fingers.

'Step aside!' Artorex ordered imperiously.

Gruffydd considered, irrelevantly, how Artorex could so easily have earned Gawayne's life-long enmity had he added the words 'little man' to his command.

He recalled the welcome given to Artorex by Lucius.

'You have grown tall,' the priest had stated unsmilingly.

Gruffydd found himself grinning at the old man's ingenuity. This priest was Roman through and through – their race had not ruled the world because they were fools.

Unlike Gawayne, Artorex had not been raised as the son of a tribal king. Nor did Artorex accept the strictures of the Roman way of life. For him, there was no glory in raising his right hand, almost hesitantly, and gripping the tang with his strong, work-hardened fingers.

'This burden is not for you, Gawayne,' he told the angry youth gently. 'Truly, I wish it were yours to take – but it is not.'

And then Artorex pulled down with all his strength, feeling the unmortared steel slide out of its stone sheath with the long hiss of an angry dragonlet.

He held its chill length in both hands before him and gazed at his fate with regretful eyes.

Gruffydd knelt on the dusty floor.

'My king!' he stated reverently.

His thoughts were of the clever Lucius, a priest who had gambled the destiny of a kingdom on a man he had not seen since he was a three-day-old babe. The bishop had wagered everything on the chance that the son would inherit the stature of his father.

Gawayne also knelt on the accumulated dirt of the floor in full obeisance to Artorex.

'My liege,' he whispered.

But the young man's face was twisted with the bitter taste of his failure.

Gripping the blade in his left hand, Artorex extended his right hand to assist Gawayne to his feet.

'You will never have to kneel to me, cousin. I understand only too well how deep is your family's hatred of my father and, perhaps, of me. I would feel the same rage were I in your shoes, for Uther used every means imaginable to take what he desired, without remorse or conscience. If you believe nothing else of me, you must accept that I hated him just as deeply as you or yours ever could.'

Gawayne looked suspiciously into Artorex's unshuttered eyes as he stumbled to his feet. The grey irises were no longer flat and unreadable. Some trace of Morgan's gifts told Gawayne that this man really did not want the kingship, but that he was harried by the demons of his blood towards a fate that would be neither fair nor kind.

Gawayne shuddered. 'I believe you, my king, and I pledge to you that I will be your man from this moment on. I am yours to command.'

'Then my first command to you is to remember, in those times when you are happiest with your friends and your family, that this burden will probably make me the loneliest man in the west.' Artorex looked at the sword once more as if the weapon was a living, venomous serpent. 'Come, nephew, we have work to commence.'

Turning to Myrddion's spy, Artorex smiled conspiratorially.

'And you also, Gruffydd. For you are now my sword bearer.'

With a casual disregard for the destiny he held in his hands, Artorex tossed the sword of Britain to Gruffydd, who barely caught it before it could tumble down the stairwell.

CHAPTER XXI

THE KEYS TO THE KINGDOM

By the time Artorex's band of men left Glastonbury, the Dux Bellorum was thoroughly irked by the unsought honours he was forced to accept. Myrddion, Luka and Lucius treated him as they always had, but every priest, monk and villager, not to mention Gawayne's bodyguard, bowed so low whenever he approached them that he rarely had the opportunity to gaze upon their faces. Even before he left that hallowed place, Artorex was feeling solitary and uncomfortable.

He refused to partake in a celebratory banquet, preferring a simple meal with his fellows of bread, cheese, fine ham and fruit. Nor did he want the potent cider made by the monks in this sacred enclave. Rather, he preferred the exceptional water of Glastonbury, filtered in the earth through the ages until its purity was like balm to his angry, tortured soul. He had a dislike for the crown, and Lucius's assurances that it had been cleansed by the waters of the pool didn't appease him.

As usual, it was Myrddion who found a way to resolve Artorex's stubbornness.

'Do you have among your holy men a worker who is skilled in shaping precious metals?' he asked Lucius.

'Aye. The man who reforged the sword is a Jew who is knowledgeable in those arts.'

The men at Lucius's table were shocked for, while the whole world knew that the Jews were the acknowledged masters of working with precious metals and gems, a Hebrew at a monastery such as Glastonbury was tantamount to a Roman king of the Saxons.

'His Jewish name was Simeon, but we at Glastonbury have always called him Simon. He is a Christian now and has come to this land expressly to follow in the footsteps of his Lord.'

He looked around the assembled group.

'I see by your faces that you consider his race accursed, but the Lord Jesus was also a Jew, so how could I bar Simon from the monastic life he craved? Simon is skilled in the use of herbs and simples, and he can cure many ailments that would normally cause death. Most importantly for your purposes, he is also highly skilled in working with precious metals. For many years, Simon would not use his God-given skills, but preferred to toil in the fields and the orchards, as if only hard, physical labour would expiate some sin in his past. He is now our blacksmith, but his fingers have not lost their cunning. I expect that Simon would make the hilt of Artorex's sword, if I ask it of him.'

All the Celts looked doubtful. The Jews were a hated race, although the reason for this loathing was lost in the mists of time. Simply put, Jews were not to be trusted, because the whole world knew they devoured infant children.

Perhaps we always need someone to bear the brunt of our own shame and anger, Gruffydd thought with sudden insight.

'Then you shall use the earrings, the gold and the jewels in the box I gave you, for they were part of Uther's most treasured possessions,' Myrddion suggested.

Artorex slammed his simple wooden cup down on the table.

'I'll not take anything else from that bastard,' he shouted.

'But, Artorex, my friend, they weren't his gems,' Myrddion replied. 'As far as I can ascertain, the pearwood box contains trophies taken from many of his victims. His servants told me how they saw Uther toying with these gems from time to time, and how he gloated over the souls of those who had stood against him and were, ultimately, defeated. The baubles weren't his to keep.'

'Then it is possible that these jewels are now the property of Morgan.' Artorex was adamant, but Myrddion knew he had the better hand in this particular game.

'The earrings belonged to your mother, part of her dowry, according to Lucius's recollections. She wore them on the night Uther first saw her face.'

'She wore them again on the night you were born, my king,' Lucius added. 'How she suffered! Trickery had brought Uther to her bed, she'd seen her husband's head set on a spear point, she'd been raped by her husband's murderer and now she was bearing her ill-conceived child. She could so easily have rejected you. Many women would have wanted to have you killed and seen to it long before they came to childbed. But Ygerne carried you to full term, and she placed those gems in her ears when she felt the first birth pangs in the palace of Venta Belgarum.'

Artorex almost gagged, so deep was his disgust for Uther Pendragon.

Lucius gazed deeply into the eyes of the new king. 'Ygerne chose to cleanse those defiled baubles with new life. She knew what Uther would do to her in the years ahead, the daily violent rapes while he was still potent, and the many indignities that she would endure to keep her daughters alive. Perhaps she hoped that you would avenge Gorlois, or nullify the death and suffering that had laid waste to her life. I could not know her mind, but her purpose was pure, for Ygerne is a frail and beautiful soul.'

Artorex was spellbound, for this was the first time he had been made fully aware of the suffering experienced by his mother.

'I was present at the birthing, Artorex. I had been summoned to assist the king's confessor, Branicus, who feared Uther above all living creatures. When you were born, poor Ygerne cried out for her baby and she managed to suckle you but once, before Uther ordered the bishop to take you away and expose you to the wind and the snow. I can assure you that she wept most bitterly for her dead son.'

Lucius paused.

'But Branicus was a true man of God. He couldn't cast a healthy child upon the snowdrifts and live to sing the Mass or shrive other souls in the confessional. However much he desired to convince Uther Pendragon to embrace Mother Church, he could not, at the last, damn his own soul for what he earnestly believed would bring the greater good. He entrusted your life to me – and the rest you know.'

'Uther's hand took the earrings from Ygerne's ears, for all that she begged to be allowed to keep them,' Myrddion continued the tale gravely. 'He would not even allow her the solace of memories. The midwife told me so. She had no reason to lie – for Uther had her murdered within the week to still her tongue. I think his madness began when he stole the innocence of Ygerne over her husband's mutilated corpse. I often saw him toy with those jewels and gloat over them, although I did not understand the evidence of my eyes at that time. He owned far more precious gems, including many baubles that vanished after his death, but not even Morgan dared to gaze upon the objects of Uther's madness.'

'It is a veritable Pandora's Box,' Lucius added to the blank incomprehension of most of the men in the room.

'As you say, Lucius, it's a Pandora's Box,' Myrddion said sadly. 'But instead of unleashing the ills of humanity on the world, these objects are symbols of defiance, love and the refusal to accept tyranny, even if denial means death.'

Myrddion examined his hands as if he saw, and smelt, traces of blood still upon them.

'Do not reproach yourself, Myrddion,' Lucius advised softly, with infinite compassion. 'You kept the dragon in check as well as any mortal could, and you diverted his worst excesses into useful pathways. Your cunning held the west safe against the Saxons and, most of all, you and your friends wrought Artorex into the man he has become. I am human enough, and sufficiently Roman, to hope that Uther rages at you still from Hades.'

'Very well,' Artorex said. 'I accept that my mother's earrings will shrive the evil from the crown.'

'And the sword?' Myrddion asked. 'The chain of power used by Gorlois, the rings, and the bands and torcs of all those nameless men who lost their lives in defiance of Uther should make a hilt for your sword that can cleanse and rejuvenate the weapon. In that way, your hands will always touch clean metal.'

'Yes, the sword as well,' Artorex replied. 'You win, old man.' His temper was still uncertain, but he was now a little mollified. 'If I'm to accept your advice, I'll require that the hilt should mirror the pattern of my dragon knife.' He pulled the weapon from its scabbard and placing it reverently on the scarred wooden table.

'Forgive me, Father Lucius, for baring this blade at holy Glastonbury,' he added apologetically.

The bishop smiled his permission and turned to one of his monks.

'Boniface, my friend, please ask Brother Simon to join us. And I would be grateful if you could bring me the pearwood box that lies on the chest in my cell. Thank you, my friend, for sparing the bones of an old man.'

Artorex marvelled at the grace of the orders given by Lucius, and how tasks were turned into pleasures under his smiling gaze.

This man would have been a better king than Uther. And he would be better suited to the task than I can be, by far, Artorex thought regretfully.

'My friend, I serve Mother Church, so earthly power is not for me,' Lucius said as if he had entered the secret compartments of Artorex's mind. 'When I was younger, and learned the cost of our losses on the battlefield, I was driven insane. I came to learn that it is only men with great strength and moral courage who can ensure that power does not corrupt. Your path is more difficult than mine, for I am not forced to test my soul with temptation, day after day, for the remainder of my life.'

Perhaps God has given this priest the ability to read my thoughts, Artorex pondered. I would not be surprised, for his sanctity is certainly beyond doubt.

Gruffydd had followed the conversation concerning Uther's relics with interest. He was surprised at the amount of wickedness that the great ones indulged in, and was even more amazed that the common folk never realized that their lords and masters manipulated them. When the crowds cried their acclaim for Uther, they had known that he had been responsible for the murder of the Boar of Cornwall, but they also wanted to believe the romantic nonsense told by the storytellers of Uther's great passion and how Lord Myrddion had used magic to deliver Ygerne into the High King's bed.

The people will believe anything, Gruffydd marvelled to himself. Still, I'm interested to see what a Jew looks like.

Gruffydd was soon to discover, with some disappointment, that there were only minute differences between Jews and Romans.

He looks quite ordinary, really, Gruffydd decided as Simon entered, his hands tucked into his homespun sleeves.

Simeon, or Simon, as Lucius called him, was a blue-jawed, black-eyed man whose face was ruddy from working at the forge.

His hands, while heavily calloused, were very delicate. Mostly clean-shaven, unlike many of his race, Simon's mouth was full and red, and his nose was long and narrow across the nostrils.

Lucius smiled a greeting towards the Jew.

'Our guest, Lord Artorex, is soon to become the High King of the Britons. He has paid us the honour of requesting a boon from you,' Lucius said.

'I'll do anything you ask, Father,' was the quiet, unemotional reply.

'The sword that you reforged for me needs a hilt that must be made as a match to this dagger, so they become paired pieces, if you like. Can you complete this task, Brother Simon?'

Brother Simon picked up the dragon dagger with an odd reverence. 'This is beautiful work, for all that it is wrought in iron. The man who forged this hilt was a master craftsman.' Simon's hands ran over the curiously shaped hilt and hand guard with obvious pleasure.

'The maker was a village smith from the fringes of Aquae Sulis,' Artorex responded with the natural pride of ownership. 'He felt he owed me a debt, and repaid me with this dagger.'

'Yes, I can make such a hilt. But the sword of a king needs embellishment, as does this beautiful knife,' Simon stated. 'I can feel the man in this weapon, for he is an artist, one who understands the fire in the metal.'

'We have "the embellishment", as you call it,' Myrddion responded.

At that point, Brother Boniface returned with the pearwood box balanced delicately on his open hands. At the direction of Lucius, Brother Simon opened the box and inhaled a small breath of appreciation when he saw the contents. Item after item was placed on the rough planks of the table, as the Jew gave a running commentary on the quality of each ornament.

'These earrings are very fine – and weren't made in these

isles. One of my race made these delicate links, and cut these garnets so that their dark beauty is softened. These rings are only large gems in raw gold,' he continued. 'They are powerful, but were wrought without any real skill. They were made in the far north. As for this chain and those torcs, they are old, very old, the little honey people shaped them once, but they have been remade, and the perfection of the metal cries out for a noble purpose. Yes, they could make a wondrous hilt for the sword – and also embellish the hilt of the dagger.'

The men around the table nodded in satisfaction.

'But lords, gold is soft, especially gold as pure as the metal in these objects. Why, this gold is almost red! A hilt and a guard of such a metal would be beautiful, but it would also be dangerous to the bearer of the sword. The first strong blow would carve through the hilt like butter.' He gazed into the eyes of Artorex. 'Lord, do you intend to actually use this sword in battle?'

'Aye. The sword is a symbol of leadership, so I'll need it in battle as a rallying point for my warriors,' Artorex replied.

'Then permit me to suggest that I make the hilt and guard out of tempered iron that is forged to a metal that is as strong as I can devise. I'd then coat the entire surface with this buttery gold. The small detail of the designs can be of pure metal, but I'd feel I betrayed you if I made a hilt that could cause your death. I've enough stones here, and enough gold, to cover your dagger many times over, so the pair should become a perfect match.' He smiled at Artorex. 'I'd prefer not to compromise so fair a weapon with any work that is unworthy of the man who originally forged this dagger.'

'Very wise words, Brother Simon,' Artorex said gratefully. 'If Lucius agrees, I'd ask you to take my dragon blade and the sword of Uther and make them into matching weapons. Make them fair and glowing, but make them strong. Shape them to inspire awe and fear in the enemy, for I'll have need of every advantage I can find.'

Brother Simon bowed deeply to Artorex and would have taken up both blades and the contents of the box had Artorex not plucked the red-gold crown out of his travel bag and dumped it unceremoniously on the top of the table.

'There's one further matter I'd like to discuss with you, Brother Simon. I don't like the crown used by Uther Pendragon. It represents many vices that I abhor, including all those faults in Uther's character that I dislike. The crown must also be reforged in a suitable design of your choosing so that it will be fair to the eye. And, once the task is complete, I'd ask Father Lucius to give his blessing to this new symbol of the British realm. Can you carry out this task in addition to the sword and the dagger?'

'Yes, my lord, I can do it. And it would be my pleasure to do so,' Simon replied with a smile of gratitude for the honour he had been offered.

'The earrings in the box belonged to my mother, so I'd be pleased if they were to become a part of the new crown. Can this be done?'

'Yes, my lord. It can be done.'

'Finally, it is my wish that the pearl on the pearwood box should be made into a ring for the thumb of my right hand.'

'That's not a difficult task, my lord. It will be done.' Brother Simon glanced up under his brows at Artorex and then down at the crown. 'Lord, you see these challenges through clear eyes. This crown is ugly, for it is heavy, cumbersome and ostentatious in its present form. I will make these objects, which will be fit for you alone, so that many men will say, I saw Artorex the Fair, and I was dazzled by the crown in his hair!' Then Simon blushed, for he wasn't accustomed to displays of personal vanity.

'They must be collected one week before the summer solstice when the coronations will take place at Venta Belgarum,' Myrddion said. 'Soon, all the world will know that Artorex is to be crowned there as the moon waxes and wanes.

Fail us not, Brother Simon, for you have but three months to complete your task.' Myrddion's face was grave, but Gruffydd could tell that his master was greatly amused at the handling of these delicate matters.

Luka broke through Myrddion's self-satisfied contemplation with a question that Gruffydd had also been longing to ask.

'Why the pearl ring, Artorex? There are stones in the box that are more valuable by far.'

Artorex grinned, and Luka could not tell if pleasure or pain was the source of his smile.

'I will use it as a reminder, friend Luka. I will only need to run my fingers over the pearl, as Uther often did, to remember what manner of man he was.'

Luka was struck dumb by Artorex's reply.

When Brother Simon had left the simple room, clutching the box, crown and weapons awkwardly to his chest, Lucius stared intently at Artorex and then slipped a plain gold ring, much worn, off his thumb.

'I ask that you accept the gift of this ring that has always been part of my secular house, Artorex. I am the only member of my family who is still alive and it would cease to be of value to any person, other than yourself, once I've left this mortal world. If you look at it carefully, the cypher can still be seen upon it, where countless paterfamilia of my house pressed it into heated wax. See? The imprint is in the form of a clenched fist.'

'I can't take your ring, Father Lucius,' Artorex exclaimed with horror.

'I should have cast it away forty years ago, for it chained me to my past when God was my only future. I've no children, and you are the closest to kin I have had since you were carried out into the snow to die. Then, when I picked you up and you clutched at me with baby fists, I thought of the cypher and its meaning. This ring prompts fond memories for me and, if at some time you look at it and remember your friend, then I will be content. You, my lord, must clench your fist around the west and never let go until death takes you.'

Artorex couldn't refuse. He slipped the ring on to his left thumb where it fitted snugly.

'While we are all in such a giving mood, I needs must give you a trifle as well, my young friend,' Luka said. He laughed. 'Are you fast, boy?'

'Fast enough,' Artorex replied in memory of the old game played with Llanwith.

'Then catch this!'

Luka's electrum torc, with the serpent symbol embossed on it, spun across the table towards Artorex's head.

Artorex caught it in a simple reflex action.

'Please,' Artorex begged. 'I can't accept this! Your torc is a proud possession of a noble family.'

The torc, of two serpents devouring each other, had always been round Luka's neck, and Artorex could not remember a time when he had not wondered at the delicacy of such a beautiful object.

'I still have my torc of kingship, which I must begin to wear more often.' Luka smiled at his young friend. 'One grows into the habit of wearing it, it's rather like the process of growing old. My son will have another made for him at the appropriate time and it will be the twin of this one. So, before you protest that this bauble rightfully belongs to him, it's worth remembering that I see more of you than I do of him.'

Once again, Artorex was forced to gratefully accept a magnificent gift.

'Now, I suppose you're going to give me something, friend Myrddion. This High King nonsense is altogether more complex than I can stand.'

'Never fear, Artorex.' Myrddion smiled back at him. 'I give

you nothing to wear, or to protect you. But I will give you a gift that will endure long after you have gone from this world.'

He paused, having gained the attention of all present.

'As High King, you must select the standard by which your subjects will know you, and by which you will be remembered, for good or for ill. When Uther became High King, he adopted the dragon symbol that was part of his own name, but I would not have you borrow anything else of his. If you'll grant me a boon, my liege, I wish to suggest your final standard.'

Artorex was acutely embarrassed. He spied the glint of a tear in the eyes of his friend, and Myrddion Merlinus had never been known to weep.

'After the summer solstice, I'll accept any name you care to choose for me. But if you choose something too unwieldy, I'll curse you throughout our lands. You may have your boon, my friend.'

'Thank you, my lord,' Myrddion replied. 'For many reasons, I ask that you be crowned as King Artor, renowned as the Great Bear, who is a noble and kingly beast. It is a shortened version of your own name that your subjects will readily adopt.'

Artorex felt tears prickle in his tear ducts, but he held them back with an effort. He knew that Myrddion had never approved of his brief marriage to the Roman Gallia. He recalled how she had called him Artor in the still of the night when they lay entwined, and how she had taught him to laugh and see goodness even in sorrow and wickedness. While he had never really considered the roots of the name, he knew that Myrddion was paying him a great honour by the comparison with an animal that, while it was known for its ferocity, was also devoted to family and to the protection of home.

Myrddion was giving him a memory of Gallia to hold close to his heart.

'Thank you, friend Myrddion. It is a noble name – and it is one with pure, golden memories for me.'

He smiled at the assembled group of friends.

'At least I shall not have to learn to listen for a name that is new to me. I have answered to the name of Artorex for as long as I can remember, so I am pleased.'

Artorex returned to Venonae where he endured the obeisance of a joyous Llanwith, and received the gift of a strange, gem-encrusted cloak pin from his friend, before resuming his defence of the mountain stronghold.

Word of Artorex's new stature spread inexorably over the land. On his return to Venta Belgarum, Gawayne told of the wonders he had seen, while Myrddion sent couriers to all the great personages in Celtic Britain, the kings of all the tribes of the west and north, all the bishops and chief Druids of the west, requesting their attendance at the coronation of Artorex as High King at Venta Belgarum during the summer solstice. There were many aggrieved and disappointed claimants to the throne, and many minor kings and dignitaries vowed they would not attend, not even if their tongues were drawn out with red-hot pincers. But all the great ones of the west knew that the princelings would take their places in the great church of Venta Belgarum – out of curiosity, if for no other reason.

Far away, in a silent nunnery in Cornwall, word came to Queen Ygerne that her son would be crowned as King Artor, High King of the Britons, and she wept tears of mingled bitterness and joy. For days, she knelt on the stones of her cold cell, until her fellow nuns feared she would die, so deep in prayer was the once beautiful woman.

Finally, bare of foot and in the white robes of a penitent, she made arrangements with the Abbess to walk the many miles to the coronation.

In Venonae, Gruffydd's new status was a wonder to all within Artorex's circle of courtiers. Who was this dishevelled red-headed man, seemingly more Saxon than Celt, who stood behind Artorex's chair at all times, along with the shadowy figures of Targo and Odin?

'Really, I cannot help but feel that Artorex should have chosen one of you to be his sword bearer,' Gruffydd apologized to the bodyguards late one night over mugs of ale.

Targo answered for both men.

'No. You're wrong. The boy is damned clever and he doesn't do anything without a good reason. Either of us would have accepted in a second, but it wouldn't be right and it would raise objections that the boy doesn't need.'

'I don't understand,' Gruffydd replied.

'We aren't Celt,' Targo responded. 'I'm a bastard Roman, and the gods alone know what Odin is. No, Artorex couldn't choose either of us, even if he wanted to. So sit back and enjoy the fun, Gruffydd. For life around Artorex is never dull.'

'Dull?' Odin looked puzzled. 'What is this dull?'

'I'll explain to you later, you dumb ox,' Targo replied in a familiar game that both men obviously enjoyed.

In the kitchens, Gruffydd was greeted with hysterical congratulations. His successes were shared, in part, by every servant in the garrison, for no one in those nether regions of kitchen, bakery and cider press had ever mixed with the great ones, least of all stood behind the High King at table.

Only Gallwyn was unimpressed with Gruffydd's new status.

'Look at you, you heathen,' she snapped. 'The Lord Artorex will be fair embarrassed by a woolly-faced ruffian in a tunic that looks like it's been dragged through a thorn bush.'

'I'm fairly sure it has been dragged through a thorn bush,' Gruffydd answered seriously.

'How will your wife and sons feel any pride in you if you are standing in the church at Venta Belgarum looking like a scarecrow?' she scolded. 'In the absence of your good wife, I will be taking you in hand.' Gallwyn folded her arms over her ample bosom.

Gruffydd's eyes opened wide, like those of a nervous horse. He had been married for several years, and his experience told him that he only understood women to the extent that he was certain that he didn't understand them at all.

'That hair has to be forced into some sort of order. It will be washed and plaited, hear? And if I'm not satisfied with the efforts you make, I'll wash you myself.'

Gallwyn had barely commenced her list of demands.

'And that beard must go.' Your master is clean-shaven so find a sharp knife and scrape off that puny excuse for a beard.'

Gruffydd growled audibly. 'Odin wears a beard.'

'Odin is a savage, and you are a good Celt,' she responded. 'Don't complain, my fine young man. At least you don't have to pluck out your beard in the Roman fashion, as I've heard the Lord Artorex does. But you have to get rid of it for the coronation.'

Gruffydd shuddered at the grotesque and painful thought of plucking out each and every hair on his chin.

'You must ask the advice of Lord Myrddion on these matters, for he will decide what you should wear that befits your station as sword bearer to the High King.'

'You're worse than my old mother, Gallwyn,' Gruffydd complained with a rueful laugh.

'Good. And no doubt she would approve of my carping. You're no longer a scurvy spy whose sole purpose in life is to look and act like a Saxon, for now you serve at the right hand of Lord Artorex, High King of the Britons.'

At that point, a rosy, almost naked young baby cooed and gurgled its way into their attention. Gruffydd noted that, surprisingly, the babe's head was still quite bald, except for an almost invisible fuzz of white-blond hair.

'Nimue!' Gruffydd crooned, seeing the tattoo upon her dimpled flesh.

'Ga, ga, ga!' the child responded, her blue eyes alive with intelligence and merriment.

'She is barely seven months old,' Gruffydd marvelled. 'My boys could not stand until they were nigh on twelve months of age. This one is crawling – and she can almost stand.'

'She is a wonder, is little Nimue,' Gallwyn replied with a loving, proud smile. 'She is so quick to learn that you wouldn't credit it, and I dread the day she speaks her first words.'

'Why?' Gruffydd asked, in the age-old ignorance of men.

'Because we'll have no more peace. I'll wager that she'll talk and talk until all the legs fall off the chairs and the tables. As it is, we had to burn her little fingers on the fire because she thought the flames were very pretty. She'd have toddled straight into the hearth.'

Gruffydd shuddered.

'Now you can see her whenever you have completed your duties for Lord Artorex.' She smiled at her friend, her cheeks flushed and ruddy in the firelight. 'You have been missed during your absence, Gruffydd,' she said simply.

'To be honest, I didn't have time to miss anyone when we were in Glastonbury. You wouldn't credit what I have seen – pools that looked like blood, and swords in stones. At times, my head's been fair addled with what was happening.'

Gallwyn's eyes gleamed with interest and an unholy pleasure.

After her kitchens, and Nimue, gossip was Gallwyn's third great love. She now had the opportunity to score a coup over the house steward, who put on airs because he was the bastard son of a Roman priest.

She crossed herself for having thoughts of such impiety and vanity. But, inwardly, Gallwyn was gloating.

'Sit down, Gruffydd, over here by the hearth where you

can be comfortable.' She held out a chair and ushered her friend into a central position near the kitchen fire. 'Perce, get the sword bearer a cup of our best ale,' she instructed her helper. 'And you girls will have no skin left on your backs if you burn that venison. You can listen – but only if you keep working.'

The kitchen maids grinned irreverently.

Gallwyn had a good heart and never really beat her staff. However, she kept a long birch cane that seemed unable to miss the tender parts of a lazy girl's rump, so the staff continued to baste and stir, scrub and boil, their ears twitching for every word of Gruffydd's story.

Turning her attention back to Gruffydd, Gallwyn nodded at her friend to indicate that he could commence the tale of his travels.

Of course, rumours of Artorex's exploits had spread through Venonae and into the countryside beyond. Even under the threat of a 'Saxon summer', a term now given for Saxon raids, the common people were enthralled by the tale of a boy who had been raised far way in the provinces, where he was protected from the enmity of his own father, and who came to achieve his birthright through the possession of Uther's magical sword. Within the next two months, Gruffydd heard the tale of the sword repeated on many occasions and was amazed at how much the story was embellished with each repetition.

The sword had been, variously, set into an ancient stone by giants, welded into an anvil by magic, or part of the foundations of the tor left by Josephus of Arimathea. In several of the stories, the sword had never even belonged to Uther, as he was judged by the gods to be unworthy of the throne of the High King. And so Uther's deranged fears became the truth at last. Without raising his hand in battle, his son eclipsed all of Uther's hard-won victories.

'People are very strange,' Gruffydd remarked to Myrddion when he went to collect three splendid sets of tunics and leggings, with cloaks, that had been designed by Artorex's mentor for the coronation. Chains of silver set with the golden bear motif had been made for the men to wear, while pins bearing a similar but more convoluted form of the beast were fashioned to hold their cloaks to their shoulders.

'People believe what they wish to believe, including what is convenient for them to understand,' Myrddion explained cynically. 'You should know that I was believed to have been sired by a demon, according to gossip, and that I am a shape-changer who used magic to build the Giant's Carol. Yes, my friend, we live in strange times when people decide that I am a sorcerer simply because I can understand many concepts that others cannot imagine. Unfortunately, people need symbols to chase away their fears.'

'Personally, I'd prefer a strong sword, a stout shield and a good battle plan, my lord. These three gifts seem far more useful to someone like me than erecting large rocks into a magic circle. Besides, the Giant's Carol has been standing out there on the plain for more than a thousand years – and you're not quite that old.'

'The making of a legend is a form of poetry, my friend, an art that is an extension of pure gossip, especially when stories are passed from one mouth into another's ear. If we could live on and on through the ages, I doubt we'd recognize ourselves in the stories that will be woven around us.'

'Well, no one's likely to remember me,' Gruffydd grinned.

'Don't be so sure, friend Gruffydd. You've played your part in the making of this new legend.'

Gruffydd left the presence of Myrddion Merlinus, wondering if the wise tactician was a little mad.

Three weeks before the coronation was to take place, Artorex began to move selected members of his household to Venta Belgarum. The kitchen staff and under-servants were not required, for Venonae could not be abandoned. Only an essential, fortunate few could be spared from the constant danger that emanated from the east.

Nor did Artorex choose to lead a large company of warriors, for those Celtic tribes who had answered the Dux Bellorum's call to arms could not supply so many battle-seasoned men that Artorex could afford to waste them on useless ceremony.

In Artorex's absence, trusted captains would hold the line, under the strong command of Pinhead, or Pelles, as he now chose to be called. The new commander was the last surviving member of Targo's scum who'd been present at the battle at Anderida two years earlier. Since that glorious day, all but Pelles had perished in battles against the barbarian hordes. Such were his survival skills that he'd earned his promotion on innumerable occasions, and Artorex trusted him to defend Venonae to the last man.

Caius had no cause to complain at being overlooked for command for he was to be a special guest at Artorex's coronation. Caius and Ector, along with other notables from Aquae Sulis, had been invited to attend Artorex's final assumption of complete power. Artorex understood Caius perfectly, and he knew that as long as his personal honour was not insulted, Caius would accept the limited measure of public acknowledgement.

Late at night, Artorex relaxed and reverted to being a hesitant young man once again as he shared ale and talked of tactics with Targo. Although his old sword master was too old to be a truly effective bodyguard, he was still the crafty mentor and practical friend he had always been. Artorex needed Targo for his bluntness of speech and his unrivalled honesty rather than the flexibility of his knee joints. Artorex had a niggling fear that old Targo would pine and die should his master send him back to honourable retirement at the Villa Poppinidii.

Odin, for his part, was enormously strong and in excellent health. His weapons skills made him the equal of four men.

'The crown and the sword may be the symbols of power, Targo, but they are just showy outward glitter that is designed to amaze the ordinary people. I wish I knew the path that leads to the hearts of so many of our squabbling tribal chiefs. We must gain an edge to forge unity, but how do we find that edge?'

'Did I ever tell you the solutions to your problems, lad? Nay, you found them for yourself. Think. How did Uther unite the tribes?'

'Through fear. With his sword and an iron fist.'

'And will that tactic work again?' Targo demanded, rather than asked.

'No. Uther was detested by most of the minor kings and his strength was dissipated as he protected his own back from their attacks. I don't have the peaceful kingdom that Uther wrestled from Vortigern and his sons. Unfortunately, that feather won't fly again, not on such turbulent air as now stirs the hearts of the Britons.'

'So how are you different from your father? What is your edge?'

Artorex pondered the problem. 'I am strong – but so was Uther. I have excellent advisers – but so did Uther. Myrddion assisted my father, as he assists me. I am the rightful Celtic claimant but Uther took the throne by force, so my birthright means nothing.'

'Go back, lad. Go back to the very beginning at Villa Poppinidii. Why were you so successful as a steward in those simple days?' Targo grinned encouragingly as Artorex forced his tired mind to search out the correct answers.

The young man stared into his simple wooden cup of ale and the strong, scarred fingers that were wrapped round it.

'I had confidence in my people and I worked at honing my skills. Uther took his skills for granted.'

'True,' Targo encouraged.

'I tried to defend the ordinary men and women who were my charges, and they were grateful. Uther didn't bother to do so.'

'That's also true, my boy.'

'I tried to treat everyone as if they were of equal status, and I attempted to use their talents as best I could,' Artorex stated uncomfortably; he found it difficult to indulge in self-praise.

'And Uther didn't,' Targo finished for him. 'He had no respect for anyone. And he didn't care if their talents were wasted – as Botha discovered.'

Artorex nodded in agreement.

'In the greater scheme of things, Uther's misuse of Botha was a minor matter for the High King. But as a loyal servant, I sympathize with Botha and how he must have felt when Uther ordered him to carry out such an ignoble task. You must always remember the example of Botha, who was faithful to his liege lord until death. Every order that you issue can hurt someone like me, or Gruffydd, a tribe or even the whole nation.'

'You're saying that even the lowliest subject should be considered when I make a decision, even if my actions may hurt them,' Artorex summarized.

'Exactly, lad,' Targo replied seriously. 'That's all leadership is, coupled with making the best of what you have.'

'Leadership can't be so simple. Although, now I come to think about it, you ask a great deal.' Artorex frowned even harder and struggled to imagine himself in the shoes of one such as King Lot. This man was married to Uther's stepdaughter, and he was expected to ally himself with his wife's enemy in a war that had little to do with Lot's kingdom – at least in the short term.

At once, Artorex felt a greater sympathy and respect for Lot, simply by imagining the situation in which the Otadini was placed. Targo's lesson became clear.

'It's also obvious that I must always be the first to lead, and the first to risk death, for I can't send men into battle without facing danger myself. The writings of the great Julius Caesar surely reflect the truth of this lesson.

'And I must understand strategy and the long view. Rulers such as Lot have little to lose at the present time, but the Saxons will eventually turn their avaricious eyes on his kingdom. It will be my task to arouse Lot's fear and imagination.

'And I must make every ally, every friend and every warrior committed to serve the one united cause, and that cause must not simply result in an increase of my power but empower those who are allied with me. They must believe that they act of their own free will and that they are my equal, even if I have manipulated their fears in the process.'

'Yes, my lord,' Targo answered simply. 'But can you do these things? There are few rulers who can bear to count their personal power as nothing.'

'What choice do I have,' Artorex countered, 'if I am to hold to the only edge I possess?'

'Why, none at all, my lord, none at all. But wasn't it ever so? I fought for Rome in battles across the whole world, without being given one single reason for all the death and destruction I participated in. But I am a happier man now that I have a purpose in my life.'

'Targo, my friend, what would I have done without you and your constant lessons?' Artorex whispered softly to his friend and companion.

Targo began to laugh, quietly at first and then louder and

louder. His mottled cheeks and jowls quivered, while his horny, scarred hands slapped his knees and tears leapt from his dark eyes.

Artorex was entirely at a loss.

'I don't understand your laughter, Targo,' he said, a little offended. 'What did I say that was so amusing?'

'My boy, did you really think I knew the answers on those occasions when I asked you to find a solution to a problem? By the gods above, half the time I didn't know the answers myself. But I believed that you had to dissect the problems for yourself so that you could devise a solution. And, most times, you did exactly that.'

'Shite!' Artorex swore. Then he, too, began to laugh. 'Do you mean that I didn't have to jump that awful fence, or fall off Aphrodite on to my arse so many times?'

Targo grinned evilly. 'Of course you did. How else would you have learned? And a little pain never hurt a growing lad.'

'You're an old fraud, Targo. I've jumped fences, I've mounted great ugly horses and I've learned to fight my way through all manner of problems because you made me devise my own solutions – when all the time you only pretended to know the answers.'

That night, when Artorex fell asleep, his body felt light and boyish. Nor was he troubled by terrible dreams and nameless fears of possible shortcomings.

When Targo checked his master's room near dawn, he found the young man smiling in his sleep and the old warrior knew that Artorex was far off in time with his Gallia.

And Targo was content.

CHAPTER XXII

A Saxon Summer

A multitude gathered at Venta Belgarum on what, by ancient reckoning, was the longest day of the year. Rain had fallen overnight and roadways, cobbles and houses seemed newly dipped in the gleam of water from tile, stone, timber and thatch. Even the cottages of the humble people, clustered like three-day-old chicks under the skirts of the city walls, were bright with festoons of branches and wild flowers, while rushes, hay and mown grass soaked up the usual mud of the roadway.

Not one tavern in Venta Belgarum could squeeze in another guest. Every building, including Uther's fortress, had been put to good use, and noble visitors were quartered wherever space was available, their flags and banners stirring in the cool breeze. The streets were alive, as if the hive of the city had been stirred vigorously and all the bees had poured forth, seeking either to work for their new master or to attack the interloper.

Artorex had not slept in the city, preferring to rest under the stars on the one night of freedom left to him before the commencement of his new life. For this last night of liberty, he preferred to lie under stout canvas, as if he was still fighting a campaign with his warriors. Time enough for soft living if he could survive the challenges he knew awaited him on the church stairs at the heart of the city.

With the aid of Gruffydd, Targo and Odin, Artorex dressed with unhurried care. His bodyguards had already donned their finery, plaited their hair and polished their arms until every piece of metal on their bodies gleamed in the sunlight. Against the wishes of his loyal servants, Artorex insisted on wearing the snowy mantle of wolf fur that he had won at Anderida more than two years earlier, although he acknowledged that it would drag in the dirt once he alighted from his horse. King Llanwith's pin held the fur together on his left shoulder and King Luka's torc gleamed at his throat like a living serpent with silver scales. His long fingers were free of ornament except for the ring gifted by Lucius on his left thumb and the pearl ring fashioned by Simon on his right.

Beneath his heavy cloak, Artorex wore a gift from Ector that had been made by Bregan, the smith who had forged his dragon blade. The gift consisted of a curious vest that clasped at the shoulders and down his sides to finish at his thighs. It was constructed of tiny rings of tempered iron that were surprisingly light for a tunic. Ector swore the smith had tried, unsuccessfully, to pierce the metal rings with daggers and swords and, although Artorex's flesh might be bruised in a battle, the tunic would deflect all but the heaviest of blades. The coat was laced at the upper shoulders, leaving Artorex's bronzed skin mostly bare, for speed depended upon freedom of movement. Targo had polished the tunic for hours on the previous night until it shimmered like silver dragon's scales under the snow-white fur.

Under the coat of iron, Artorex wore a snowy-white tunic in the Roman style. His bronzed legs were bare except where his new boots were laced up to his calves and Odin had ensured that the leather was as soft as linen and as burnished as bronze. Targo told disgusting stories of Odin's use of lamb's brains and the other concoctions that made the leather as pliant as any woven fabric. Odin himself had even elected to wear boots in honour of the occasion and plaited his beard into two rather frightening fangs.

Alone, except for his three companions, and with neither sword belt nor scabbard, Artorex rode Coal into the outskirts of Venta Belgarum. With the wolf pelt cloak cast back over his right shoulder, to trail over the shining black flanks of his horse, Artorex was an imposing sight.

His hair, unbound and waving in the breeze, spread out over the pelts like red-gold silk.

At each village, the populace stared at him with their mouths agape for, in their simple imaginings, he seemed like a hero out of legend who had returned to the earth. But then he grinned boyishly at the villagers while bowing deeply to the left and the right. The villagers shook the air with their cheers, while maidens ran to strew flowers from the fields beneath the feet of his horse. Daisies, lavender, buttercups, mint and late-flowering bulbs scented the air as Coal strode proudly over a carpet of colour.

As Artorex entered the fortified walls on the outskirts of the city, he continued to smile, wave and bow his head to the elderly without a hint of Uther's sullen disdain. He gave special smiles to the children and gratefully accepted their offers of flowers. The crowd loved the sight of their heroic warrior king, while many of the populace joined the procession of townsfolk that followed behind him in a multicoloured tail.

Before Artorex reached the fortress, the gates swung inwards. The noise increased as, on cobbles thick with flowers laid out before him by young women and girls, Artorex made his stately, courteous passage through the narrow streets. One old beldam, dressed in her best finery, stopped him and offered him a circlet of daisies, and the young man bent his head low over the horse's mane, allowing her to reach up her old arms and place it over his head. Then, when he kissed her arthritic fingers, the crowd howled its approval.

The closer Artorex came to the stone, cruciform church, the heavier the air became, and fewer bursts of new cheering rose to greet him. But with each step that Coal took, Artorex maintained his smiling demeanour and exhibited an impenetrable courtesy. He even smiled when King Lot stared ostentatiously over his head from the top of the church steps, and Queen Morgause pointedly turned her back on him.

Lot was dressed with eye-popping gorgeousness in a vast woollen skirt of woad blue and dull green stripes and checks of various widths. His huge chest was encased in a richly embroidered, woollen shirt under a breastplate coated with gold. Gargoyle faces with open, leering mouths decorated the breastplate, which was laced over his broad girth with cords of gold and silver. His cloak was bound at the shoulder with an enormous pin that was intricately carved and decorated with cabochon gems. It was as large as a grown man's hand span.

Beside Lot's huge bulk, Queen Morgause seemed tiny, but she could never be negligible. Unlike her husband, her dress subtly implied mourning, for her overskirt was of pale grey gauze over a heavier kirtle of dark, sanguine red. She had covered her hair with a confection of golden wire and red wool, while her whole ensemble was covered by a long black cloak that puddled at her feet.

Her sister outdid her in funereal black, without even the pretence of jewellery as ornamentation. Because she was a maiden, Morgan wore her hair unbound and her long, raven tresses, as straight as a spear shaft, hung down her back to her knees. That hair should have softened Morgan's appearance but, instead, it merely heightened her unnatural glamour.

King Leodegran of the Dobunni tribe wore a toga and cloak edged, quite inappropriately, with imperial purple. His hair was curled around his smooth face and his hands dripped with rings and chains of gold and precious gems. By comparison, his companion, King Mark of the Deceangli, was elegant in a simple robe of grey wool with borders of black and silver. Mark's lack of ornamentation was reflected in his pursed, disapproving lips and his womanish eyes.

En masse, the collection of kings, nobles and their ladies appeared in a tangle of colours and styles that were as contrasting and as conflicting as they were. The King of the Silures wore fur and leather, braced with plates of bronze, while the Dumnonii queen, wife of Gorlois's brother, wore gauzy linen that had come from the looms of Egypt by trade ship. Few would even deign to speak to their nearest neighbour for it was only the old pacts enforced by Uther that had brought them together.

The clerics conspired to stand as far from each other as possible. The Druids wore homespun and carried tall, intricate staffs. Some had decorated their long hair and beards with garlands of mistletoe or ivy while others wore bands of gold or silver across their foreheads. Some Druids appeared to have walked, barefoot, out of the wild places, while others were obviously intellectuals and sophisticates.

Some of the Christian priests wore black that was slashed with red to represent the blood of Christ, while others, like the monks from Glastonbury, were dressed in unadorned homespun tied at the waist with simple rope. As with the rest of that great gathering, no unifying thread of shared thought, belief or empathy joined the clergy into one.

Artorex gazed at his guests who were so symbolic of his divided, complex and vital people, and felt a very natural thrill of inadequacy.

But no hint of his inner turmoil was reflected in his calm face.

Artorex dismounted at the steps of the church and climbed the shallow incline to a curule chair of the Roman style, chosen specifically by Myrddion because it suggested power without the grandiosity of a throne. Artorex then turned to face the assembled kings, princes, priests and bishops, while Myrddion stepped forward to speak of the crowning of the king that would be.

Myrddion wore sable black which emphasized his white streaked hair. He wore no ornamentation, needing no embellishment other than his fine-boned face and his fierce, dark eyes.

The crowd hushed as Myrddion stepped before the assembled guests and townsfolk.

'You know me, great lords of Britain, priests and proud people of Venta Belgarum. I am Myrddion Merlinus, once called the devil's spawn and, later, to my shame, I was Uther's hound. But ever have I fought for the freedom of these lands and, sometimes, the weapons that kept you safe in your warm beds were unworthy of you. Uther Pendragon was one such weapon that I used in defence of the realm. Above all other men, I knew the depravity of his various sins, but for all that Uther was a cruel and unscrupulous man, he won your safety with many years in the saddle, as he fought tirelessly to drive away the barbarians and the Saxon hordes.'

Myrddion paused and his eyes swept the kings, Druids and priests with faint scorn.

'Uther forced us to fight our enemies as a single, undivided people. You, the tribal kings, had squabbled amongst yourselves for generations, allowing the Saxons to decimate our peoples and to destroy our villages and farms. Without Uther, flawed as he undoubtedly was, you would not possess the luxury of your various realms. You would be forced to flee into the mountains to starve in the snow. Uther was, indeed, High King.'

Myrddion allowed his voice to soften, so the honey of his words slid easily into the ears of all those souls who listened, except for the most obdurate who would never trust the servant of Uther Pendragon.

'Here sits Uther's son, Artor, who has come to this place to claim his birthright as High King as successor to his father. He is made in the likeness of Uther, is he not? But Artor is not his father's man. Cast out by his sire, he was raised in the Roman lands to our north. He came to you two years ago and was named the Warrior of the West. Later, Uther gave this young man the title of Dux Bellorum.'

Myrddion paused, and looked directly at his audience. Each person felt, irrationally, that Myrddion was speaking to him or to her alone.

'Why, do you ask? I can tell you. Not one inch of Celtic earth has been taken by the Saxons since Artor took up the sword against them.'

A rumble passed through the great multitude, mainly from the townsfolk and the villagers, but several kings nodded in agreement as well.

Still, Myrddion recognized that many faces were stony with disapproval.

'And yet too many of you turned your backs on your fellow Celts. You sent no men to serve the Dux Bellorum. And you gave no thanks to a man who, like Uther before him, risked his life in a hundred skirmishes so that you could feast and drink daintily, and safely, at your tables, without the need to risk your own skins.'

A growl of dissent came from the assembled nobles, but Myrddion ignored their outrage.

'He now comes before you with the sword of Uther reforged, bearing the crown of the Britons remade. Speak now, those among you who would deny Artor's claim to his throne, or accept his right by birth, and by battle, to rule the Britons as High King.'

King Lot stood and moved to address the multitude. His great girth was impressive in the yards of tartan edged in gilt thread, and his grey beard and hair framed a face that was reddened with passion.

Artorex sat like marble in his white cloak and watched.

'This pretender to the throne is Uther's bastard child at best. How are we to know that he has any right at all to rule the Celts? And why should we place our futures in the hands of a man whom even his father did not trust if his father was, in fact, Uther Pendragon?'

Some sections of the assembled nobles roared out their agreement, so that Gruffydd felt himself redden and tense in response to Lot's carefully staged insults. On the fringe of the assembly, Prince Gawayne cringed in shame, but Artorex continued to smile courteously and sit at his ease, his back ramrod straight.

Myrddion would have answered, but a thin, white-clad nun stepped out of the portals of the church behind him, supported by Lucius of Glastonbury.

Wearily, she ascended two steps, to stand directly in front of Artorex. She turned and kneeled in deep obeisance before her son. Artorex would have lifted her to her feet, but she rose painfully and turned to face King Lot and the huge assembly. Her voice was larger than her thin body suggested, and the crowd leaned towards her to capture every word.

'You know me well, Lot of the north, for you married my daughter, so don't insult me with your slurs and innuendo. Did you believe I wouldn't make the long journey from my convent to see my son assume his rightful place as High King of the Britons? Are you so cowardly that you'd think to blacken my reputation in my absence?'

'I didn't intend . . .' Lot began, but the frail woman raised one pale hand to silence him.

'I am Ygerne, widow of Duke Gorlois, the Boar of the Dumnonii. Uther Pendragon murdered my husband and raped me while I was forced to gaze upon the bloody head of my beloved Gorlois. I, alone, may speak of the birth of Artorex and if he was, indeed, born as the true son of Uther Pendragon.'

Ygerne paused to control her shortening breath.

'I quickened with child and Uther wed me, seeking to take Cornwall without more effort in lives and time. And I agreed, to ensure the safety of my living children. How I loathed the child I carried within my womb. How I wished us both dead. God forgive me for my acceptance of marriage to Uther Pendragon, for I was destined to spend many grim and bitter years as his possession, and I allowed hatred to eat my heart away.'

Tiring, she paused yet again.

'Then, as the child stirred within me, I found my heart had not quite died. When I bore the child, I saw his ruddy hair and long limbs that were so much like those of his father. But he also had the eyes and features of my own dead father, and I found I could hate the child no more. For many years, I believed my son was dead and I mourned for him bitterly. My proudest day came when he returned to Venta Belgarum as a fine and strong young man, a warrior who'd been cleansed of the poison that came with Uther's seed.'

Behind Artorex, Gruffydd watched Ygerne's pale face that was nearly as white as the coif that covered her shaved head. She had been a famed beauty, Gruffydd had been told, and he could see the last of that loveliness with his own eyes. But the singers of songs had never spoken of her courage, which Gruffydd now witnessed as she exposed the deepest feelings of her heart – her disappointments, her tragedies and the long, patient years as she was forced to sit on a cushion at the feet of a monster.

'I am Ygerne, Queen of the Britons – and a humble penitent,' she continued. 'Hear me, my people. The man who will soon become King Artor is the legitimate son of the Pendragon line, and of myself. His is the throne – by right of birth!'

The crowd was utterly still as Lucius led the thin, fading woman away.

As she passed Artorex on her painful journey into the portals of the church, Artorex rose, knelt before her and kissed her tiny, bandaged feet. One hand fluttered lightly over his hair – and then she was gone.

Like the slow thunder of a breaking wave, the crowd murmured at the courtesy and gentleness shown by the Dux Bellorum.

'The question of parentage is settled, unless one among you chooses to doubt the queen's word,' Myrddion dared the angry faction of the crowd. 'Who else will speak against Artor?'

A woman in black stepped out of Lot's retinue and a storm of protest cried out at the effrontery of this hated woman who dared to speak before the assembly.

She threw off her cowl, causing many of the townsfolk to hiss in fear as Morgan pointed one white finger at Artorex.

'Would you order me to be silent, Artor? I, Morgan, am the eldest child of Gorlois of Cornwall. And I'll speak here today, for the murder of my father at the hands of Uther Pendragon gives me that right. My father had no son to stand for him.'

Artorex nodded his head in agreement. He rose to his feet.

'You have earned the right to speak, my sister. But I would remind you, Morgan, that you yourself are not without guilt.'

As the crowd murmured in agreement with Artorex's words, Morgan and Myrddion faced each other. They were so alike in features, but so different at heart.

Then she pointed at Artorex, and addressed the crowd.

'This man took Uther's symbols of kingship by trickery and

he will bring us all to ruin, just as his family dishonoured my father, Gorlois of Cornwall. This man is the poisoned seed of a diseased tree. I have known the face of the dragon, and it is evil! Myrddion's ambition placed Uther's sword into the hands of Artorex, for only dreadful wickedness would dare to place the crown upon the head of a child of Uther. Uther's hound conspired with Uther to trick my mother so this man could be conceived, so how can you trust the word of Myrddion Merlinus? Did Myrddion not conspire with Uther to make every day of my mother's marriage filled with pain, indignity and humiliation. How can you depend upon the decency of Uther's son? Beware, people of the west, for you've been warned!'

Again, the crowd rumbled, but this time with disapproval, not because Morgan was female but because her vitriolic diatribe was obviously motivated by hatred. Morgan had made the error of exaggeration.

Myrddion answered her charges in a ringing voice that could be heard from one end of the great square to the other. He won the immediate attention of the crowd.

'Trickery? Evil? Wickedness? No, woman, it is obvious that spite and hatred distort any truth in your words, so that all men who look upon your face flee as if you were a leper. Your words are emptied by hate and you play with innuendo as if it were a lute. You claim prophecy, but how may we trust your words when you blind your eyes with a strip of skin from the spine of a child, a penance demanded by your masters in return for your evil gifts? Does evil not lie? And your foresight belongs to those who practise the black and arcane ways of wickedness.'

Before the crowd had time to shudder at his words, he continued, but in a voice that was sad and slow.

'Yes, I counselled Uther. I even mixed a sleeping draught so he could insinuate his way into Ygerne's bedchamber. I discovered his plans for Gorlois far too late to warn your father. Yes, I felt shame when Uther showed Ygerne the head of her husband and she discovered that she had opened her body to her husband's murderer. Yes, I shuddered with guilt when I learned that he raped Ygerne while Gorlois's dead eyes watched this cruelty. Yes, I would have given your mother up to Uther for a single night, if that would have kept Uther's feet on the path that protected the people of the west from the menace of the Saxon hordes. But did I trade my soul to the Dark Ones for the honey in my words? No! My sins, my errors of judgement and my dishonour when your mother was raped were my own transgressions, they weren't the work of demons. I was too young to bear the mark of prophecy that we both wear.'

He pointed to the white band in his hair.

'But never, woman, would I wantonly sell my soul for the satisfaction of revenge.'

Morgan seemed to shrivel in her black robes at the loathing in Myrddion's voice. Without giving her an opportunity to respond, Myrddion glanced across at Gruffydd, who was standing directly behind Artorex.

'Stand forth, Gruffydd, sword bearer of the king-to-be and loyal warrior against the Saxons,' Myrddion roared, so that all people in the great open space could hear.

He held his open arms out to the crowd.

'I beg leave that this servant should speak. For he was present at Glastonbury when Artorex successfully recovered both symbols of Uther's power. Only Gruffydd, Prince Gawayne and the pious Bishop Lucius of Glastonbury Monastery can bear witness to the validity of Artorex's claim of being the rightful heir to the throne of High King of the Britons.'

At last! many in the crowd thought. Now we shall hear the truth of this matter from one who was present when the hand of God revealed the location of these magical relics.

'Let him speak! Let him speak! Let him speak!' they cried aloud as one.

Morgan knew the force of her words had been eclipsed, so she backed into the crowd, where even Lot's retinue avoided her shadow.

Gruffydd stepped forward. He was obviously nervous and his first words marked him as an ordinary man of the people.

'I am Gruffydd of Venta Silurum and, for ten years, I have served Master Myrddion Merlinus in the Saxon cities, collecting information of planned attacks by our enemies. My hands are not clean of Saxon blood, for I have often needed to kill those barbarians who crossed my path, especially those who were a danger to our cause and to our people. For the blood I have been forced to shed, I am a sinner in every sense of the word, but the gods themselves chose me as a witness of what occurred at Glastonbury.'

Then Gruffydd told what he had seen, simply and eloquently. He repeated the decree given by Lucius, that only the true High King of the Britons could find the sword of Uther and draw it forth from the stone. Even as Gruffydd spoke, Myrddion felt the mood of the assembled kings begin to waver, for Glastonbury and the relics themselves married both Christianity and the old religion, so none were untouched, regardless of their faith. Yet the real force of the truth of the tale was Gruffydd's simplicity, his sense of awe and the rightness of events as they unfolded. No man doubted that Gruffydd believed he had seen a prophecy fulfilled.

Only one other king stood forth to make a belated attempt to muddy the waters of Artorex's claim to the throne. The crux of King Mark's complaint was that Artorex was tainted with the old Roman ways of the past. Ector bristled at the slur and would have replied himself, but the Magistrate of Aquae Sulis restrained the old man.

The magistrate stepped forward and took Ector's place on the stairs.

'Hear me, people of Venta Belgarum! I am Vestus of the Vestulii, Chief Magistrate of Aquae Sulis for a decade or more. I am of Roman lineage. I am also a proud Briton, and I serve our people to the very best of my ability.'

He paused.

'You speak of the taint of Roman culture, but much of what you are comes from your Roman past and the gifts the Romans brought to our peoples.'

The magistrate had the attention of the entire assembly.

'But on this occasion I come to this assembly of notables not to speak of the glories of ancient Rome but to tell you a tale of a simple steward who braved a terrible evil to save the life of a child.'

This tale was new and the crowd sucked it in greedily.

'At the time of which I speak, Artorex was still a youth. He had barely reached manhood when he became aware of the activities of a vile band of monsters who were involved in the ancient practice of pederasty. This cult, led by the Severinii, a powerful family who lived near Aquae Sulis, had inflicted torture, starvation and death on a number of young male children who had been stolen from the local villages. By defiling these young children, and starving their victims to death, they crossed the boundaries of what any Roman community would accept.

'When he became aware of the vile activities of the Severinii family, Artorex determined to bring the perpetrators of these crimes to justice. With the aid of his foster-brother, Caius, Artorex entered the lair of the Severinii and saved the life of Brego, a child of the local village, from certain rape, torture and death. Brego was ten years of age, and he was the sole surviving captive. The bodies of a number of previous victims were recovered at the same time.

'I ordered the criminals to be crucified and their villa burned to the ground. Artorex could have made a great fortune, for he was given the opportunity to plunder the store of precious objects collected by the Severinii, but he scorned to touch such tainted things. Instead, he permitted the elderly slaves of the Severinii, who were free of guilt, to take what they needed and depart. Do you want magnanimity? Do you want courage? Do you want compassion in your king? All these qualities were present in the attributes of this young man who bravely accomplished this task.'

The magistrate assessed the mood of his audience.

'The bodies of seven murdered children were recovered and burned that night. I watched the face of the young Artorex as he endured this trial. He was sickened – as any decent man would be – but he acted as a witness and returned the ashes of the lost children to their humble parents. Who among you great leaders of the west would have cared so personally about the kin of the murdered children? Who among you would have chosen to bear witness to their pain and offer comfort to the families of those children? Who among you would have *bothered*? But this man did! His Roman upbringing – and the honourable teachings of his Roman foster-parents – did him no harm.'

Vestus, with his Roman toga firmly in place, and with the seal of his office around his neck, pointed proudly to Artorex.

'The remnants of Roman Britain will fight for Artor and for the west. We will go to battle with no other leader. None of the tribal kings have earned the right to request our loyalty.'

The nobles were silent. No more voices were raised in argument, although Myrddion was not fool enough to believe their opposition was finished, merely driven underground by the howls of protest emanating from the warriors and the assembled population.

'I call the Bishop of Venta Belgarum to crown the king-to-be before you,' Myrddion called out loudly. 'And those who choose may take Mass on this most auspicious of days.'

The doors of the stone church opened wide and the Bishop of Venta Belgarum, accompanied by Lucius of Glastonbury, came forth.

The bishop lifted the crown high above his head with both hands, so that the awed and amazed townsfolk saw it for the first time.

Brother Simon had changed the design entirely, so that now the massy band consisted of a dragon motif, with the beast centred at the brow and the wings rising for flight over the head of the wearer. All the garnets and rubies had been placed upon the dragon, with the largest in its eyes and in the centre of its forehead. The smaller gems decorated the scales of the beast so that they seemed to glister in the morning sunshine, as if the animal was alive and about to belch forth fire. The band itself was of simple gold, except where the beast's clawed feet roosted on it.

'Stand forth, Artor of Aquae Sulis, Dux Bellorum, and accept your birthright as High King of the Britons!'

Artorex knelt on the stone steps, so that the bishop could place the exquisite crown over the daisy chain that adorned his brow. The incongruous pairing ought to have been amusing, but when Artorex turned to face the people, the ruddy dragon rose aloft out of a nest of flowers.

'Hail Artor, High King of the Britons! Hail!' the bishop roared.

'Hail Artor, High King of the Britons! Hail!' the crowd responded in turn. Their faces were flushed with excitement that was mingled with awe.

Then Lucius came forward, beckoning Gruffydd to his side.

'Kneel, Artor, High King of the Britons, and accept the weapons that will hold the west in safety.'

Artorex knelt and Gruffydd fastened a great belt of gold-studded leather around the king's hips.

Lucius held the dragon knife aloft, with its hilt and pommel in the form of a twisted dragon, now sheathed in gold.

'This is the dragon knife of King Artor,' he informed the assembled nobility. 'It was forged by Bregan, a smith, as a gift to the High King for saving the life of his son.'

Lucius then turned to face Artorex.

'Sire, please accept this knife in your left hand, and swear that this weapon will not rest while Saxons raid our lands.'

'Thus do I swear,' Artorex replied.

Then Gruffydd slipped the knife into its waiting scabbard.

A priest handed Lucius a long leather-wrapped bundle, which Lucius unbound to expose a huge and glittering blade.

'Sire, this is the sword of King Uther that has been reforged to become the weapon destined to be worn by the High King of the Britons. Do you swear, King Artor, that it will not rest while enemies assail your peoples?'

Lucius held up the sword that bore the identical hilt and pommel as the knife, but which was now cunningly adorned with gems so that the dragon seemed to twist and turn while the light played on it.

Latin script ran down the flat sides of the blade.

' "He who bears this sword is the rightful King of the Britons," ' Lucius translated in a loud, stentorian voice.

'Do you accept and swear that you will use this sword in the rightful pursuit of all that is noble for the welfare of your peoples?'

'I do!' Artorex replied. He turned to face the assembly, fully armed and incandescent in his acceptance of his destiny.

Myrddion stepped forward. 'From the Isle of Apples at Glastonbury monastery, the place of the Blessed, comes this Holy Sword which I name Caliburn, the Dragon of Britain.'

'Go forward then, King Artor, Golden Bear of the Britons,' Lucius stated proudly. 'And let the dragon take flight to protect the lands of the west both near and far!'

The people roared their approval, as Artorex handed the weapon to Gruffydd who then lifted it high in both hands. The rays of the sun were reflected from the metal, so that flame seemed to burn down the edges of the blade.

'And now to Mass, for those among you who choose to enter our Church,' Lucius concluded. 'We shall then feast the coming of King Artor, High King of the Britons.'

The dignitaries in the crowd, both pagan and Christian, surged forward to gain places within the Church. The ordinary citizens, barred from the ceremony by the sheer weight of numbers, clustered on the forecourt in a great sea of colour. A surge of joy, excitement and, beneath the fervour, a tide of relief, set men and women to dancing, casting flowers or cheering with abandonment. The smallest child would remember until its deathbed the feeling of hope that poured into the hearts of the revellers on that golden day. Peace would come again, and security would enrich the land with the crowning of a new king.

Over the babble of the crowd, the bells of Venta Belgarum began to ring. Trumpets added their brazen voices and every musician contributed to the sweet chaos and the cacophony.

Ostentatiously, Morgan turned her back on the ceremony and departed.

Artor noted her passing with a sigh.

The feasting was long, and Artor became very tired by the evening's end. He had utilised his edge until his face felt frozen into an empty smile. He had eaten a little of thrushes in honey, of eels in aspic, of whole roasted deer, boar and steer, as well as the delicacies of the sea and the fruits of the orchards until he felt ill. He had found something praiseworthy with which to flatter every tribal king and had accepted advice from old and young, no matter how banal and impractical those opinions had been. Now, as the gigantic meal drew to a close, Artor knew it was time to put the first part of his plan into action.

As he rose to his feet from a long trestle table where he was surrounded by clerics and his kin, he gazed down the other tables in the room that were crammed with the aristocracy of the Celts. Flushed faces stared back at him, some in admiration while others were closed and secretive.

The noise rose upwards towards the smoky, painted ceiling. The laughter of women, the booming conversation of animated men and the tinkle and bray of musicians competed with each other in the din. Over the sounds of merriment in the King's Hall rose the dull roar of the celebrating citizens outside the hall, like the rolling, muffled sound of the ocean. Artor pressed one palm against the walls of the hall and he felt the very structure of Venta Belgarum close around him like a mantrap.

The mood was joyful and abandoned.

At least Morgan is honest! Artor thought as he forced his tired lips to smile. She refuses to eat at my table because she is my enemy. How many of my guests pretend?

His inner voice answered him fairly.

Many. Perhaps, most. But if you win against the Saxons and gift these sycophants with rich spoils, they'll come to love you for it.

Artor wasn't prepared to voice his doubts, preferring to spread his arms wide so that he seemed to embrace the whole hall, all of Venta Belgarum and the wide lands beyond it.

The nobles within the hall fell into attentive silence as Artor began to speak.

'Friends, regardless of your station, I ask that you accept my thanks for your generosity. I also call on all men of heart who wish to stem the Saxon threat to join with me at Cadbury Tor, the ancient fortress of our people, which shall be my headquarters in the years to come. There, among the ruins, we will rebuild a symbol that shall rally all Britons to join hands as one united people. There, with advice from all the leaders of our peoples, we shall determine the paths we must take to strike the Saxons at their heart.

'And, at our table, all shall be equal and all shall speak their minds and be heard. If we are to be one – Celts, Romans and Britons all – then we must work in concert.

'My kings and my captains, on the seventh day from this evening, we meet at Cadbury Tor.'

The long day was over at last, and Artor attempted to sleep in Uther's quarters – in rooms that had been scrubbed, re-fitted and cleansed by water, fire, salt and air. As he lay in a bed of unparalleled luxury, Artor couldn't sleep. He knew that his warriors stood guard outside his door, but he didn't fear a stealthy attack. Rather, he was crushed by the weight of responsibility that lay on his shoulders and on his heart. He knew that to be alone would be a luxury from this day forward. And to be totally safe would be impossible.

'So our many dreams, my sweet Gallia, have come to this pass. Better I should mingle my dust with yours where the flowers bloom at Villa Poppinidii, than rest on fine linen in this gilded bed, for the weight of my duties may overwhelm me.'

Neither the long dead Gallia, nor the night itself, chose to answer him.

The flowering face of Licia, his unacknowledged daughter, came to him during the night. She was laughing and playing at some childish game with string around her fingers.

'This is why we fight for our survival,' Artorex told the night. 'Surely this girl is the reason why Artor has been born anew.

'For the people, the children and the future,' he swore, as the first light began to filter through Uther's window, 'I will take up this impossible sword so that the land and the Britons can grow and flourish. This, then, shall be my purpose.'

Then Artor left Uther's chamber in Venta Belgarum without regret. He never slept in its illusory luxury again.

Author's Note

After twenty years of researching the Arthurian legends for various university courses, I became something of an expert on most things pertaining to Arthur, historical or otherwise. Again, and again, friends suggested I should use my knowledge and extensive private library to produce a work of fiction based on the legends.

For years, I resisted the impulse, feeling that there was little left for anyone to write. I had no desire to branch into science fiction or fantasy and, still less, to produce a romance. I had watched all the latest films and was amused by the various interpretations, but nothing really sparked my imagination.

Then, in an obscure text, I discovered a rather vague reference to a noted historical incident that occurred during medieval times when a grave was exposed at Glastonbury monastery during a period of civil strife. The accuracy of the reports has to be taken at face value because the grave – and the interred remains – has been irretrievably lost.

This particular reference translated the stone tablet found within the grave as:

> Here lies Arthur, King of the Britons,
> And Guinevere, his second wife.

I was, of course, familiar with the more usual translation of the stone, which merely adds the words 'and Guinevere, his wife', so the use of that evocative word, 'second', caught my imagination and gained my immediate attention.

Apart from that one, rather odd reference, I have found nothing else among all my research material that even hints at a first wife.

Who can know? At the time the grave was found, Arthur had been dead for some six hundred years.

However, I began to wonder once more about the Dux Bellorum of the fifth and sixth centuries.

Learned scholars have shown over the passage of thousands of years that enduring legends often have a kernel of truth at their heart and that great events in the lives of human beings are embroidered during the telling and retelling of heroic deeds. But I always wondered why any part-Celt, part-Roman war chief could avoid being married at a young age, as was then the custom. Historically, children were wedded in arranged marriages before they reached puberty. Logic dictates that such an important young man could have been married many times, especially considering the high mortality rate of girls and women during the Dark Ages.

So, from a simple reference, this novel evolved. From that point on, I was free to create whatever plot lines I wanted, subject to keeping close to the spirit of the legends. The only parts of the story that define Arthur's early years refer to a foster-father, Ector, and his son, whom I named Caius (the Sir Kay of later legends). They were guardians of some vague, unchronicled place called the Old Forest.

Not wanting to travel down the exceptional paths explored by T. H. White in *The Once and Future King*, with its empathic, beautiful mix of medievalism and fantasy, I determined to remain within an area of which I am familiar – the Roman world. Nor did I have any desire to follow the path of Mary Stewart and her magnificent history of the life and deeds of Merlin.

I tried, then, to imagine the lost years after the Roman legions abandoned Britain during the Dark Ages.

I make no apologies for using the original Roman names for cities and towns of the period that are used during this work. Aquae Sulis is, of course, Bath, a city most likely to have retained its Romanized flavour far longer than many other cities in Britain. Venta Belgarum is Winchester, a prominent city in the Arthurian legends, so it seemed appropriate that it should be Uther Pendragon's winter quarters. Other cities are placed on the maps provided.

Lucius of Glastonbury has no part in any version of the legend, but Glastonbury (under many names) was a Christian centre for a very long time, so it follows naturally that there would have been a bishop, regardless of his name. I would like to think that he was my Lucius.

The link to the Fisher King and Joseph of Arimathea gives Glastonbury its pedigree as a holy place, so it seems feasible that a High King who wanted to be rid of a babe, but wished to keep his own hands clean, would use a Church dignitary to solve his problem.

Romans, on the other hand, used fostering frequently as a part of their social system. Yet Ector, by name, appears Celtic in derivation. To use the Roman link, I determined to marry Ector to the last child of a powerful British family of Roman descent. Therefore, Livinia had equal status with Ector in many ways, although like many sensible women, she always deferred to his opinion in public.

And so my story grew. I suppose the real fascination of any legend, for me, is the strange translation from human to hero that the protagonist experiences. No man willingly chooses such a path, so my Artorex is pushed, coaxed, bullied and, finally, brutalized into the role selected for him. The ambiguities in Arthur's supposed character have to be explained somehow. How could he not act with such intelligence and sympathy in so many instances, yet attempt to murder the infant Mordred and tolerate the infidelities of Guinevere that are starkly evident in the later legends? I had to create a pragmatist who was born to be a decent man.

I have a feeling that Uther was such a man, one who was charismatic, intensely human and passionate until power destroyed his finer self. I therefore made my Uther an object lesson for the young Artorex, a warning of what the corruptive influences of hubris and absolute authority can be.

Gallia is totally Roman in nature, so she is joyous, sensual and practical. She is untroubled by some of the brutalities of life and yet is able to find useful conclusions to even dire situations. In fact, Livinia is much the same type of woman, only with greater gravity and dignity and infinitely less laughter. Julanna is more enigmatic and mercurial. Like all frightened women, she can be frightening as well.

Perhaps I had most fun with the characters of Targo, Gallwyn and Frith. Frankly, the wholly northern name, Frith, was too much of a temptation to ignore, and so I was forced to create her whole story around the origins of her name. She is all wise women, all older women with their physical weaknesses, but with all of their magnificence as well. Of course, a slave would be drawn into caring for an unloved foster-child. Of course, she would have enormous pride if she had refused manumission. This woman was alive in my mind before I wrote a single word. And I hated having to kill her off. I hope she touched you!

Targo utters the types of words and ideas that aristocrats don't use, in public at least. The empire, and beyond, was full of such men. They were the flotsam of war, looking desperately for a flag to follow to give meaning to their lives. Perhaps he could have been cruder, but I rationalized that Artorex would not have liked his more pungent statements. I found Targo was good fun and this practical, ordinary man was rendered memorable for me because he was Everyman.

Gallwyn is a commonplace woman who is neither beautiful nor tragic. Nor can she be any kind of threat or power. Too often, women are paragons or monsters within the Arthurian legends, and I prefer to deal with the truth where I can. Besides, Gallwyn is naturally noble when she faces down frightening, powerful people for the sake of love.

Nimue, with her ghastly birth and her part in the later legends as a seducer and a female monster has always worried me. Perhaps I simply hate the idea that women are typecast as wrong-thinking or wicked within the legends, especially in this post-modernist era when such concepts are not socially correct. At any rate, my Nimue is neither wicked nor wilful – she is simply alien in a society that has little time for a strange female, one with brains and beauty. Her grisly birth is feasible, as is her upbringing.

Perce, later to become Sir Percivale, makes his emergence in the kitchens, as some versions of the legends state, and I found his ordinary goodness to be the perfect foil for Caius and his flawed sadism.

Unfortunately, my Caius, or Sir Kay as he becomes known in the later legends, is a very unpleasant person. Every story needs a villain and I feel sufficient sympathy for Morgan to try to understand her violence, rather than damn her out of hand. Therefore, Caius will have to do.

In the French romances and the Grail legends, the romance writers indicated that they never liked him much anyway.

Please note that the old Arthurian traditions avoid all mention of Lancelot, who is an invention of the French romances – and later developments in medieval courtesy.

On the other hand, Gawayne was frequently the court hero, as in *Sir Gawain and the Green Knight*, the famous alliterative poem of medieval times. Mordred is also a supposed lover of Guenevere, so I am holding to this older tradition.

I hope the reader can see that my characters lived and breathed for me. They developed lives that were quite separate from mine, their creator. However, it would be wrong to state that my beliefs are not embedded in this book. I believe in the best and worst aspects of human nature, and that a streak of violence exists in the most pacific of us. I also know that spite and hubris are alive and well in the human condition. I have seen – and felt – their ugly powers.

But I also believe that hope is the single greatest impetus to human courage. I suppose the three travellers became the symbols of that belief. Merlin, Llanwith and Luka set out to create a weapon borne out of hope. Nor are they so callous as to leave their tool to survive as best he can after they have placed him in harm's way. They risk themselves as well as Artorex, because hope requires self-sacrifice. Their rootless lives, as they plot Arthur's elevation to glory, is proof of their dedication to a selfless quest.

I believe that Arthur had no choice. Circumstances made Arthur assume the role of High King of the Britons because he was a victim of his birth, his natural gifts and the dreams of others. I wanted to illustrate that he lost his own dreams because of the needs of his people. For me, that was always the tragedy at the heart of the Arthuriad, as it was for Homer's works, *The Iliad* and *The Odyssey*, or any other heroic cycle you may care to examine.

Incidentally, when I veer away from the legends, I have done so deliberately for there is no inalienable truth in the fine detail of my plot line. For instance, wouldn't Gallia's garden be a remarkable thing? Wouldn't such a tribute to love be the highest art of human endeavour, perishable as it is?

I give you Morgan's vindictiveness and Uther's cruelty as the ultimate examples of impotence of spirit. There is very little that is built out of such petty human feelings. Only greatness of heart lasts, as was proved in the modern-day battle at Rorke's Drift or in the stubborn courage of those few Jews who survived the concentration camps of the Third Reich. The monster, Hitler, died like Uther, frightened, hiding, haunted by his crimes and his wholly reasonable belief that all decent human beings would turn their backs on him. Who really cares where Hitler's bones lie, or how he died, as long as he is safely dead?

Now, in the twenty-first century, Karl Marx's grave in a London cemetery is no longer a rallying cry to the poisoned idea that the end justifies the means. We shall never know for certain where Arthur lies, or if he even lived. If he was a myth, then it was necessary for human beings to invent him.

Hail, Arthur, King of the Britons!

I wish another hero would take your place, now that the west has such a need of you.

An Interview with
M·K· Hume

Writing is said to be something that people are afflicted with rather than gifted, and that it's something you have to do rather than want to do. What is your opinion of this statement and how true is it to you?

Long before I considered writing seriously, I always wrote for pleasure, and I've got the writer's callous to prove it. I started writing when I was eight years old because I adored heroic poetry (e.g., *Horatio at the Bridge* and *Hiawatha*). I enjoyed entering competitions as a child and wrote a diary, although it's patchy. Because I painted as well, I was able to keep the writing itch at bay. Later, when I became a teacher, I wrote gruesome stories for students and even when babysitting, I adored inventing and telling stories.

I am a storyteller by inclination, and I'd hope I'm also a song-master. I think all good writers have to be, to describe the internal world that goes on, waking and sleeping, inside our heads. I'll tell the tales, write them and paint them – but first I have to birth them! It's like breathing, I suppose. A friend once called me a Pied Piper because of it. I love to paint with words, to choose the correct words and to find the most apt, unusual imagery, or to try to discover a way to turn what I see behind my eyes into pictures that readers are forced to see as well.

PS I hate the postmodernist idea that the author has no place in text, and that it's the reader alone who matters. Yes, the reader makes us or breaks us as commercial successes, but I'd still write even if I didn't sell a single book. Writing and painting is, for me, a more important guide to my thoughts than what I say when I speak.

When did you realise that you wanted to be a writer?

When I was a child, I had a particularly vivid dream (in colour) where I was riding a black horse across a wild landscape. I recall I was wearing a necklace of black diamonds in white metal (silver, I guess) and I was being pursued by something. I tried to write down the details of the dream at the time, but I didn't have the skills. I still remember the details of the dream.

It is often said that if you can write a short story you can write anything. How true do you think this is and what have you written that either proves or disproves this point of view?

From my perspective, a short story demands a brief burst of incredible discipline. I wrote short stories from childhood for personal pleasure and, when I was teaching, I wrote gruesome little short stories of all types as examples for teenagers. I entered competitions, and won quite a few (just small local ones). I really enjoyed the discipline of stretching myself out for seven hundred to a thousand words.

I also believe that it's the best starting point for allowing a writer to set their imagination free. Why can't Harlequin and Columbine dance in Times Square at midnight? Could an incubus stalk a man and only be seen on a light-reflective surface? What would have happened if Pontius Pilate had set Jesus free?

I eventually found writing a full-length novel to be relatively easy because I'd been writing short stories for years, and I was surprised by how free and exciting I found novel-writing to be. But I also believe academic, business and short story writing provided the discipline that has ensured that I pay attention to the vocabulary I use.

I self-published all my short stories some years ago under the title, *Little Tales of Light Madness*, and I was surprised by how many sold through word of mouth and in spite of completely inadequate marketing skills.

If someone were to enter a bookshop, how would you persuade them to try your novel over someone else's and how would you define it?

Initially, I'd show them the cover. Unlike many books, the cover is a reflection of the contents in this case. I'd tell them that it is a different view of King Arthur, not medieval or magical or constrained by the rather distant, idealized and, dare I say it, wimpy image of Arthur. My Arthur has flaws, is violent and capable of savagery – but he's a real man! A hero must be attractive, charismatic and brave. He/she must have real enemies, not monsters or ill-defined, magical threats. The invasion of the Saxons seemed to me to be an enormous problem that Arthur could pit his valour against. Besides, if Arthur existed, the Saxons really were his enemies.

I'm really passionate about this topic, and I'd trust my enthusiasm to help persuade someone to try my novel. Also, I believe in my Arthur, who is not a prototype idealized king. Nor are my other characters the traditional, legendary forms. I tried to create some sense of truth to explain why this man and his adherents would be preserved by the ancient methods of story-telling.

How would you 'sell' your book in twenty words or less?

Valour, vice, death and despair! A man's heart holds the only salvation for his people but he must give everything!

Who is a must-have on your bookshelf and whose latest release will find you on the bookshop's doorstep waiting for it to open?

The Lord of the Rings (Tolkien) is my favourite book, closely followed by *Tea With the Black Dragon* (R. A. MacAvoy) and *The Black Angel* (John Connolly). I adore the writing styles of John Connolly and Carol O'Connell and I pursue their books passionately.

PS I also re-read *Judas Child* (Carol O'Connell) every year as well.

When you sit down and write, do you know how the story will end or do you just let the pen take you? Do you develop character profiles and outlines for your novels before writing them or do you let your ideas develop as you write?

I never know how the story will end. In my defence, however, I spend ever so long creating my characters before I pick up my pen. I can tell you about their ancestors, their parents, where they've grown up, everything, whether I use it or not.

Then, when the characters are more familiar to me than my own family, I pick up my pen and follow them through my story, recording what they say with my imaginary video camera. There are times when I become quite desperate because my hand can't keep up with them as they charge through the world I've invented for them.

No, I don't create character profiles. It's all done internally. I've been told that I should follow a plan, but this method works for me. Of course, I have some idea of the broad time period and the overriding conflict, as I've done a great deal of general research before hand.

What do you do to relax and what have you read recently?

I read a book a day and I hunt through thrift shops for treasures. I write letters (as distinct from emails) because I love the rituals of letter writing. I hunt for gifts for friends or, if I have more time, I paint.

I've just finished *Dexter by Design* (Jeff Lindsay) and I'm also reading *Myth* (G. S. Kirk) as a refresher. To keep my wits sensitive, I'm also reading Dante's *Purgatorio* with the Salvador Dali illustrations. I dip into it occasionally as I can't pretend that I can read it in one hit, but it's normal for me to be reading half a dozen things at the same time.

What is your guiltiest pleasure that few know about?

I don't think I have too many guilty pleasures – I'm depressingly open as a personality, so the world generally knows everything I do. However, I have been known to derive enjoyment out of (mentally) punishing certain people who have harmed me or mine, and planning how to get away with it successfully. Once I've 'killed her off', I find they don't bother me any more! Pathological, I suppose, but it's fun to imagine how 'the worm could turn' – and how I'd go about it.

Many writers have pets. What do you have and what are their key traits (and do they appear in your novel as certain characters?)?

Animals like me. I have an eighteen-year-old miniature terrier called L.G. (for Little Girl) who was given to me when she was eight because her owners had died. She's convinced she's a Rottweiller and I admire her courage and her loyalty.

I own a cat called Salem who is eight and she was given to me when her owner had to move to an apartment that didn't permit pets (Yes, I'm a sucker!). She's a black-haired, green-eyed killer who has been fitted with bells because she insists on trying to feed me birds, mice, lizards, geckos etc. I also have a very large black cat called Satan who comes to visit on a daily basis. He's lazy, indolent and capable of bursts of enthusiasm for food and cuddles.

I inherited my son's goldfish that live in a huge six-foot deep, fifteen-foot diameter plastic pond and are now an average of twelve inches in size. I feed them when I remember, but as they have a living environment, they'll never starve. I don't know if fish have ears, but they rise to the surface when I call out 'fishie!!!'

I don't consciously use my pets in my stories but I guess I admire courage, loyalty, ruthlessness, devotion and power – so I guess that explains me.

Which character within your latest book was the most fun to write and why?

Targo is my idea of a real man, and I had a great deal of pleasure creating him. He can say all the things I'd often like to say, with impunity. He's certainly mine because there are no equivalent characters in the legends.

How similar to your principal protagonist are you?

I wish I were like the young Artorex, although I wouldn't enjoy the price he pays to achieve greatness. I'm drawn to people who struggle with great troubles and strife, and I'm relieved when a person breaks the constraints of society and rises above their condition.

Despite my best efforts, I've never really fitted in with my various peer groups throughout my life. I suppose outsiders are therefore important to me and, now that I reflect on it, many characters are outsiders in *Dragon's Child* and the other two books that follow. Even my villains don't fit comfortably into their societies. I'd like to believe that the aliens amongst us are the one who achieve, because they don't have the comfort of people who fit into the shapes that life makes for them. Artorex is a 'square peg', but is a really superior example, as are Myrddion, Targo and Odin. Even Caius is alien, and his vices reflect an inability to understand his peers.

What hobbies do you have and how do they influence your work?

I read anything and everything. Obviously, wide and catholic reading really helps with all sorts of scraps of information. Art has provided me with habits of observation, the use of colour and an ability to visualize. Thrift shops provide a means of collecting people from all walks of life. I am an inveterate chatterer and even while sitting and having a cup of coffee, I collect fragments of conversation, pieces of faces and gestures, all the minutie that creates good characterisation. Even bad experiences are grist for the mill.

Where do you get your ideas from?

Anywhere and everywhere! With the trilogy, I obviously had the legends to go by, even though I had to find realistic ways to translate these legends into prosaic life. I loved that challenge.

I like to write all kinds of genre. I would hate to have to write historical epics until I died, although I love them. It's the stories and the characters that fall through the cracks that appeal to me. For example, what happened to Nefertiti? How would you feel if you were a survivor of the Charge of the Light Brigade? What would your life be like after you had won fame as a war hero? Did Pontius Pilate commit suicide at Lake Geneva? Where did Keats get the idea for *Bella Dame Sans Merci*?

Do you ever encounter writers' block and, if so, how do you overcome it?

No. That's not to say I don't write absolute rubbish on some days, but I can also tear up what I don't like and keep what I do. For me, the trick is to keep writing. Some of it will be useless, but some will be fine. Therefore, I write every day because I have a 'real job'. Many people think that being an author is a kind of hobby, and I believe that's a dangerous path for any writer to follow. I write between 6 a.m. and midday, at least, every day, and I don't ever get writer's block.

Certain authors are renowned for writing at what many would call 'uncivilised' times. When do you write and how do the others in your household feel about it?

I write as above, but that doesn't mean that thoughts of a book don't go with me everywhere I go, so I can get things down or write a few pages. Having a quiet drink at a pub or a coffee break when I'm shopping, or midnight when I cannot sleep – I just write whenever the mood takes me.

Sometimes pieces of music seem to influence certain scenes within novels, do you have a soundtrack for your tale or is it a case of writing in silence with perhaps the odd musical break inbetween scenes?

I write to the music of TV, my invalid son's never-ending calls for real or imagined needs, the cat's insistence on sitting on the page I am working on, and the occasional talk-back radio programme. I enjoy music in the background, when I am afforded the opportunity, and I suppose I like stimulating stuff such as Meatloaf, Chicago, Leonard Cohen, Lily Allen, etc. Once again, I like a wide range of music as long as it stimulates – but I can do without it!!!!

However, I believe very strongly that the written word has its own musicality and I read my work aloud to make sure that the sound is true to what I am trying to say. Certain words and phrases can drive me crazy – because they damage the music and the song.

What misconceptions, if any, did you have about the writing and publishing field when you were first getting started?

My biggest misconception was how long it all took. I knew there would be a great deal of work involved, but I never expected that it would be quite so much. This is not a complaint, as I rather like the challenge and the discipline. What I didn't realise was that when your publisher's core business is historical literature, they expect perfection in the research that you present to their public – and if you come close to achieving their standards, then they will do everything in their power to 'achieve the grail'. My agent has the same exacting standards.

What I never expected, as an Australian, was how genuine, clever and committed the people in the publishing industry can be. In Australia, writing is an exclusive club and you aren't expected to apply unless you belong. When I first met my agent and publisher in London in 2008, it was with a great deal of trepidation.

When they told my how much they appreciated my work and the standards that I was setting, I'm ashamed to say that I doubted them because of the 'Australian Cultural Cringe'. Even now, I don't belong to 'The Writers' Club' or the 'Literati of Australia'. I don't think I ever will, because I fervently believe that there's no sin in writing material that the public want to read.

If music be the food of love, what do you think writing is?

Writing is the food of my life! If we can agree that life is a very mixed bag of joy and tragedy, virtue and vice, heroism and cowardice, and anything else you care to mention, then writing records, analyses, enlightens and ennobles life in all its vividness. It's my food anyway!

What can you tell us about the next novel?

Each of the volumes in the trilogy approximates a decade in the life of King Arthur. The first volume, *Dragon's Child*, is set in Artor's teen years up to the point where he becomes king at about twenty years of age.

Part two in the trilogy, *The Warrior of the West*, chronicles Artor's success in his wars against the Saxons, his unfortunate marriage and the building of his fortress at Cadbury Tor (my Camelot). This volume is set in Artor's thirties. Targo is back, but he is very old. Nimue has grown into an adult and Perce has become Percivale, Artor's purest and most decent warrior. Artor is at the peak of his powers, but he is constantly on guard to avoid the pitfalls of absolute power.

Part three of the trilogy, *The Bloody Cup*, chronicles the final decade of Artor's life, leading up to his death in his late fifties.

What are the last five internet sites that you've visited?

www.lifeinitaly.com/beauty/cosmetic-history-rome.asp
www.pantheon.org/articles/t/taliesin.html
www.ynysprydein.org/bran/bardic_notes.htm
http://en.wikipedia.org/wiki/Picts
www.omegawatches.com

Did you ever take any writing classes to learn the craft?

I learned most of my writing skills by immersing myself in
literature, and have come to appreciate that you must study the
good, the bad, and the very ordinary, to appreciate the
differences between them.

How did you get past the initial barriers of criticism and rejection?

Nobody likes rejection, but any Australian writer gets used to it
quickly. I always had the feeling that life would work out if I
could just get someone to read my stuff. I soon realized that it's
getting an agent that's hard (impossible in Australia) because
ninety-nine per cent of all published works are contracted
through an agent. If you're a tyro (beginner), nobody wants to
read you – so you don't reach first base.

To get my writing career off the ground, I wrote a Mills &
Boon style novel. I was frustrated to find that I passed through
the hands of several of the company's readers before I was
eventually rejected. I wasn't actually upset by the rejections,
although I badly wanted to see myself in print.

I then proceeded to write a Georgette Heyer-style novel (it
was an excellent read but remains unpublished). This was
followed by two historical romances set during the Australian
gold rush. These also remain unpublished despite the fact that

one of them won second prize in the Random House/Australian Women's Day Literary Competition of 1996. The book won $5,000 against a Melbourne Cup field of almost 3,000 entries from Australia's best novelists.

Basically, we have a situation where writers set themselves up for rejection as soon as they begin to write. As happens in all the creative arts. You can't enjoy the praise without the criticism. Yes, it hurts, but you have to learn from it and roll with the punches.

In your opinion, what are the best and worst aspects of writing for a living?

I've been lucky enough to enjoy a salary – because writing can be an endeavour that you do for love – and nothing else! I'd hoped to make a living out of writing and then my life would be perfect!!!! I love being the master of my own destiny, and I'm prepared to suffer the drawbacks that come with this freedom. I am also drawn by the opportunity to say something that will outlast my lifetime. Some writers do have the opportunity to become immortal.

Headline Review would like to thank http://falcatatimes.blogspot.com for allowing us to reproduce this interview with M. K. Hume.

We hope you have enjoyed *King Arthur: Dragon's Child*.
Artor's exciting and compelling story continues in
King Arthur: Warrior of the West, coming soon
from Headline Review.

Here is a preview...

CHAPTER I

BLOOD GUILT

Then all the councillors, together with that proud tyrant Vortigern, the British king, were so blinded, that, as a protection to their country, they sealed its doom by inviting in among them (like wolves into the sheepfold), the fierce and impious Saxons, a race hateful both to God and men, to repel the invasions of the northern nations.

Gildas

Artor stood on the summit of the imposing earthworks of Cadbury Tor and stared down at his domain. Below him, like the peeled skin of an apple, the ramparts and cobbled roadways leading to the flagged fortress curled around the tor. Regular redoubts guarded heavy log gates that could be closed and barred to seal any enemy between its walls of wood and stone. If any fortress could be considered impregnable, then Cadbury was one such, for in its long history it had never fallen.

As he stared down at what he had rebuilt, Artor recalled his first, crucial campaign against the western Saxons twelve years earlier.

Older Celts still remembered, and resented, the foolishness of King Vortigern who had been so lost to reason that when the strong, golden legs of Rowena, his Saxon queen, were wrapped round his waist, he was prepared to accede to her every request. While in her thrall, Vortigern permitted the Saxons to settle in the lands of the Demetae, and for generations Celts and Saxons had dwelt together uneasily, until the Saxons had eventually sought to extend their power by forming an alliance with Katigern Oakheart in the east.

But, early in his reign, Artor had ridden north out of Cadbury and defeated the invaders at a time when he was still untried, both as a king and as a leader. For the first time, and in bloody attrition, Artor had used his cavalry against that most fearsome of barbarian tactics, the Saxon shield wall.

A double line of Saxons wedged their circular wooden, bull hide and bronze shields together in unconscious imitation of the old Roman tortoise. But the Saxons stood well over six feet in height, unlike the Romans who were rarely taller than five and a half feet. The second row protected the heads of the front with their shields, and once the shield wall was engaged, the warriors refused to retreat, holding the line until every last man was dead. Like the ancient Spartans, the Saxons worshipped individual heroism and prowess in battle, but without the leaven of Spartan iron discipline. Wild for glory, Saxon warriors courted death and heroism, while the Romans had always been pragmatic, professional and sanguine fighters.

Artor had viewed the shield wall from a convenient rise in the ground above the forked Roman road near Magnis. He had sighed, anticipating the slaughter that it presaged. The Saxons were accustomed to absorbing the shock of fiercely attacking men, but Artor had changed the rules of engagement. The High King ordered his cavalry to pound the wall in wave after thundering wave of charging horseflesh. No man, no matter how large, can absorb the shock of a galloping horse. As the cavalry disengaged, Celtic spears were used to deadly effect to slaughter fallen men. Inevitably, many horses perished as the berserk Saxons risked everything to gut the animals, but the wall was weakened and eventually broke. The remaining Saxons fled into the inhospitable mountains. Through inexperience, Artor had mercifully permitted them to escape.

'You'll have to crush them sooner or later,' Targo, his old sword master, had grunted as he cut the throat of a horse whose leg dangled at an unnatural, painful angle.

'True,' Artor replied philosophically, and stepped to one side to avoid the jet of arterial blood as the horse kicked convulsively, and then died. 'But I must soon face a larger Saxon force in the east, and I don't have the men to deal with enemies on two fronts. These curs will keep till a later time.'

'You'll not succeed with cavalry so easily again,' Targo warned softly. 'Still, I suppose there're many ways to trap a rabbit, as my old sergeant used to say. They'll continue to breed until they become a problem once again.'

'Give over, Targo!' Artor snapped, his eyes momentarily cold. Then he laughed ruefully. 'I still lack the stomach for carnage.'

'You'll learn,' Targo replied without a trace of humour or rancour in his cracked old voice.